Fahrenheit 666

FAHRENHEIT
666

Andrew Harman

LEGEND

Published in the United Kingdom in 1995 by
Legend Books

1 3 5 7 9 10 8 6 4 2

First published in the United Kingdom in 1995 by
Legend Books

Random House UK
20 Vauxhall Bridge Road, London, SW1V 2SA

Random House Australia (Pty) Limited
20 Alfred Street, Milsons Point, Sydney,
New South Wales 2061, Australia

Random House New Zealand Limited
18 Poland Road, Glenfield
Auckland 10, New Zealand

Random House South Africa (Pty) Limited
PO Box 337, Bergvlei, South Africa

Random House UK Limited Reg. No. 954009

Papers used by Random House UK Limited are natural, recyclable
products made from wood grown in sustainable forests. The
manufacturing processes conform to the environmental regulations of
the country of origin.

Typeset by Deltatype Ltd, Ellesmere Port, Cheshire
Printed and bound in Great Britain by BPC Paperbacks Ltd
A member of The British Printing Company Ltd

ISBN: 0 099 49881 0

Fahrenheit 666

The temperature at which
devils are happiest.

Contents

Mind over Mammals 1

Psalmed and Ready 44

Destig, destig. One, two 96

Some Deadly Sins 125

Of Blueprints and Hair-nets 156

The Suspicion Bells 202

Of Beavers and Catastrophic Converters 239

This one's to the unsung heroes of a massive Legendary team. Without the massed ranks of devoted enthusiasts that are Random House UK I'd probably be unemployed . . . and you probably wouldn't be reading this.

A few special thankyous to, in the Editorial Corner, John, Nicola and Jules, take a bow . . . in the Publicity and Sorting Things Out Corner, Kate and Tracey, Hoorah! In the Art Department, Dennis and his team, massive applause! . . . and a huge 'mmmmwah!' to everyone in the Getting the Books on the Shelves Corner, step into the limelight Ron, Paul, Michael, Kate G, Graham, Rod, Mike, David, Gill, Kate R, Peter, Debbie, Alan, Jeremy, Chris and Arne. Keep it up, please . . . I hear a bank manager . . .

And last, a very special, and hugely overdue squeal of public delight to one chap without whom my books almost certainly wouldn't look half as pretty. An artist who now hasn't got any orange or yellow paint left after all those flames. Thanks, Mick. Now, about this next cover . . .

Mind over Mammals

He opened his eyes, stared in the mirror and decided he was going to enjoy being a woman. Especially whilst clad in such interesting lingerie. Three weeks of total nymphomaniac pleasure awaited him and he was damned sure he would make the most of every debauched minute. But first there were just a few essential things to get the hang of. At least, that's what the holiday brochure had told him. First, seduction.

Experimentally, he flicked his waist-length flask-blonde hair, fluttered his three-inch raven-feather lashes and attempted to affect the perfect pout. He failed. Five hundred years toiling with a pick-axe in the steaming mines of Helian had somehow never provided him with a chance to practise. Well, not with teeth anyway. And learning to pout seductively with a mouthful of yellowing fangs and a chin the colour of a well-used leather armchair was not a simple task. The demon decided to give the pout a miss for a while and concentrate his devilish efforts on generating the consummate coquettish giggle.

Nervously he inhaled deeply, intoxicated with the feel of gently tightening whalebone-reinforced undergarments and a whole host of interestingly positioned straps. Mentally he formed a picture of the sound he wanted to issue from his beautifully feminine lips; a soft, becoming squeak, rising an octave effortlessly and ending in a sharp intake of breath. Alarming yet appealing (in an irresistibly charming way), guaranteed to have droves of eager suitors smashing down the door.

To anyone but the demon, it was way off key. In fact, a herd of donkeys at the slaughter would have been a symphony in comparison. But, remarkably, it worked.

With a grin of anticipation, he thrilled at the sound of feet storming down the corridor outside. Nonchalantly the demon licked a tiny finger, traced his deliciously plucked eyebrow and smoothed the front of his basque.

Seconds later the door was kicked off its hinges and a host of eager men burst in. The demon raised a curious eyebrow as he noticed that they were all wearing cassocks. He knew they went in for odd things in Southern Hedon, but cassocks? Ah, well, in for a groat . . .

'Hello, darlings!' he shouted appealingly. The floor vibrated with the hellish racket, but still they came.

General Sinnohd, bedecked in full crimson robes of office sprinted into the room laying down a suppressing fountain of 100 proof Holy Water. Three monks fanned out from behind him, snatched the grotesquely pouting woman and hurled her on to the bed kicking and screaming. The men from the monastery knew they had another victim red-handed.

The demon from Helian fluttered his eyelids as he was overwhelmed, he hadn't expected his coquettish giggle to be *so* effective. Well, not without a little practice, anyway.

It was only as the straps tightened against his wrists and ankles, the candles were lit and the incense burner was set up on the portable field altar that he realised maybe – just maybe – they weren't all here for an evening's seduction.

General Sinnohd cracked his knuckles, grinned the grin of a fanatic and issued the words that every holidaying demon dreads. 'Okay everybody, are we ready to exorcise?'

For Alhf the Demon, the next hour and a half was sheer hell.

Squatting on the far side of the Talpa Mountains' pristine snow-covered peaks, like something a thousand-foot-long incontinent dragon had passed, lurked the seething mass that called itself Cranachan.

And deep within Cranachan's labyrinthine intestines could just be heard a heavy sigh laced with the decorations of despondency and alcohol.

Miserably the Really Reverend Unctuous III tugged the cork out of a second flagon of communion wine, which was

2

way past its bless-by date, poured himself yet another vast gobletful and sat glumly in the rat-smelling chaos of the vestry. A twitching set of whiskers poked out of the gloom, squeaked and awaited a chunk of the bluest of cheeses.

Unctuous sighed again as the cheese arced into the darkness, was snatched and voraciously nibbled at. Held in that single chunk of mouldering dairy produce were the entire hopes of him ever having a congregation to which he could preach – hopes which would be back to haunt him in a few hours' time, masquerading as tiny black pellets of rat droppings.

Nobody ever came to the Public Chapel of St Absent the Regularly Forgotten to worship. Fifty years and not a pair of psalms to rub together.

The Really Reverend Unctuous III had been a hysterical optimist way back then, but he had quickly discovered the Cranachanians' attitude to religion. And almost equally as quickly made up a reasonable approximation of the truth to explain why nobody ever came out to pray. It wasn't *really* that Cranachanians didn't believe in things they couldn't see or touch or talk to. Oh no. It was simply that they didn't have enough belief spare to spend on religion, he told himself, and then illustrated it with a convenient example of simple Cranachanian life. Take, he had insisted to himself over and over again, a typical Cranachanian housewife. After believing for the first few minutes of the day that the north-easterly drizzle wasn't any worse than yesterday's constant downpour; then spending the next few hours insisting vehemently that she wouldn't get mugged on the way to market; then traipsing round said market struggling in the firm faith that there would be enough money in her wallet to buy a sufficiency of turnips to feed the kids; and then passing the rest of the evening convincing herself and the rest of the family that the turnip gruel was a) the finest meal they had eaten in their lives and, after a brief examination of the purse, b) would be an ongoing feast that would last for the rest of the week, well, there wasn't really enough faith left for luxuries like gods and things.

And this was reflected perfectly in the size of the congregation habitually attending the Public Chapel of St Absent the Regularly Forgotten.

Each week the number of the faithfully devoted attending for worship could be counted on the fingers of a convicted thief's right wrist-stump.

It had been like this for the last half-century and had the Really Reverend Unctuous III not been baptised in the Sea of Tranquillity and shunned for ever the use or knowledge of the word 'tantrum', he would now have been spitting fury and hurling candlesticks in month-long fits of rage.

Why he felt so particularly gloomy tonight he wasn't sure. Could be the wine, could be the weather, or it could just be that he was bored. After five decades with yourself, a dozen candlesticks and a couple of rodents for company, the conversation does tend towards repetition.

Now, if he had a decent novel to read . . . But he'd cancelled his membership of the Scroll Club years ago after they insisted on sending him that nonsense about . . . oh, what was it?

His mind lurched drunkenly back thirty-odd years through the musty archives of his memory. His vision shimmered as he looked back, back, back . . .

He'd been cleaning candlesticks, again, and at first he hadn't recognised the sound. Two swift sharp knuckle collisions on the oak panel of his door and then silence again. He'd looked up from the wax-splattered brass he'd been polishing and checked for rats. Nothing. He shrugged, started back at the candle and then leapt out of his skin as he realised that knocks meant knuckles and knuckles meant people! In a second he'd vaulted over half a dozen pews and was sprinting to the door, grinning widely with expectation . . . ahhh, those were the days. He could still sprint then . . . He recalled snatching the handles, tugging hard and sweeping the floor with a long bow of greeting, the complex pattern of gold braiding on his skullcap glinting in the light from his candle.

It was only after a minute and a half of extreme lumbar

4

discomfort and a total lack of entering worshippers that he had stood creakily and tutted.

Imagination playing tricks, must be!, he had thought all those decades ago.

But then his eyes had fallen on the tiny rectangular hessian parcel leaning against the edge of the doorpost. Incredibly it had been addressed to him. Scratching the side of his pale, round head in acute bafflement he'd squinted up and down the corridor, then snatched the parcel, slammed the door shut and vanished into the cluttered, rat-smelling chaos of his vestry.

He grinned wistfully and took another swig of wine as he recalled how his hands had trembled as he feverishly began to unwrap the parcel, his eyes filling with tears of eager hope as he tore at the hessian.

The recommended title from the Scroll Club . . . It had to be! The latest highbrow modern literary classic from the quill of Jh'leek Hooper. He quivered expectantly. It had been months since he had ticked the order form, strapped it eagerly to the last of his pre-paid Scroll Club homing-pigeons and waited for delivery of *Nubile Nymphs Ride Bareback Polo Ponies* and now it was here. Happy, happy, joy, oh joy!

He tore off the final wrapping, flung it into a far corner and stared at the back of the tiny, dull manual before him. Strange choice of cover, he had thought. Then he'd turned it over and screamed as he read the title:

TEACH YOURSELF TELEPUSHY
Suggestive Mental Assertion in Twenty-Four Easy Lessons

The wrong one! He hadn't ordered that. Nobody in their right mind would want to read anything so dull and boring as that. He wanted *Nubile Nymphs* or nothing. In a fit of youthful pique he had flung the manual away and forgotten about it.

Until now . . . Decades later and he had read absolutely everything else he could lay his hands on in this tiny chapel. And he was far from being in his right mind. He was desperate for something, *anything* new to read. He leapt to his feet, swayed a bit and dived into a heap of large boxes that hadn't been moved for . . . oooh, thirty years or so. Spiders fled, woodlice trembled and several single-parent rat families were suddenly plunged into homelessness as the aging containers were hurled aloft in Unctuous's desperate search. And miraculously, after five minutes of scrabbling, there it was.

He could hardly control his quivering hands long enough to open the first page and begin to read.

Congratulations on your choice of scroll and welcome to the future of almost limitless possibilities! You are standing on the brink of a learning experience which will transport you to the World of Your Choices; A World where YOU are no longer the passenger; Where YOU have the controls! Come with us on an easy-to-follow twenty-four step journey into the realms of Telepushy.

Yes! Stick with us and you will no longer have to wait to be served at the bar of life. Learn our lessons and the Champagne of Success will overflow your cup. Follow us and golden opportunities will dog your every footstep.

Yes! It's true! With Suggestive Mental Assertion you can have that devoted congregation you've always dreamed of.

Focus your mind the S.M.A. Way and Telepush life's problems away!

. . . and there were three hundred and six more pages just like that. Oh joy!

Razor-sharp talons gleamed redly, drumming irritably on the document-strewn table, counting off the last interminable seconds of the day. Then they stopped abruptly, pushed a few sheaves of scorched Nognite Parchment around the obsidian table, snatched listlessly at a boil-point pen and tapped that for a change.

Nabob narrowed his crimson eyes, scowled at the mound of immigration documents and tutted miserably. All the corners of the latest batch were scorched. Every single one of the damned things. Pathetic! He knew he really ought to send them back – Nognite Parchment was supposedly guaranteed 'Scorch-Free at ambient temperatures. Will not wrinkle, char or calcine. Honest'. He really *should* send them back, he just couldn't be bothered. He had *far* more important things to consider. If everything went to plan, he'd be out of here very soon. Fast track to the top.

Flicking ash off several of the sootier corners he tutted, snorted a blast of sulphurous breath and cursed apathetically. It was typical of the way things were going. Just another example of the state of the underworld today.

Suddenly a flash of ultra-violent crimson blasted through the micro-thin plate-quartz windows. For a split second he was silhouetted at the desk; a nine-foot black-scaled creature in a corona of vermilion. The flash was followed moments later by a screaming crash of thunder. And then the weather really began. Sheeting torrents of flame flashed down from above, bouncing on the teeming pavement, dancing on the countless roofs and gurgling down the woefully inadequate guttering.

Nabob cursed again as he watched the meteorological pyrotechnics outside. He should have known it would turn nasty. The day he'd left his flame-cloak at the dry-cleaners it starts flashing down. And all he had was a tired old cinderella that had an irritating habit of turning inside out in high winds.

'Who'd work for the Sinful Service?' he thought miserably, and stared out of the office window. His slitted pupils misted over as he thought back to when he had first joined.

Ah, such enthusiasm! He was going to work his way up through the infernal ranks, skip gaily through 'Occult Accounts', leapfrog 'Torture Timetabling' and keep going onward and upward towards the *real* power. But, somehow things had gone wrong; somewhere along the line he'd ended up in 'Immigrations' filing records on the latest entrants to Mortropolis, capital of the Underworld Kingdom of Helian. He'd been at it for centuries, trapped in a boring no-promotions backwater. Stamping entry visas and checking passmorts was no career for a demon with drive.

With a sly grin he stared at the notice pinned to the board.

Things were about to change. Ha! After the elections, *everything* would be different . . .

Suddenly a plume of superheated steam erupted from a long tube outside the window. In seconds it was joined by a stream of others, each bellowing in a discordant cacophony.

Nabob squealed with delight as he heard the shift-change whistle echo across Mortropolis. In one leap he snatched his cinderella off the peg and clattered away down the spiral stairs, his cloven hooves striking sparks off each one as he skittered along.

Years of experience had taught him that if he didn't get out before the crush he'd be stuck there for hours, trapped in the seemingly endless queue backed up the stairs. And tonight it would be worse. It always was if it was flaming. The idiots from accounts took ages fiddling about with their cloaks and 'cindies'.

With a final skittering of hooves he spun off the last stairs, raced across the foyer, swerved through the rotating doors and plunged into the seething streets. In seconds he was up to his armpits in the crowds, the black scales of his skin and the curling pair of horns marking him out as one of the ruling class. Snarling angrily, he shoved through the masses of bodies, and headed for downtown Tumor.

'Out of my way!' he snorted with barely contained fury. 'Move!' He snatched angrily at one of the countless pairs of shoulders before him and hurled their owner sideways. Unclenching his fists, he pawed his way through the jam of bodies with all the efficiency of a leper in the January sales. There were far too many of them. And they *still* came over the River Phlegethon. A decent war or famine and the ferrymen would be carrying hundreds a day.

Choosing a sluggishly moving pedestrian at random he wound himself up and delivered a hefty crack across the back of its head. The head turned, stared up at the snarling devil in the perfectly tailored skin of black leather, received a swift uppercut to his jaw, ricocheted sideways and arced into oblivion. Nabob sneered and waded on through the heaving streets.

It took him an hour and a half before he finally got into the middle of downtown Tumor and, as usual, he instantly regretted it. Nobody in their right mind visited the district if they could help it. His ears pounded with the sound of the infernal machines of the Phlegethon Ship Yards, the heat was unbearable – way up in the high six-eighties – and there were even more bodies down here. He had been assured that the reason the Transcendental Travel Company Ltd had their office in downtown Tumor was based on shrewd finance. Rent was cheap.

Angrily Nabob hurled three ex-sailors out of the way, dashed down a narrow back alley and burst through a pair of heat-purpled steel doors, anticipation rising inside him as his cloven hooves powered him up the seemingly endless flights of steep stairs. His thighs were throbbing as he reached the top floor of the strata-scraper, shoved open the door of the Transcendental Travel Company Ltd and stepped into the middle of a raging argument.

'I booked three weeks!' yelled a huge demon leaning over the manager's desk. 'Three weeks. And what do I get? An hour and a half!'

'I'm sorry, sir. It's a risk you have to take with this type of vacation. Were you insured?' whimpered the scaly figure behind the desk.

'Yes!' screamed the angry customer, slamming a sheet of pristine Nognite Parchment on to the obsidian desk.

'Ah,' grunted the manager as he licked his talon, flicked through the document and tried to calculate the degree of protection the desk could offer.

'Well?' growled Alhf the demon, his forked tail flicking angry red.

'This is the Standard Cover,' answered Flagit nervously and began to realise why he had been the only volunteer to step into the manager's recently vacated shoes.* This

---

* Rumour had it that he had either been arrested by the Malebranche for infringement of Helian's strict Transcendental Traffic Control Regulations, or been viciously murdered by a very dissatisfied customer. Whatever the truth, everybody felt certain that he was never coming back. Such were the dangers of operating a holiday business.

9

twelve-foot axe-wielding demon was his fifteenth complaint that day and he had a horrible feeling that he knew exactly what it was about. 'This covers you for cancellations, double-bookings and any third-party criminal proceedings arising from your period of possession.'

'And?'

'It does not cover acts of war, gods or . . . er . . .' He wasn't going to say it.

The demon went several shades of vermilion darker, telegraphing its feelings of extreme displeasure very succinctly. 'Look, when I booked a three-week possession of a teenage nymphomaniac in Southern Hedon I expected to have some interesting experiences which I could share with my mates down the bar. I did *not* expect to open her raven-lashed eyes . . .'

Here it comes, thought Flagit, beginning to tremble.

'. . . then find myself tied to a bed, staring into the face of a priest,' ranted the demon.

Definitely. Number fifteen. Flagit cringed.

A thin line of saliva dribbled unchecked from the edge of the demon's fuming mouth. 'And spend an hour and a half being exorcised *senseless*! D'you call that a holiday? I want my money back!'

Inside, Flagit screamed. *Another* exorcism. It seemed that the recently promoted General Sinnohd was settling well into his role of Exorcist General. A little too well.

Flagit crawled sheepishly behind the defensive screens of the insurance document, shrugged and said as inoffensively as possible, 'I'm sorry, sir, but without the Extended Anti-Exorcism Warranty I am unable to . . .'

The demon made a horrible growling sound and leaned even further forward, its claws flexing wildly, dithering between snatching at his axe or Flagit's throat.

'B . . . but, er, under the circumstances,' whimpered Flagit with a cheesy grin, 'I can offer an alternative. We've just had a cancellation. How would you like three weeks narrow-boating on the Phlegethon, hmmm?'

Three of the lower office minions scrambled through a far

door. A wisp of steam trickled angrily out of the demon's nostril as one claw stroked the handle of his pick-axe.

'I take it that's a "no"? Er, how about a long weekend lava surfing in the Arrhenius basin?'

The demon leapt forward and snatched Flagit firmly around his scaly throat. The erstwhile clerk threw up his arms in defeat, waving them frantically, 'Okay, okay. Let go!'

The demon dropped him back into his swively stone chair with a crash.

'Look,' croaked Flagit conspiratorially, 'how about if I say you were double-booked. I mean, it happens sometimes, especially with the nymphomaniacs, they're very popular at this time of year. You can claim on your insurance then. See?' Flagit massaged his crushed larynx and, not for the first time, wondered if his promotion had been a good thing. Okay the money was better, but the idea of spending the rest of eternity with a crushed windpipe was less than totally appealing. He'd never sing another aria.

'That mean I can have another holiday?' growled the demon suspiciously.

'Of course, anything from this brochure. Anything,' whimpered Flagit handing over a thick glossy. 'Er, please, take your pick.'

Still grumbling, the demon grabbed the brochure.

'And if you're not entirely satisfied with the selection available we can arrange to refund your hard-earned money, minus a small handling fee, of course.'

The demon grunted and, temporarily satisfied, lurched off into a corner to begin squinting through the brochure.

Flagit wiped steaming sweat off his scaly brow and breathed a sigh of relief. It was short lived.

Out of the corner of his slitted eye he saw Nabob stalking towards him.

Flagit's infernal heart leapt a beat. He knew just by looking that Nabob had come to collect.

'Hello, Flagit,' he growled. 'Got anything for me?'

'Er, what did you have in mind?' Flagit answered, still rubbing his leathery throat.

11

'You tell me. You should know what I can get for fifteen thousand obuls these days.'

Flagit swallowed apprehensively, reached behind him and nervously fingered a small sack. He knew better than most that fifteen thousand obuls was a good few truckloads of sold souls. But you try buying state of the art equipment at black market prices. It was hell down here. Nervously he patted his sack and hoped it would be enough. Nabob was expecting something pretty spectacular, and the price for winning elections was very high. 'Delivery time,' growled Nabob eyeing the sack. 'I've had enough waiting. Three months of your feeble excuses does little for my patience. It's time for results. And you'd better make them good!'

With a flick of his wrist Flagit beckoned the demon and left the room, heading quickly for a small storeroom in the far corner of the top floor of the strata-scraper.

Flagit swung his sack carefully on to the heat-stained desk and wiped his brow. It was hot up here, even for him. That was the problem with top floors of strata-scrapers. They were always too hot. Life in the Underworld Kingdom of Helian was always hot but here, jammed against the enormous canopy of the rock ceiling (affectionately known as the stratasphere) it was very hot indeed. There were times when it could get into the six-nineties. But that would be remedied soon. His first decision as the new manager had been to get air-conditioning fitted quick smart. Why be a manager *and* sweat?

'What do you wish to know,' croaked Flagit, his throat still smarting and a rivulet of sweat dribbling down the scales of his back.

'You know damn well! Fifteen thousand obuls!' shouted Nabob slamming one scaly fist into another. 'Fifteen k you've had. Show me the goods!'

Flagit fidgeted and wiped his brow. 'Research and development is a bit pricey. Especially if you want it to win the elect . . .'

'Did I ask for excuses? Did I? Just shut up and show me why you've been avoiding me for the last three months,' snarled Nabob leaning far too close to Flagit's ear.

Flagit swallowed hoping that his latest results hadn't

melted. 'Why meet here?' growled Nabob. 'It's too hot. And I hate Tumor!'

'I gotta business to run and besides, *your* place is too hot. Seirizzim's devils are everywhere. If he gets a whiff of this . . . phew, it doesn't bear thinking about. Seirizzim for Undertaker-in-Chief, uuuurgh! Do you want what I've got, or not?' snapped Flagit. He swallowed once more as Nabob sneered, then nodded and wiped his furrowed brow with the back of his scaly hand. Flagit grinned and pulled a small rectangular obsidian base, six gleaming steel balls, a tiny wire frame and several bits of No-Glow string out of his sack.

'Hurry up!' snapped Nabob as he watched Flagit attach the frame to the base then thread string through each of the balls and hang them on the frame in a perfect line.

'Voilà!' proclaimed Flagit.

'And what is that supposed to be?' growled Nabob, the tip of his pointed tail flicking irritably. 'Or more pertinently, how is that heap of scrap meant to make His Infernality, the Dark Lord d'Abaloh eternally indebted to me and therefore crown me Undertaker-in-Chief of Mortropolis over all other candidates, hmmmm?'

'Watch,' said Flagit, wishing fervently that he could control his endocrine system and ooze confidence from every pore. There was no guarantee he would walk out of his meeting on both hooves if Nabob was displeased.

With his talons shaking only very slightly, Flagit grasped the suspended ball nearest to him, pulled it gently away from the other five and let it drop. As if by magic, the sixth ball shot away from the pack, arched and slammed back into the remaining five, catapulting the first away and starting the entire cycle again.

Nabob began to seethe as the clicking of the balls grated on the shreds of his already inflamed temper. Flagit forced a grin, stopped the cradle, grasped a pair of balls and repeated the exercise. 'You can do it with three as well,' he added, hoping that it helped his case.

'What is it?' bellowed Nabob, steam flaring out of his broad nostrils.

13

'Er, the perfect relaxation aid for stressed-out rulers of the Underworld. You see, the principle of conservation of momentum is harnessed to offer a soothing repetitive cycle of collisions and . . .'

'Shut up!'

'. . . so aid restful sleep.'

'Shut up!' screamed Nabob turning a very crimson shade of stygian black. 'I gave you fifteen thousand obuls three months ago and that's the best you could come up with?'

'Oh no. How about this?' declared Flagit, producing a foot-long transparent tank filled with an orange and a crimson liquid. In a flash he settled it on a longer base and released a small switch. The clockwork mechanism whirred in the base and the tank rocked gently back and forth, the denser crimson granite lava surging in slow-motion minia-ture tidal waves beneath the layer of immiscible orange. 'I've been working on putting a tiny surfer in there but it always flips over and melts. I think it's more relaxing this way, though. Don't you? . . . oh.' Flagit caught a face-full of seething hot breath as he turned and looked up. 'Well, I've got an idea for a little steel ball on the end of a string that you can use to knock down little cubes of rock . . . No? Ha! Silly idea. Of course, er, what was I thinking of . . .'

'Thinking? Thinking?' yelled Nabob. 'Cognitive mental reasoning had nothing to do with it. When I suggested that d'Abaloh might perhaps like something to help him relax after a hard day's deviltry, I had in mind something a little more punitive. A new torment to add to the Malebolge, perhaps, or . . .'

'What about a new set of gleaming pitchfork sharpeners,' interrupted Flagit. 'Or this?' he grinned, tugging a picture of a beaming bearded face out of his sack. 'Top of the range deity dartboard?'

'No, no!' squealed Nabob, his voice edged with acute barbs of victimisation. 'I'm ruined! My entire career in tatters. Seirizzim'll walk into the Undertakership unchal-lenged and I'll be counting blasphemers by the end of his first week in office. I'm ruined. Ruined! And it's all your fault!'

Suddenly self-pity switched to anger and revenge. Nabob's face contorted from wide-eyed fear to the snarling calculating sneer of malevolent evil. 'Ye-eeesss,' he purred and, snatching Flagit by the throat, pinned him to the wall. '*Your* fault. You let me down with your pathetic feeblemindedness!' Nabob's threatening leer slithered into the realms of ultimatum. 'Let me ask you a simple question, Flagit. What do you think will happen to you if, due to some unforeseen circumstance, I happen not to manage to secure the post of Undertaker-in-Chief of Mortropolis, hmmm?'

Flagit's mouth worked as he tried to follow the thread of the threat. 'Er . . .' was as far as he got.

'Think about it, idiot!' screamed Nabob. 'But not too hard. I want results. And you've got a week to find them!' he squealed tyrannically, flinging Flagit across the storeroom, storming out of the door and down the hundred feet of stairs, slamming into a knot of trudging pedestrians. He wheeled around, sprinted back up the stairs, poked his head back through the door and bellowed. 'And do something about all these . . . these *creatures*! The place is crawling with 'em!'

She hitched up her bright red nightdress, tucking it expertly in the straps of her panties, checked the rope and swung. Air rushed through the scruffy bunches of her hair as she arced between the rafters, wooden dagger clenched firmly between her nine-year-old teeth. This time she would get to the treasure. Nobody could stop her.

With the lightest of slaps she landed in a squat on the dusty rafter of the cluttered printer's shop and poised as she calculated the distance to the 'skyland'.

If we were to view the 'skyland' through the critical lenses of adult logic we would see a dust-covered wooden shelf raised or lowered from the print shop ceiling by a complicated series of pulleys and ropes, thus offering a substantial increase in the room's storage capacity. To Alea it was a swinging patch of land floating above the clouds and the crocodile pit accessible only by the most daring feat of bravery – leaping for the rope. No swashbuckling hero had ever flown like Alea, no matter how many times they'd whisked the heroine off by convenient chandelier. As she squatted on the rafter, dagger between her teeth, eyeing the rope dangling motionless six feet before her, Alea knew that *this* was real adventure.

She'd done this hundreds of times and knew, after more bruised knees than she would admit to, that the secret of getting across the gap was momentum. Aim high, swing hard and there's no problem. Low and limp and you'd be found by the enemy, dangling helplessly above the crocodile pit and slipping ever closer.

Alea knew that evil lurked everywhere and had been made incarnate in the form of everyone over the age of ten and/or anyone who told her to 'stop being a nuisance and go to bed'. She'd almost been caught a few minutes previously when her father had unexpectedly poked his head around the door and squinted through his inch-thick crystal glasses while she had been shinning up another rope. Only a vast amount of luck and her ability to freeze motionless had saved her from the deathly perils of being sent to bed early. Game over.

But now, seconds later, she was *far* from motionless. Every fibre of her tiny body had suddenly released itself in a single explosive leap towards the rope, her hands flailed then snatched firmly around the hessian and prepared to swing her over the crocodile pit. Then, disaster struck. The 'skyland' rope dropped suddenly two feet straight down, halting in an arm-wrenching jerk and the sickening sound of a rack of multi-coloured inks being catapulted ceilingwards. Sabotage! Somebody had *deliberately* not tied the brake on. Disaster. She wouldn't get her treasure.

There was only a short period of silence between the endless cacophony of shattering pots, splashing inks and the answering roars of fury from her father. Footsteps smashed angrily towards the door, growls and curses mingling with bellows of 'Alea, if that is half as bad as it sounded, then you're really for it! What have I told you about playing in my workshop?'

Swallowing nervously she squinted down at the growing

16

puddle of colour and tried to work out if it was any worse than last month's 'mishap'; the one that had ever-so-successfully ruined eight days of her father's work in a fraction of a second. She winced as she thought of the slab of painstakingly carved lithochip text as it tumbled off the shelf, smashed into the chain-mail overcoat and exploded into countless tiny fragments. She still maintained that it shouldn't have been balanced so precariously on the shelf. Then she thought of her father's face and how it had managed to produce such an amazing range of reds and purples of rage. She looked at the puddle below and, on balance, decided that it wasn't quite as bad as that. She hoped. She'd been condemned to three weeks of holding Daddy's hand and wearing a skirt. Sheer Hell!

The door exploded and her father stood silhouetted in all his wiry rage. Alea dangled helplessly red, green and vermilion-handed above an ever-expanding sea of rainbows, and attempted to muster her sweetest of heart-meltingly innocent grins. Sadly it didn't work around the dagger.

'What have you done?' shrieked Gravure, his hair seeming to crackle with shock.

Alea spat out the dagger. 'Er . . . slipped,' she muttered as a streak of pink escaped from the end of her nose.

'Slipped?' parroted Gravure hopping from one foot to the other. 'Is that all you have to say for yourself?'

'Er . . . game over,' she admitted and would've shrugged her shoulders had she not been clinging to the rope for dear life, her mind whirring as she looked for ways of lessening her sentence to mere death. Denial – nope, a teeny bit too much evidence stacked, or rather puddled against her for that. Mitigating circumstances – plead that the rope should have been securely fastened then none of this would have happened, dodgy without an extremely good defence lawyer and an especially pretty smile. Then it struck her. The Constructive approach. What possible benefit could a multi-coloured pool of expanding inks be to the printing industry as a whole?

Alea cleared her throat, slipped a few inches down the

rope and started talking, fast. 'It's a good thing. If you pass me a sheet of parchment, any colour you like, I'll show you the fastest way ever to do foot painting and it'll be really, really pretty you'll see and everybody will think it's lovely and you can sell it and make lots of money in art shops and you'll be rich . . .' She faded out and decided that, just now, a full working demonstration may not be the right thing. 'Er, how about, it makes the floor look nice.'

'How about, I've got to clear it up?' he snarled.

'Oh, would you? That's nice,' she grinned and then wondered if she'd said the right thing.

A minute later when the third bucket of icy water was hurled over her head as she sat in the bath facing a sentence of three weeks early bedtime without supper and no recourse to lawyer or court of appeal, she realised that maybe another choice of words would have been more appropriate.

Flagit loved fruit-flies. They had to be his favourite possession. So delightfully simple and irresistibly sneaky. They always gave him a buzz. Especially after a hassle-packed day in the Transcendental Travel Company Ltd.

In the tiny booth, a thousand feet beneath the Talpa Mountains, he grinned a grin blessed with far too many teeth. A tiny fraction of his mind buzzed about inside the fruit-fly above, his mental projections focused with pin-point accuracy through the large mesh-like dome above. To the fruit-fly he was an undetected mental passenger, watching every move, sensing every insectile sensation. A cerebral voyeur.

Right now there were countless demons and devils plugged into similar booths all over the Underworld Kingdom of Helian. Each one acting out their own fantasies through the bodies of their possessed – for a weekly rate, of course. Even the lowliest of the labourers in the Phlegethon Ship Yards could plug in and *be* a prince regent for a week, or a nymphomaniac for a month, or more. All you needed was enough obuls to pay the fare.

And a ticket.

That was essential. No ticket, no possession. The rules said so. Well, it was the only way to keep control. 'V-space' was getting crowded. With so many cerebral voyeurs going 'topside' the chances of re-entering some other devil's body were growing exponentially. The tickets enabled Voyeur Traffic Control to keep tabs on everyone.

Flagit had been there once. A darkened room with a huge black sphere at its centre, covered in tiny glowing lights and a string of numbers dashing here and there. Each one the main consciousness of a holidaying demon, steered carefully through the galaxy of others, directly back to its own body.

The demonic psyche was helpless in its acorporeal state. Yank it out of its body and it wouldn't stand a hope in Helian of finding its way back. Not on its own.

But Flagit knew of little sneaky ways around this. He'd worked in the Transcendental Travel Company long enough to know that if you're careful and you leave most of yourself behind, you can possess anything you want and return safely.

So far he had only ever released two-fifths of his consciousness to cerebral voyeurging. And so far the trace on the Voyeur Traffic Control sphere hadn't been picked up. Unfortunately that meant the only things he could easily possess required an intellect slightly less than that of an Ammorettan Death Lizard. With a lobotomy.

But now he lay back and watched the endless corridors of the intestines of Cranachan swirl by in grainy compound visions. Today's little jaunt wasn't merely a necessary relaxant for Flagit. Today he was looking for something. Something to save his neck from the vice-like grip of Nabob.

Suddenly he felt a wave of disgruntlement trickle through the antennae of the fruit-fly, and in a flash he sat bolt upright, the inside of his nostrils quivering with anticipation. Disgruntlement was a good thing in Flagit's eyes. Whilst the old adage about devils and idle hands may certainly be true, it is also a fact that the underworld doesn't hold anywhere near all the copyrights on the inventiveness of the truly hacked off. Even the most battle hardened of trained exorcist's knees would turn to jelly if they'd seen the horrors that could be perpetrated by the meekest lamb in the foulest of moods. Not many people know that.

Rubbing his talons eagerly he closed a mental circuit and the fruit-fly arced through the open door of the Chapel of St Absent the Regularly Forgotten, swooped through the vestry door, perched itself on the edge of a long unlit candlestick and stared with more than usual insectile curiosity at the figure in the gloom.

With an eager grin of unholy fervour the Really Reverend Unctuous III slammed shut the *Teach Yourself Telepushy* manual and readied himself for his first attempt at suggestive mental assertion.

He was certain he understood it; well, he'd read it from cover to cover five times. But just to make sure he flicked to the chapter entitled 'Mind over Mammals: First Forays into Rodent Control', and read it again, his mind seething with thoughts of the future. If only he'd read it thirty years ago then this chapel of St Absent the Regularly Forgotten would be heaving with eager worshippers desperate for a psalm or two, clamouring for catechisms, screaming for holy teachings and begging for their very own bibles to bash.

An hour later, his brain fizzing with pent excitement, he burst out of the vestry (followed by a tiny fruit-fly which settled on the back of a convenient pew). Reverend Unctuous hurled a large square blanket on to the tiled floor and, with a struggle of aching arthritis settled himself into the requisite yogic posture. According to the manual, tying one's legs into unnatural positions was supposed to focus one's mind on the matter in hand. Personally, Rev. Unctuous had his doubts. So did his knees.

But he harboured not one coracle of doubt about the efficacy of Suggestive Mental Assertion. He knew for certain that it worked. Well, the manual had told him so. Just like it had told him so many other fabulous things. Unctuous knew that if he had the time, inclination and glue, he could make a small five-sided pyramid and, just by thinking sharp thoughts, he could hone as many blunted razor-blades in it as he wanted. He also knew that talking to plants to encourage them to grow was a complete waste of breath and would only end in jaw-ache. The *real* way to encourage and sustain improved botanical propagation was through continued mental communing with all vegetable companions. It was all there in chapter nineteen, 'Ferns and Buds and Brains'.*

And so here he sat, squarely in the centre of the tiny storeroom sized chapel of St Absent the Regularly Forgotten, ready and eager to begin. With a final squint under the pews he closed his eyes, mentally reached out and leapt into the cerebral Pied Piper's costume. Following the detailed instructions in the manual to the letter he imagined his skull as a transparent beehive, his thoughts whirling and buzzing within. And he imagined it getting hotter. Right on schedule the walls of the hive began to glisten, melting, growing thinner. The cerebral bees buzzed louder, excited now as rivulets of molten hive began to run down the domed surface . . .

And suddenly a hole appeared, followed a millisecond later by a single neuronal bee, flitting in fizzing apian abandon. In a flash it was gone, out through the walls and away, seeking eeking rodents just moments ahead of the rest of the swarm.

Had anybody been watching the activities of the Really Reverend Unctuous III, they may not have noticed anything unusual. In truth there wasn't really anything unusual to see, well, apart from the fact that he was sitting on the floor in the

---

* Actually all of this is not strictly true. There was one teensy-weensy smidgin of doubt held warily in the back of Unctuous's brain. It concerned the footnote in the chapter regarding rodent control. Now what had it said? Ah yes.

'*Editor's note*. Extensive field trials have shown that telepushic manipulation of any creature above lizards on the evolutionary ladder will be found to be impossible. This, however, can be overcome by the use of the No-Slip Telepushic Enhancer available from the Scroll Club at the bargain price of five hundred and twelve groats plus thirty two groats pigeons and packing.'

Then it had shown him a scrappy diagram of a funny, hairnet-shaped thing. Upon seeing this, Unctuous had tutted loudly, shaken his head in incomprehension and turned the page. It was glaringly obvious to him that this piece of claptrap had been added later. For one thing it was simply a cheap excuse for the Scroll Club to extract more hard-earned cash from gullible punters. And for another, anybody in their right mind knew that there was no such thing as evolution. So, animals and stuff changed shape sometimes, of course they did, that was just the god's way of keeping things interesting for zoologists.

lotus position with his palms upturned, moaning gently. With the exception of the very unholy puce glow emanating from the network of hand-sewn gold braid covering his tiny skull cap, you could easily have been forgiven for thinking he was just meditating.

'He's just meditating,' thought the current owner of two jet-black compound eyes angrily as it peered out from the back of a suitable pew. 'Meditating! Damn, damn, damn! Another dead end.'

Miserably, it turned away, unenthusiastically thinking about drawing-boards and going back to a place called 'square one'. Desperation had made it search so far afield. Three days left . . . and still nothing to show. The fruit-fly spat angrily and launched itself once more on a weary search.

Then suddenly its attention was snatched by an unexpected skittering of claws on stone. It turned and stared as a dozen rats flooded into the chapel and screeched to a halt in front of Reverend Unctuous. They were joined seconds later by a countless wave of eager rodents, tails twitching, whiskers buzzing, their thoughts dominated by the fact they knew they had to be there, right now, because if they weren't, well, er, well . . . All right, so none of them were really sure *why*, but they all knew it was vitally important that they attended. Definitely. Yup. This was the place. Just here.

The Reverend opened his eyes and stared at the swarming grey carpet of fidgeting rodents. Under any other circumstances he would have leapt out of his skin if he had opened his eyes and found himself in that situation. Right now he shrieked with euphoric delight and the puce glowing of his skullcap vanished. Mentally he gave himself a huge pat on the back for seeing right through that cheap, and woefully inaccurate, footnote.

Before the echoes of excited happiness had died in the tiny chapel, the telepushic field had shattered, the cerebral Pied Piper called his last tune and a thousand terrified scraps of ratkind had woken up to the fact they didn't want to be there no matter what anyone had told them and had scurried into a million different holes.

'It works!' shrieked Reverend Unctuous as he watched countless ratty tails vanish. 'Suggestive Mental Assertion works!'

'Suggestive Mental Ass . . . What kind of . . . ?' squeaked a tiny buzzing voice.

'Brilliant! That's what kind of. Well, not quite, they've all scattered now but seeing as I thought I'd just sit there and get cramp,' answered the Reverend failing to realise that the voice had come from a tiny fruit-fly hovering a scant inch from the end of his nose. In truth Reverend Unctuous probably wouldn't have noticed anything unusual. Not with the mood he was in now. Ecstasy rattled around his swirling mind. 'I really did it! Summoned all those rats just by thinking of cheese. Ha! What do they think they know about evolution!'

Summoned? thought the fruit-fly eagerly, mentally rubbing a scaly hand over its chin and seeing a sudden usefulness in the situation.

'Oh, what would I give to do *that* to real people!'

'What, precisely *would* you give?' buzzed the fruit-fly schemingly. An eagerly whining egg of a plan hatching in its tiny sizzling mind.

'Oooh. Anything!'

'Anything?' buzzed the fruit-fly again.

'Absolutely anything!'

'Absolutely anything at all?' parroted the tiny insect. One more time and he'd have him.

'Yup! Absol—' He didn't get a chance to finish.

With a whoop of uncharacteristic enthusiasm not normally associated with your average winged insect, a section of the floor exploded, plumes of superheated steam billowed out, dozens of scaly black talons thrashed wildly and a second later the Really Reverend Unctuous III was gone.

Then the floor reformed with a squidgy crackling noise and a small fruit-fly suffering from a dreadful headache crashed into the side of a recently polished candlestick.

Miserably, it shook its head, tugged at the bottom of its eyes, examined the colour of its proboscis in the reflection

23

and vowed never, ever again to have a night out on a fermented peach. The last three days were a total blank.

Somewhere in a crimson gloom the Really Reverend Unctuous III opened his eyes, stared at a vast figure in the darkness and snapped them shut again six times faster. 'It's a bad dream,' he tried to convince himself, 'a very bad dream. Far, far too much wine. As soon as you open your eyes it will have gone because things like that just don't exist in reality, okay? Now, after three . . .'

It was still there, standing nine feet tall in its stocking hooves and glistening malevolently beneath a perfect body stocking of black leathery scales. Its mouth was crammed with a mismatched collection of far too many teeth for its own good (or anyone else's for that matter), and, alarmingly for Unctuous, it was staring intently at him with the type of greedy calculations that made Cranachanian tax-collectors famous throughout the Talpa Mountains.

'Neat trick with the rats that,' it said and winked menacingly.

Reverend Unctuous screamed and blacked out, but it was very difficult to tell precisely what order he did them in.

When he came round and had plucked up enough courage to open his eyes again, the thing was still staring at him.

'How d'you do it?' it asked in a deep rasping voice that whistled creepily just before it opened its mouth. 'The rat-trick, I mean, eh? How's it done?' An arrow-headed tail lashed casually in the air behind him.

'W . . . w . . . w . . . w—' began the Reverend Unctuous in a bout of stunning coherence.

'With mirrors?' guessed the thing. 'Oh, surely not.'

'Wh . . . wh . . . where . . .'

'Wearing silly clothes? C'mon how d'you do it?'

'Where am I?' squeaked the Reverend.

'Ohhh!' it roared disappointedly, at a pitch several dozen octaves below the hearing range of bats. 'Can't you do any better than that?' It curled back its glistening upper lip and showed just how disappointed it really was in the Reverend's standard of questioning. 'I would have thought the answer was obvious!' it gloated, pointing casually around the stygian cavern at the apex of the strata-scraper with a nonchalant talon. A small patch of rock cooled above his head.

'C . . . can I h . . . have a clue, only I'm n . . . not feeling myself t . . . today,' whimpered Unctuous as he spotted the thing's horns and matching pointy tail.

'Well, let me see. You're at least a thousand feet below your usual location, the number of teeth in the guard dog's jaws is exactly divisible by three and, oh yes, if you listen carefully you should just be able to hear the sound of countless souls suffering in an eternal torment of their own making.'

The Reverend's jaw landed on his chest.

'Oh, yes,' continued the thing, 'And, er, you might not be alive any more. Sorry about that but, well, needs must and all that.'

'You're the d . . . d . . . dev—' blubbed Unctuous.

'*The* devil. Oooh, no. Tut, tut!' it admonished. 'Thought you of all people would've known that. No, no I'm just your humble common or garden little minor devil. Name's Flagit, by the way. Now, about that thing with the rats . . .'

'But I'm a man of the cloth. I shouldn't be down here,' shrieked Unctuous.

'Were,' corrected Flagit. '*Were* a man of the cloth. Past tense. It's all right, you'll get used to it. Now, the rat-trick?'

'Why am I here?' Unctuous squealed.

Flagit rolled his eyes wearily. 'Do we *have* to go through it all? Oh, well. What's the last thing you remember after the rats, eh?'

Reverend Unctuous narrowed his eyes and delved into his memory. 'I . . . well, my entire life flashed . . .' began Unctuous.

'No, no,' tutted Flagit irritably. '*Before* that. C'mon, think!'

Unctuous screwed up his eyes and concentrated harder. 'Well, I did sort of wish that I could summon a whole

25

congregation,' he confessed to his feet. Or more exactly, what had once been his feet.

'I think you'll find the *exact* words,' offered Flagit, 'were, "Oh, what would I give to do *that* to real people!" and I said, "What, precisely would you give?" and you said . . .'

'You mean . . . ?' croaked Unctuous, a look of total horror springing unbidden into his eyes as understanding dawned over a barren future of extreme desolation.

'No, no. It was "Ooooh. Absolutely anything!" I think,' supplied Flagit helpfully. 'Said it three times on the trot, so, zzzappp, here you are.'

'You kidnapped me?' whimpered Unctuous, dreading the answer.

'Nah. Don't be silly . . .'

The Reverend breathed a sigh of relief. Not kidnapped! So there was still hope, still a tiny glimmer of optimism shining around the edge of the door of total defeat.

'We made a pact!' finished Flagit happily. The door slammed shut with a resounding crash. 'A binding contract witnessed by me, happens all the time. You know, folks wanting to play the violin a bit better, chaps painting portraits and jamming them in the loft while they stay young forever . . .'

'And all because I wanted a congregation?' spluttered Unctuous, the furrows on his brow deepening desperately.

'Yup! You're here to stay 'cause of them,' answered Flagit, and showed the vast majority of his fangs as if to prove the point.

'How big?' asked Unctuous.

'Eh?'

'How big a congregation?'

'Oh, I dunno. Besides it doesn't matter now.'

'Excuse me, but I think it does matter,' said Unctuous, feeling indignation rising in his lower colon. 'I mean, if this is one of those pact things and I'm d . . . d . . . ahem, part of it, well, I think it's only fair that I should know how big my congregation is. Hmmm, come to that, where are they?'

'Er, they're around,' answered Flagit uncertainly.

'Around? What kind of an answer is that? They should at least be well within a reasonable preaching distance, you know, with me in front of them, teaching, doing things that men of the cloth are supposed to do! Not them up there and me down here. Understand?' fumed Unctuous.

Flagit rolled his slitted eyeballs wearily and sighed. 'Oh, I see. Umm, you should have made it a bit clearer. Too late now, sorry.' Flagit shrugged non-committally and attempted to dismiss the matter.

'Now look here,' shouted Unctuous having none of it. Forty-five years he'd waited for his very own congregation and he wasn't going to let some nine-foot scale-ridden demon with horns and halitosis stand in his way. Well, at least not unless he actually thought about it. 'I didn't agree to any of this. I want to see who's in charge! I want my body back!'

Flagit suddenly twitched guiltily and peered anxiously over his shoulder. 'Ssssh! Not so loud!' he croaked hoarsely. 'You don't want to make a fuss about all this.'

'Oh, but I do!'

Flagit's mind whirred. If anybody else found out that he'd kidnapped a man of the cloth . . . He shuddered.

'C'mon!' insisted Unctuous bubbling with righteous indignation. 'Where's the devil in charge, hmmm? I want to see him, this instant!'

Flagit searched through the untidy depths of the recesses of his scheming consciousness. How could he keep the Reverend quiet? What did men of the cloth understand? He racked his brain harder and harder and . . . Truth! That's it. Tell him the truth and he'll be jelly in your hands.

Flagit took a deep breath, his thoughts desperately focused on the rat-trick and how to find out how it was done. Truth, he cringed momentarily. This wouldn't be easy. Years of constant neglect had left him very rusty on the old 'truth' front.

'You're here because . . .' *Rats* 'Er, well, because of . . .' *Rats* '. . . the thoughts in your head,' whispered Flagit finally through clenched teeth and tight-lidded eyes. 'You know,'

27

he added helpfully. 'The book.' He held his breath and listened for the screams of indignation.

It didn't really have the effect he had anticipated.

True, the once-Really Reverend Unctuous III had stopped demanding to see whoever's in charge and this, for Flagit, was a definite improvement. But he hadn't expected the surge of self-pity that flooded unchecked out of the man of the cloth.

'I only *thought* about it!' he moaned. 'I didn't do it, ever . . . Well, I read about it, but I didn't think that counted. Not really . . . All right, so I have got a vivid imagination and I admit that I could imagine the nubile nymphs riding bareback on polo ponies but it was all *clean* fun. Especially in the shower afterwards with the foaming water running in bubbling rivulets down their firm young bodies . . . ahem.'

Flagit shook his head and simply stared at the ex-Reverend. The truth had never been *that* confusing the last time he'd tried it. True enough, that had been a few centuries ago, but still. He shook his head and tried a different tack.

'Look, about these rats?' he asked.

Unctuous shook his head in shame and turned redder as nubile nymphs cantered seductively around the arena of his thoughts, slapping thighs and cracking whips against the barest of backs.

A thousand different hues swirled before his eyes as Gravure shoved the mop through the sea of ink, lifted and wrung it into the waiting bucket.

There was no denying that Alea was a little devil. Hardly a week went by without something being shattered or split or ruined or . . . Ah, but sometimes it had marvellously inspiring consequences.

Whisper the word 'Inspiration' randomly into anyone's shell-like ear and you can guarantee the images that leap to mind will tend to involve the sudden ignition of vast 40-watt light bulbs, or ageing mathematicians exploding from an afternoon bath and dashing naked down the street shrieking 'Eureka!' It is only very rarely that whispering 'Inspiration' will conjure thoughts of bulbously throbbing toes, chain-mail overcoats and a battered dust-pan and brush.

In fact the only mind into which such images would spring was that of Gravure the once less-than-marginally successful owner of his eponymous 'Cairn, Headstone and Memento Emporium'.

He smiled now as he recalled that time, late one uneventful evening when, bathed in the guttering glow of a candle, he had just been adding the final letters to a vast polished slab of Talpine Slate. Three dozen taps of his favourite cold chisel and there! It was done. Eight solid days of chipping and filing to produce one thousand perfectly carved words in lithochip bold to a depth of a quarter thumb-nail. He grinned. It could have been one of his finest headstones, except that all the letters were back to front and there was a number in the bottom right-hand corner.

It had taken him quite a while to get used to carving backwards – the S's were the hardest to crack – but that evening, four months or so after mastering the complexities of a mirrored ampersand, buying his 'Random Hovel' franchise and launching himself into the world of tome publishing, well, he could carve anything. Borders of interlaced angels, margins of cavorting cherubim, strings of seraphs . . . you just name it! All that was left to do with this eight-day slab of work was load it into the press in the corner, plaster it with a layer of white ink and squash as many sheets of black parchment on to it as he possibly could. He was constantly amazed the way the white miraculously formed letters upon the black surface. If only it didn't take so long to make each slate in the first place . . .

With a satisfied grin he pushed back his chair, stood and was about to lug his masterpiece over to the press when disaster struck.

Disasters are known to take many forms: earthquakes, tidal waves and so forth. This one was nine years old and wearing a bright red nightdress tucked indecorously into the straps of her panties. And it came whistling out of the rafters on a rope, let go and landed with a neat slap on the top of a nearby cupboard. Gravure was screaming even before the vibrations hit the lithochip slab, sending it crashing to the floor, shattering into countless thousands of worthless pieces, taking a chair and a chain-mail overcoat with it and dealing a deadly blow to one of Gravure's toes.

The dust settled faster than the screaming tirade of fizzing-blue edged blasphemies that lanced around the workshop.

Right then he could cheerfully have run screaming through the chaos of his tiny workshop, axe in hand in hot pursuit of a certain nine year old. But she had scarpered to her favourite hiding cupboard under the stairs.

The better part of three-quarters of an hour's cursing later, his toe throbbing in pulsing agony and his hair covered in thin grey dust, Gravure decided that the slate would not get around to clearing itself up. He grabbed his dust-pan and brush, swore again and attacked the quarry of letters on the floor, clearing a good half shovelful away before stopping and staring in drop-jawed amazement.

Inspiration was moments away from Gravure as he gazed at three tiny fragments of slate that had somehow lodged in the elbow of his mail overcoat. He rubbed his disbelieving eyes and stared again. They were still there, a triplet of letters cheerfully spelling out the greeting '!iH', which, to anyone who had just spent over a week concentrating solely on a thousand words of lithocarving, was instantly recognisable as 'Hi!' Trembling he reached out and grasped the 'H', pulling it out from between the links of the mail and then shoving it back. A little squeak of wonder burst from his lips as he did the same with the 'i'. In a second he had removed the '!', grabbed a handful of letters and jammed them into the mail, creating the message '!ereht iH'. A quick dab of white ink, a scrap of black parchment and Gravure had produced the first ever example of chipset printing. It only took a month (three weeks of which had Alea confined exclusively to wearing a skirt and holding his hand in public), and he'd chipped out eighteen full sets of the alphabet and hacked his overcoat into mesh squares.

'Finished my order yet?' snapped the figure in the long cloak and pristine white collar as he slammed the door to the Printer's Shop and shattered Gravure's reverie. His voice was somehow tetchy and pious at the same time and obviously more used to conversations regarding the end of the world than anything so mundane as printing orders.

Gravure looked up from the hypnotic swirls of colour, spun around and squinted up through the inch-thick crystals clamped to the end of his nose. 'Eh? Oh, oh Reverend Screed. You did make me jump.'

'Finished my order yet?' repeated the Reverend with an ounce less piety and scowled at the vast stain of inks drying on the floor.

'Not quite, no. Sorry, I got a little, well, inspired . . .'

'Is that what you call it?' grunted the Mostly Reverend Vex Screed of the Haranguist Mission with even less piety and a distinct half teaspoon of annoyance.

'Er, I had this accident and dropped . . . well actually it wasn't me . . . I . . .' began Gravure.

'I take it this is the beginning of an excuse. Shall I sit down or will it be brief?' muttered Reverend Screed irritably.

The wind trickled pathetically out of Gravure's sails.

'My, that was brief,' snarled Screed. 'Now, for the third time of enquiry, have you finished my order yet?'

'No,' Gravure admitted sheepishly.

'Mr Gravure, may I remind you that you are dealing with the living now. Delays are far less tolerable . . .'

'You saying I'm slow? I'll have you know, I never delivered a headstone late in all my life! There was that mausoleum that arrived three weeks after it should've, true, but it wasn't my fault the cart axles couldn't take it. I said it'd be heavy but they wouldn't listen . . .'

'Mr Gravure, when will my order be ready?'

'Er,' he squinted over at the array of slate letters poking out of the remains of his chain-mail and shrugged. 'Two weeks or a fortnight, whichever's soonest,' he grunted.

'Ach! That will be too late,' snapped the Haranguist Missionary, calculating on his long fingers.

31

'Too late for what?' asked Gravure.

'Cha! For *whom*.'

'For whom, then?'

'Dozens, perhaps hundreds of lost souls. The heathenish wandering clans of the D'vanouin Tribespeople,' replied Reverend Screed, his eyes clouding over as he seemed to stare into the south.

'Oh, they've wandered back here again, have they?' sniffed Gravure and began to mop at the ink again. 'Don't do no one any harm.'

'Harm?' whinnied Reverend Screed, whirling around dervishly. 'They do me harm. They are heathens, unbelievers, infidels! . . . Ahem.' He smoothed his hair and struggled to calm himself. 'Once they have seen the good word flowing in full D'vanouin translation, which you should have finished printing weeks ago, they will be converted. Otherwise . . .' Images of infernos whirlwinded inside Screed's mind. 'I shall return in seven days to collect three hundred copies of the Red Proselytic Manuscript of St Lucre the Unwashed as ordered. Goodnight!' He whirled and headed for the door.

'A week? There's still a hundred pages . . . thousand words a page . . . Coooh! Laws of chance . . . I can't guarantee there won't be any chipping errors. I mean, there's so many vowels in D'vanouin . . .'

But his words failed to reach the Reverend's ears which were now on the far side of his reverberating front door and accelerating away.

'Oh well,' grumbled Gravure, 'he'll just have to take it as it comes. And lump it.' He thrust his mop deep into the ink and watched as it turned a vicious shade of turbid brown.

Slowly he shook his head. All the experience of work with inks and he still couldn't fathom why such pretty colours combine to make such a mess.

Sinday morning rose across Mortropolis with its usual lack of splendour. The dawns and sunsets in Helian were not known for being spectacular. Unsurprising since the only sources of light here, one thousand feet underground, were the constant ruddy glow of the lava lamps and the occasional flash of lightning before a flamestorm.

'You certain there isn't something you're not telling me?' growled Flagit as he leaned over the terrified Reverend Unctuous and uncurled a nine-inch talon menacingly.

'Like I said, that's it. I've told you everything,' he whimpered, hoping that his memory hadn't in fact failed him. He had always prided himself on his memory of scripture. In fact during his training in the cloisters of Abbey Synnia he had consistently won at Trifling Quest, snatching cheeses whenever he was asked questions from the Vulgate Bible. What he couldn't recall probably wasn't even written.

But that had been when his mind was focused and free of distractions. Right now there were other things on his mind than simply trying to recall the entire contents of *Teach Yourself Telepushy* after reading it only five times. One of them was nine feet tall and kept showing him his excessive fangs, horns and claws. The others insisted on cantering around the inside of his brain, flexing whips and flashing firm thighs at him. The worrying part about the nymphs was that they seemed to be wearing far less and to be even more nubile now than they had been an hour ago.

'You sure that's all I have to do? Just make little bees in my head, burn down the hive and then I'll be able to control every single creature that lives up there?' growled Flagit for the fifteenth time.

'Well, that's a rather crude précis of over three hundred pages of text, but yes,' answered Unctuous with a wince.

'That's absolutely all there is to it?'

Unctuous nodded.

'So how come it doesn't work, huh?' snarled Flagit. 'Fifteen times I've tried the rat-trick and got nothing! I know it works, I've seen you do it. What aren't you telling me?' Flagit's temper snapped its leash, fear of Nabob driving it onwards, spurring it in the knowledge that in a few hours Nabob would be coming to collect. Snarling, the devil leapt across the cavern, seized the Reverend and smashed him against the wall.

33

Through clenched teeth Unctuous squeaked, 'I've told you absolutely everything. I wouldn't lie to you. I'm . . . I'm a man of the cloth!' But somewhere, buried deep at the back of his mind he knew there was a teensy-weensy scrap of reason why Flagit's attempt at Suggestive Mental Assertion had been so overwhelmingly unsuccessful. It was something to do with ladders and evolution and stuff, but he really wasn't sure what. Guiltily Unctuous kept his lips tightly shut. Offering himself a thoroughly criminal confession he kept incredibly quiet. Oh, the shame. He'd been in Helian for a matter of hours and already his devotion to absolute truth was slipping. An image of a nubile fetlock being caressed with a bull-whip flashed distractedly across his mind.

'So why doesn't it work then?' snarled Flagit tightening his grip around the Reverend's throat. 'Am I stupid, or something?'

Unctuous flailed and shook his head frantically. 'No, no. The rats might be just too far up . . . er, away, that's all. Signal too weak, that sort of thing,' he winced.

'What, like the rock's blocking my thoughts?' growled Flagit.

Desperate Unctuous nodded his head, agreeing with such eager amplitude that the scorched remains of his skullcap leapt off his perspiring scalp and crashed to the floor.

'What's that?' growled Flagit and snatched it on to the end of a glinting talon, squinting suspiciously.

'Mine. Part of the uniform.' A dubious spark of memory flashed into his head: a scrappy picture of a funny hairnet thing that had something to with . . . what?

At the same instant a flicker of intuition pricked in the stygian gloom of Flagit's brain.

'Uniform, eh? So you'd've been wearing it at the time?' he mused and rubbed his chin slyly, his thoughts flashing to the Transcendental Travel Domes in the rooms off the corridor outside.

Unctuous tutted and rolled his eyes. 'Well, of course I was wearing it, that's why it's here. You didn't make a pact with my wardrobe!'

'Yes, but you wore this and the rat-trick worked. I didn't and *it* didn't. Ha!'

In a flash Flagit dropped Unctuous and slapped the gold-braided skullcap on the top of his head, between his horns. And closed his eyes. Then, for the sixteenth desperate time he conjured images of mental bees, each desperate to harness the will of a single rodent, each wild with the desire to dominate. Around the bees the hive began to melt, and this time, for the first time, Flagit felt the heat singe at the buzzing neuronal bodies.

Nervously Unctuous watched as the skullcap began to glow a pale puce.

Suddenly there was a purple flash across the inside of Flagit's eyelids, followed by a shower of green stars and a shimmering haze appeared across the bottom of his field of vision. With a squeak of joy he realised that he was staring through the eyes of a single white and vastly overfed rat. It was only with the slightest squeak of rodent terror that he noticed the vast, ring-bedecked hand sweeping out of the sky in his direction.

In a shady street at the base of the strata-scraper Nabob tugged his flame-cloak collar hard up under his horns and scowled around the corner. Thousands of miserable souls trudged head-down through the burnings streets, some moaning, some wailing and all gnashing their teeth. All, that is, except one who stood in the ring of light cast from a lava lamp and simply gnashed its teeth.

Nabob cursed and pulled back out of sight. The gnashing monster had been there continuously from Thornsday morning, watching. Ever since Nabob had put himself forward as a candidate for the elections to Undertaker-in-Chief of Mortropolis, it had been there, keeping any one of its hideous three eyes peeled and reporting back to the dread head of Immigration, Seirizzim. Even as Nabob stood in the pouring flames, he knew that there were similar nameless figures lurking in shadows watching his and Flagit's caverns. At first he had been mildly flattered that the hated Seirizzim was taking such an interest in him, but now it just got way up his flared nostrils.

Suddenly, somewhere miles away, a lever was tugged, a valve flipped over and countless cavernfuls of hyper-heated air scorched down miles of piping, rattling and surging around corners to erupt from innumerable openings in a hissing squeal. The first shift of the day was over, and in a moment crush hour would begin again.

For a brief second Nabob's attention drifted to the trudging throng before him, and as one they changed direction and shuffled off towards some other unattainable destination. All around him cries of anguish could be heard as the doors of punishment chambers were hurled open and banished souls were flung on to the street to shuffle away across town and their next shift of torture. And then a question popped unbidden into Nabob's thoughts. Why had the streets not been empty before the shift change? They used to be, years back. Okay, so you'd possibly spot a few devils staggering home after a serious Satyrday Night on the town, but for the Damned out so early . . . ? Between shifts? Didn't they have a hole to go to? Had immigration really let that many of them in? Could Seirizzim . . . ?

A tidal wave of sinners exploded, coughing and spluttering from eight hours' headstanding in a cesspit and lurched towards Nabob filling the street in an almost impenetrable wall of reeking misery. Nabob grinned, tugged his flame-cloak tighter and crouched down to an uncomfortable five feet. Lastly he took a deep breath, judged his moment and vanished into the jostling tumult unseen by Seirizzim's trioptic thug. Bodies swarmed around him, pushing and coughing, carrying him past the scorched steel doors of the strata-scraper in a wailing torrent. At the last moment he reached out, snatched at the door handle and was blasted inside by the pressure, his momentum spinning him across the stairwell. The demon took a deep breath to clear his nostrils, chuckled and sprinted up the stairs towards the offices of the Transcendental Travel Company Ltd.

Ninety-nine floors above Nabob's pounding hooves, deep

inside Flagit's seething mind, understanding was beginning to spread tiny grey mycelia and tug facts together. It had only taken him a few terrified moments to realise that the warm sticky feeling being exuded by the long-haired rat was not an action resulting from acute fear working on bowel movements. It was, in fact, affection. This was a pet rat. And grossly overfed. In the last ten minutes he'd had scraps of fifteen different cheeses rammed under his twitching whiskers and been 'coochee-cooed' at more times than he could count.

Flagit had just about had enough. It was time for action. He beamed a host of thoughts ratward. The rodent looked up and stared about it. Flagit saw the huge pin-striped sleeve of an expensive suit stretch away before him and peered down at the enormous continent of a polished wooden table below. He watched as the massive, heavily-ringed hand swooped ponderously down towards a bowl and absently removed another blue veined chunk of cheese.

No, no! thought Flagit in panic. Not more flaming Dragonzola!

In a flash, a battery of Flagit's wild thoughts raced unstoppably upwards . . .

A scream echoed through the vast marble hall of a huge mansion as ratty talons sliced through expensive pin-striped sleeve and buried themselves in fleshy forearm. Khar Pahcheeno, the Head of the Cranachanian 'Family', leapt out of his vast leather chair, hurling rat and cheese in all directions. The white pet somersaulted three times before crashing on to the polished wooden table as the door was flung open and three vast bouncers thundered in. Maliciously the rat zinged a claw to full extension, smirked at the polished wooden surface and began to scratch. Khar Pahcheeno stood sucking his forearm as Fhet Ucheeni the bouncer scoured for intruders. The sound of claw on wood rasped louder and then abruptly stopped. All eyes turned on the rat as it stepped casually sideways and grinned back devilishly. There, scratched a quarter of an inch into the gleaming grain was the unmistakable image of two fingers raised in the eternally insulting salute. Flagit snatched the Reverend's skullcap off, threw back his head and roared with demoniacal laughter. Such fun, such power. What a plaything! What a . . . !

Suddenly, a cloven hoof kicked the door open, to admit a feverishly panting Nabob who clattered into the room and snatched the shrieking Flagit warmly by the throat.

The Reverend Unctuous squeaked and scuttled behind a convenient Nognite basket, crossing himself wildly and murmuring anything vaguely holy that happened to spring to mind.

'Well . . . ?' snarled Nabob. 'It's time!'

Flagit made a strange gurgling noise and stared at the claw tightening around his throat. Had Nabob ever made a detailed study of 'Guttural Vocalisations; Pure and Applied' he might just have realised that Flagit was attempting to communicate the desire to be allowed to breathe. Please.

'What have you come up with? More balls on strings? A red-hot poker cosy, hmmm? More delightful things that will guarantee to get my name at the top of d'Abaloh's bad books, eh? A little something that is absolutely *certain* to swing his casting vote my way? You've had almost a week. Show me what you've done!' shouted Nabob, dropping him. Flagit collapsed in a scaly heap. 'Show me now!'

Flagit took a deep draught from a fizzing jug of brimstone and treacle. 'Tan-naaah!' he fanfared, producing a tiny cap of gold mesh from behind his back.

'So? What is it?' growled Nabob. 'A gold-plated lava lampshade, perhaps?'

'Ooooh no, no! I have in my hand here *the* finest plaything ever to come yours, mine or even Dark Lord d'Abaloh's way. If *this* doesn't secure you total election victory, then d'Abaloh's corruption is far from absolute!' yelled Flagit.

'Ssssh!' whimpered Nabob glancing nervously over his shoulder. Demons had been known to mysteriously disappear for muttering things far less controversial than that last little outburst. Despite himself Nabob found he was getting excited. If Flagit was prepared to hurl risky sentiments around then it must be good. He listened to the speechifying demon feeling himself being swept along on the rising cadence of his words.

'. . . control over every living thing, bend and subjugate the conscious mind and manipulate the psyche! Why, only a few seconds before you arrived I made a rat put a *very nasty scratch* in a lovely shiny table . . .'

'What?' screamed Nabob. 'You did what?'

Flagit looked flustered. 'Er, I made a rat . . . er . . .'

'Rats always scratch tables,' observed Nabob.

'Er, no, no. I think you'll find that's cats. Something to do with keeping their claws sharp . . .'

'Rats, cats, so what?'

'Er, I think you might be missing the . . . I might not have made myself clear,' winced Flagit, seeing the glare in Nabob's slitted eyes and feeling that the conversation wasn't really going precisely the way he would have liked. 'This wasn't just any old random slash-and-run type wanton vandalism . . .' he began in a different vein.

'Oh no? What then? The entire works of Ronnie Musbosch? In marquetry?' cackled Nabob flippantly.

Flagit snarled deep inside and stomped forward angrily, raising the first two talons of his right claw in an offensive 'v'.

'Temper, temper!' shouted Nabob.

'*That* is what I made the rat scratch. A quarter of an inch deep in the gleaming surface of an ancient, and very valuable, walnut table too!' Each word was emphasised by a significant waving of the insolently rigid digits.

For the first time since his percussive entrance Nabob was actually silent. It didn't last long. 'Don't believe you,' he snarled, but with definitely less bluster. 'Show me.'

Barely containing his excitement Flagit dropped the mesh skullcap on to Nabob's head and settled it carefully between his horns.

'Now, close your eyes,' he whispered.

'What? You seriously . . . ?'

'Close them and listen carefully.' Flagit whispered strings of detailed instructions into Nabob's ear, guiding him hypnotically through the almost meditative mind-state necessary for Suggestive Mental Assertion to work.

As soon as Flagit's commentary ended, strange images flashed into Nabob's sceptical mind, bouncing into focus like eager spaniels with a bone.

He whimpered and snatched his eyes wide open.

'Guess it works,' croaked Flagit. 'D'you see the purple flash and all them little stars?'

Nabob nodded limply. 'What the . . . ?'

'Try again, keep your eyes closed and watch for the whiskers.'

Nabob covered his slitted pupils and the same picture dashed enthusiastically back. He whimpered, fighting the urge to open his eyes, wallowing in the crystallising images of an alien world a thousand feet above . . .

'Can you see the whiskers?' asked Flagit's voice.

'I, I, no,' grunted Nabob trying to figure out exactly what it was he could see.

Directly above him dark strips of some strange organic compound crossed each other and held up a flat region of an expanse of carbonates and mineral deposits. To his left a silvered sheet of super-cooled calcium silicate shone dimly in the midnight gloom.

'What about the table? Can you see that?' pestered the voice of Flagit whispering in his ear. 'Look around.'

Suddenly the image reeled wildly in Nabob's head, swirling uncontrollably.

'Keep your eyes shut!' snapped Flagit as Nabob whimpered and gripped the arm of the chair. 'Tight or you'll lose it!'

The vision of a table swam nauseously into view, set out with a cracked mirror, a small stack of parchment and a collected mound of dead beetles. Nabob thought about standing and staggered towards the table. He had to see this scratch. He turned and cried out as he saw a face in the mirror staring back at him. The face of a curly haired nine-year-old girl full of freckly innocence, above a bright red nightdress.

This girl's my oyster, thought Nabob evilly. It's fun time!

And the lip on the face in the mirror curled back into a grin far too devilish for your average nine-year-old; her eyes narrowed, her fingers flexed and she started to cackle uncontrollably.

Week-old tabby kittens sprang and bounced across candy floss clouds, chasing pink cotton-wool balls and gleefully swatting at dandelion clocks. Day-old chicks peeped encouragingly to the pneumatic lambs. It was a nine-year-old's picture of cutesy happiness. It wasn't a patch on fighting pirates for treasure, but it had sufficed for as long as she could remember.

Until tonight.

What started it she would never know, but in her mind's eye, the tabbies grew teeth and from each padded paw sprang razor claws. Feral snarls licked across their once-innocent kitten faces as they noticed just how tasty the chicks looked. Horns germinated on the lambs' heads, erupting in curly terror with a cracking of agnine skulls. Madness poured into her dreams. Bleating and babbling, a single lamb grew claws and tore at its pristine wool, ripping madly in a frenzy of mutilation, exposing the glistening black scales and the red slitted pupils . . .

Mmmmm, she thought. *This* is more like it!

Alea leapt out of bed and dashed for the mirror. Her eyes narrowed, her hands flexed and she began to cackle. Her pulse quickened as she heard the sound of her strangely-changed voice, blood surging hot through her juvenile veins, throbbing with mounting delinquency. Something inside her young mind stirred and fidgeted, thrashing about and kicking up clouds of devilry like a dogfish in a pond. Desires began to spin uncontrollably through her heart, concepts she had never heard of before . . . vandalism, destruction, ruin, not doing homework. Every fibre of her body ached to be tearing and wrecking. Each limb throbbed and longed to be smashing and laying waste. A wisp of fear flashed through her seething mind. What was happening?

Was this puberty?

Not knowing why, she suddenly wanted to spin on her heel, dash into the other room and do something very wicked.

Within the second she was standing in the centre of her father's workshop, humming with damage potential. She stared at the colours and hues crying for attention on the shelves. The flasks of ink primaries vying with pots of dried sub-shades, clashing with the fifty-eight tons of black glaring menacingly at peach blossom and apple whites, as if despising their warmly natural charm.

Images of spinning pots ricocheting off the walls and splattering rainbows of indelible destruction across the workshop filled her mind's eye. But this time it would not be accidental. She cracked her eager knuckles, cackled wickedly, headed for the crimson and stopped, suddenly doubting her actions.

Flinging gallons of lurid inks around the workshop, destroying her father's work and putting back the printing schedule weeks was bad, even detestable, but it wasn't the *worst*. Too small, no knock-on effect. Lacking in sinister subtlety or deadly finesse. Just petty vandalism really, not a very *original* sin at all. She rubbed her hands together, scowled thoughtfully and assessed the printer's shelves for the heights of potentially magnificent malfeasance.

Her fingertip ran across a huge stone-edging decorated with fairy cakes. Fidgeting, she scowled at the lyrically lilting chipset prose and accompanying intricately carved illustrations for page sixty-three of *Scone, but Not Forgotten: the Cook-it-Yourself Guide to Reincarnations and Immortality*.

She tutted and moved on, her fingers strolling over another stack of rock borders just returned from the proof-reader and ready for printing. She grinned as an idea crackled into her head. In a few seconds she was scrambling up the stack of stone letters and mesh. A surge of undiluted naughtiness flooded her nine-year-old body as she set to work with an everwidening grin, plucking out and re-arranging hosts of chipset lettering.

Exhibiting a penchant for wickedness and a fluent understanding of D'vanouin that was way beyond her years she calculatingly rearranged the letters in the illuminated handy field edition of the Red Proselytic Manuscript of St Lucre the Unwashed. She also found time to draw moustaches on all the angels. She thrilled with nefarious delight as she wantonly vandalised the plates for tomorrow's print-run.

And, a thousand feet below her bare toes, something enjoyed itself far more than it had done in centuries.

Psalmed and Ready

Coloured streaks of moted light flooded through the lupin window in the north transept of Abbey Synnia, bounced off the gleaming tiled floor and cast a million shadows for the guard-monks to hide in. Peeled eyes peered out from the dark rectangles lurking under each pew, attention fixed on the main door, ready, waiting and primed for the invaders. Behind them gleamed the priceless glory of the Chalice of Wyndarland, miles from home and vulnerable.

Unseen and unheard a tiny nasturtium of glass wriggled and dropped silently out of the lupin window. A second later a head topped with hair the length of freshly mown suede appeared in the gap, peered eagerly around and grinned. No one in sight. But he knew they were all down there, arranged in the classic Sacred Deployment Number Three. He'd done the training; he knew. And besides, his perfectly utilised intelligence sources had informed him that twenty-five guard-monks were secreted under the pews forward of centre and three dozen behind the cloister screen, with half a dozen scattered discretionally around the baptismal font and the pulpit. Oh, the naivety of that fossil Pope Uri the Thirty-Third. Did he really expect to thwart them with that old tactical chestnut?

Tying off the rope he had lowered, Friar Succingo flexed muscles hardened through weeks of shinning up thirty-foot bell-ropes and abseiled expertly into a confessional. Seconds later the other five invaders were with him, hearts pounding, caterpillars pupating excitedly in their stomachs. They all knew what they had to do. They'd had their orders from above, delivered this very morning by pigeon, seal unbroken. The final climax of months of preparation.

Then, in response to the barest gesture of command, two intruders slipped off their sandals, leapt for the cast-iron candle-holders protruding from the vast pillars, swung over the bar, sprang and landed on the first-floor cloisters in a flurry of cassocks. Instantly they vanished, one east, one west.

Three . . . two . . . one. Right on cue, a pair of high-intensity incense burners hit the centre of the main aisle and exploded in vast plumes of choking blue smoke. Slamm J'hadd tugged his cowl over his head and trembled in the confessional. Why did they have to be *so* loud? All the months of training and he still hadn't got used to it.

Accelerated by the impatient heel of Friar Succingo's assault sandal, J'hadd cannoned through the carved door under cover of the smoke screen. With cassock akimbo he sprinted for the high altar as a hulking guard-monk erupted from beneath a pew. Succingo spotted him, expertly unlaced his counterweighted stole and began spinning it, calculating trajectory and strike potential. Terrified, J'hadd snatched his stole, jammed his eyes shut and hurled it desperately at the oncoming onslaught. That was it, game over. There was a thud, a crash and nervously J'hadd dared open his eyes. Miraculously the guard-monk was down, ankles bound, buried in a bonfire of shattered pews. Maybe he was getting the hang of this stole-throwing after all.

Above him, his counterweighted weapon dangled from a candle holder.

In a flurry of three more stoles and cloister bombs from above, the rest of the Abbey resistance folded. But the alarm had been raised. Carillons of bells boomed around the vast interior, tocsins of terror poisoning the air. Sacred security systems screamed into action. Automatic bolts slammed across the main door and sealed off the bell-tower. And a vast ornate screen dropped out of the sky, landed atop the altar-rail and formed an impenetrable barrier eighteen feet high.

J'hadd chewed his nails, and winced as the smoke stung his eyes. Suddenly, a pew landed before him at the base of the altar steps, then another was hurled across it, forming a makeshift see-saw facing the altar screen. Friar Succingo snatched at him, shoving him kneeling on to the top pew, sprinting past and scrambling up the altar screen with another invader. They climbed six feet, stopped and leapt backwards on to the raised pew. In a second J'hadd was squealing as he arced over the screen with barely an inch to spare.

'Grab it!' shrieked Friar Succingo through the railings, pointing desperately at the Chalice. Dazed, J'hadd reached for the artefact and instantly lassos fell from above, slid tight around his limbs and hauled him up to the first-floor cloisters, shrieking.

Two more incense-diary devices blasted out choking screens, followed by three more cloister bombs and in seconds J'hadd was swung through the lupined glass clutching the Holy Chalice of Wynderland.

He burst into the gleaming sunlight screaming and hit the cemetery grass with a dull thud. In a moment Succingo's hands snatched the Chalice and he sprinted away, the thrill of a successful mission pounding within. Suddenly, he saw movement out of the corner of his eye and a purple-clad pursuer broke cover from behind a convenient mausoleum. Momentary panic surging through his rotund body, the Friar tucked the Chalice under his camouflage cassock. There shouldn't have been anyone there! Especially not someone who could run that fast. The purple cassock of General Sinnohd flapped noisily as he gained on Succingo, slashing the distance by the second. Then he unexpectedly leapt, roaring, and clamped his arms solidly about the Friar's knees. The graveyard hit him at full tilt and in that single muddy moment he knew it was all over. He'd been set up, betrayed, double crucifixed.

'Give it back!' commanded a voice as another purple-clad figure stepped out from behind a mossy gravestone. Succingo looked up at the mitre and crook and realised that this was Pope Uri the Thirty-Third. 'C'mon! Return the Chalice!'

'Never! cried the Friar and thrust it deeper within his cassock.

'Very well. We'll do it the hard way,' snarled the Pope and attempted to click his arthritic fingers. Muttering miserably he jammed two digits into his mouth and blasted a short sharp whistle. An eclipse of Abbey Synnian guard-monks erupted from countless gravestones and buried the Friar alive.

Hands snatched at his body and pulled. Succingo was helpless in the mêlée, powerless to prevent them raising him aloft and striking up a rowdy chant of 'Party, party! Hallelujah!' All around him he saw other groups of guard-monks raising his team victoriously and hurling banners skywards. Something didn't feel quite right any more. If this *was* a lynching, then why did they all look so pleased with themselves? Were they really that sick?

He didn't have a chance to find out before he was plunged into the gloom of the Abbey, carried up the aisle and hurled into one of six waiting chairs hastily assembled at the bottom of the altar. In quick succession his team were by his side, facing the entire might of the Abbey Synnian Security Service.

With only the slightest of shoving Pope Uri and General Sinnohd pushed their way through and stood glaring at the audacious six.

'So!' scowled Pope Uri a slight curl of cruelty twitching at his lip. 'Try to steal the Chalice of Wyndarland, would you?'

'N . . . n . . . n . . .' whimpered J'hadd, shaking his head. Succingo's elbow rattled against his ribs.

'Try?' yelled the Friar defiantly. 'Ha! We succeeded. I have it here!' He patted his cassock victoriously.

'Oh yes, then what, pray, is this?' answered the Pope, whisking a gleaming chalice from beneath his acres of ancient vestments in a manner which J'hadd found far too showy, under the circumstances.

'A fake!' grumbled Friar Succingo, trying desperately to ignore the looks of growing doubt on his team's faces. J'hadd chewed his thumbnail.

'Certain? Take a look at your own,' purred the Pope revelling in each torturous moment.

Nervously, Succingo tugged an identical copy into the light. 'This is the real Chalice!' he cried and received a pathetic ripple of supporting whimpers. J'hadd stared at the ominously twitching lips of the Pope and decided that he really didn't like being there any more.

'Uh-huh. Turn it around,' whispered Pope Uri with none of the holiness one might normally expect from a man in his position.

Dreading what he would see, Succingo obeyed. Read the five words and screamed. There, etched neatly into the replica chalice, was the legend:

CONGRATULATIONS
WELCOME TO THE SAS!

Pope Uri and General Sinnohd exploded with pent hilarity and six monks tugged on ropes releasing a thousand festively coloured pig's bladders painstakingly inflated over the last few days.

'Well done, Succingo,' spluttered the Pope. 'Nobody's ever got away with that before. Had that copy made decades ago.' Casually he handed the real chalice to the guffawing figure of General Sinnohd and turned back to Friar Succingo. 'Sorry about our little joke, but after eighteen months training I thought a few more minutes of sweating wouldn't make any difference. It's good to have you on our side! Welcome to the SAS, Friar-Captain Succingo and your daring team!'

'Welcome to the SAS!' squeaked Slamm J'hadd around his thumb. 'We did it?' They were the four little words that every novice priest and friar would eagerly give their life's supply of ninety-proof communion wine to hear. Ooooh, he could have genuflected for joy. Stacks better than 'Well done, you're Pope!' and leagues ahead of 'Congratulations on your new Sainthood!'

It was the uniform that did it, of course. Well, you only had to look at it. None of this flowing acres of passé purple robes or yards of plain chaste white vestments made from finest bleached sackcloth. No, no. Not for the SAS.

48

We are talking head-turning top-of-the-range designer camouflage cassocks. Twenty-eight concealed pockets, holy webbing bandolier, bible belt . . . the works. No expense was spared on the Special Aisle Service.

It was the law. And had been for the last five hundred and three years. Ever since, in fact, a particular chance meeting which involved two royal houses, a secluded waterfall, some overactive hormones and a wild boar – although not necessarily in that order.

It is a well-documented fact that King Stigg of Rhyngill was a keen hunter of wild boar. Up until 1017, centuries after his death, the main banqueting hall in Castell Rhyngill was decorated with the mounted heads of some six hundred and twenty-two of the beasties which he had bagged over the numerous years of his rulership. But of all the boar he had slain or given chase to, never had he faced the fabled screaming boar of the southern Talpa Mountains. It was said that once seen, it haunted your every waking thought, twisting every conversation or discussion back to that one obsessive subject with mind-numbing repetition.

And so it was on the trail of the screaming boar that King Stigg found himself wandering way off the beaten track, getting an eyeful of the sight of a beautiful waterfall leaping off a cliff, arcing vertiginously downwards and crashing seductively over the naked body of the teenage maiden Princess Natis of the Non-Aligned Tribes of Talpa showering herself below. Something surged in his loins and, all thoughts of boar forgotten, he dragged her off kicking and screaming to be his bride.

In a rare flash of common sense, Stigg somehow suspected that the chances of a peaceful marriage ceremony were pretty slim and since his loin-stirring had continued unabated he decided that it might be prudent to gird them thoroughly. To this end, the twenty-four biggest and ugliest monks serving in Abbey Synnia at that time were issued with special knives and ordered to patrol the aisle, eyes peeled, ready to jump on even the merest whiff of trouble from any of the bridal entourage.

49

It was a total success. Almost. After a tense and very brief ceremony, three poisonings and a violent fracas involving an axe and two of the bridesmaids, the King dragged his wife off to the conjugal bed, loins thankfully intact.

The next morning King Stigg, exhausted but extremely happy for once, issued a decree ensuring that the Special Aisle Service remain eternally vigilant so that this conjugal victory could be repeated as regularly as he felt up to it. And on that day, before vanishing once again upstairs, he issued the SAS motto: 'Who girds wins.'

It had been an honour then to serve in the SAS and it still was.

'Friar-Private' Slamm J'hadd, as he was now known, was stunned that they had actually managed to pull it off.

But as he sat before the altar of Abbey Synnia, Slamm J'hadd cursed. Two years in the planning; eighteen months, five thousand gallons of sweat, blood and tears in the execution, and here he was. Exactly where he didn't want to be. It really shouldn't have gone this far. He should've wrapped it up ages ago. He'd failed again. And if he didn't get his finger out in the next few weeks he'd be directing wagon trains on Knavesbridge for the rest of his life. Or worse. As Friar-Captain 'Tucky' Succingo waved the counterfeit chalice in victory, Slamm J'hadd slouched miserably and tutted.

The goats saw him first. Each one took it in turns to break off their endless search for nibbles, stare long and hard through the wriggling heat haze at the approaching figure, spit uninterestedly and continue their grubbing about for anything remotely edible in the rocks of the Ghuppy Desert.

Old Git was the last to notice his approach. It wasn't surprising since this seemingly immortal relic of goatkind was far from sensually perfect. Cataracts, deafness and a tendency for his front left leg to spasm for no apparent reason all conspired to make him wish that the outside world would leave him alone. Although he could make an exception if a wild female ibex with a penchant for dirty old goats

50

fluttered her eyelids at him becomingly. However, seeing as the black-robed figure sweeping across the rocky desert appeared to be carrying a case of books and not a wild female ibex with a penchant for dirty old goats, Old Git dismissed him from his limited field of interest with a derisive snort of boredom and wondered what lichen tasted of.

Behind the goats a clump of brightly coloured tents encircled a patch of ground very much like any other patch of ground in a hundred-ell radius and flapped gently in the breeze. Quite what primeval restlessness drove the D'vanouin nomads to up sticks twice a week, trudge all day across the trackless desert and set up camp around another undistinguished patch of rock, no one had a clue. This was generally because no one survived long enough to ask. Rumour had it that their wanderlust was due to the fact that the rock was greyer on the other side of the hill, but folklore disagreed, suggesting that since they'd been doing it for longer than anyone could remember it was now an instinct, like hibernation or pupating. Myth disagreed and even had the audacity to suggest that it was entirely due to the vast string of bad debts they were fleeing from. Whatever the reason, every couple of days, come sunshine or sunshine, they'd kick the goats off and follow them until they gave up and sat down somewhere. Today, unfortunately, that place happened to be here. Right on the path of the Mostly Reverend Vex Screed, Chief Haranguist Missionary for Southern Rhyngill.

'Have you heard the Word?' he cried snatching open the nearest tent's flap and stomping inside. 'I have come from far,' he declared leaning back to demonstrate the point, 'but now I'm . . .' he dashed towards the most senior looking D'vanouin and thrust his face an inch away from his nose. '. . . near!' With a grin, he stood and dashed back to the entrance slit. 'I was far,' he repeated. 'But now I'm . . .' he scurried forward, '. . . near! See? Far . . . near!'

The D'vanouins stared at the black-robed madman and passed around a bowl of sheep's eyes.

Reverend Screed shrugged the pack off his shoulders and

51

began handing out piles of gleaming new red books to each of the gathered nomads. 'Take one and pass them along. If there aren't enough you'll have to share one between two.' He dived back into his sack, withdrew a battered-looking tambourine and shook it with an ominously hearty grin. 'Hope you'll all be in good voice later. I feel the urge for a "Kumbayah" coming on!'

The sheep's eyes continued their unblinking circuit of the tent.

'But first, a short lesson from the Book of Apophthegms,' declared Reverend Screed, flicking open his own personal, but highly battered, copy of the Red Proselytic Manuscript of St Lucre the Unwashed. He pointed to the page number and began to read. There was a brief desultory rustling of pages accompanied by several 'harrumphs' of acute uninterest from the older D'vanouins.

Why such disinterest? Well, they'd seen religion before. Tried it in hundreds of different forms. That was *the* major snag about constantly wandering aimlessly about in the wilderness – spend more than forty days out here and missionaries would be flocking to save you. The older D'vanouins had really had enough of flocking missionaries.

Some religions had seemed like fun at the time. Once they'd run across a Blikni Yogi from the Meanlayla Mountains on his annual recruitment drive and been introduced to communal co-operative self-deception. By lying to oneself with sufficient conviction one can make oneself believe that everyone else in the room can fly. With enough people arranged in small groups being supported by others' beliefs in their aerial abilities, periods of sustained co-operative flight could be achieved. The D'vanouins soon got bored with this after discovering the difficulty of concentrating on everybody else whilst hovering precariously thirty feet off the ground.

Over the years, some religious zealots had been run out of camp far faster than others. The current record holder was a delegate from the Anti-Numismatic Missionary who lasted a full twenty-seven and a half seconds after declaring that everyone would be happier and live longer without coinage or monetary tokens of any sort. He got as far as saying, 'Here, place your evil currency in my sack and be free of sin!' before seventy-six ceremonial yataghan daggers were whistling after his fleeing heels.

Now, it wasn't that the D'vanouins hadn't the capacity to believe. Oh no. They'd believe as deeply as the next man, just as long as it didn't involve giving up any fragment of the perfectly honed lifestyle of debauchery to which they had grown immensely accustomed, running up debts as and when necessary in the pursuit of a good time.

Give them a spiritual doctrine that offered all that and their piety would know no bounds.

Little did the unsuspecting Reverend Vex Screed know but right now he was, in fact, introducing the D'vanouins to their hearts' desire. It was there, translated in black and white before their very eyes.

The nine year old translator poked her demonic face under a tent flap and watched with almost as much avid interest as the devil below. All around the tent there were nudges of attentive elbows, the wagging of fascinated fingers and the intake of astounding breaths. There, in the books before them, written in perfect D'vanouin was the message.

Yea, though I walk in the alley of debt, I don't give a damn.

The first giggles of conversion chuckled around the tent as amazed eyes beheld legions of moustachioed angels cavorting in the margins of the illuminated text. And over the page, in block capitals, was a tale of an itinerant deity who insisted on getting parties going by zapping buckets of water into groaning barrels of twenty-five-year-old whisky.

Blessed is the pure grain spirit for it is the water of life.

And the shrieks of reformation rang loud, for over the next page was a declaration that struck powerful chords of conviction in the souls of those gathered. It offered the security of religion and the promise of a chaotic havoc-wreaking session to put the word 'mayhem' to shame. For there, written large, the sacred call to arms . . .

> Fear ye not the darkest depths of night;
> let ye lambs of devotion burn bright.

With a cry to strike terror into the hardiest of sheep-farmers, the D'vanouins snatched wholeheartedly at their latest religion. This one had to be good, it offered parties, it demanded sacrificial lambs and, if there was enough left over for kebabs afterwards, well, who could blame them?

Alea rubbed her hands as for the first time in his life the Mostly Reverend Vex Screed had a hundred per cent conversion. It was only with the slightest of doubts that he watched the tribesmen tug maps of Southern Rhyngill out of saddle-bags and begin pointing eagerly at the least protected of the sheep farms.

He should have been an awful lot more concerned.

Especially when, with whoops and screams of excitement, they dashed out of the tent, hurled ropes, nets and boxes of yataghans on to the backs of their camels and thundered enthusiastically away in a vast cloud of dust, each waving a red tome.

Panting with the effort of the chase, the warthog slunk around the back of its quarry and halted, snout close to the grass, tense breath moving several dozen blades. Generations of instinct whirred through its mind as it calculated the best line of approach. They were skittish; one false move, one misplaced trotter-fall and he'd lose the lot of them. But if he snuck around the back of that boulder, then down that little rivulet and came up over . . .

A sharp whistle shattered the silence, blasting a coded message across the valley at the speed of sound.

The warthog shook its shaggy, tooth-encrusted head in disbelief. Back behind the tree stump? Surely not. Catch one glimpse of me and they'll be off for certain . . . ah, unless . . .

The whistle dotted and dashed another hail of distant commands.

All right, already, thought the warthog, I'm off! It stood and sprinted for the stump. A large ram caught sight of the motion and dashed down the slope, starting a fluffy white avalanche of ovine panic. There was a blast of whistle and . . .

Hah! Perfect! thought the warthog as his partner swooped out of nowhere and cut off the line of escape. The flock of sheep bleated and trembled in woolly anxiety, while the warthogs licked their expectantly salivating jowls. They had them, gripped in a tightening pincer that your average Ogmiran Mega-scorpion would give its right stinger for. The warthog snarled and, as if this had been the starting pistol, the sheep bolted, skittering and bouncing down the hill in a flocculent surge of fluffy self-preservation, through that gap between those two poles and . . .

With one bound a figure leapt from nowhere and slammed the gate shut behind them. And the crowd went wild. Bunches of ribboned flowers arced into the arena and were snatched up by the beaming pair of warthogs as Torrve, the shepherd bowed and waved ecstatically. He was the crowd's undisputed favourite, thrilling them year after year with his faithful herding partners, Vyll and Dheene.

Despite the light, but irritatingly incessant, north-westerly drizzle, a large crowd had gathered for the annual Lammarch Warthog Trials. On the same day every year people flooded into this natural bowl to stand in their rain-cloaks and oooh and aaah in amazement at the almost telepathic link forged between one man and the hogs. Such intelligence! Amazing the way they could be trained to herd sheep. But, if the truth were known, these domesticated beasts used only a tiny fraction of the hunting and herding skills of their wild cousins. Now, it takes a real warthog to track down and capture the wily Feral Talpine Truffle. Sheep? Phooey. Mere pedestrians compared to the semi-sentient mountain-dwelling fungi prized for their fabled aphrodisiac and hallucinatory properties.

Suddenly, the crowd rumbled, heaved and exploded in screams of protesting indignation as four pairs of score-parchments were held aloft. Five point three for technical ability from the Rhyngillian judge. Scandal. Were they blind? Get the referee! Clods of turf zoomed judgewards, flipping and spinning with deadly, if soggy, accuracy, and the crowd took a menacing step forward.

The top notch on the leader board hung in the balance . . . it was all down to the marks for artistic merit. The Rhyngillian judge looked up from the bench and swallowed nervously as he saw the expressions of the sod-wielding public. As one, the three other judges hurled their score-parchments aloft, proudly holding six point noughts as high as they could for everyone to see. All eyes turned on the Rhyngillian judge, swiftly calculating trajectories and target areas for maximum effect. The other judges dived under the bench as with a whimper and a limpid grin he revealed his score-parchments. Five point two.

'Sod him!' ordered an irate member of the audience and several acres of turf sprang gleefully into the air, spinning towards their intended target with devastating effect.

But before the crowd had a chance to re-arm themselves, disaster struck.

Hosts of screaming bed-sheeted warriors galloped into the amphitheatre on battle-camels. They waved glinting cut-lasses around their heads and wielded huge nets on sticks. As one they surged towards the sheep-pen, swinging the nets. And before anyone could react the D'vanouins scooped their bleating prizes from the woolly crush and vanished over the far horizon with them, whooping and cat-calling obscenely.

Suddenly, to the gathered crowd, squabbling over first place in the Warthog Trials seemed not a little on the trivial side.

Warm scented breezes of sublime joy swept across the delighted tundras of Reverend Screed's heart. Today was a good day, he mused as he sauntered through the sand-dunes at the edge of the Ghuppy Desert, heading towards Southern

Rhyngill. An entire tribe converted, whoosh, just like that! They must have been *so* desperate. Days like this were what made it all worth while, spreading contentment and joy and the Word.

In his glowing fog of self congratulation, the Mostly Reverend Vex Screed failed completely to notice that a nine-year-old girl in a red nightdress was currently unfastening the latches of his back-pack. Carefully she reached inside, snatched one of the books and tugged it gently into the open with a wicked grin.

'. . . I said "Hello",' she repeated a few moments later as she hopped up and down in front of him.

'Eh? Oh, hello, little girl,' grunted Screed absently. To Nabob, the nine-foot horny devil squatting in a tiny cavern in Mortropolis, being referred to as a 'little girl' came as something of a shock. But he recovered quickly. He was having *far* too much fun! The willingness this little girl was showing to the suggestive thoughts he sent was amazing.

'What's this word?' he mouthed through Alea as she raised the book in her hand and pointed randomly.

'Eh? Er, that's, ummmm . . .' began Screed, attempting to read one of the serpentine squiggles squirming across the D'vanouin edition of the Red Proselytic Manuscript of St Lucre the Unwashed.

'. . . and this one?' squeaked Alea eagerly flipping a few pages. 'Can't read this one either, what's it say?'

Screed shook his head and tried to follow as she kept up the incessant bombardment.

'. . . and this one? Is it pronounced "Nnnnnnnnjeeyah" or is it "Nnnannnjyahhahh"? Cause I think that little squiggly thing above the "nj" makes it a "njya", hmmmm?'

'What are you doing with that?' asked Screed in confusion.

'Trying to read it, 'sept it's hard, see?' answered Alea and put her head on one side like a spaniel that's just done a good trick. Nabob chuckled to himself as he added this final touch.

'Well, I'm not surprised. It has undergone thorough literal translation into a dialect known as D'vanouin,' answered Screed still trying not to let go of his warmly successful mood.

'Eh? Wassat mean?'

'Oh, er, it's foreign. Hard.' And with that he took a few strides forward and settled back into self-congratulatory mode.

There was a brief skittering of tiny feet, a scuffling of pages and then Alea's voice shattered his relaxing reverie. 'So what's *that* word, then?' she asked, bouncing up and down before him. 'I want to read it.'

'Oh, now look here, try this one. You might find it easier.' And with that he snatched Alea's book and thrust his very own copy into her hands. 'Read that and keep quiet,' he added, striding off with her in tow.

'Thank you,' she grinned and skipped cheerfully behind him.

Nabob rubbed his hands together wickedly. Everything was turning out wonderfully, a little suggestion here, a nudge of persuasion there . . . Now, if camels gallop as fast as I think, then . . .

Suddenly a whole host of battle-bactrians erupted over a dune, ridden by dozens of screaming, bed-sheeted D'vanouins. Plumes of sand flew from hooves as they charged towards Screed and Alea, bearing down on them with daggers drawn and war cries raw in their throats. Screed opened his mouth to scream as legs and knees filled his field of view . . .

And then they were past, thundering away back to camp.

'Dune-hogs!' shouted Alea. 'Nobody ever teach you look where you're . . .'

'Now, now. Er, let them be,' stuttered Screed in his most pacifistic manner.

'What? They just nearly flattened me!'

'Ah, yes. That's the word, you see? *Nearly*. They're simply full of the joys of the word of St Lucre and are showing it in a method of their own choosing. It's . . . er, a bit of a *boisterous* choosing I must agree, but, well, there's no harm done.'

'Oh, no?' growled a deep voice edged with a country-style burr. 'No 'arm? Don't s'pose you'd be 'appenin' t'see what they was carryin', hmmm?'

Screed whirled around and stood face to face with a

58

countless mass of sweating and miffed-looking countryfolk. He couldn't yet be certain but they did seem to bear a remarkable resemblance to shepherds.

'C . . . carrying?' he spluttered.

'Yup.'

'Sheep,' whispered Alea.

'Er, sheep?' hazarded Screed.

'He knows! Get 'im, Neame!' squealed a voice from the back.

'No, no. It was a lucky guess,' whimpered Screed, waving his palms and backing away.

'You sure? See, me an' the boys've jus' 'ad our Warthog Trials disturbed by them camels an' we don' like tha', do we, boys?'

A hearty chorus of rustic disapproval echoed back.

Screed wanted to ask what warthogs had to do with sheep but decided against it just now.

'Now, we's peaceful 'onest folk who only get together once a year for a bit of a party after the trials an', well, 'avin' it messed up 'as really gotten our goat . . .'

'Or sheep!' shouted Alea from behind Screed.

'Ssssssh!' whispered Screed sharply.

'Who you tellin' to sssssh . . . ?' growled the shepherd, Neame, and took a step forward. But then he glanced down as his foot struck something in the sand, something hard and red. 'What's this?' he asked, mostly to himself as the other shepherds shuffled a threatening pace forward.

'A book. Fell off the back of a camel,' answered Alea and stepped into view. 'I saw it.'

'Ssssssh!' snarled Screed.

'Camel, you say?' asked Neame, glaring at Screed, then smiling at the pretty little nine-year-old who was being very helpful.

'Oh, yes,' answered Alea. 'It nearly ran me over when lots and lots of them came over that hill carrying lots of sheep.' At mention of that fluffy five-letter word a dozen indignant growls broke out. 'I only noticed the book 'cause I thought it was funny,' she ended cryptically.

'Funny?' grunted Neame. And in the privacy of his own cavern, Nabob squealed with delight. Mortals! Pah, so predictable!

Alea looked straight into the shepherd's eyes. 'Yes. Well, don't *you* think it's funny that he's got lots of them books in his pack?' she said pointing directly at Screed.

Evidently, by the look on their faces, they didn't. Neither did Screed who, on balance, deciding that distance was the better part of survival, spun and legged it.

Seconds later, Alea stood on the side of the sand-dune alone and giggling, smirking evilly to herself every time a distant 'Help!' or 'Get 'im! C'mon, faster!' drifted into earshot. Then she hitched up her red nightdress and skipped off towards Abbey Synnia to wait behind a suitable bush.

In his cavern. Nabob's ribs were beginning to ache with his screeching laughter. Oh, it was so *good* to be bad!

Away across Mortropolis in the top storeroom of the Transcendental Travel Company Ltd, the Really Reverend Unctuous III was having problems with being dead. It wasn't the fact that he was dead, that was all right, I mean he'd done everything to sort himself out, given himself the Last Rites (better late than never) offered himself a full Requiem Mass and even murmured a few comforting words of remembrance to himself. And, apart from the fact that he'd have to be a qualified contortionist if ever he needed a shoulder to cry on in the coming months, the only real snag was that the Underworld definitely wasn't what he'd expected.

Well, superficially it was – gloomy lighting, infernal heating, screams of eternal torment, devils and demons stamping about and shouting a lot, you know the sort of thing. There was even a three-foot black insecty-thing in a cage over in the far corner that ate rocks. It seemed to be some sort of a pet and his skin crawled every time it scuttled forward, snatched a chunk of granite off the wall and gulped it whole. But, despite everything, Unctuous couldn't help feeling that, well, something was missing.

It was uncomfortable down there and the sight of that devil

crooning over his pet stalag-mite had really put the willies up him, but, from what he'd seen so far he couldn't really describe the Underworld as an infernal cycle of torment and torture. In fact, if he actually admitted it to himself, he was more bored than anything.

'Er, what are you doing?' he asked the devil that called itself Flagit as it leant over a mass of infernite wires pinned to a large sponge.

'I'm busy, go away,' it grumbled staring confusedly at the coloured pairs of stones dangling from the ends of the strands of wire.

Strange, Unctuous thought, it'd been at that ever since the other one had slapped it on the back and dashed out of there wearing the remains of his skull-cap, convinced that something was in the bag. *And* it didn't say thank you.

'I'm bored,' wheedled Unctuous. 'I thought you devils were supposed to find things for idle hands to do.'

'Pah! Not today. It's Sinday, day of rest,' scorned Flagit irritably, his slitted eyes not moving from the intricate design before him. Noisily he scratched his head with an index talon, shrugged his vast shoulders and passed a ruby bobbin over a pair of sapphires and an opal, then threaded an amethyst through a loop and pulled. A scream of irritation erupted as the infernite lattice unravelled itself gleefully before its crimson eyes and was hurled across the cavern. 'Damn that thing! Why does it always do that?'

Unctuous picked it up and looked. 'Er, well, you didn't lock your warp thread in place securely before looping that flying trans-weft into . . .'

'Oh, I see, expert on lace making are we?' snarled Flagit looking as menacing as he could with a pair of blunting thimbles on his left claw.

'Well, as a matter of fact, yes, I thought it might be handy for setting up a woman's institute or something. You know, Tuesday morning around a coffee, and biscuits and, er . . . Oh, no. I don't suppose you do. Er, what is it anyway?'

'None . . . none of your business,' growled Flagit snatching it back swiftly. 'It concerns matters way beyond the understanding and comprehension of that tiny organ which you call your mind.'

'Hmmm, there's a lot of that about down here,' mused Unctuous. 'But it does bear an uncanny resemblance to an attempt at copying the gold braid trimming off my skullcap, which your friend seemed to take a liking to,' he said pointing at the unravelled infernite wires.

'Hmmph, you don't need it anymore. Why should you be bothered?' snarled Flagit attempting to quash the Reverend's suspicions by appearing totally uninterested.

'Your uninterest doesn't fool me for a minute! I've seen the concentration you've put into trying to get it right. Nobody, not even a devil, puts that much effort into something he's not bothered about. Now, am I correct? Why are you trying to make a larger version of the gold braid from my skullcap?'

Flagit stared at him angrily. Unctuous was asking too many questions and answering them far too accurately. What answer could the devil possibly give that would allay his suspicions and throw him off the track? 'Okay, you're right. It's a present for a . . . er, a friend,' confessed Flagit.

'Oh, lovely. And I bet I know why you kept it all so quiet! Ooh what a ribbing you'd get if your friends found out that a big lad like you was making lace . . .'

Flagit nodded warily, unsure where he was leading now.

'. . . for your mother,' finished Reverend Unctuous. 'Well, we're not going to get it finished off by throwing it across the room now are we? So I'll help you and it can be our little secret. How's that?'

Flagit's jaw was on his chest as he nodded weakly.

'Well, come on then, pick it up!' commanded Unctuous.

Flagit was shocked to find that he was actually obeying and in a second the infernite lattice was on his lap.

'Now, see that pair of amethyst bobbins, well the tension on those is shocking! Mummy's not going to be pleased if her nice little hairnet unravels itself as soon as she puts it on, now is she?' wittered Reverend Unctuous in the first ever lace class to be held in Mortropolis.

'Sanctuary, sanctuary!' screamed the Mostly Reverend Vex
Screed as he hurled himself through the front door of Abbey
Synnia and sprinted up the aisle. Hot on his sandalled heels
surged a clump of a hundred seething shepherds brandishing
crooks in a manner that did not look friendly.

'Kill him!' screamed one.

'Roast him!' yelled another.

'Dip him!' shrieked a third, missing the point entirely. A
lifetime spent sitting on the side of a hill watching sheep
gently nibbling grass and bleating soothingly hadn't really
prepared him for the harsh reality of the lynch mob.

Before the panting intruders could reach the high altar,
ropes dropped out of hatches in the ceiling and half a dozen
armed SAS monks abseiled rapidly down, bounced once at
the floor and stood shoulder to shoulder with their ceremonial daggers drawn.

'Who bargeth unbidden into this here Abbey and
demandeth ye ancient right of sanctuary,' bellowed Friar-
Captain 'Tucky' Succingo stamping his foot in the tradition-
ally sacred manner.

'Me, me, me!' shrieked Screed, trembling as he scurried
behind the monks with a screech of sandalwood on marble.

'From what plaguing evil dost thou requireth sanctuary?'
asked Succingo following the letter of the lore as he was
supposed to.

'Them!' squealed Screed, pointing a shaking fingertip at
the swarming mass of enweaponed shepherds glowering at a
stand-off in the aisle. 'I should have thought *that* was
obvious,' he added.

'And why dost ye ravening horde seek to basheth ye to
little bits and stampeth gleefully upon them in an orgy of wild
abandon?'

'Ask them,' whimpered Screed, 'All I know is I'm walking
home after a hard day's word spreading when I nearly get run
over by a camel stampede, then those shepherds point at me,
scream "Get 'im!" and the chase is on. You going to give me
sanctuary or not?'

Slamm J'hadd scratched the top of his suede-covered head baffled by a strange feeling of shocked disbelief. It all sounded *too* violent. Not his scene at all. Now give him a good mystery to solve . . .

'You telling me that you haven't a clue why a hundred shepherds suddenly get the urge to mash you?' bellowed Friar-Captain Succingo.

'Haven't the foggiest,' whimpered Screed. 'Mistaken identity? Stopping to ask didn't really seem like a good idea, you know.'

J'hadd chewed a nervous nail as Succingo whirled around to address the ravening horde of shepherds. 'Ravening horde of shepherds, why dost thou seek to bash this man of the cloth into little bits and stampeth gleefully upon them in an orgy of wild abandon, hmmm?'

A hundred different answers exploded from a hundred different mouths in a blast of extreme irritation. Surprisingly though, there was one word that kept popping up in all their cries of protest. The word . . . sheep.

J'hadd shook his head in confusion. Sheep? Could this be why I've been sent here after all? Was this the 'sad case' that Sergeant Vertex had mentioned as he'd signed the parchments and sent me away from the Religious Undercover Crime Squad after nearly twelve and a half years as Pious Constable without solving a single act of transgression aforethought? Could this be the case that would elevate me to the ranks of Chaste Inspector?

It all started to make sense to him now. In a surge of pride he suddenly had to admire Sacrosanct Sergeant Vertex back in Cranachan. He had planned this *so* carefully. Making such a fuss of 'washing his hands' of me; telling everyone what a 'worthless waste of space' I was; shrieking so perfectly when I suggested that I really did want to make a career for myself in the RUC – and all to create the perfect cover. Oh, Sergeant Vertex! What an intriguing web he had woven. This was *real* undercover work, so far under that even I didn't know my real calling.

Slamm J'hadd tapped his chin thoughtfully. Aha! So *that*

was why in the eighteen months of solid SAS training and his unstoppable service in the Cobblery Division he had never found any sign of illegal trading in souls. It was part of something bigger, something beyond the boundaries of the SAS! J'hadd grinned to himself, swelling with pride. *I knew I'd a feeling that Sergeant Vertex – bless him! – had me on a fast track to Chaste Inspector ever since the end of my first day. Well, why else had his face lit up with delight when, after spending hours in a dark corner, I'd returned to report that I'd had a 'long stand', moreover, why else would he fall about with uncontained joy after I'd searched through every single drawer in engineering to find a left-handed screwdriver. What an impression I must've made! And now I'm here in the midst of a deep cover infiltration operation to solve . . . well, what?*

Suddenly his thoughts were disturbed by a purple-clad figure bustling forward towards the throng. 'Now then, now then, what's going on here?' shouted Pope Uri stamping on the hem of his ancient robe,* tripping and landing face down with a muffled curse, sending his mitre spinning across the floor.

A hundred and seven different answers exploded from a

---

* The robes had been tailored over three hundred years ago for the now legendary 'Soup Pope of Abbey Synnia'. Thirty decades into the incensed past, His Holiness Pope Uri the First decided to celebrate his recent accession by hiring the bespoke clerical tailor for a new set of purple togs. Following a harrowing series of fittings, adjustments and tweakings that wasted vast tracts of episcopal time and tried the papal patience to its very limits, he vowed never again to have to put up with the agony of a thousand pin-pricks. Once the garments were tacked to the necessary standards of Papal Decorum, he issued a forceful decree ensuring that they would never be altered again. He had intended to add the phrase, 'in my lifetime' but his jaw locked solid in a spasm of tetanus contracted from the tailor's six thousand rusty pins. He lived out his days on a diet of thin soup and totally incomprehensible sermons.

Three centuries later his edict was still in effect, much to the chagrin of the current Pope. It wasn't the overwhelming tattiness of the purple silk that irritated Uri the Thirty-Third so much, nor the gaping holes in the knee area. It wasn't even the emergency green patch glued under the left armpit that got on his wick. It was the angry bruises emblazoned across his shiny forehead that did that. The first Pope Uri had stood almost a foot taller, and weighed about fifteen and a half stone more than this current, osseous creature. The slightest lapse of concentration, he'd catch a toe in the hem's endless acreage and go bunion over tonsure, adding another bruise to his constantly swelling collection. And he simply detested the way bruises clashed with purple.

65

hundred and seven different mouths as the SAS monks and Succingo joined in.

'Sshhhh. Hush. Silence!' squealed the Pope, hauling himself to his feet, his face turning a very similar colour to his papal robes. 'Succingo, explain!' he ordered.

'Well, Your Eminence, it would seem to have something to do with sheep going missing . . .' began the Friar-Captain, before being interrupted by Southern Rhyngill's largest shepherd lurching his way to the front of the lynch mob, tapping a small tree-trunk idly on his palm.

''E did it!' growled the shepherd, somehow managing to hit the natural frequency of the long transept and making it boom. ''E made 'em steal my flock!'

'And mine!' agreed another.

'Mine too!'

J'hadd flipped a small hymnal out of his cassock pocket and began furiously making notes.

'All mine 'ave gone, as well!' yelled another, hopping up and down.

'I didn't!' squealed Screed, protesting his innocence from behind a thin pious line of SAS monks. 'I don't know anything about it.'

'Liar!' growled the earnest shepherd, 'You're in it up to your eyeballs!'

'Be quiet!' shouted Pope Uri.

'I was preaching!' whined Screed. 'Giving them the Good News!'

'What "Good News"? Where to find the best sheep in the Talpa Mountains?' yelled Neame the shepherd lurching another fuming step forward. There was a flurry of angry agreements.

Unseen, a nine-year-old girl in a red nightdress strolled casually up the aisle brushing leaves from her hair, hand in hand with a terrified monk carrying a crook.

'Shut up!' screeched the Pope at the shepherds, banging a gold offertory plate furiously on a pew until he was rewarded with at least a modicum of silence. 'Do I understand from this overloud fracas that Brother Vex Screed here stands accused of inciting the D'vanouin tribespeople to kidnap your sheep?'

'Too right!' yelled the huge shepherd amongst a veritable plethora of agreements.

Pope Uri held up his hands for silence. 'And did you, Brother Screed?'

'No! I just gave them my usual spiel and they embraced the Good News with total conviction. In fact they were so enthusiastic about it all that they pulled some maps out, had a quick discussion, which I didn't understand a word of, saddled up their camels and galloped off. Well, I thought they were going to tell their friends and . . . Oh dear, I've just remembered. They all had very large nets tied to the saddles on their camels.'

'Sort of sheep-sized nets,' added Alea helpfully and gently tugged the quivering form of Brother Ovine through the crowd.

The shepherds growled and simmered.

'Worry not, Brother Screed. 'Tis only a few hundred that are lost,' declared Pope Uri, ascending the final step into the pulpit and spreading his arms evangelically wide. 'A small woolly price to pay for the lesson that must be learned!' he cried pointing accusingly at the mass of shepherds. 'You who are so quick to resort to duffing people up in the name of vengeful justice, *you* are the ones that have lost your sheep!'

'Oh dear,' muttered Brother Ovine.

'But we,' shouted Pope Uri, 'men of the cloth, followers of faith, gleaming motes in the eyes of the gods, *we* have our flock cheerfully grazing in the fields outside even as we speak.'

'Oh dear, oh dear,' muttered Brother Ovine and a dewdrop of perspiration squeezed through his prematurely enlarging tonsure.

'Does that not strike you as interesting?' continued Pope Uri. 'Does that not smack of the mysterious ways one hears so much about the gods acting in . . . ?'

Reverend Screed stared up at the spouting mouth of Pope Uri and was dead impressed. He had to take his cowl off to him, that's some dashed fine haranguing going on there.

'Take this lesson to heart and learn it well,' ranted Pope Uri fervently, 'Let not you weep who have lost your sheep and do not know where to find them. Leave them alone and they shall come home, wagging their tails behind them! And now, open your hymn tomes at page fifty three . . .'

'Ahem . . .' coughed a nine-year-old throat.

'. . . and we can have two verses of . . .'

'Ahem! . . .'

'Get that girl a glass of water . . .'

'*AHEM*! I think somebody would like to tell you something,' shouted Alea.

'Confessions are on Thursdays at . . .' began the Pope.

'Erm, I don't think you'll want to wait that long. Will they, Brother Ovine?'

Meekly the coldly sweating heap of monastic shepherd shook his head.

'Your Holiness . . .' he choked, clutching at his crook of yew with white-knuckled hands. 'Your Holiness . . . the sheep are gone!'

Reverend Screed swallowed noisily, whirled on his heels and sprinted for the far cloisters and any hope of mortal freedom.

'Get him!' shrieked Pope Uri, vaulting out of the pulpit, snatching a large brass candlestick and sprinting after the fleeing Haranguist Missionary, his mind seething with thoughts of bashing the traitor to bits and stamping on the pieces.

Alea grinned as the Pope Uri vanished through a cloister barely a second ahead of the rest of the mob.

In the crimson gloom of his cavern, lit only by the bubbling glow from his lava lamp, Nabob hurled back his head and laughed long and loud. Everything was going splendidly. Absolutely wonderfully. One more push and the election would be well and truly in the bag.

Well, how could Dark Lord d'Abaloh possibly refuse him the Undertaker-in-Chiefship when the shimmering gift of telepushy was dropped between his curly horns? The

Underworld had never seen such stunning deviltry potential and Nabob knew it.

He chuckled malevolently as he looked at what he, an amateur when compared to d'Abaloh, had achieved in the last three days. Simply by manipulating the actions of a nine-year-old girl, he had single clawedly brought the D'vanouins, the shepherds and the entire monastic population of Abbey Synnia to the very brink of war. One more shove and they'd be over the edge, screaming and charging into the roaring inferno of uncontrollable rage. What fun d'Abaloh could have!

Nabob, all thoughts of Flagit fading, allowed himself another flurry of wild self-congratulatory cackling as he mentally patted himself on his scaly back. What a genius he had been to bring telepushy to the Underworld! The future had never looked so bad.

Panting and wheezing like a geriatric tortoise that had just been trounced by an arrogant hare, Pope Uri the Thirty-Third collapsed through the door of Abbey Synnia's west wing and lurched along the cloisters towards his rooms.

It had been a hard chase, pounding wildly down the twisting confines of the cloisters in hot pursuit of that damnable Haranguist Missionary. Uri had been gaining ground and would have caught him had he not erupted from the far door with such velocity, tripped over the bottom corner of his ancient purple robe and gone bouncing away, sock over mitre. It was frightening how fast the ground had come up to meet him.

What he needed right now was a nice long soak in a hot bath to get rid of the bruises all down his back from where the SAS monks and a hundred irate shepherds had trampled over him. Yeah, a nice long soak and a bottle of ale and the peace to plot exactly what he would do to that sheep-stealing lump of putrefying . . .

'. . . I said, "Did you catch him?"' repeated the little girl, looking up at him expectantly, her face crowned with plumes of red hair and a pair of red and white ribbons tied in bows.

'Does it look like it?' snapped Pope Uri angrily.

'I only asked,' whimpered Alea, looking hurt and pouting for all she was worth. Once he was on her side it would be easy.

A lance of guilty regret speared Pope Uri's heart. 'Oh, er, sorry,' he said. 'I didn't mean it to come out quite so harshly, but . . .'

'Oh, it's okay,' answered Alea with a maliciously consoling smile. 'You're upset about having all your sheep stolen, aren't you?'

'Is it *that* obvious?'

'And you're ever so concerned about all their little helpless lives being snatched from your caring surroundings . . .'

Pope Uri nodded.

'You're worried that your faithful band of caring monks will not be fed properly . . .'

'Too right!' He nodded again, this time showing more annoyance than remorse.

'. . . you're distressed that there won't be enough darning wool to mend your brothers' socks in the coming chilly winter months . . .' Another, more vehement, nod.

'And . . .' A harsh edge formed around Alea's words, '. . . above all, you're desperately angry about having been made to look a complete fool during your finest spontaneous sermon for years . . .'

'Yes! I was on a roll there,' blurted Pope Uri, his upper lip trembling. He took a deep breath, feeling evangelical indignation ignite inside, stoking the fires of irritation and blowing on the smouldering coals of unholy anger. 'Damn! What a sermon!' he cried, slamming his papal fist into opened palm with a slap. 'Yeah! I was a river of words foaming in full spate,' he yelled, hurling his arms wide in tortured melodrama. 'I could have converted them, shown them all the light, led them out of the wilderness of woe and into the bountifully heaving pastures of pleasure!' A note of pleading sounded above the angst-ridden ranting. 'I *had* taken their adversity and was showing them the stars! One

70

more minute, just one, and their spilt-milk-sobbing would have become cries of ecstatic rapture, I *could* have . . .'

'So what you going to do about it, huh?' snarled Alea.

Pope Uri stopped and stared at the girl. 'Do . . . ?' he gulped, aware that the evangelist within was eager for retribution.

'Yup, do,' she confirmed. 'They've not only nicked all your sheep, but publicly made you look like an idiot, *and* stopped you converting a hundred shepherds. So what happens now? You going to let get away with it, huh?'

Desperately he tried to keep control. 'Er . . . Once we've captured the Reverend Screed then we'll beat a confession . . . er, offer to let him confess what he's done with the sheep, and . . .' stuttered the Pope, failing to notice that Alea was now talking in plurals.

'Won't do any good,' she tutted. 'Never get your sheep back that way.'

A glint of madness flashed across Uri's face. 'A good beating . . .' he shrieked before controlling himself. 'Er, it's worked in the past, a listening ear can . . .'

'Hah! Not this time. He hasn't got 'em,' snapped Alea. 'Screed's been working with the D'vanouins!'

Nabob screeched with feral laughter as he saw the Pope's mask of shocked horror. He knew what effect the mention of those heathens would have on the man of the cloth.

Barely controlled fury erupted within Uri. He could just about cope with being made to look a fool . . . but *not* by a bunch of heathens!

'Yes!' snarled Alea, putting the Pope's seething thoughts into carefully inflammatory words. 'Those damned heathens have stolen *your* flock! Their blasphemous tongues are salivating at the thought of *your* lambs . . .'

Uri went pale as the truth hit him. His hands flexed, mentally reaching for knives, swords, pitchforks . . .

Nabob readied his embroidery of lies and leapt into Alea's mind, focusing his own on a vibrant image of whirling D'vanouins dancing round blazing fires at sunset, roasting succulent lambs on spits. 'Right now,' growled Alea

71

devilishly, 'they are building up the fires, sharpening their knives, slicing pitta breads!'

Pope Uri's lips curled back in anger as he turned in the cloister and began to stamp towards the Abbey Armoury, thoughts of a Holy War rising like a dense fog in his mind, drowning out the voices advocating a peaceful settlement and perhaps the opening of a lamb trade in return for . . .

Nabob readied himself for the ultimate shove, the last kick to set Pope Uri skittering down the slippery slope. In these final few minutes before Uri actually declared war every word had to be chosen carefully. He paused to think, knowing that Pope Uri was teetering at the top of a helter-skelter of emotions. It would be so easy for him to hand back the mat . . .

And in that instant of hesitation, the momentum was lost. For the briefest of moments Alea slipped a thought in sideways.

Nabob's eyes rolled as he felt his control on the little girl slipping, distraction chiselling its way between the fingers of his grip of evil. Alea's will wriggled and fought, suddenly realising that it had a chance for freedom. She kicked and bucked frantically, as containable as a greased eel . . .

'It's time for action . . . or your flock is kebabs!' tele-pushed Nabob along with a picture of the wildly dancing D'vanouins.

Alea opened her mouth to speak. 'It's time for act—' she stopped and put a thoughtful finger to her chin, then shook her head. Below, Nabob swore and concentrated harder. 'It's time for act—' Alea repeated and looked at the cavorting after-image in her head. Romantic thoughts of a desert adventure swept through her impressionable mind. 'Time for act—actually, it sounds quite nice. A bit of a kebab freshly grilled under an open sky . . .'

Nabob's jaw dropped as flashes of sparkling interference flashed through his mind, there was a brief crackling in his ears and then, abruptly, total silence. Well, except for a single dull tone ringing disconnectedly in his ears. He had lost her.

72

'. . . bit of dancing and camel riding, and then a night under canvas, lulled to sleep by the gentle chirping of desert insects,' finished Alea in a tone of voice more suited to a nine-year-old. 'Not as exciting as stealing treasure from my skyland, but it could be fun!'

Pope Uri shook his head at the words, a look of shame crossing his face. And, at the top of the helter-skelter that could so easily have led to outright war, the Pope handed back his mat. 'You're right. They're a peaceful race whose only interest is dancing and the finer points of lamb. Their meagre existence doesn't allow them to afford to purchase . . .' he whimpered and scuttled off towards the altar, firing up his finest preservative prayers and readying himself for a long night's kneeling.

Nabob squealed and raged helplessly below as he snatched off the tiny gold braid net. Broken! His new toy had malfunctioned. Screaming and smashing his fists on to the obsidian table he cried out in frustration. His cast-iron guaranteed election victory lay shattered and rusting before him, irreparable, useless . . .

And it was all Flagit's fault! It had to be, he was the one who had come up with such a half-baked pile of steaming claptrap. He slammed his fists on the table once more, hurled his chair across the cavern and sprinted out of sight in a flurry of angrily clattering hooves.

Alea shook her head in bewildered disbelief as she watched Pope Uri sprinting away from her. She hadn't a clue where she was, or how she had got there. In fact, the last thing she remembered for certain was being sent to bed in disgrace following a certain inky accident . . . Sent to bed. That was it! This was a dream, a startlingly realistic figment of her imagination. Funny the way she knew that she was dreaming, though. Still, who cared. She was safely tucked up in bed, nothing dangerous could happen. Now, where was she up to?

She watched Pope Uri dashing away and thought of prayers and hours of kneeling. Then pictures of D'vanouin annihilation flashed startlingly to mind, swords wielded in anger, knights charging in full battle array, leagues of archers loading bows . . .

'Wait!' cried Alea to the rapidly receding figure in purple robes. 'Come back! The Armoury's that way! Get some swords and knives and things, they're much more fun! Oi! This is *my* dream. I'm in charge, and I want swords and knives and stabbing, oooh, yes lots of stabbing, and . . . Oi! You listening? Come back!'

'Sorry, we're closed,' said a demonic clerk of the Transcendental Travel Company Ltd as Nabob erupted through the door and stamped across the floor towards the manager's office. 'But, if you'd like to pop in tomorrow, I'd be delighted to take your booking . . . yurgh!' she grunted as she was hauled out of her desk and pinned to the back wall. 'I take it that's a "no",' she croaked as Nabob snarled and ground his teeth for effect.

'I've come to see the manager,' he growled, dropping her back in her seat. He kicked open the other door and slammed it shut behind him.

The clerk massaged her throat and tutted to herself. 'No manners, you try a bit of politeness and see where it gets you . . .'

Flagit looked up from his desk in horrified alarm and swallowed as Nabob clattered towards him, seething anger from every scaly pore. Before he could move, the intruder raised his claw, screamed and slammed a tiny gold braid skullcap on to the obsidian desk.

'Broken!' cried Nabob, his claws skittering on the shiny table top as he leant over it and stared accusingly at Flagit. 'You've failed me. Without that the election victory is Seirizzim's!'

'What hap—?'

'It was in my claws. I had it there. One more push and he could never have denied me! It could've been a glorious war! But no,' wailed Nabob writhing in tortured angst. 'Lost contact . . .'

'What're you on ab—?'

'One week to the election,' Nabob screamed and turned from the desk, almost doubling over in anger. 'Next Firesday and it'll be all over. It's too late. Seirizzim's unstoppable now . . .'

'Tell me what happ—'

Nabob stamped a cloven hoof, whirled around and caught Flagit by the throat. A blazing tornado of barely contained fury lashed at the back of Nabob's eyes as he stared wildly into Flagit's trembling face. 'You have three days to supply me with a sure-fire election winner. Three days. D'you hear?'

Flagit nodded once and was hurled out of Nabob's grasp with a snort of disgust.

'But, what went . . .' began Flagit as the door slammed shut again. '. . . wrong?' he finished limply as another clerk screamed outside.

Flagit's trembling claw snaked over the edge of his desk, hooked the gold braid net on one talon and vanished again.

Shaking, he stared at it and tried to work out what Nabob was so miffed about. Something about losing contact and it being broken. He struggled to his hooves and skittered out of his office. It was time for another word with the Reverend Unctuous.

Nabob was already two-thirds of the way down the stairs of the strata-scraper, accelerating and cursing himself in no uncertain terms. 'What was I thinking?' he snarled in the stairwell. 'War, up there, with those apathetic mortals? Started by a nine-year-old? Bound to fail! Why didn't I see it? Should've hung election victory on something with a decent chance of success. Stick to what you know, Nabob, you idiot! Stick to what you're good at! A decent bit of dishonest corruption, bribery and sabotage!'

He whirlwinded out of the back door and, unseen by Seirizzim's heavy who was watching the front, galloped off towards the offices of a certain Captain Naglfar, ferrymaster over the Phlegethon.

She pointed frantically in the opposite direction and tugged harder at Pope Uri's cassock. For a dream character he was being particularly stubborn, thought Alea as she kept up a constant barrage of arguments for turning around, opening up the Armoury and having a damn good scrap. If she didn't persuade him soon it would be morning and she'd never have a chance to stab anyone. 'Look,' she shouted. 'You can't just stroll up to the D'vanouins and *ask* for your sheep back, you know. You need weapons to stab them with. Lots of them! Empty the shelves!' Alea's voice cracked in desperation as she was dragged along the floor. 'Arm all your monks to the teeth and storm the heathens. Give me a sword, I'll show you. Run them through. Burn them all. Stab them! Hack them into little bits! You have no choice. It's war or nothing!'

Unheeding Alea's incitements, Uri dashed on down the cloisters, his head buzzing with suitable psalmic pleas. At full tilt, he wheeled around a corner and smashed into the purple-robed figure of General Sinnohd. It was the first thing Pope Uri had noticed in the last five minutes.

'Fine welcome this is,' grunted the Exorcist General as he tried to right himself and smooth down his moustache. 'Thought everyone'd been kidnapped or somethin' . . .'

'What news?' pressed Uri, snatching the General by the collar and staring urgently into his eyes. 'Have you caught him?'

'Eh? Caught who? What you talking about?'

'Screed? Do you have him?' Uri pleaded, aching for news of his flock.

'You feeling all right?' asked the General. 'Did some major catastrophe happen while I was away casting out spirits from the poor defenceless virgins of Cranachan? It's a long hike over those mountains you know, and I'm famished. Any nosh about? I could kill for a bit of roast lamb!'

Pope Uri turned a strange colour in response to Sinnohd's question. 'Now's not a good time for lamb, General,' he choked.

Suddenly Alea's ears pricked at the mention of the word 'General'. She racked her brain as she tried to think of what that meant. She knew it had something to do with wars and battles and things, if only she could get him to persuade the Pope, then . . .

'What?' spluttered Sinnohd. 'It is Wednesday, isn't it? Don't tell me you lot have scoffed it all?'

Pope Uri shook his head.

'D'vanouin ram-raid!' piped up Alea helpfully. 'Stolen the lot of 'em.'

General Sinnohd's nostrils twitched as he sniffed a waft of something far more interesting than mere exorcisms. Ten years retirement from the SAS spent casting out devils from all and sundry had left him itching for something with a more military feel to it. Exorcism was all well and good, but it didn't have quite the same adversarial feel to it as a fully fledged war. Nope, when it came to the crunch you just couldn't beat a good pincer movement. General Sinnohd's moustache began to quiver.

'You let D'vanouins get away with our flock?' he shouted, half-disgusted and half far-too-excited about the whole thing to let intelligence enter into the argument.

Pope Uri nodded. Alea's heart quickened a beat or two.

'Well, let's saddle up and show them varmints what happens to flock-rustling heathens!' shrieked Sinnohd a little too enthusiastically. Alea cheered.

Uri clenched his teeth at the word 'heathen'. 'I can't do that,' he protested 'It's not a religious matter.'

'Boooo!' added Alea.

'They're our sheep. That makes them Abbey property and therefore the lambs of the Gods!' shouted Sinnohd evangelically. Alea nodded fervently and gave another little cheer.

'No,' countered Pope Uri as firmly as he could. 'This is a civil matter. The Black Guard can deal with it.'

'Pah! You'd trust Achonite with a matter as severe as this? With his record for unrivalled speed?' Sinnohd crowed sarcastically.

Alea snorted to herself and, still convinced that she was dreaming, tried to work out how long it was until morning. Having decided that they were wasting far too much time she

77

decided to change tack a little. She stood up and, giggling, pointed at General Sinnohd's left foot.

'You've got a hole in your sock.'

The General blushed for a moment and stared at Alea. 'Yes, I've been meaning to get it fixed for some time, but . . .'

'It's too late now,' smirked Alea as if she had some vital information that he didn't.

'No, no. Winter is two months away. I'll have Brother Textor rustle me up a new pair . . .'

'What with?' burst Alea, her thoughts firmly on swords and knives.

'Wool . . .' began General Sinnohd and looked at Uri accusingly.

The Pope shrugged.

Sinnohd growled.

And Alea punched the air with joy.

'I take it that without a nice flock of happy little sheep to fleece, socks are less than freely available,' growled the General.

Uri nodded.

'Saddle up!' snarled Sinnohd.

'I hardly think socks are cause for . . .' began Uri and caught sight of the General's smouldering expression.

Sinnohd growled to himself as his itching for battle grew, but justifying a war on the basis of a footwear shortage was a bit extreme. Irritably he rubbed his chin and fumed.

Alea, undaunted by this slight hiccup, and more determined than ever to get a decent scrap going before breakfast, smiled up at Sinnohd and said, 'I often have holes in my socks, but I don't mind. I just put my feet up in front of the fire. And watch my dinner cooking. You know, things like roast lamb sizzling merrily away . . .'

The Pope stared at the General as identical imaginary scenarios leapt into their minds.

Alea's commentary continued unabated. 'Sprinkle over a little more fresh rosemary, baste the crispy browning skin with more honey and ginger . . . oh, smell that succulent flesh . . .'

The Pope whimpered and wiped his chin.

'Golden potatoes roasting in the rich basting juices. The carving knife slipping through the perfect leg of lamb . . .'

The General's stomach rumbled in favour of the army marching.

'Savour that aroma, revel in that heavenly smell, wallow in the thought of it melting in your salivating mouth. 'Cause that's all you'll get!' bellowed Alea.

Uri jumped and his eyes snapped open.

'By the Gods, she's right!' bellowed General Sinnohd. 'No more roast lamb until Achonite gets off his fat backside and retrieves your sheep. It'll be too late by then! Do you really want unwashed heathens sinking their blasphemous fangs into our chaste lambs? Are you happy at the thought of lonely potatoes huddling together on your trencher for warmth, pining for the tender company of a rosemary soaked plattermate?'

It was too much for Pope Uri. 'Damn those flock-stealing D'vanouins!' he cried. 'Saddle up! It's time for retribution. This means WAR!'

'Yes, yes, yes!' squealed Alea gleefully and skipped up and down. Had Nabob been watching, he would have been so proud.

Flagit dropped his desperate head into his claws and exhaled an exhausted sigh. He'd been here for hours, stuck in the tiny storeroom, jammed between the top of the strata-scraper and the countless tons of rock above, and the heat was really getting to him. It was in the high six eighties up here, it had to be.

He stared at the Reverend Unctuous spouting chapter and verse from the book of telepushy and swore under his breath. What was he looking for? What had gone wrong?

Over the last eight hours he had tried over a hundred times to raise something with the gold braid net, anything, he'd even settle for a rat. And every time he received the same dull monotonous whine, buzzing incessantly in his ears. What had that damned Nabob done to it? And how dare he come barging in like that, scaring all of Flagit's staff and denting his nice door panel? He wasn't Undertaker-in-Chief yet. Oh no. Not by a long way, and without my help, he never will be, you can be certain of that, Flagit, my boy, he told himself. Not ever.

A tiny inkling of a thought began to sparkle in the ooze of his mind. A minuscule reaction to being cooped up in this stifling heat, working his talons to the quick, searching for an answer that would enable someone else to reap the masses of rewards to be had from untold power.

Anyone can stand for elect—!

And just as quickly, he stiffled it, looking around nervously. Don't ever let anyone catch you thinking thoughts like that. It's dangerous, he chastised himself. That's mutiny, that is.

Unheard, or just ignored, a tiny fraction of his will shouted, 'So what's wrong with a bit of mutiny, eh?'

Abruptly, Flagit shook his head, stood quickly and stamped over to Unctuous who was still droning out sections of *Teach Yourself Telepushy* in a dull, mantraic fashion.

'. . . system of control that can occasionally achieve overwhelming mastery of another's mental capacities. Throughout history it has been the goal of untold generations of rulers to maintain their hold over the peoples . . .'

'Whoa, whoa, stop!' cried Flagit trying to get his unruly thoughts back on track. 'This is getting nowhere. Start again.'

'Again?' grunted Unctuous incredulously. 'I've already been through it . . .'

'I know. And this *still* doesn't work, does it?' snarled Flagit lashing the stuffy air with the gold braid net 'I don't want to hear any more of your questions, all right? Just do it!'

Unctuous shrugged. 'Very well,' he grunted, took a deep breath and began. '"TEACH YOURSELF TELEPUSHY. Suggestive Mental Assertion in Twenty F—"'

'Stop!' shouted Flagit suddenly. 'What did you just say?'

Unctuous rolled his eyes wearily and tutted. 'TEACH YOURSELF TELEPUSHY. Suggestive Ment—'

'Suggestive!' cried Flagit as a continent of clouds lifted from his mood. 'Suggestive. Ha! That's it!'

'Eh?'

'Anything, and I mean absolutely anything, can ignore this if it wants to.' he enthused, waving the net. 'You can only persuade someone to do something, you can't force them. They can just switch off and look the other way if they want to. Of course, that is it!' Flagit ran towards Unctuous arms flailing, snatched him up, planted a single enormous kiss on his forehead, then wheeled on his cloven heel and galloped through the door whistling tunelessly.

'Nabob never could handle girls!'

It may have been his religious background, or simply his dislike of demonic whistling, but Unctuous was rather worried about suddenly having a nine-foot devil feeling rapturously happy about something he'd just told it.

For General Sinnohd, deep in the crypt, it was definitely shaping up to be the best breakfast he'd eaten in years. Okay, so the food wasn't the best – a few dozen rabbits, no matter how well braised, baked or deep fried couldn't ever make up for one perfectly roasted lamb with apricots, honey and rosemary. But somehow the total absence of anything even remotely resembling sheep-kind added to the fevered piquancy of the occasion. The lack highlighted the immediacy of the ensuing battle, helped to focus the mind wonderfully.

But for 'Friar-Private' Slamm J'hadd, the last thing he wanted was a war. The suede-length hair on the back of his neck prickled as he fumed quietly. Twelve and a half years in the Religious Undercover Crime Squad and eighteen months of Special Aisle Service training to get here, and now, on the eve of renewing his own personal fight for truth, justice and the Cranachanian Way in the name of Sacrosanct Sergeant Vertex – bless him! – the banners go up and it's war.

The General stood on his Chair of Honour at the head of the table and surveyed the men, each wearing their gleaming SAS Divisional badges – a single figleaf crossed by two tightly locked hands and the motto 'Who Girds Wins'. His blood boiled with the anticipatory glee of battle being joined by these newest recruits, and he was igniting fires of anti-heathenic passions within the gathered group. '. . . and so it falls firmly on to your young and strong shoulder to avenge this insult, to rectify this reprehensible wrong that has been wrung,' shouted General Sinnohd passionately, cringing only slightly at the grammatical blasphemies he had just uttered. It was a sign of just how riled he was. No man of the cloth should start the day without his roast lamb. At least, that was what Sinnohd thought.

'Raise your goblets, men!' he cried, then leapt on to the table, uncorked a flagon of cask-strength metheglin and sloshed huge measures into each man's glass. He swigged a vast gulp out of the flask and grinned. At least there was metheglin for breakfast – it wasn't all gloom and despond. The gathered troops necked their drinks with deepest piety.

And then, with a turn of speed that defied his portly bulk, General Sinnohd leapt off the far end of the table, spun around, stamped on the hard rock floor and yelled, 'Preeeesent psalms!'

Sandalled feet slammed on to the floor as all present leapt to correct attention. With perfect precision tiny black field-edition psalters were snatched from cassock holsters, slammed into receptive psalms, flicked open and readied. Without a word of command, which thrilled Sinnohd immensely, the crypt began to echo with the precision pounding of soles on rock at one hundred and eighty beats a minute. The SAS monks paired up and jogged out at double-time. And then Friar-Captain 'Tucky' Succingo raised his voice and launched into Psalm 936, freshly written over a gallon or so of mead last night.

'We're gonna kick them D'vanouins'
And the troops shouted back;
'We're gonna kick them hard and win!'
'They stole our sheep and ran away,' led Succingo.
'We'll make 'em suffer the Crusading Way! Yo, yo, yo!'
Psalmed and ready the Abbey Synnia detachment of the

SAS stamped and chanted their enthusiastic way out of the crypt and off into battle. General Sinnohd wiped a single tear of pride from his eye and thanked all the deities he could count for the good fortune of not being D'vanouin.

And then he saddled up and rode off to fetch reinforcements.

The River Phlegethon oozed blackly past under the hull of the ferry and slithered away into the stygian gloom of Helian. Dozens of other craft fired their infernal combustion engines and belched noxious fumes into the choking atmosphere, struggling through the syrupy river with their cargos of souls.

'So what's in it for me and the lads?' growled Captain Naglfar across the top of his ferry's wheel.

'You'll have your reward,' growled Nabob back.

'Uh-huh. And how much of a reward d'you have in mind?' snarled Naglfar, his eyes smouldering beneath his peaked cap with as much intensity as his blazing pipe.

'Enough,' answered Nabob and spat for effect. This was hard bargaining and he was prepared to act the part. Hard.

'I like lots . . .'

'You'll have lots.'

'. . . and so do the other lads,' finished Naglfar with a satisfied tug on his pipe. Nabob swallowed and looked at his hooves briefly. He'd stepped in too quick, too eager! This was really going to be expensive.

'You keep this going till the election and I'll see you all get a raise. It's been one obulus a soul for too long and you know it,' growled Nabob in his finest negotiatory tone.

'That on top of our "reward"?'

'Of course.'

Naglfar went grimly silent and dragged hard on his flaming pipe. 'That count for our brothers over Styx way?' he asked, piercing Nabob with his glowing eyes.

'Here's a down payment,' snarled Nabob intensely, swishing back his flame-cloak and hurling a vast sack on to the floor with a satisfying rattle of coins.

A sneer of delight crossed the Captain's scaly face. 'That'll do for expenses, banners and posters and such like.'

Nabob gagged. Another fifteen thousand obuls! 'You'll do it?'

Naglfar grinned and patted the sack. 'Got yourself a strike. One hour and we're all out!' He reached up and tugged on a vast horn. Three long blasts, two short and a final long drone reverberated across the Phlegethon. Barely had it died than it was met by a hail of cacophonous response as all the Captains recognised its meaning.

'Strike meeting in ten minutes!'

On the edge of the Ghuppy Desert, shoots of dense marram grass trembled then parted with a swish. Two quivering eyes stared down the dune at the huddling mass of tents, blinked twice and withdrew. It was just as that little girl had said. There weren't any guards.

Neame, the enormous shepherd, growled a couple of commands, snorted half a dozen angry orders and prepared to attack. It was a plan stunning in its classic simplicity. Storm down the sand dune, snatch back the sheep and leg it as fast as their en-sandalled tootsies would carry them. Elegant, refined and only possessing one tiny snag. It was doomed.

Responding to a growled order from Neame, the shepherds unsheathed their fleecing daggers, leapt out of the marram cover and sprinted wildly down the dune. Arcs of sand sprang from their heels as they bounded towards the D'vanouin camp, momentum clawing at their feet, each step longer than the last.

And then the D'vanouin alarm was raised. A single reedy blast through a curling goat's horn. It was a sound that should have struck quivering terror deep into the marrow of the attackers' spines. It should have halted them in their tracks and caused them to stop and think about just how valuable the average flock of sheep is when compared to, say, the immense agony potential of countless freshly sharpened ceremonial yataghan daggers.

It should have . . . but it didn't.

Neame grinned as he stormed onwards across the edge of the Ghuppy Desert. Having the alarm blasting out across the heathens' encampment and allowing them to arm themselves in battle-hardened readiness for the ensuing fracas, was all part of his cunning plan. You see, it mattered not a jot how horribly enweaponed the D'vanouins were, or so Neame's reasoning as an expert shepherd went. After years of experience he knew that the only thing that made the biggest of nasty, curly-horned rams really dangerous was its irritating ability to charge. It was well-known fact that no shepherd had ever been mauled savagely by a casually strolling merino. But give it a few hundred yards' run-up . . .

This is why shepherds herd sheep in such tightly packed flocks. Health and Safety, see?

So, to defeat the D'vanouins it was just a matter of herding them so tightly together that they couldn't swing their deadly yataghans. Round 'em up and skin 'em. Easy.

And had they been attacking a flock of heathenic sheep it would certainly have worked. However, there were two tiny details that Neame hadn't considered. One, sheep don't, as a rule, ride battle bactrians and, two, sheep have never ever successfully deployed a perfect three-pronged outflanking pincer movement.

After thirty seconds of furious stabbing and slicing Neame realised that, perhaps, he had been a little hasty regarding his strategy formation.

Another D'vanouin-backed camel surged towards him, spitting and screaming . . .

If you ignored the incessant whooshing of the magma under-flood heating; the odd screams of countless souls swirling in torment; the thundering crush hour surge below and the evil tapping of frustrated talons on an obsidian tabletop, then the silence in the office would have driven you mad. Especially if you had turned and looked at the expression of pure evil on the face of the figure with its scaly back to the lava lamp. With eyes tightly squinting in rapt concentration it sneered and ground its teeth with angry glee.

Nabob lined up another sharpened stalactite, focused on the portrait on the far wall and hurled it. With a whistle and a thud, the projectile lanced through the air and embedded itself in the head of Immigration's jugular to a depth of several inches. Twenty-five other stalactites jutted angrily from the illustration. He cursed volubly, wishing that it could have been the real Seirizzim over there. Then there'd be no competition, the Undertaker-in-Chiefship woud be his, total control of Mortropolis would be in his claws and he could get out of this damned office.

The rules were clear: he had to prove his worthiness for the role in the finest and noblest traditional manner – trial by subornation. Or outgrease thy neighbour.

It was an ancient skill, a dextrous balancing act and a ruthless game of skulduggery rolled into one. The politics of palm-oiling. And there was nothing in the rules about sabotaging your opponent. In a few minutes' time all traffic on the Phlegethon would grind to a stubborn halt. No more souls would enter Helian, no more fares would be collected and no more money would enter the coffers of a certain Foul Lord d'Abaloh. And nobody, not even Seirizzim would be able to get the system moving again.

Well, nobody, that is, except little old Nabob, who, in return for consideration for the post of Undertaker-in Chief . . .

Another stalactite left Nabob's claw, zipped across the room and ended its trajectory quivering in a facsimile of Seirizzim's left nostril.

Suddenly the door burst open and a junior clerk struggled in under a heap of freshly filled out Nognite parchment forms. He staggered a precarious zig-zag path towards Nabob's desk barely able to see over the top sheet. Amazingly he dropped the stack without incident, wheeled around and struggled in with the other half.

'What the . . . ?' cried Nabob as he glared out from behind the mountainous wall of parchmentwork.

'Just come in,' panted the clerk. 'Latest admissions.'

'So many?' spluttered Nabob, shocked.

'Yeah, looks like a plague or a war's broken out up there . . .'

'A plague or a W—' Nabob leapt to his hooves and glared at the 'cause of death' on the top sheet. 'Spear wound'. The next was 'decapitation' and this was followed by three 'piercings of major organ by foreign body such as sword'. Nabob yelped with joy and hurled another stalactite at the portrait of Seirizzim. He didn't know much about the precise workings of bubonic plague or leprosy on the biochemistry of the average body, but he was certain it didn't normally involve spears or decapitation.

Nabob squealed with delight and punched the air with clenched talons.

The clerk gulped and scarpered. He'd never seen anyone react quite so joyously to a mound of parchmentwork.

How it had started Nabob hadn't a clue, but it was a war. His war! Snarling ecstatically, he took a step nearer election victory. A war *and* a strike. Ooooh goody!

Sixteen miles from Abbey Synnia and they were still in good voice. Monastic metheglin was powerful stuff. The pounding double-time jogging underpinned their battle psalms with devastating precision.

'Stab them hard and slit their throats!' screamed Friar-Captain Succingo.

'Save our sheep and kill their goats! Yo, yo, yo!' shrieked the troops enthusiastically.

Suddenly a hand raised its feeble self above the horizon of the sand dunes ahead and waved desperately. As one, the SAS monks stopped, slamming their sandalled feet to a snappy attention.

Friar-Captain 'Tucky' Succingo trotted forward to the injured man and barely stifled a gasp as he recognised the recently irate shepherd, Neame.

'Go back!' he croaked. 'Turn around, run away, flee!' His breath kicked up little clouds of sand as he shouted.

'We're on a mission from the Gods!' proclaimed Succingo proudly, his chest swelling with religious fervour.

'But they've got camels and swords and pincers,' gibbered Neame.

'Pincers?' thought J'hadd. 'Don't like the sound of that. Perhaps he's been out in the sun too long.'

'And they've got our sheep!' bellowed Succingo. 'Don't you forget that, men! Our innocent fluffy companions are in the evil clutches of those heathen D'vanouins! Don't forget, it goes against all that is decent and noble and right!' He whirled on his heel, tapped his toe twice on the ground and instantly the pounding of crusading feet sprang into the air.

'Psalm 936, verse ninety-three!' declared Succingo, then yelled. 'Loose our lambs and save our sheep!'

The faithful troopers screamed back. 'Free our rams and bash those creeps!'

Within a few seconds the pounding of feet and the yells of 'Yo, yo, yo!' were just distant echoes.

Two midnight dark figures struggled for supremacy in the dim glow of a single lava-lamp, its liquid granite contents casting a ruddy lambency over the inside of the store-room. One thrust after another was parried, each lunge for victory defended, every stab countered in the fight for priority.

'No, no, no! Me first!' shouted Nabob.

'Me, me, me!' whined Flagit for the hundredth time.

'Oh, all right. Go on,' conceded Nabob grudgingly. 'But be quick about it!'

Flagit's face lit up and he produced a strange device decorated with peculiar coloured beads. At least that's how it appeared to Nabob.

'Guess what it is,' shouted Flagit cheerfully.

'I give up,' moaned Nabob. 'Now, my turn . . .'

'No, no, you've got five more guesses.' chirped Flagit, fluttering his scaly eyelids.

Nabob scowled at the tiny wire mesh object bristling with printed runic circuit boards. 'An automatic colander,' he snarled, eager to give Flagit more orders.

'Wrong!' chimed Flagit, 'Guess again.'

'A proximity sensitive cod-piece.'

'Nope. Guess ag . . .'

'Tell me!' Nabob smashed a clenched claw on the table top. Flagit rolled his eyes and tutted.

'Now!' demanded Nabob, steam curling out of his devilish nostrils.

'You sure?'

Nabob's eyes narrowed angrily, his lip curling back in practised malevolence.

'Okay, okay, just checking,' said Flagit raising his palms in submission. 'Hold your breath . . . This is the object you have been waiting for, the undisputed bridge over the chasm of election defeat. *This* is an infernite lattice!'

'A what?' groaned Nabob thoroughly underwhelmed.

'Infernite lattice. The latest advance in my telepushy research programme. This takes the whole . . .'

At mention of the word telepushy, Nabob shuddered. 'Stop right there! I won't hear anymore about it!' he shouted, clenching his claws. 'It doesn't work! I have faced near disaster through that . . . that . . .' fuming he swept his forearm across the desk, sending the infernite lattice crashing to the floor. Flagit squeaked in alarm, leaping up to retrieve it. 'Leave!' bellowed Nabob. 'That's irrelevant now. Sit and see something of *real* importance!'

Flagit's mouth opened and closed with pent fury. He wanted to scream out loud that it did work, if you used it properly and besides he'd fixed it now so that . . . But, rarely for him, no sound came out.

'*I* have the election in the bag,' shouted Nabob, much to Flagit's overwhelming irritation. Corpuscular blobs of light from the lava lamp lit his sneering face, highlighting the curve of his horns and the searing flare of his steaming nostrils. Nabob's eyes flashed wider with seething pride as he leaned forward and glowered at Flagit.

'Ever heard of the Flock Wars?' he growled in a startlingly self-congratulatory manner.

Flagit shook his head.

'You will. Soon those two words will be legendary. Every single resident of Helian will have heard of the Flock Wars and I will be Undertaker-in-Chief of Mortropolis because of them!'

Flagit stared in bewildered blankness.

'In the last two weeks I have been getting up to some first class deviltry,' he rubbed his talons against the hard scale of his pectorals and strutted round the storeroom. 'Nine-year-olds are *so* vulnerable, you know,' he grinned devilishly, his lip curling back to reveal pin-sharp teeth glinting from wine-dark gums. 'Put temptation their way and they lap it up! Oh, it was a delight the way she added those moustaches to the angels and, ahem, "edited" certain sensitive texts. Sweet Alea, so pretty. She'll grow up to break a few more laws, I'm sure. Damn shame she's got that stubborn streak . . .'

'Wh . . . what are you on about?' choked Flagit, finally regaining his voice.

'Gah . . .' snarled Nabob, trying to hide his fuming irritation at losing Alea. 'Do I really have to spell it out? *I* started the Flock Wars. Me. Nabob. It was I who put the ideas into Alea's head. She *never* would've thought of it herself, oh no. It was I that guided her tiny impressionable hand. Me. And it will be me who'll win the election as soon as I offer d'Abaloh the gift of such power.' He strutted away, claws behind his back, shouting.

Flagit's mind whirled with questions at mention of Alea. What was he talking about? Why did he sound like he was defending himself? Nine-year-old girls can't start wars, can they? He opened his mouth but Nabob whirled and shouted.

'D'Abaloh won't be able to refuse me! Nothing that Seirizzim can offer will come anywhere near! All I need is the proof that I started it.' He glared piercingly at Flagit. 'And *that* is precisely where you come in!'

'You couldn't control . . . ME?' Flagit shrieked and swallowed twice as he realised what Nabob had just said. 'Proof?' he whimpered and had the terrible feeling he was going to regret it.

'Yes, proof! It's dropping in thick and fast even as I speak,' cackled Nabob his eyes staring greedily into a rosily thorny future.

'I don't follow . . .'

'Think, Flagit!' screamed Nabob slapping him hard across the back of the head in a manner schoolteachers would give their eye teeth for. 'War means fighting. Fighting means injuries and death! And where do the souls of the dead end up . . . ?'

All Flagit could do was point vaguely east to the distant banks of the Phlegethon and the queues for the ferries. He had a very nasty feeling he knew what was coming next.

'My *dear* Flagit,' growled Nabob, advancing, his talons flexing and clawing the air with pent glee as they twined about his shoulder. 'You . . . get over the far side of the Phlegethon. I don't care how, just do it! Grab any new arrival that knows anything about why they're fighting and bring 'em back here in time to prove my case at the election.' He whirled on his cloven heel and headed for the door. 'You have three days!' he added.

'But, what makes you think d'Abaloh'll believe . . .'

'Flagit! Don't be so stupid.' he shrieked through the closing door. 'Everyone knows the dead can't lie!'

Flagit scooped up the infernite lattice from the storeroom floor and stood rocking back and forth in a paroxysm of fuming rage. 'Fetch me a witness,' he growled under his fetid breath, 'get across the Phlegethon. Pah! He can wait for it. I've got something *far* more important than a couple of dead shepherds. I'll show him real power. Oh yes, soon he'll see *real* control!'

A head bristling with suede-length hair peered cautiously over the top of a large sand-dune and stared at the scene below. Both eyebrows scrambled up his forehead trying to escape, his hand slapped across his mouth barely holding back a squeak of alarm as his eyes bulged at the size of the D'vanouin encampment below. Acres of pointy tents stretched away as far as he could see, each sporting a different banner, each bulging with far too many weapons. The lookout trembled, attempting to gauge the strength of the gathering force and almost wet himself. He had expected to see a few of the enemy keenly mustered in the valley, but not that many. Not eight thousand scimitared madmen, sporting full D'vanouin desert garb, swirling restlessly around a flock of terrified sheep. Things, he concluded as he ran out of numbers he knew, really had got way, way out of hand – twenty-three raids this week, barely a sheep to be had for love nor money in the whole of Southern Rhyngill. And it was still only Tuesday. Still, there were no signs of the pincers.

With a whimper he elbowed his way back from the edge of the dune and crawled towards the waiting division of troopers.

'Report, Private J'hadd,' barked a figure sporting an even more severely stubbly head.

Slamm J'hadd stared at Friar-Captain Succingo and the group of missionaries mustering behind him and cringed. It didn't look good.

'It doesn't look good,' he reported. 'More of them than you can shake a stick at, Sah.'

'We don't shake sticks, Private. We've got these,' bellowed Succingo patting the muzzle of his newly issued Uri 9 mm Anti-Heretic Cross-bow. 'Any hostages?'

'Bupple ob bields . . .'

'Stop chewing those nails, Private!' shrieked Succingo glaring at J'hadd.

'Er . . . Couple of fields' worth, Sah.'

'Damn them. Why couldn't they have left our flocks alone? . . . Fingers!'

Succingo glared forcefully at J'hadd, who made a very embarrassed strangling sort of noise, turned strangely pink and thrust his tempting fingernails deep into the folds of his cassock. Life in the frontline could be harsh. And so could Succingo's stares. It was quite surprising just how swiftly he had got the hang of them. Such was the pressures of command.

Unseen, a nine-year-old girl watched from a clump of marram grass and mentally marked out the biggest and noisiest of the SAS missionaries. What a prize he would make, agreed Flagit a thousand feet below.

With a series of gestures and a final blessing Friar-Captain Succingo turned on his heel and vanished over the top, his SAS desert missionaries tracking every expertly placed step. He sprinted down the dune, knees almost to his chest, dodging covertly behind stalks of marram grass, and dropped silently into a trench. The twenty-four devoutly armed SAS missionaries followed in their camouflage cassocks.

Beyond the trench, lambs bleated in woolly panic as strips of blue touch-parchment were wrapped around their middles, their legs tied to stakes and hoisted suddenly aloft. Slamm J'hadd winced as a bank of oil-soaked torches scorched into flaring orange life. Squeals of delight raced around the D'vanouins as the flames illuminated their swarthy faces hell-bent on unholy acts of mass agnicide.

Just how far out of hand the Flock Wars had become, in so short a time, J'hadd still couldn't quite believe. And he'd been in it from the start. Right since the very first of the 'Ram-raids' as Cranachan's popular press, the *Triumphant Herald*, had christened these incursions.

J'hadd squinted between clumps of grass, furiously scribbling 'evidence' in his hymnal. Then his attention was recaptured as a roar of devotion cheered from the D'vanouins. Adrenalin surged through Friar-Captain Succingo's heart as the desert raiders tugged at their collars, flipping white conical hoods over their evil faces. He had to act soon. Otherwise another four hundred baby sheep would be toasted alive . . .

How could the Haranguist Mission have been so blindly irresponsible? It was so unprofessional. If they would insist on preaching the holy word to impressionable desert nomads they could have at least spelt it properly.

Another dozen bleating lambs were trussed, touch-parchmented and hoiked skywards with a cheer.

'Let ye lamps of devotion burn bright!' . . . Well, that's what it should have said. *Lamps*. Okay, so the technology for high-volume illuminated manuscript print runs was still in its infancy but . . . what the hell were proof-readers for?

Suddenly a gap appeared in the ranks of the surging mass of torch frenzied kebabarians (another *Triumphant Herald* epithet), and a single figure swaggered imperiously forward whirling a blazing firebrand wildly around his head. In a second the hair-triggers of 'Tucky' Succingo's righteous consciousness had him marked. Almost without noticing, the Friar-Captain's hand flashed to a quiver of Cruci-Flyte Crossbow bolts and expertly flicked one into the groove of his weapon.

Unseen, behind a D'vanouin tent now, a tiny nine-year-old girl in a red nightdress grinned and started to have another flood of extremely wicked thoughts. The grin turned to a sneer as she waited for the time to be just right. The D'vanouin with the firebrand strode towards the streamers of blue touch-parchment maypoling in the evening breeze and slashed randomly. In a flash dozens had caught, sparking wildly, scorching unstoppably lambwards. The gathered heathens cheered raucously.

And in that instant, twenty-four camouflage-cassocked SAS missionaries leapt over the top, each loosing a six-round hail of pious retribution. With a single shriek from Succingo, they drew their standard Abbey-issue ceremonial SAS daggers and charged, cassock hems swirling above steel toe-capped sandals, puffs of sand springing behind their feet.

Fearless of the personal danger Succingo plunged through the swirling bedsheets of the D'vanouin ranks, racing for the lambs in distress. He skipped and dodged over the discarded piles of St Lucre's text, cursing. His ceremonial dagger thrust out uncountable times, its twelve-inch blade and nine-inch spikes halting screaming tribesmen in their frenzied tracks. All around him blade clashed with flaming brand, cinders flying in crimson pyrotechnical streaks. And suddenly the crowd parted. He surged forward and stood face to hood with a single brand-wielding figure. Succingo recognised him in an instant as the heathen he had marked to suffer for such acts of mass flock destruction.

Nobody noticed as a tiny nightdressed girl patted the nose of a large camel, shinned up its flank and spurred it into action. These were the dreams she liked best. The ones where she really felt as if she were taking part.

Two hundred sheep bleated as if in encouragement as Succingo circled his opponent warily. 'Filthy swine of the desert, scum of the shifting wastelands . . .'

Slamm J'hadd scribbled desperately in his hymnal, trying to keep up with the Friar-Captain's speech. This was all 'evidence'. Sacrosanct Sergeant Vertex would appreciate every word – bless him!

Two eyes stared back at Succingo malevolently, bloodshot anger through a linen letterbox.

'. . . not too late,' growled Succingo, 'let the sheep go . . .'

Flames scurried up the blue touch-parchments and the D'vanouins roared.

Suddenly J'hadd realised he had stopped writing. Desperately he sprinted forward.

For the Friar-Captain, time was running out.

'What's after "scum of the shifting wastelands"?' shouted J'hadd.

Succingo didn't answer, he had to act. And now.

He feinted left, thrust right and would have been clubbed to the ground and flattened by a charging red nightdressed warrior on an assault dromedary had it not been for her unexpected collision with the back of Slamm J'hadd's head.

The entire desert slammed into J'hadd's face, blasting all the oxygen from his lungs, kicking him into submission. The ground was torn open before him, claws snatched at his cassock and, before he could whimper, kick or wriggle in protest, he disappeared.

Destig, destig. One, two . . .

A hunched figure shivered violently in the pre-dawn light of another talpine morning and tugged impatiently on the lead tied around a laden llama's neck. The burdened beast snorted, trotted across a lichen-encrusted boulder and started a small avalanche of rocks. Steam rose from the figure scowling over its blanket-covered shoulder and spitting irritably through chattering teeth. The saliva whistled through the gloom, hit a large rock and fizzed.

'It's freezing,' he thought, his mind swirling with dark infernal thoughts. 'How can anything possibly live at this temperature?'

A gentle breeze yawned sleepily across the scene, dozily stirring the fronds of heather beneath the llama's hooves. Goose-pimples erupted across the stranger's scales like an acute case of acne. He spat once more and tugged the sixteen blankets tighter around his shoulders, cursing himself vehemently for not wearing any boots or gloves. It would take days to get the feeling back in his hooves. And as for his talons . . . it'd be weeks before he played the violin again. The sooner he was back in the warmth the better.

Miserably he breasted the top of a small hillock and stared down into the valley beyond. His spirits wriggled, flicked their tails and raised themselves from the stilted depths of discomfort. There ahead was the target, and this was as close as he was going to go. He scowled at the ornately decorated building, curling his lip derisively as he laid slitted eyes on the gargoyles leering malevolently across the valley. 'Pathetic,' he snarled, 'If they knew what they *really* looked like, they wouldn't dare stick 'em on rooftops.'

Controlling his shivering hands for a moment he turned to the llama, checked the fastenings on its load, hung a small parchment note on its ear and whacked the beast across the buttocks. It skittered over the rocks and sprinted down the track for a few yards, before giving up and trudging the rest of the way.

His job done, the blanketed stranger blew hot breath across his freezing claws, whirled around and vanished down a small crack between two boulders with a sneeze. His limbs ached desperately for a nice hot mud-bath.

There were certain times that Xedoc, the trainee priest, hated. There were others he detested. And there were some that he despised with a fulminating vehemence that could be measured on the Richter scale. This was one of the latter.

Miserably he flicked the tiny finger bells for the six thousand three hundred and fifth time that morning, scowled and burned laser beams of scorn into the back of the mitre-crowned head before him.

It was four o'clock in the morning, he was wearing a sack, clutching a twenty-pound incense burner and ringing a bell every time the Pope moaned. It was one of those cere-monies.

At four o'clock in the morning any normal twelve-year-old should be tucked up in bed dreaming of leading crack squadrons of cheering crusaders into battle heroically to crush heretics once and for all, or . . . swooping down from trees to beat the stuffing out of a band of brigands, save the kidnapped princess and receive his just rewards. To Xedoc's smouldering mind he should most definitely *not* be kneeling in a draughty vestibule, ringing bells and watching old Popes stare fixedly at shelves of skimpy nighties. Okay, so it was the tri-annual Re-dedication of the Sacred Lingerie of St Mykle and someone had to keep ringing the bell and wafting incense about the place. It was just . . . well, why did it always have to be him? When would he get to the interesting parts of his training like Crusade Strategies, Catacomb Tactics and Clerical Weapons Deployment or stuff like Exorcisms in Theory and Practice?

His Holiness Pope Uri the Thirty-Third moaned once more as he surveyed the fastenings on a particularly tasteful black basque from the Temple of Marxsan Spensah. Xedoc dutifully chinged the bells, his forehead wrinkling in an ever deepening scowl. It was starting to get light outside.

Suddenly there was a screeching of decelerating sandals on stone, the slap of a palm on marble and a frantic monk swung around a pillar and panted into earshot. 'He's back!' he croaked.

Xedoc's eyes exploded into fascinated circles of awe. Precisely who it was that had returned and why his travelling habits should be of interest to the Pope he hadn't a clue. But it did sound remarkably promising. Infinitely more interesting than the last three and a half hours had been. And besides, nobody ever disturbed the Pope unless it was really vital.

Pope Uri wrenched his eyes away from a particularly becoming pink satin teddy and glared at Pasterr, the clinical cleric. Xedoc hedged his bets and chinged the bells, just in case.

'A survivor,' enthused the monk, looked at the Pope's expression and added defensively, 'You asked to be kept informed if . . .'

His Holiness grunted, gathered his vast purple robes around him moodily and stood with an ominous creak of joints. With a final wistful gaze at an array of delicately frilled undergarments he swivelled around, leant on his curling Staff of Office and shuffled out, wiping his nose noisily. The monk followed, as did Xedoc, barely containing his torrent of curiosity.

Pope Uri scraped arthritically down yards of corridors, each pair of footsteps counterpointed by the thwack of his ferruled staff on cold stone, acres of purple silk hanging from his skeletal body. Then he stopped, pushed open a door and staggered down a narrow passage. Xedoc's spirits rose considerably as he snuck in after the monk. He'd never been in this part of the Abbey before. Ahead there was the creaking of another door and the Pope, the monk and Xedoc entered a large room furnished with twenty or thirty hammocks stretched between the pillars of the cloisters. At the far end, one hammock was surrounded on three sides by pale blue curtains.

It was to this corner that the Pope made, all ahead full shuffle, and disappeared through the curtains.

Xedoc dashed around the far side and squirmed under the drapes.

'Yeuch,' grunted the Pope as he stared at the body on the hammock. 'That's a nasty looking forehead,' he said, peering at the crosses of cat-gut holding the top of his head on.

'No need to get personal,' admonished Pasterr.

'It's horrible. What hit him?'

'Haven't a clue,' began the monk. 'But he won't need a haircut for a while.'

'Damn those heretical D'vanouin! Are there no limits to their unforgivable depravity? First sheep and now . . . this!' snarled the Pope. 'Anybody see what happened?'

'You mean apart from the D'vanouin? Haven't a clue,' grunted Pasterr and stared at his sandals. The light from a small candle glinted momentarily across the tonsured curve of his scalp.

'What? Well ask someone! Quick!'

'Er, who?' asked the monk shrugging his shoulders.

Uri snarled angrily, snatched back the curtains and stared at the empty hammocks. 'You discharged them without debriefing? Call them in. I want eye-witness reports!'

'How good are you with ouija boards?'

'Eh?'

'You'll need to be first class if you want answers from his team.'

Uri removed his huge purple mitre and scratched the middle of his head in utter confusion. 'You mean . . . ?'

'Yup. Friar-Private Slamm J'hadd's the only one who came back . . .'

There was a sharp intake of startled breath from beneath the hammock. Slamm J'hadd, the only one? Xedoc knew all about Slamm J'hadd. Well, hardly a day went by without reports of his latest inept exploits in the SAS echoing around the cloisters amid guffaws of laughter.

'He was strapped to the back of that,' finished Pasterr, pointing at a baffled-looking llama which was chewing at a hammock. 'And he had this around his ear.' The monk handed Uri a small parchment tag.

' "Yours, I believe",' read the Pope in a very baffled voice.

'Oh, Gods, even the D'vanouin don't want him,' muttered Uri.

Suddenly J'hadd's eyelids flipped open with a slap, pupils darting frantically around his sockets like goldfish under attack from a feral kitten. But they didn't see the faces of concern above him. His eye/brain interface whirled around frantically, searching for something to focus on, something he recognised. And in a heart-stopping second he worked out that wherever the latest battle of the Flock Wars was raging, this certainly wasn't it.

In his mind's eye the all-too-recent memory of a light, the colour of molten lava, swung nauseously above him. Clenching his fists he desperately tried to fathom what the D'vanouin had in store for him. What evil deeds had they constructed? Torture? Interrogation? Well, they'd get nothing out of him. Just name, rank, hymn number and maybe a particularly insulting psalm or two, if he could remember any. Strange, but just for a moment everything seemed to be a bit distant. Yeah, but they'd still get nothing out of him.

And there and then he vowed to tell them so. Dimly he recalled hearing a strange gurgling sound as his throat failed to produce anything even remotely coherent.

Silhouetted against the crimson light, a distorted face wearing a handkerchief over its nostrils peered through banks of cooling steam, shook itself dismissively and tutted. Then it checked on the dozen and a half tubes which snaked across J'hadd's field of view before disappearing.

Sickeningly, J'hadd became abominably aware of a regular squishing noise throbbing in time with his heart, and would have sworn on several psalms that the liquid pulsing through numerous tubes was bright oxygenated red; and that the face behind the mask was covered in black chitinous scales; and that the person to whom the face belonged was holding a brace and bit, and . . . But that was only a wicked trick of the light. Er, wasn't it?

He tried to move his head for a better look. Something growled angrily and one of far too many vice-like claws clamped his forehead tightly to the table. Panic surged through him as he realised his wrists and ankles were being held down by more burning claws.

Something dark and scaly flashed across the edge of his peripheral vision in response to a growled order that sounded something like 'Sthetic!' The scaly something snatched a large thorn off a table, dipped the tip into a dark bowl and advanced. In a second, hot claws had tugged up his cassock sleeve, gripped the inside of his forearm and plunged the thorn into a conveniently throbbing artery.

J'hadd's pupils quivered, dilated and rolled into the top of his head. It was almost as if they were trying to see precisely what the creature up to its elbows in the squishier parts of his prefrontal cortex was trying to do.

In the Abbey hammock, his hands swirled wildly around his head, swatting imaginary demons as they dive-bombed him, his body squirming and writhing on the swinging hammock. 'No, no, not the sthetic, no more, no . . .'

And then suddenly, the hellish images vanished . . .

'. . . oh. Hello.'

Pope Uri stared at the oscillating Friar-Private, who swung to-and-fro in the hammock. 'Er, where am I?' whimpered J'hadd, in the age-old plea of victims awakened from a very long period of unexpectedly enforced unconsciousness.

'Back at the Abbey.'

'Oh, in that case. Pious Con . . . er, Friar-Private Slamm J'hadd reporting for . . . What's that llama doing there?' he cried, staring at the hairy beast as it investigated the edible potential of a four-pack of bandages.

'Er, we were hoping you might be able to clear that one up,' said Pasterr.

J'hadd stared blankly up from the hammock. 'Eh?'

'It brought you here.'

'But, I can't ride,' whimpered J'hadd.

'Er, you weren't riding it. You were out cold.'

'Er . . . but I would've fallen off.'

'These might have helped,' said the monk, holding up the straps that had secured him to the llama.

'Are you saying I was . . . baggage?' spluttered J'hadd, his head aching as the llama polished off a second bandage. Pope Uri frowned at the beast, feeling certain that somewhere deep within its genes was more than a smattering of goat. It didn't really surprise him though. Those D'vanouin would get up to anything.

'Oh, the shame! Ignomy! Ignomy! I've shamed the noble aisles of the SAS,' cried J'hadd, clutching at his chest before rolling his eyes and lapsing once more into fitful unconsciousness.

'Oh dear,' muttered Pope Uri. 'That bang on the head is worse than I thought. No more crusades for him, I'm afraid.'

And underneath the still-swinging hammock, Xedoc sensed that somehow the Pope's words marked the end of an era for the SAS.

If he had in fact known what wide-reaching consequences that particular 'bang on the head' would have in the very near future, and how vast the shock-wave sphere of its influence would become, Xedoc would have been screaming in panic, tearing his hair out and dashing up the Talpa Mountains to join the next flock of lemmings now leaving precipice 3b on a non-return trip to oblivion.

Over the numerous years that Cranachan had lurked in the Talpa Mountains nobody had actually sat down with an acre of parchment, a theodolite and detailed contour maps of Cranachan's undulations, armed themselves with half a dozen quills and actually designed the drainage system. Over those same years, scholars have debated this phenomenon for at least a minute and a half and concluded that the reasons for it are probably that a) there are, in fact, no detailed contour maps of Cranachan, or b) nobody is precisely certain what a theodolite is, or c) nobody could be bothered to design the drainage system since nobody had, in fact, complained of a lack of adequately designed drainage facilities. I mean, if it ain't broke, go to the pub. The latter is probably the most likely since most Cranachanian's attitude to waste disposal is to dump it out of the window and wait for it to dribble down the street, washed away in the almost incessant north-easterly drizzle.

Uncannily, if someone were to undertake a survey of the actual routes of current waste disposal throughout Cranachan, it would be found that it trundled downhill, following the exact same lines as that of the streets until it reached a small hole in the bottom left hand corner of Pitt Square and vanished over a cliff.

Right now, next door but one to this small hole, sparks where flying. A cacophony of metal striking metal echoed deafeningly above the grunted exhalations of extreme effort and the gurgle of yesterday's vegetable peelings vanishing out of town. A sweating silhouette swung his mallet up to full speed and plunged forward, delivered another flurry of deadly blows, snatched at the sword blade and plunged it into a bucket of water. Plumes of steam billowed forth, vanishing up towards the cobwebby rafters of Spam Smith's Smith's Shop. It was just a normal day for the blacksmith of Pitt Square, a day spent cursing profusely as a twelve-pound lump hammer bounced off his left thumbnail; an afternoon spent dancing around the anvil as yet another hot coal sprang on to his already scorched toes; and a lunchtime of shrieking colourful profanities as another four-pound llama steak shrivelled up and ignited on the forge.

Had you ever let your finger walk through the yellowing pages of the small ads in the *Triumphant Herald* you would have heard of this fine establishment. Amongst attention-grabbing advertisements from expert used-cart dealers offering special finance on getaway gigs ('Buy Now! Pay With Robbery. It's a Real Steal at Hugh Lett's Wheels!'), or bespoke assassins ('For Take-outs and Stake-outs, He's Number One. Call 'Deathwish' Ikhnaton – and get the Job Done!'), lurked one for a 24-hour horse reshoeing service ('Is your horse a hobbledy horse? Give your steed feet of steel. Hop into Spam Smith's Smith's Shop – approved percheron spares dealer – insurance claims a speciality'). Not only was Spam Smith extremely good at knocking up a quartet of horseshoes in under an hour but, surprisingly, he'd recently discovered that he could rustle up the finest two-handed salamanka broadsword you'd hope to find anywhere this side of the Ghuppy Desert. It took a certain amount of skill to fold the curved blade over two thousand times in order to offer the unparalleled rigid flexibility and humming sharpness known and loved by the *crème de la crème* of murderers. And for Spam Smith, it was a skill born of inevitability. The inevitability that if he didn't manage to come up with the goods then, tonight, tomorrow, or some time soon his spleen would be viciously organ-napped as he strolled casually down a dark alley. Since a good ninety-six per cent of the alleys in Cranachan are decidedly on the dark side (and since the man who wanted the salamanka happened to be Ikhnaton the Assassin), Spam Smith had learnt swordcraft remarkably swiftly.

He pulled the salamanka out of the bucket, stared admiringly at the crinkly blade and, despite his throbbing toe, he grinned. Deadly dangerous, he thought, rubbing his calloused thumb affectionately down the sword's corrugated length.

Suddenly the smith door was kicked open with a shriek of irritation and creaking hinges. Spam jumped, and a host of hunting spiders scuttled for cover, as a black-clad figure lurched in from the drizzle. With a whimper of embarrassment the smith jammed a coaly thumb in this mouth and sucked miserably on the newly crinkle-cut digit.

The intruder stomped irritably forward, growling as he swatted skeins of ropes and pulleys out of his path. Spam trembled; the assassin had come to collect. With a click of heels on stone the stranger halted before the vast anvil and dripped miserably. 'Drizzle! I hate it,' he growled. 'Ruins my armour!'

Spam looked him up and down and ended looking down.

Now, it *had* been dark when he had been 'commissioned' by Ikhnaton down the back of Penury Place, and Spam knew that he was well above your average stature, but he felt certain that he remembered the Assassin as being lots taller than this gent. And the ponytail had gone right the way down his back.

'. . . and the things it does to scabbards!' growled the intruder in a voice that rattled the anvil. 'I'm going to have to stay up all night greasing my weaponry!' he snarled, shaking fountains of water off his matt-black leather armour.

'Er, I have an extensive range of watertight scabbards in a range of sizes and colours, sir,' offered the smith, sniffing a sale through the tangle of unruly hair that inhabited the lower half of his face. The stranger had come in for something, after all, why not try to get some money out of him while he was there?

'Colours? Colours? What would I want with coloured scabbards, hmmm?' barked the stranger. His voice would have made calving glaciers sound angelic. He stepped forward into a pool of light.

'Well, coloured scabbards are very attrac—' began Spam and stopped dead. The layers of sooty sweat coating his vast shoulders turned alarmingly cold. 'Oh, sir I didn't recognnnn—'

As his lips curled back Spam Smith's backbone froze as he identified Commander 'Black' Achonite, the leader of the Cranachanian Black Guards.

Amazingly a cautionary throttling was withheld, his apology was accepted with little more than a seismic rumble of disgust. Quite how any throat could be capable of such tectonic vocalisations no one had the faintest idea. Not even Achonite. But he was the last to care. A throat like his made bellowing orders at the Black Guards both extremely effective and deliriously pleasurable. Oh, the joys of haranguing a raw recruit's lily-white lobes following the slightest procedural *faux pas*! It made being Commander so worthwhile.

'I can offer a full range of tasteful *black* scabbards, sir, guaranteed invisible only minutes after sundown . . .'

attempted Spam once more, trying to put off finding out what it was the Commander of the Black Guard wanted with him. It was bound to be unpleasant. He had a reputation to uphold. 'The Stygian Stormtrooper Selection is very popul—'

'Is this your usual sales ploy?' growled Achonite staring at the slightly blood-stained salamanka in Spam's enormous hand. 'Only I don't normally *like* pressure selling. Especially at swordpoint!'

The smith whimpered and hurled the sword hastily behind him, brushing his hand on his apron as if to remove any trace of it that remained.

'Better,' grinned Achonite. 'Now, I am not interested in scabbards, swords or weaponry of any kind! I want something a little more unusual,' he growled, curling his lip once more to reveal the tooth tattoos of command.*

'I shall endeavour to help in any way I—.'

'Hah! Course you will!' chuckled Achonite – a sound not too dissimilar to a series of minor earthquakes. 'When I ask, people always do!'

Spam swallowed nervously and reluctantly asked. 'How can I be of service, sir?'

'Rats,' growled Commander Achonite by way of explanation.

'Sir?' choked Spam wondering if he had heard properly.

'Need to stop them. They're everywhere!'

Spam scratched at the top of his head and looked around worriedly. 'I can't see . . .' he began. And stopped himself in mid-vowel, recalling the first motto of the Black Guard as

---

* Dental Displays of Rank and Honour among the Cranachan Black Guards served many useful purposes. They swiftly negated the need for sewing fiddly coloured patches of cloth to shoulder-pads – a practice which Commander Achonite found extremely suspect in an active security force, not only ruining the totally menacing stygian appearance of the uniform but teaching his band of hand-picked men dubious pastimes like sewing, threading needles and cross-stitching. You never heard of assassins taking up lace-making.

Intrabuccal Rank Discrimination was also a boon for discipline enforcement. Demotion within the Black Guards could be an extremely messy and painful business. Not easily forgotten.

Especially if one has a deeply ingrained fear of a mouthful of pliers.

coined by Commander Achonite himself: 'Disagree and Die'. '. . . seem to think . . . er, have you tried rat-traps, sir?'

Achonite made a strange tectonic gurgling noise, scowled from behind half-closed eyes and strode menacingly forward. 'Stop them! Not catch them!' he insisted.

Spam's palms sweated coldly despite his sudden proximity to the forge. His mouth worked pathetically. 'St . . . op, sir?'

'I'm twenty-three Black Guards short today because of the damned things!' growled Achonite, flexing his gauntlets vexedly and staring into the middle distance.

'Rats, sir?'

'Yes, dammit! Are you listening?'

Spam nodded mutely and attempted to calculate his chances of completing this conversation alive. He didn't get far.

'Those tunnels and passages are full of rats. Haven't been fed in months by the looks of my Guards' ankles. Damn things! I've had to rewrite my patrol schedule four times!'

Ever since the discovery of a vast subterranean network of hidden tunnels criss-crossing the very body of Cranachan and swiss-cheesing the Imperial Palace Fortress, the Black Guards had been working shifts to find out precisely what was down there. Apart from a vast hoard of priceless treasures, invaluable artworks, ancient heirlooms, jewels and fifty-eight tons of a particularly energetic ambulatory slime-mould, the guards had come up with nothing except several dozen rat-gnawed ankles. And this was ruining efficiency, as Achonite was now graphically demonstrating on Spam's left foot with a large pair of pliers. 'I want my Black Guards to be rat-proof!' snarled Achonite, assaulting the smith's big toe.

'Ahhhh . . . But how?'

Achonite leapt up, snatched a sheet of parchment out of his armour pocket and slapped it on to the anvil. Scribbled figures covered the entire surface. 'Shoe sizes and inside leg measurements for the whole of the platoon. I want two pairs of forged steel, thigh-length boots for each of them by Monday!'

'But there's eighty-nine of them!'

'Best get started then, eh!' growled the Commander, heading for the door.

'I can't possibly have all this finish . . .' squeaked Spam, staring at the list.

'Oh, but you can!' grinned Achonite with a flash of tattoos. 'And you will! Otherwise I'll have you for interfering with the course of justice. See you Monday!' and the door slammed shut.

Spam groaned miserably as he nursed his throbbing toes.

Suddenly there was a squeal of hinges and the door burst open again. 'And don't forget,' growled Achonite seismically, 'paint them all matt black!'

Of all the things that could have happened during Slamm J'hadd's mentally-outlined career rise to Chaste Inspector, this was definitely not what he would have chosen. It was bad enough having to lie there in his hammock staring at the cracked ceiling of the Abbey hospital, on his own with only the occasional ministrations of Pasterr the cleric to break the monotony, but, on top of that, well, his head hurt. It throbbed and pulsed wickedly and felt as though his skull was suddenly far too small for its contents. And then there were the voices. Endlessly repeating the same thing all afternoon, over and over again, time after time . . .

'Destig, destig. One, two . . .'

There it was again. That damnable voice inside his head. Coming through shatteringly unignorable with every consonant, bellowing every vowel in its strangely distorted way, sounding like a public announcer with screaming pneumonia.

'Destig . . .'

J'hadd whimpered, rolled over, rammed his head under the pillow and sobbed pathetically in the darkness, swaying gently from side to side. This was not helpful. Sacrosanct Sergeant Vertex was relying on him to solve . . . er, whatever it was he had to solve and here he was with noises in his head. And time was running out.

If he didn't solve it by 08.00 a week next Thursday, then his promising career would be terminated. He'd be out on his ear, chasing peasants for non-payment of alms or tracking down penance shirkers.

Pious Constable Slamm J'hadd of the Religious Undercover Crime Squad, moaned miserably under his pillow. He wanted to be working undercover, not lying under them. It *was* a wonderfully promising transgression-busting career, he told himself. He'd been promising Sacrosanct Sergeant Vertex he'd bust one for fourteen years now. Fortunately for Vertex, the standard twelve years and two was the absolute limit of RUC patience. It was all written in the Force Scriptures.

and Pwarroh didst search for twelve years and two in the wilderness, turningeth ye stones of ye desert for answers until he reachedeth ye last one. And there he beheld that before him layeth victory! Yes answer and eternal glory, his praises sung by hosts of heavenly cherubim throughout ye halls of eternity, fame! Or defeat and having to bloody well start again.

The RUC ran by the Book, every action, choice or question could be carried out, decided upon or answered with reference to any one of the thirty-three thousand and seven Parables of the Lore. And Slamm J'hadd also ran by the Book. Mainly because he had heard that if he stepped out of line they would throw the Book at him, and he didn't want that because it was very big and would give him a very nasty bruise.

His head throbbed again and screamed 'Destig. One, two, two . . .'

It wasn't fair. How was he supposed to work with his head doing that? Wars and screaming headaches. Arghh! A PC's lot is not a happy one.

The oil-black surface of the River Phlegethon bubbled as it slithered behind the fuming crowd. For the first time in countless centuries nothing moved across it. The irritable mob had been there for hours; tempers, voices and hackles all rising together, following in the ancient and dangerous ritual of negotiation.

'No, no, no!' shouted an exceedingly agitated Captain Naglfar, the Chief Shop-Steward of the Underworld Ferrymen's Coalition for Arguing, Shouting and Generally Being Narked. He tugged his cap peak down over his eye sockets, stamped his bare hoof on the stone quay with a click and tugged long and hard on his reeking pipe. 'Ain't you heard a single word I've screamed? Me and my brothers are here to discuss pay and conditions, not listen to your tired and empty promises regarding working hours!' He snarled and took a menacing step forward. The others followed solidly behind him, angrily bashing huge oars against their palms. Their black cloaks swirled restlessly round the bleached surface of their ancient ankles.

The enormous figure they faced stood its ground, folded its vast scaly arms and turned its slitted eyes a few shades redder for effect. 'Gentledemons!' roared Seirizzim, the single remaining representative of the Sinful Service. The others had scarpered hours ago when the oars had started to be brandished threateningly. 'You don't appear to realise precisely what I'm offering? Go back to your boats now, resume work at full strength and I will accommodate you in respect of your request for extra time off.'

'What'll that mean? In real terms?' growled Captain Naglfar scowling as he thought of the fun he was having. He hadn't enjoyed himself quite so much in a long time – making the hated Head of Immigration sweat *and* getting paid for it! Infinitely preferable to hauling boatloads of ungrateful wailing souls across the river for a mere pittance.

'I will allow you an extra half an hour off on Firesdays, to be phased in over an agreed period of increased soul transportation,' declared Seirizzim glaring levelly at Naglfar.

'Well, whoopee!' growled the Captain, oozing sarcasm. The other strikers roared with laughter.

'That may not seem overly generous, but if you take a

moment to *think* . . .' Seirizzim's diplomatic patience was wearing thin. 'With the benefit of a shorter working week, you can scuttle back to your caverns earlier, have a longer weekend, spend more time with your wife and kids!' He finished his speech over a wall of chuckling growls and palm-slapping oars.

'But, I *hate* my kids!' screamed a snarling figure from the middle of the knot of ferrymen, his eyes flashing red as he clawed threateningly at the air.

'I hate my wife!' bellowed another amid a cheer of raucous approval.

'Er, well you can use the extra time to relax then, play golf . . .' shouted Seirizzim, beginning to wish he'd had the sense to leg it quick-sharp with the other councillors when the talks had turned to yells and bellows.

'Play golf?' screamed Naglfar spinning on his heel and addressing the crowd angrily. 'What kind of a decadent bourgeois suggestion is that, brothers? Wasting our time sticking wrinkly balls down holes and taking them out again? That's typical of the class-ridden arguments we have been dogged with throughout the last few hours of negotiation. Golf! What chance do ferrymen have of being allowed membership of upper-class golf clubs, I ask you?' he shrieked rhetorically.

'Oh, it's easy if you go to the Tumor Mortropolitan Field on a weekday . . .' began a voice in the crowd before fading away in a puff of acute embarrassment and half a dozen elbows in the ribs.

'What about bowls?' snarled Seirizzim hoping that would be a little more use as a bargaining chip. 'That's more your level!'

The squeals of devilish outrage suggested not.

'You listen here, Seirizzim!' bellowed Naglfar, stamping forward with a terrifying click of heel on stone. 'My brothers and me ain't interested in an extra half hour a week, all right?' His bony nostrils flared beneath the brow of his captain's cap and black cowl. 'And we of the Underworld Ferrymen's Coalition for Arguing, Shouting and Generally

Being Narked don't care about improved canteen facilities either. *And!* I can categorically state beyond any shadow of the slightest doubt that my comrades and I are vehemently opposed indeed to the idea of repainting and refitting our ferries. For your information, Mr Sinful Servant, our craft are supposed to be deathly stygian black and the sails are meant to hang limply in shredded tatters from the creaking masts of bleached bone. It's all part of the traditional corporate image as passed by the original board of governors in the first annual general meeting!'

A chorus of enthusiastic agreement echoed around the closing circle of the entire ranks of the P&A Ferry Company.*

'What do you want?' asked Seirizzim reluctantly. The first signs of defeat were starting to show. He had asked a direct question and in so doing had broken the first rule of negotiation; Tell them what *you* want them to have. 'Pay-rise!' screamed the unified answer conducted by the power-mad index talon of Captain Naglfar.

'No, no, you've got a contract . . . all legal and binding and . . .'

'Drawn up over fifty centuries ago!' snapped Naglfar, wheeling around with a screech of heel bone on granite.

'Charon struck a good deal for you,' whimpered Seirizzim, shuffling his cloven hooves nervously as the thirteen ferry-men closed in.

'Pah!' spat Captan Naglfar. 'Back then it might have been worth the slate it was scratched on, but now . . . one obulus per soul transported! Well, it's exploitation, innit?'

'Slave labour!' agreed one of the others.

'Scandal!'

For the first time Seirizzim had the sneaking suspicion he was glad that the other staff from Immigration had scarpered. They wouldn't be there to see his rapidly approaching

---

* Named after the main areas of business over which they operate, the Rivers Phlegethon and Acheron. The P&A Line was formed five thousand years ago when the family-owned cross-river company Acheron Aquatics was snapped up by the might of corporate Townsend Phlegethon.

112

defeat. 'You should be happy,' suggested Seirizzim hope-fully. 'Your ferries are always full. Every year there's a decent virulent plague or a few bloody wars . . . you've got no shortage of passengers.' That was true, and Seirizzim knew it. Every minute the strike lasted, the more backlog stacked up over the river, and what with these Flock Wars going on . . .

Captain Naglfar took another step forward and seized Seirizzim by his scaly throat. 'My comrades and I work our bones to the bone, offering a vital service to the Underworld at large. We ferrymen can barely hold our skulls above the constant surging stream of souls queuing desperately for transport. Our skeleton staff cannot cope with the demand. Our ferries are overloaded. All those feet tramping in and out! The repair bills are rocketing!'

'It's true!' shrieked a ferryman.

'Rowlocks!' cried another seething with emotion. 'Cost me nigh on two 'undred obuls to 'ave 'em relined last week.'

'But Charon signed the deal . . .' choked Seirizzim.

Captain Naglfar screamed as if he had been stabbed with a red-hot poker. 'Call that a deal?' Oh he *was* enjoying this. He dropped Seirizzim and made a series of very graphic gestures to two enormous ferrymen at the back. Within seconds they were ploughing their skeletal way through the throng, erupting before Seirizzim with an ancient-looking demon dangling between them. Naglfar turned on the twitching white-haired figure.

'Charon,' he screamed an inch from his ear. 'Mr Charon, hello?'

A glow of red peered out through centuries of cataracts as he dodderingly raised his head and said, 'Eh?'

'Hello, Charon? Sorry to bother you, but my brothers and I of the Underworld Ferrymen's Coalition of Arguing, Shouting and Generally Being Narked, of which you are a founding member and life peer, well, we were wondering could you tell us what inflation is?' shouted Naglfar.

'What?' snapped the fossilised remnant of the legendary inventor of the flameproof coracle.

'Inflation,' yelled Naglfar. 'Can you tell us what it is?'

'Speak up. I'm not deaf!'

'Inflation!' squealed Naglfar and the rest of the crowd.

'No need to shout!' snapped Charon, scowling at them through rheumy eyes. ''Course I know what it is. You callin' me senile, eh? Eh? I know your sort.'

'No, we're on your side,' screeched Naglfar.

'Ask 'im a few questions 'til 'e gets one wrong then it's woomph straight in the nut'ouse and out the way,' grizzled Charon, 'Well you won't get me that easy.'

'Inflation?' reminded Naglfar.

'Yeah, Yeah. Dreadful stuff. Get it all the time, look!' he held out his shaking, oar-worn hands, which bulged at the joints.

'No, Charon. That's inflammation!'

'Yeah. Shockin' in't it? I know! Hah! Can't lock me away for that.'

Captain Naglfar turned on Seirizzim. 'See?' he bellowed. 'Hasn't a clue now and he hadn't a clue then.'

'What are you trying to say? That Charon's a senile old . . . ?'

Countless sharp intakes of hostile breath cut him off.

'That deal is worthless and is stifling ferrymen's ability to eke out the honest wages that they so richly deserve.'

'Who said "dessert"?' crackled Charon. 'I'll have some rice pudding.'

Captain Naglfar attempted to ignore the interruption and glared at Seirizzim more intently than ever. 'Inflation! Five thousand years ago nobody knew it existed; so it wasn't drawn into the contract; so centuries later you pay us one obulus instead of . . . instead of, er . . .' he clicked his fingers behind him.

'Nine hundred and forty-six,' answered a terrified accountant peering through huge bug-eyed glasses.

'Nine hundred and forty-six obuls per soul! Now at eighteen a trip, ten minutes turnaround time . . .' Naglfar's crimson eyes rattled inside his skull as he swooned before such large numbers. 'That's a load of obulus we aren't getting paid, isn't it, brothers?'

'But what can I do?' whimpered Seirizzim, sensing that something was about to start which he wasn't going to enjoy explaining.

'Give us the money or we stay out!' growled Naglfar with a supportive banging of oars into bony palms.

'But . . .' began Seirizzim as images of war-torn souls flooded into his mind, backing up for miles across the river.

'Hear that comrades? All out, stay out!' screamed Captain Naglfar. 'Strike!' And in that moment the P&A Ferry company, and therefore the entire Underworld ferry services, remained at full ahead halt.

In the sweating confines of the Transcendental Travel Company Ltd's storeroom the Really Reverend Unctuous III was annoyed and his ears buzzed. For the last eight hours or so, excepting lunch and tea breaks, the corridors had echoed with sawing and banging and the walls had resonated with a sickening chewing noise that sounded just like diamond-tipped teeth gnawing through solid granite.* But worst of all, something had been whistling. Vhen Tacxia, the demon heating contractor always whistled while it worked, famous throughout Helian for it. Claimed it kept his stalag-mite happy as it gnawed its way through the rock.

Unctuous wasn't the only one who'd breathed a sigh of relief when Vhen Tacxia had declared it home time, whistled his stalag-mite into his cage and scarpered down the stairs. All the clerks had broken into spontaneous cheering and left. But the most relieved was undoubtedly one Flagit. Not because of the staff complaints, nor the customer complaints forcing him to refund half a dozen irate tourists' money. No, Flagit was relieved because at last he could try out his new device properly.

---

* Once heard, never forgotten, the stalag-mite is blessed with six hundred and twelve diamond-tipped teeth for gnawing through solid granite. Now domesticated, they are used extensively around Helian for burrowing out cavern extensions, laying air-conditioning and have even been known to make loving pets.

Trembling with anticipation he burst into the storeroom, snatched a large box from a shelf and sprinted out again, slamming the door. It was the most action Unctuous had seen all day.

Flagit dashed into the manager's office, dropped the box onto the desk and sprinted over to the obsidian drinks cabinet. In seconds he had poured himself a large brimstone and treacle and drained it in one gulp. Fixing himself another he glared at the tools strewn everywhere, drills, strange-shaped vents and a small windmill-like device, and wished it was all over. Another week of it.

He necked the last of the second brimstone and treacle and stood motionless, only his nostrils quivering. Then, uncontrollably he snatched a small breath, then another, then a third, and suddenly exploded in a single vast sneeze overturning the table and scattering parchments everywhere.

He sniffed miserably, dived over to a smouldering bowl and shoved his head under the towel, inhaling the fumes. He wished the sulphates of potash would start to have some smidgen of effect on his cold. Damn that world up there, he thought miserably and sneezed. Nowhere had a right to be *so* cold? And if he had anything to do with it, it wouldn't. A few degrees warmer wouldn't go amiss. That world had given him a cold and as his first gift, he'd give them a bit of a warm.

He sneezed explosively once more and cursed. Bah! he snarled. Chilblains and a dose of double pneumonia. What a price to pay for *the* greatest discovery ever to land in the smouldering lap of devil-kind! He shrugged. The brink of the greatest moment in his life and he felt absolutely horrible. It wasn't fair, life was hell.

Taking a last final sniff of potash he skittered eagerly over to the desk and dragged a mesh device covered in coloured beads out of a box. For a few moments he fiddled with the silver-grey strands of the lacy cap, arranging it carefully between his horns, then flipping two circular crystals down over his eyes, settling them carefully into place with the thin wire clips that hooked around his ears.

'Sid back, relax and bake yourselb cobfortable to enjoy a

hands on debonstration of just what, *sniff*, an infernite lattice is capable of!'

It was a good job no one was there to hear this sinusitic announcement. Flagit hoped it would sound a little more impressive when he showed it to other interested parties. And there were bound to be some . . . possibly even Foul Lord d'Abaloh himself.

Nabob had enjoyed fiddling about with his own 'pet' nine-year-old, suggesting that maybe, if she really wanted to, she could vandalise that, or do this. But that was Suggestive Mental Assertion . . . All well and good, as far as it went and if she wanted to go along with it, but . . .

It wasn't a patch on a bit of TLC – Total Limbic Control.

Suggestive Mental Assertion could never have made that little girl handle a camel so effectively or do things against her will. Ask any parent and they'll tell you tales that'll make your hair curl about the evil that nine-year-olds can inflict on others in the name of fun. Stabbing each other with pencils, pouring wax in little Johnny's ears, stringing Lucy up on the flagpole . . . all good clean wickedness. But ask them to strangle their kitten in cold blood? No chance, never in a million years.

Not unless you have a Total Limbic Control link . . .

One day Flagit would get round to fitting a link to Alea, but right now his practised thoughts raced through the lattice crowning his head. With ease he began to produce complex cerebral patterns, plucking easily recognisable neuronal networks out of his imagination, moulding them, enhancing them and finally broadcasting the result, flinging it direction-lessly across the cerebral airwaves. It was a shame he hadn't thought about tight beam streaming.

Inside the receiver web wrapped around the limbic system of Slamm J'hadd's brain a word formed and blasted through his brain.

'Destig . . .'

'Oh, no,' moaned J'hadd. 'Go away!'

But it was too late. The testing was over, the mental floodgates were open, the barriers were down. It was impossible for J'hadd to resist as some part of his mind elbowed him out of the way, snatched his body and leapt out of the hammock. His feet slapped across the cold stone floor, he grabbed the door and in seconds he was away, off over the Talpa Mountains heading for Cranachan, a sneer of malevolence sweeping his face.

Alea didn't know why she woke up so suddenly that night, but then, she never did. Well, she wouldn't, I mean, did anyone ever try to tell you all about the effect of stray omnidirectional telepushic signals when you were nine?

All she knew was that tonight she had a craving. A weird craving. A sudden and complete need to be . . . where? Her nine-year-old mind whirled as images of sparks and hammers raged wildly and her heart surged with nefarious pleasure. She was having those naughty feelings again, that half-heard voice in her red head that just made her want to do things. Bad things. In a moment she had a complete picture of a place which she quite simply had to be. Now!

If anyone had asked her where it was she would have shrugged and played shyly with the bottom of her red nightdress, the way she always did. But instinctively she knew *exactly* were to find her vision and, as if she had been born from an unbroken six-generation-long line of Cranachanian cartographers, her race memory *insisted* that straight out the front door, second left, fifth right was the way she should start out. Immediately!

Sparks raged and flew in angry coronas, fireworks in need of an audience cavorted as Spam Smith rained hails of sweeping blows down on his trusty anvil. His brow gushed buckets of smoke-stained sweat as he tossed the piece of steel he was working on into the roaring inferno of his forge. A few more beatings and it would be complete. Then there'd only be six more size twelve full-length security boots left to make. Half a dozen case-hardened toecaps stood between the Cranachanian Black Guards and being totally rat-proof.

With a sigh that echoed off the walls of his smithy he wiped the back of his blackened hand across his dripping brow and expertly tugged the steel boot from the fire. In a flash it was on the anvil, its shin being set upon wildly. Then it was arcing through the air and landing in a barrel with a satisfying blast of steam.

Way gone midnight and another day just over.

Erupting in a bellow of relief, he closed down the vent on the forge, spun on his heel and triple-locked the door behind him.

Already the prospect of the first of many flagons of Hexenhammer was tugging at his soot-blackened tongue. He deserved it after all that banging.

In Transcendental Travel's office, a midnight-black figure's jaw dropped open, awestruck, as ghostly images flashed into his spectrecals. High-definition scenes blasted directly through his optic nerve undegraded by rods and cones, lancing brainwards in stunning eerie reality. Oddly the first thing that struck him was just how low the viewpoint appeared to be – just under six feet above the ground, he would estimate.

Suddenly, the image of a dark back alley swayed. A hand had appeared in the bottom corner swinging a grappling hook, winding up the momentum and hurling. In seconds, two muscular forearms were tugging strenously at the rope, the wall of the building slipping by below. Then, roof tiles. A crowbar ripping the catch from a small skylight and flinging it open.

With instinctive nosiness Flagit leant forward, peering inside through the spectrecals, letting out a squeak as, unexpectedly, the point of view of the image moved with him. He pulled back and very nearly fell off his chair. The comforting claustrophobic confines of the cavern were gone. Instead, he was perched precariously, and extremely sickeningly, on a steeply inclined slate roof. Staring at a forty-foot drop. Without a harness. Or safety net.

Vertigo wrestled agoraphobia for supremacy, pinning it down in an over-arm leg lock and cheerfully pounding its head on the canvas. 'Dhe space . . . !' sniffed Flagit as he started to enact the action above. He scrambled across the table and leapt on to the far side. He wasn't sure whether to scream with exhilaration or sheer terror. It was far more realistic than he had expected, he felt as though he were virtually there.

'So mudch space!' he yelped as he mimed dropping through the skylight and landing on a wooden beam. His senses were immersed in the scene playing a thousand feet above him, his eyes peered through the eyes of an intruder edging along a two inch beam and stepping carefully over a host of counterbalance sandbags. The smithy spread out below.

Half a mile up the road, Spam Smith's tongue dribbled expectantly as he scuttled through downtown Cranachan. Pavlov would have been proud of his salivary gland's response to thoughts of Hexenhammer on his way towards 'The Gutter'. Okay so it wasn't the classiest hostelry in Cranachan but it had two real advantages over any of the others. It never closed. And the floor shows were legendary; 'The Gutter' was almost always the scene of some of the most spectacular brawls anywhere this side of the Talpa Mountains. Hardly a night went by without some alcohol-enriched argument blossoming into a full riot, or without someone being messily assassinated in the Gents for the most trivial of matters.

Suddenly the inside of Spam Smith's mouth dried up, all thoughts of a relaxing flagon dashed. With a quivering curse he slapped his blackened forehead, spun a full hundred and eighty degrees on his heel and dashed back the way he had come, keeping a terrified eye constantly flicking over his huge shoulder. How could he have forgotten it? Of all the days for two-handed salamanka broadswords to slip one's mind, why did it have to be the day for delivery. Nobody breaks a contract with an assassin for very long; especially one who has just trekked up from Fort Knumm to take personal delivery. And even more especially if that particular assassin happens to have had several hours quaffing time with the legendarily temper-shortening Hexenhammer.

As Spam Smith reached the nearest he had been to sprinting in the last ten years, he failed to notice a pair of eager eyes watching him from a side alley. A sly grin of nefarious mischief flashed across the face of the nine-year-old girl in the red nightdress as she checked for witnesses and dashed after the blacksmith.

A quarter of a mile ahead, a cowled silhouette wormed its way along the narrow rope-strewn world of the rafters, each movement controlled from far, far below. Flagit wobbled nervously along the table edge, miming stepping over coils of snaking hemp and slinking around counterweight sandbags until he found a likely spot in the field of view offered by the spectrecals. Swaying only very slightly he snatched at an imaginary rope, bent and cursed as the sound of ripping flooded into his devilish ears.

Just his luck. He was practising Total Limbic Control with a body that was overweight! Strange he hadn't noticed that during the operation.

Nervously he checked the integrity of his trousers and stared bewildered at the intact camouflage cassock and a growling pile of sand at his 'other' feet. Not daring to turn around on the two inch rafter he felt up the sand bag and winced as his finger caught the edge of 'his' ceremonial dagger jammed up to its hilt and prongs in the sack. One tug and it was free. He lay it on the beam, swung on one of the ropes and landed on the floor with a splat of bare feet. He whirled around and slapped away towards the deep ruddy glow of the forge.

In a second Flagit had mimed tearing open the air vents on the forge, had hurled tons more peat and coal on and was working away at the bellows with ferverish glee. A thousand feet above, it had all been played out to devilish perfection.

Flagit was rewarded with ten-foot tongues of lashing crimson flame, plumes of swirling dense smoke and the sweet smell of cracking hydrocarbons. And the temperature began to rise.

Unseen, a tiny red-nightdressed figure swung in through the open skylight, landed on a beam and grinned as the smithy door was kicked open by the panting owner. Spam surged in like a frantic tsunami, ducked around the anvil and snatched a sheathed two-handed salamanka broadsword off the wall. Behind him brimstone bubbled within a fissure in a coal, pungent fumes hammering for release in the fiery forge. A crack, an explosion and a meteoric fragment bounced off the back of Spam Smith's head. He wheeled around and glared at the forge which was belching flames uncontrollably. He sprinted towards the vent handle, he had to shut it down.

'Leave it!' snapped a whisper from a patch of shadow. Spam wheeled around, shock lancing icicles of fear through his heart. Had the assassin come to collect? 'But it's ready . . .'

'Get away from the forge!' chimed Flagit and the throat a thousand feet above.

'But . . .' The smith wiped a small trickle of sand away from his shoulder.

'Stop arguing!'

'It's ready. I've got it,' shouted Spam drawing the salamanka with a susurous swipe of corrugated steel. 'See? Take your head off in a second.'

'You threatening me?'

'No, no!' squeaked the smith, waving his hands in panic, slicing through a dozen ropes in seconds. Suddenly twelve counterbalance sandbags screamed out of the rafters, missing the intruder by inches.

'Uh-oh,' whimpered Spam, beginning to sweat. Terror tugged at his heels and he took a pace backwards.

A fragment of Flagit's consciousness flashed a signal almost reflexively and unseen, the red-nightdressed girl scampered across the rafters, watching the action with a glint of madness in her eye. In a flash she had wound a slip-knot into a loop and dropped it on the floor behind the retreating smith.

'Look, it was an accident!' squealed Spam, waving the salamanka tip at the sandbags on the floor. 'I didn't mean . . .'

'. . . to drop a couple of tons of sand on my head. Oh no!'

Spam Smith stepped back another pace and far too many things seemed to happen at once.

The girl in the rafters, obeying her desperate need to wreak havoc, shoved her sandbag off the beam, the loop snapped tight around Spam Smith's ankle and he spun on to his head and shot upwards in a cloud of abuse. Alea leapt up and down with feral glee, dislodging the intruder's ceremonial pronged dagger. It spun off the beam, lodging itself in the squishy part between Spam Smith's fourth and fifth ribs. The salamanka crashed to the floor.

And with a shriek of crimson Alea sprang out of the window into the night air.

The intruder snatched his dagger from the dangling smith, banked up the forge with anything burnable he could find and sprinted out of the front door. Had he been in anything approaching his 'right mind' and seen what he had just done, he would have a) wet himself, b) chewed his fingernails to the first knuckle in under thirty seconds, c) screamed, or d) all of the above, simultaneously.

With a squeal of protesting brakes and the muffled splat of a particularly sluggish rodent meeting its maker beneath a large wheel, a cart slewed to a halt in a tiny alley and Commander 'Black' Achonite leapt off. In two strides he was at the door, pummelling it into submission with the knuckles of his matt black gauntlets.

'Never here when you need him,' growled Achonite seismically, pacing about and gnashing his teeth as Captain Barak of the Black Guard skittered up behind. 'Well, today's the day. If he's not ready . . .' Achonite clenched his gauntlets, wheeled around at the door, winding himself up to deliver another round of pounding impatience, and fell through the open space.

And almost immediately he was back on his feet again, looking around and glaring at Barak, challenging him to repeat anything about that if he dared. It was then that the heatwave hit them, the white-hot tips of searing convection currents breaking across their brows in a flash.

In the centre of the smithy, the forge spewed sheets of lashing flame high into the air, its vent jammed fully open.

Wind rattled about Achonite's ankles, tearing oxygen unstoppably into the infernal conflagration, torching everything in the roaring forge.

Achonite stomped through the swirling smokescreen, seemingly oblivious to the chaos, and snatched one of his rat-proof boots off a peg on the wall. And then with a squeal he dropped it, the ruddily glowing toe-cap dinging on the stone floor. Sixteen of the others had buckled irreparably in the heat.

And then through the smoke he saw him. 'Smith!' he bellowed above the whistling of incomplete combustion, 'What've you done to my boots? My men can't wear these! Stop swaying while I'm talking at you . . . oh.'

'Typical!' growled Achonite at Barak a few moments later as he lurched out of the smoke, sweating under the load of the smith. 'I ask him to do a simple job and he goes and gets himself murdered! Murdered, I ask you. Careless!' He flung the smith on to the cart.

'All right, Barak,' he growled. 'Put that fire out and round up the usual murder suspects.' He whipped the rhinos into action and skittered off up the alley.

'Now where, oh where, am I going to get rat-proof boots?'

124

Some Deadly Sins

His eyes danced wildly beneath taut lids as he fought to comprehend the images bombarding his whirling senses. Flames. Forges. Crowbars. Breaking and entering.

His body shook as the events scrambled and fought for attention. He shook again as no sense came forth. Then again, harder, more insistent, demanding.

'Hey? Anybody in there?'

His eyes slapped open with a start, blinked through crispy lashes and blurrily focused on the monster of a man shaking his shoulder impatiently. The dream images slithered miserably away into the back corners of his unconsciousness, folded their arms and waited impatiently for his next night's sleep.

'Don't recognise me? Shame on you, soldier!' snarled General Sinnohd through a forced grin, thumping Slamm J'hadd in the shoulder playfully. He winced at the sound of his voice and hated himself for it.

General Sinnohd's crusading career had earned him almost countless rewards for bravery and courage above and beyond the call of duty. Even now his chest chinked with the Victorious Cross he had earned after single-handedly rescuing ninety-seven captured SAS hostages from the siege machines of Temple Mephitic; his epaulets glinted with the Honourable Stick Pin of Exquisite Doughtiness for unbounded grace under battle pressures; and his earlobes rang with the Pearl Butterflies of his hundred ell breaststroke award, through pirahna-infested pools. Publicly there was nothing that frightened General Sinnohd.

Privately, and you really would have to pry to get this far, he would admit to being scared witless by just one thing – the smell of monastic hospitals. Nothing else ever came anywhere near to bothering him even remotely. Well, unless you

125

included spiders . . . his skin would shin madly up and down his spine every time he even so much as thought of the way they had of wiggling their huge hairy monstrous legs. Come to that, he wasn't *too* fond of stick insects, slugs, millipedes and a whole host of things you normally find huddled under large rocks.

'Oh! General!' began Slamm J'hadd, attempting to snap a salute from his hammock. 'Er . . . How are you, Sah?'

'No, no. How are *you*?' Sinnohd cringed.

'Er, ready to resume my duties,' J'hadd lied, looking confusedly at the glistening marks of recent burns which peppered his hands.

'No. No, er, that's fine, you just rest,' mumbled Sinnohd and stared blankly at the floor. Visiting time. Visiting time! General Sinnohd was totally convinced that visiting time ran slower than any other period of temporality. It was a dull green backwater of chronology's most sluggish flow, covered in leaves and algae and the wreckage of shopping baskets. Slower even than Wet Sunday Afternoon time . . .

'Did you want to see me?' asked J'hadd.

Sinnohd almost succumbed to the temptation of shrieking 'No, no, just passing,' whirling on his heel and high-tailing it out of there, double-time.

'Er, thought you might like to know how the, er, battle went, you know,' he mumbled through clenched teeth. 'Sorry to hear about the head, by the way,' he added with a grimace that failed remotely to resemble the comforting beam of warmth and well-being it was supposed to be. There was really no way that Slamm J'hadd would ever be a heart-throb from now on, not with those cat-gut scars holding the top of his head on. Maybe with an understanding wig-maker . . .

'Was it a glorious victory, Sah?' asked J'hadd, hoping it was the right question to ask a General whilst in a hammock.

'Medal material,' answered Sinnohd, his confidence growing as he back-pedalled toward firmer, familiar territories. 'Should have been there, man . . . oh, ahem, figure of speech.' He grinned limply, tugged at the base of his cassock tunic and continued hurriedly, eager to relive his most recent glorious moments. 'Swooped down over the dunes a few hours after Succingo's utter def— er, negative attack opportunity. Eighty-five battalions of crack SAS troopers from the United Missions lay down covering fire of Cruci-Flyte bolts, then 18th Organ and 385th Psalmed Divisions deployed in Archangel Ground Attack Wings, rounded the heathen D'vanouin up with vigorous use of Cloister Bombs and suppressing small Fire-Psalms cover. Hoiked the ringleaders up on Golgotha-Poles, showed them the error of their ways, gave them a good dusting off. Even got a few converts out of it.'

'It has the air of a historic success,' crooned J'hadd, tears of emotion forming on his strangely singed eyelashes. 'Would that I hadn't fallen foul of the enemy's evil tactics so early in . . .' he whimpered, thinking more about his Undercover Crime work than any SAS duties.

'Mmmmm, yes, well, just be more careful next time,' the General grunted through nostrils attempting to jam themselves shut. He stood, snatched a rolled parchment out from under his arm and flung it on to J'hadd's hammock. 'You can read all about it there.' He gagged as the hospital smell assaulted his olfactory organ, spun on his heel and sprinted out into the infernal heat of the Abbey kitchens and the reassuring waft of crisply roasting lamb.

Slamm J'hadd swung gently on his hammock and stared at the newsparchment. Eagerly he snatched at the front page of the *Triumphant Herald*, clamouring for the information regarding the end of the Flock Wars. He flicked it flat and was hit between his shoulder blades by a screaming headline.

His eyes stared, widening with shock. His pulse raced coursing with adrenalin. His jaw dropped.

Blackened Smith in Bungled Burglary Blaze!

The dreams . . . He dropped the newsparchment as if it too were incinerating in a blast of crimson flames. The dreams . . .

He snatched at his head, winced and stared at hands which were peppered with burns, his palms scorched by the frantic rope-slide getaway, his feet covered in sand and ash, his cassock and pyjamas smeared with the grubby stains of a smithy.

Somehow he had the sneaking suspicion that something odd had happened last night.

A thousand feet below, in the offices of the Transcendental Travel Company Ltd, Flagit lay down the infernite lattice and stared at it, shaking. Inside his head, Euphoria fought Shock against a background of spinning adrenalin. Half of his mind whooped and cheered with victory and exhilaration, the other sat and chewed its mental fingernails. A possession holiday had never been *that* realistic! He'd gulped three double brimstones in five minutes and was really hoping they would start to do something soon. Very soon. The ranting of Euphoria was beginning to irritate him.

'Don't you see?' insisted Euphoria, tugging at the lapels of Shock's flamecloak. 'This is it. Our big chance!'

Shock tried to back away. He didn't like the way bright yellow showed maniacally around the edge of Euphoria's eyes.

'Just think what d'Abaloh'll give for this, eh? Think! Do you have any idea at all how long he's been trying to get his talons on anything like it? Do you?' Euphoria's claws trembled as he spoke.

'I didn't know he was look . . .'

'Ooooh yes. Possessions, that's as far as anyone's ever got! And how far can you go with that, eh? Even the most idiotic tourist knows that one decent exorcist on your patch means you're snookered. Not to mention all those messy rejection side effects, you know, rotting skin and bad breath . . . I tell you, d'Abaloh'll be eating out of our hands!'

'Yes, I'm sure he will,' grunted Shock dismissively, 'But . . . well, what can you actually do with this total Lipstick Control?'

'Limbic! Have you been paying any attention at all?'

snarled Euphoria rolling his eyes. 'Stick an infernite lattice around the most vulnerable part of the brain, the limbic system, the bit without all that namby-pamby "conscience" stuff – no guilt, no dithering, just action – do that and you can do anything, lie, cheat. Even kill! They can't resist! You saw what happened in the smithy.'

'But that was an accident . . .' Shock pleaded.

'Ha! I even fooled you. Did you think it was just *coincidence* that our dear little nine-year-old happened to be passing? Oh no. I did that. I planned it all. Down to using her to get the SAS officer!'

'*You*? But you said he was d—'

'Ooooh no! You mean you didn't stop to think why we were pulling his skull apart in the cold-room?' snorted Euphoria, vibrating with excitement.

'I . . . er . . . felt sick . . .'

'We had to keep him alive, of course. They can't survive at Fahrenheit 666 . . .'

'Alive?' Shock cried and raised his claws in alarm. 'But that's . . .'

'Illegal? I know, I know,' snarled Euphoria with a grin. 'But look who makes the rules? Convince d'Abaloh of it all and he wouldn't be bothered about a couple of illegal entries . . .'

'A couple? Two!' choked Shock. 'Who?'

'Just some priest who wanted to make a pact.'

Shock screamed and grabbed at his head.

'Where d'you think that natty little hair-net came from, hmmm?'

Shock grabbed at his head and shook. 'This is all far too much. I need a holiday,' he whimpered.

'Well, you're talking to the right chap,' leapt in Euphoria with both hooves. 'Where d'you fancy. C'mon, on the house, courtesy of Total Limbic Control!' shrieked Euphoria wildly as he saw the complete vista of possibilities expanding before his very mind's eyes.

'What? Oh, er, no I . . . I don't think I could stand being inside another head *quite* so soon . . .'

'No need. Anywhere you like in the comfort of our own head. Get away from it all. Nice little chalet in the Krataoan Basin, dip our toes in the lava, ambient temperature of 666° F all year round, lovely!'

'You're raving!' squeaked Shock backing away from Euphoria's frightening yellow-rimmed eyes. 'There's no way we can get me to Krataoa . . .'

'Not yet, no. But c'mon, use Imagination! See the big picture beyond the flares of your nostrils. Fleets of slave labourers all under Total Limbic Control beavering away to build us perfect little pads!'

Shock stared. An infectious spark of possibility crackled. 'Are you mad . . .'

Viral images of possibilities flashed faster through Flagit's mind as the three double brimstones, instead of damping down his whirling thoughts, seemed to free them and encourage wilder speculation. Pictures of a gleaming future shot into his seething mind, whirlwinding in uncontrollably. And then he caught sight of the litter of air-conditioning equipment. His optic nerve snatched the image and tossed it before Euphoria, hurling a log of inspiration on to the already scorching fires of possibility. There was a crackle, a spark and in a second he saw the future.

'And why stop in places that are already hot, I mean volcanoes can get a bit boring after a while. We could get the slaves to redirect lava beds to spots of outstanding natural beauty. Or build d'Abaloh a holiday palace! We could, couldn't we?' Euphoria grinned wildly.

And suddenly for the first time, Flagit knew that he really had something that Seirizzim would never outbribe.

D'Abaloh's very own private holiday palace.

But already, deep inside his mind, Euphoria's wildly tilting windmill of thoughts had gone way, *way* beyond that. Flagit picked up a tiny turbine lying on the floor and flicked it, thoughtfully.

One of the hundreds of feral ravings* which lurked about the

* The nights in Cranachan are long and, strangely enough, dark. Especially in

myriad nooks and crannies of the Imperial Palace Fortress of Cranachan swooped miserably out of the dull north-westerly drizzle.

A storm-cloud typhoon of rage swelled inside a darkened room two-thirds of the way up a sheer four-hundred-foot wall.

The raving soared for a soggy second on a brief updraught, unaware of the brooding eyes that tracked it across the slate-grey sky.

A black gauntlet creaked as an index finger curled back and locked against a thumb. Inside the hand, myosin fibres tensioned, whitening the knuckle, trembling with the strain. The hand edged fractions of an inch closer to the craggy pebble on the table.

The raving cawed raucously on some short-sighted avian whim and swooped a bit more.

With a squeal of leathery friction the hand released its trigger finger, flicking the pebble through the window with pin-point accuracy. The raving squawked, dropped three hundred feet out of the sky, bounced on a springy bit of winter,

which coincidentally, is the breeding season for the myopic Talpine Raven, a bird which believes its plumage is a sort of dull mottled black and it has a large beak and sweeping tail. But with a focal length of three-quarters of an inch, it was dashed hard to be certain. On the other hand, the female members of the Tor Tellini Crowned Starling know beyond a shadow of a doubt that their plumage is a rich, dark British Racing green with a huge crimson plume stretching over the back of their necks all year round. They are absolutely certain of this fact since they tend to spend most of the hours of daylight staring narcissistically into any conveniently reflective puddle.

For ninety-eight per cent of the year everything in the skies above Cranachan is fine. The myopic ravens bumble about in the air barely scraping past the unseen mountains. And the Crowned Starlings ignore them, gazing admiringly into their favourite puddles.

But for the other two per cent of the time, the female myopic ravens are in full breeding cycle. Their necks blossom with bright crimson neck horns and they begin to release wildly aphrodisiac pheromones on to the air currents. The males go crazy, dive-bombing out of the skies and occasionally mistaking a pouting crowned starling for a horny raven. An easy mistake under the circumstances.

The resulting offspring, known simply as ravings, or more correctly as *Narcissari forlornus*, are the most miserable bird in the entire history of the Talpa Mountains. Ravings can be constantly seen swooping forlornly about the place constantly searching for a reflective surface that will show them as more than bedraggled blobs of smudged fuzziness. They are desperately awaiting the invention of the contact lens for birds.

heather and landed upside-down in a crumpled heap with a splitting headache.

Inside the darkened room Commander 'Black' Achonite continued to grind his teeth without even the merest glimmer of satisfaction. He'd taken a dozen or so ravings out at pointblank range in the last ten minutes and he still didn't feel any better. Normally raving bating was his favourite way to relax.

Not today. He was in a bad mood. He was waiting and he *hated* waiting. It wasn't that he was impatient or anything, oh no. He just wanted everything NOW!

He was also in a bad mood because he had lost on the boxer shrimps. He had a dead cert. Destroyer weighed five ounces and was six and a quarter inches long. It should have been a walk-over. He'd smashed all-comers up until now and Achonite had stuck a whole month's wages on it against Sacrosanct Sergeant Vertex's Crippler . . . pah! As if that shrimp could even hope to defeat Destroyer. Why did he have to lose to Sacrosanct Sergeant Vertex of all people? Damn the RUC! Damn the smug way he'd grinned when he couldn't pay up and cackled, 'Ha! Achonite! You owe me one!' Damn everything!

Behind him, masked by the thick oak of the door and the seismic grinding of his molars, a nervous breath was taken. Then the door was tapped.

'Enter. Now. Report!' screamed Achonite. 'Now!' he added as an eternal millisecond ticked by before the door opened. 'C'mon, c'mon! Report!'

Captain Barak shuddered, recognising the Commander's mood in a blink of white-hot terror. His palms flooding with cold sweat, he gritted his teeth and stamped across the bare stone floor with as much noise as possible. An inch from the flimsy protection of the vast oak table Barak halted, raised his right knee as high as it would go and, grimacing, stamped his steel toe-capped boot on to the stone floor with a deafening collision. Before the echoes had died he launched into his report at a full military one hundred and twelve decibels.

One of the things Barak had learned about the military mind was that noise formed the most important aspect of reports. Never mind the quality, feel the din. You could be barking up an entire tropical rainforest of erroneous trees, but as long as you shouted loud enough about it, everyone was happy.

'. . . current conflagration state of deceased's premises – raging inferno. Whereabouts of weapon, or other device, utilised to administer cessation of life – unknown. Precise reason for demise of deceased – unknown. Total pool of eyewitnesses – none. Number of sets of serviceable rat-proof boots currently available for immediate usage – none, Sah!' yelled Barak, his fingers crossed that his vocal cords wouldn't snap under the strain.

'Give me some good news!' screamed Achonite.

'Location of usual suspects – dungeons twelve to fifteen, inclusive, Sah!' he shouted, maintaining his gaze at a regulation six inches above Achonite's head.

'Damn that smith!' roared Achonite seismically as he thought of all the parchmentwork this would mean; suspect inquisitions, torture chamber bookings, fuel requisitions for all the red hot pokers . . . and he still had to find a source for rat-proof boots. It was getting too much. 'Charge him with wasting Black Guard time and interfering with my temper! Off with his head!'

'But, Sah! He's already d—!'

'Details, details! Off with his head. Where is he?' grunged Achonite.

'With Rensic, Sah!'

'Aaargh! How much longer will he be? I want that smith's head!'

'Hard to say, Sah!' yelled Barak. 'Divination's far from an exact science, especially for Rensic, Sah!'

Achonite slammed his fists on the table, launched a strafing series of pebble volleys after a raving swooping past a far window and roared as the closed pane shattered.

'First witness!' he growled and stamped off toward dungeon twelve, molar grating molar in tectonic fury.

What little sunlight that ever managed to slither its way through the constant curtain of north-westerly drizzle and beam limply over Cranachan, was just a rumour down here. Buried deep in the bowels of the Imperial Palace Fortress, the only light that shone within this cold cavern came from tallow candles and a small fire.

This was Rensic's lab and it had to be kept cold. Things would rot if it ever warmed up.

Four years ago if you'd whispered the name Thor Rensic to anyone they would have shrugged blankly, but whisper 'The Exhumer' and you'd get a far different response. Fear and hatred would have sprang to the fore fuelled by a fulminating loathing of the most wanted serial grave-robber ever to stalk Cranachan. Many have attempted to break his running total of enforced resurrections. None have succeeded – at the height of his 'career' Rensic was snatching up to three bodies from their final resting-place in one night . . . every night. Only to return them a few days later covered in neatly sliced dissection scars.

For almost a year the *Triumphant Herald* ran daily lists of the most recent disinternees and public fears grew. They feared what they didn't understand . . . why did he do it?

Grave-robbing they could understand. Happened all the time, tombs broken open, graves ruptured, mausoleums ransacked. And every single scrap of value pinched.

But nobody ever nicked the body!

And no body was safe from Rensic's shovel. Rich or poor meant nothing to him, rank or marques of distinction were ignored. He had only one criterion for selection – freshness.

It was only the courage of one low-ranking Black Guard officer, lying in wait, six feet under after his own highly publicised funeral that finally stopped the 'Exhumer' in his macabre tracks. Mercifully, Rensic was true to form, he hadn't had to wait long before leaping from the coffin and slapping the handcuffs firmly on the 'Exhumer's' soiled wrists.

Captain Barak's career had come on a long way since then.

But Rensic still gave him the creeps with his unhealthy attitude to why things stopped living. It was this fascination that had driven him to the very brink of good taste; his constant striving to discover why it was that simply by holding somebody underwater for a few hours they choked and ceased breathing; his amazement to discover that you could lose a finger in a fight and it would hurt, you could lose a kidney in a fight and you'd not be very well, but lose a small red bit of plumbing from the middle of your chest and it was curtains for sure.

He had to get volunteers where he could and, well, no one wanted them any more, and he *had* washed them and put them back.

The jury let him off and the judge vowed that he could continue his work. But *only* on criminals.

Captain Barak shuddered as he clenched his fist, knocked on the door decorated with the notice 'Thor Rensic's Syense Lab', walked in and looked around.

The walls were lined with shelves, each one crammed with bottles of pallidly preserved entrails or the odd limb. In the far corner, dimly visible in the pool of tallow lamp-light stood a single battered-looking skeleton dangling from a single peg hammered into the rock. Over the years Barak had become used to most of the scene in Rensic's lab. But there was one thing that always threw him, lancing straight to the tiny area of his brain that was in charge of nausea. His stomach flipped like a gasping haddock as he stared at the body of Spam Smith stretched out on an enormous stone slab. Around it was drawn a huge circle, its circumference decorated with letters and symbols, each figure chalked meticulously before a small tallow lantern. It looked like the closing seconds of some demonic cult's ritual sacrifice – the body on the altar, the ring of candles, the bottled entrails. The only thing that wrecked it was the rabbit.

That and the string of carrots placed carefully in front of the chalk letters.

Thor Rensic stared intently at the lop-eared bunny, his

quill poised expectantly above a parchment clipboard as it sniffed suspiciously at a carrot.

Barak cleared his throat nervously, wondering at the immediate mental stability of Rensic and whether he shouldn't, in fact, just back up out of there and leave the nutter to it. After all, it wouldn't be *that* bad if he came back in a few hours, or days, or . . .

'Ahhhh, Barak, I've been expecting you,' oozed Rensic, somehow making the innocent phrase sound far more suspect than it had any right to be.

Rensic returned his attention to the rabbit as it flared its nostrils, whirred around and padded towards a different carrot. Cautiously, its hind feet quivering in readiness to thump alarm and scarper, it nosed the vegetable poised in front of the letter 'q', liked what it sniffed and took a tentative nibble.

Rensic exploded with frustration and hurled the clipboard at the bewildered bunny. 'Arghh! All I need on a day like this is a dyslexic rabbit!' he squealed as a white tail vanished behind the stone slab. 'My tests, my tests! Ruined. Hours of work down the drain . . .' His fleshy face quivered in the gloomy light, puffs of hot breath floated momentarily in the cold air.

Barak thumped the side of his head as if it was some complex mechanical device that suddenly, stubbornly, refused to work properly. 'The rabbit? You're blaming the rabbit?' he gagged, incredulity dripping off every syllable.

'And what is wrong with that, hmm?' snapped Rensic, spinning and staring angrily up at Barak. 'The damned thing *is* to blame, after all. A "q"? I ask you?' he growled rhetorically. 'Why not a single vowel, any vowel?'

'. . . . ? . . .' whimpered Barak incomprehensibly.

'Haven't a clue have you?' Rensic scorned, suddenly feeling a seed of arrogance blossom in his heart. 'Has "Thor Rensic's Syense" advanced *so* far since your last visit, hmmm? Hast thou not heard of lepomancy?' probed Rensic almost theatrically.

'Lepomancy . . . ?' spluttered Barak and then stared

from the expression of serious study on Rensic's pallid face to the tiny white rabbit peeking nervously from behind the stone. 'Oh, no. Are you telling me that you're using rabbits for . . .'

'Divination. Of course!' declared Rensic snapping a pair of thin white gloves off his hands with a flourish, scrunching them up and hurling them across the room. 'With those noses they can spell out the cause of death of any subject. At least most of them do!' he squealed and glared fanatically at the fluffy bunny twitching its nose at him. 'The ones that *can* spell at least. Look at this, look!' he snatched the clipboard off the floor and thrust it under Barak's nose. There in black and white, under 'cause of death', it clearly stated 'zxrrtq'.

'Useless!' Rensic threw his arms in the air. 'I might as well tug open any of those volumes and pull out the first name I find,' he snarled irritably, flicking his finger at the shelf of leather-bound manuals.

'But what about the more, er, invasive techniques you used to use?' asked Barak thinking about the scalpel-happy day of the 'Exhumer'.

'What do you think this is? The dark ages? This is the modern way, no more blades and goo and pots of smelly squidgy gunk. I've gone beyond all that stuff. Lepomancy is just as accurate and a *stack* easier to clear up after.'

'Accurate?' snorted Barak.

'In conjunction with other mantic techniques, yes,' sulked Rensic. 'What you doing down here anyway?' he asked grumpily.

Barak almost smirked at the change of mood. He didn't need a degree in Thor Rensics to know when he had touched a nerve. 'It's Achonite . . .'

'Don't tell me? He wants these results three weeks ago, I know. It's always the same, so impatient!'

'No, he wants the smith. He's been charged.'

'Hah! Who did it? . . . no, no, let me guess,' enthused Rensic suddenly, rolling a set of coloured dice, closing his eyes and waving his hands for silence.

'Spam Smith. Chopping block at dawn . . .' said Barak

most definitely not in the mood for playing guessing games. Especially if his opponent was someone with a tangible faith in the divinatory power of rabbits.

'Really? Damn, I had my money on that Hack D'ripper. Nasty piece of work he is.'

'Nah! Can't be him,' snapped Barak, his patience rapidly running out. 'D'ripper only does girls.'

'Oh, yeah, silly me. Smith? Now, why's that sound familar?' mused Rensic. 'You mean suici—?' he gasped unbelievingly. 'Oh no. That's cheating!'

'Idiot!' snarled Barak, shaking his head. 'Have him ready for collection in two hours. Achonite's orders!' Barak stamped his heel, spun round and slammed the door behind him with a gasp of relief. Inside the lab a high-pitched crooning could be heard. 'Here, bunny. Here, little fluffy bunny. It's time for a bit of extispicy, come on. I'm sure your entrails will tell me something useful, come on.'

Barak fled.

Giggling maniacally like a crazed banshee on some new-fangled hallucinatory chemical, Flagit screeched to a halt at the apex of a dead-end. His head glistened with the combined sheen of a layer of steaming sweat and the gold braid of a tiny skullcap. Chuckling evilly he placed the six-foot cage on the rock floor and, keening in a strange high-pitched way, reached inside and pulled out three feet of horribly clawed, blackly glistening insect. Its dimly remembered ancestors had once been a fraction of an inch long, gibbous white and lived on a diet of cheese. But generations of reproduction on the banks of the Phlegethon, in an environment of such seething evil, had turned them into this. Exoskeletoned, snarling, granite devouring stalag-mites.

It only took a couple of seconds for Flagit to grab hold of the simplistic insectile mind and impress upon it his over-whelming will. Countless hours of fruit-fly possessions coupled with the enhancing power of the braid mesh made this the proverbial piece of victorious sponge cake.

Then with a sneer he dropped the stalag-mite on the floor

and watched as it flexed its ten-inch stygian claws, all eight of them, cracked the knuckles of its dozen pincers, warmed up its already salivating mandibles and leapt at the passage roof. In moments it had vanished in a blizzard of granite chips, boring frantically through the rock leaving a rough hole leading straight up.

Flagit grinned, waggled his talons in anticipation and leapt after the stalag-mite.

A thousand feet above, in a tiny alley, in the lowest part of Cranachan, a small crowd had gathered to look at the flames. They stood out really well through the jagged hole in the dark slate roof of the smithy and contrasted prettily with the dark of the night.

'Look, go away! There's nothing to see here,' snarled a hulking Black Guard from behind the single string of blue and black stripes.

'Ooh, yes there is!' answered a small girl from the crowd. 'There's all them big flames to look at and there's you and all these ropes. It's 'citing!'

'Yeah well. Apart from that there's nothing to see. So clear off,' insisted the guard.

'No. I want to see the body . . .'

Deep within the scorching crimson flames of the un-controllable forge, something moved. It purposefully hauled itself upwards, claw over claw from a thousand feet below, revelling in the comforting licking of pure flame on its scaly skin and thrilling in the anticipatory glow of coming sin.

Unseen by the argumentative girl or the guard outside, a fistful of nine-inch talons snatched a hold of the forge's edge and hauled. Curly horns, flaring nostrils and infernal slitting eyes erupted from the flames. There was a skittering of cloven hooves on the forge rim and in a second Flagit was standing in the middle of Spam Smith's shop. He stared around, eyes peeled, searching the empty smithy, wincing only very slightly as the cold stabbed up through his hooves. Swiftly he recalled the images seen from below through J'hadd's eyes, trying to gauge where precisely the body should be hanging . . . the body of his next recruit. Talons flexing eagerly he clip-clopped around the forge to where he knew it would be. There, just behind that enormous post, dangling forlornly, waiting for him . . . nothing! Flagit snatched a sharp shocked breath and coughed as the cold air battered his lungs.

He rubbed his eyes noisily, blinked and stared again. The pain of truth hit him . . . Spam Smith was gone!

Flagit stood there, baffled, motionless. Nine feet of flabbergasted devil.

Then voices filtered through the door, one large and insistent, the other small and wheedling.

'Little girls like you shouldn't be so interested in murder,' insisted the guard. 'It's not natural. Go 'ome an' play with your dolls or somethin'.'

'Sexist!' squealed the little girl. 'I bet you'd let a boy in!'

'Yeah, well boys is different. Boys is supposed to be 'orrible. They like worms and spiders and stuff.'

'I like worms, look!' insisted the girl.

'Yeuch! Where'd you get them?'

'In my pocket. And I've got some grubs somewhere, too.'

'I don't care if you've got a whole termite's nest in there, you can't see the body.'

'Why not!' squealed the girl with a stamp of her feet.

Flagit's ears picked up even higher than usual.

''Cause it's not here. Taken away for examinations.'

Within the smithy Flagit squealed, slammed his talons against a pillar in frustration and dived into the searing flames of the forge.

Taken away for examinations? Questions blocked his way. What sort of examinations? Where? How could he find out?

And then he remembered the Reverend Unctuous. He would know. Right then Flagit vowed to get the answers in any way he could.

He had to have the smith. All his plans depended on him having a competent and very dead smith. Who else could possibly make the wrought iron gates for d'Abaloh's holiday palace?

Or the miles of security fencing which he was sure to need?

'Nurse, nurse!' screamed Slamm J'hadd in a state of almost rigormortic terror. His knuckles gripped at the folds of the *Triumphant Herald*, his eyes staring endlessly at the headline, the explosive blows of the alliterated 'B's pounding into his throbbing skull like heavy-psalms fire across a field of marram. 'Blackened Smith in Bungled Burglary Blaze!'

'Nurse!' he squealed, echoing plaintively throughout the empty ward. He had to tell someone, he'd run his life by the Book for the last fourteen years and he wasn't about to stop now. He knew perfectly that it was every criminal's duty to come clean and confess their transgressions.

'All right, all right!' grumbled Pasterr the medical monk, shuffling across the stone floor, his hand still clutching a large lamb leg wrapped in a vast trencher of bread. 'How many times have I told you there aren't any nurses here? Bad distraction what with all these hammocks going begging . . .'

'I did it! Fetch Pope Uri. I want to confess,' squealed J'hadd, transfixed by the newsparchment.

'Did what? What are you on about?' grumbled Pasterr, his sandwich floating half-way towards his mouth.

'This,' J'hadd shouted, shaking the tabloid front page. 'This! I can't get it out of my mind! Oh, the shame.'

'Whooo! Not surpised with a figure like that,' grinned Pasterr as he caught sight of the titillating caption declaring 'Buxom Bertha Beautifully Bare!' 'But, you're on the wrong page. C'mon turn over . . .'

J'hadd shook the newsparchment angrily, his knuckles still locked tight. 'No, that there. The headline!'

'Yeah, I know you were in the Wars. Take a look in the mirror if you ever forget,' offered Pasterr with a smirk and took a bite of his lamb sandwich.

'That headline. I did it. Me! I want to confess. I am a crimin—'

Pasterr barely managed to control his mouthful of lamby bits as he guffawed and creased up double, coughing. 'Oh, that's a good one, Slamm. You got me there, ha!'

'I did it. I killed Spam Smith! Lock me away. Throw the book at me. I deserve it.'

'No way,' dismissed Pasterr wiping roast sheep off his cheek. 'You've had your joke. Now go back to sleep.'

'Do I have to spell it out? I did it! Fetch the Pope. I'll pay my debt to society. I have no alibi. I'm as guilty as if I'd been caught with hands redder than . . .'

'Oh, shut up! You were here all last night, tucked up all cosy-like in your own little hammock,' grumbled Pasterr, tiring rapidly of the joke and wondering just quite how buxom Bertha really was.

'I killed . . .'

'Whoa, whoa! All right, wise guy. What makes you think I should grab Uri out of his evening feed to come down here and listen to your ridiculous rantings? The rantings, I hasten to add, of someone who very recently had their brains splattered all over the desert.'

'I've got evidence,' insisted J'hadd in a strangely conspirational tone of voice, wondering if by solving this case he would be allowed to stay on in the RUC, in prison as some sort of undercover spy foiling plots . . . hmmm, maybe not. 'Look!' He finally unclenched his fists and showed Pasterr the burn marks of the ropes from the grappling hook. Then he tugged back his covers and waved his filthy feet at him. 'See? And there's all these dirty marks on my pyjamas . . . I did it. I'll come willingly . . .' He held out his wrists to be cuffed.

Pasterr stared boredly around a mouthful of lamb. 'And that's it?' he mumbled. 'That's your evidence?'

'What more do you want? These are all things from his smithy and . . . and, well, I *remember* doing it. Fetch the Pope, I want to confess!'

'You remember it all quite clearly, eh?'

'Yes, I woke up and . . .'

'. . .it was all there, right at the front of your mind,' interrupted Pasterr.

J'hadd stared, unsure whether to be deflated or exhilarated. 'How did you know?'

'Somniprescience,' he grunted, accidentally spitting a soggy piece of bread on to the floor. 'Well documented. Quite common after a trauma.'

'Somni . . . what?'

'Cor, I would've thought you'd know all about that. Didn't you ever hear of it in your classes? "Behavioural Manifestations of Post Militaristic Engagement Trauma and Possible Monastic Repercussions". At least, I think that's what it was called. It was bit heavy, all that parapsychology stuff, but I like that sort of thing.'

'Was that one of those forty-day course, double period after Matins things?' asked J'hadd.

Pasterr nodded. 'Lead up to the Festival of Globular Deities, last year, yeah.'

'I did double Exorcism. Now, what's this somni whatsit?'

'Yeuch! You like all that squidgy possession sort of stuff?' winced Pasterr, thinking about all the horror stories he'd heard about exorcism practicals going wrong. 'Sicko!'

J'hadd snarled and stared at Pasterr's neck, flexing his hands meaningfully. 'Look, are you going to tell me, or do I have *another* murder on my hands?' he threatened with the spitting fury of an irritated week-old labrador.

'Ha, er, somniprescience, yeah, I was getting to it,' whimpered Pasterr, swallowing the last of his sandwich against a swelling tide of amusement and wiping his hands hygienically on his cassock. 'Heard of somnambulism, sleep-walking? You know, where people's subconscious grabs 'em and takes 'em for a bit of a stroll . . .'

'Yeah?' whispered J'hadd, suddenly awestruck, and concentrating hard. This had big words in it, it must be important.

'Well, somniprescience is like the mental equivalent. You hitch a ride on someone else's subconscious, see?'

'But that's got nothing to do with these?' J'hadd pointed wildly at his feet and waved his hands around.

'Patience,' admonished Pasterr. 'I was coming to that, too. In some cases of extreme trauma, like being bashed about in a battle, losing all your colleagues and being the only survivor, for example . . . '

Slamm J'hadd scowled for a moment.

'. . . well, in cases like that, it's not uncommon for the "dreamer" to want to imitate the "carrier". Now this is where the theory gets a bit weird, and I'm not really sure if I understand it all,' confessed Pasterr. 'Some people reckon that the imitation is all psychological, you know, the brain producing funny blotches on the skin that look like burns and things. And there's some that reckon it's sort of "make-do-with-what's-to-hand".'

J'hadd sat still for a moment, his finger on his chin, thinking. Then he took a deep breath and began. 'Are you trying to tell me that my subconscious is so traumatised by the Flock Wars that it runs away and pretends to be someone else at night, and that, instead of being concrete evidence, these marks on my body are merely manifestations of my own feeble cry for help?'

'Yup,' grunted Pasterr cheerfully. 'Someone else killed Spam Smith. Fancy a sandwich?'

In that moment Slamm J'hadd lost what little faith he had ever had in any branch of medicine with a 'psych' in it.

Thor Rensic had found that the first major advantage of using the divinatory powers of rabbits over more traditional methods of post-mortem examination is the ease of clearing up afterwards. The second major advantage is purely culinary.

By following a strictly defined Hierarchical sequence of lepomancy, extispicy, empyromancy and adaptive gyromancy, he had developed a highly satisfying and nutritious approach to post mortems. It went something like this.

Having nurtured a single rabbit on organically grown vegetable produce and observed the order in which said produce was consumed (lepomancy), the second stage of divination – extispicy – can begin. By casting the entrails of a recently deceased animal into a pot and squinting hard, other divinatory insights can be obtained. Often pictures may form, or letters, or, on rare occasions, whole words. Further information can be had by completely skinning the beast and roasting gently over a roaring fire with a few herbs, eggs and flour. Empyromancy, in the form of the regular crackling of roasting rabbit, can give important aural clues as to the attacker's identity. Finally, and this was undoubtedly Thor Rensic's favourite procedure, there was adaptive gyromancy. Normally gyromancy involved scribbling as many causes of death as Rensic could possibly think of in a circle on the floor, then spinning around until he was dizzy and fell over. The answer was then there before him. Adaptive gyromancy was pretty much exactly the same, except for the fact that the falling over involved large amounts of strong wine consumed after devouring the remains of the rabbit.

It was two-thirds of the way down the fourth bottle of red, during an in-depth and highly scientific session of adaptive gyromancy, that strange things started to happen in Thor Rensic's Lab.

In a distant dark corner, three flagstones began to vibrate as if something were pushing at them, or licking at them. The lines between them began to glow a deep crimson as if a thermic lance was burning its way through centuries of accumulated muck. Thin wisps of smoke rose as superheated gases filtered out through the gaps, which grew by the second as black stalag-mite claws scratched and devoured, stealthily. A startled woodlouse was nibbled before it realised. Then one of the flags moved slowly upwards, scraping cautiously against the others, and was slid to one side. A wave of infernal heat surged silently into the room as talons scrabbled on the stone floor and hauled a black scaled head into the lab. And there it halted, chad-like, peering at the whirling figure of Thor Rensic as he swayed and lurched around the lab in the last uncontrollable moments of gyromantic rapture. Flagit watched spellbound as with a final hiccup Rensic tripped and collapsed, grinning helplessly.

After ten minutes of total inactivity from the prostrate divinator, Flagit hurled the other two flags out of his way,

145

patted the stalag-mite affectionately, erupted from the hole and clattered across the lab towards the equally motionless form of Spam Smith.

It was just as Unctuous had told him, pots, murky, entrailed vessels and the body on the central stone.

Less than a minute later only the first two remained. And three hastily re-cemented flagstones in the far corner.

General Sinnohd grinned to himself privately as he turned the last corner and marched up towards the door to the chapel of St Absent the Regularly Forgotten. It had been the best part of forty years since he had paid a visit to the Really Reverend Unctuous III and his tiny chapel buried in the lower intestines of the Imperial Palace Fortress of Cranachan. So he thought it was just about time to make an appearance. And if the conversation just happened to turn to the latest victory over the heathen D'vanouin and how General Sinnohd had led the 18th Organ Battalion in for the final glorious assault then so be it. Good job he'd brought his entire supply of tin vicars to illustrate the strategies. He was extremely relieved to see that nothing had changed. Including the lock on the Pseudogranite door which led to the secret monastic access tunnel.

Apart from a few extremely uninterested woodlice, six zebra spiders and a pair of earwigs no one had witnessed the General, four llamas, two assistants and a large box of tin vicars on wheels disappear through the secret door.

As Sinnohd had led the way, twisting and turning through the seemingly endless passages with his tallow candle held high, he also calculated the expected value of Unctuous' chapel franchise backpayments – thirty-eight years at twelve hundred groats and six hail mary's. And then there was the Crusades Supporting Surcharge for the Flock Wars, not to mention the SAS Benevolent Fund and a host of other unimportant but nevertheless very expensive donations required of Unctuous. And so it was with not a small flurry of fiscal expectation and bursting with strategies untold that General Sinnohd raised his holy fist and pounded on the chapel door.

It was only after allowing his assistants to beat their knuckles red raw that he realised he wasn't going to get any response. With a snarl of irritation he turned the handle and strode in.

As his feet hit the stone-floored interior several dozen rats scattered and disappeared beneath numerous pews. They were the only things that moved.

'Unctuous!' yelled Sinnohd angrily as he stamped towards the vestry. 'Where are you?' he demanded, bursting through the door and startling another dozen rats making the most of the scraps that came to claw. For a moment General Sinnohd was taken aback by the sight of the best part of a case of empty communion wine bottles lying strewn about the floor, but then he saw the collection box.

With a flurry of keys he unlocked it and emptied the contents joyously into his palm, thrilling with the anticipated cascade of wealth. Two discontinued gold coins bounced off his palm.

Sinnohd squealed as he realised why Reverend Unctuous III's recent communion wine orders had been so low. He'd done a runner!

Mouthing a great many things a man of the cloth shouldn't, General Sinnohd wheeled on his heel and stomped out, turned right and pounded down a different corridor with a stride that meant trouble for a certain missing Really Reverend when he found him.

And he'd been so looking forward to playing soldiers.

Reverend Unctuous III (deceased) peered out from behind a large curtain in Flagit's storeroom and had a horrible feeling that things weren't right. A vast black-scaled creature stamped angrily back and forth across the floor exuding an air of extreme irritation, cursing noisily as plumes of icy air fell from a complex series of hastily cobbled pipes in the corner.

'Where in Helian have you been?' screamed Nabob as the door was kicked open.

'Busy!' grunted Flagit, shedding a cloud of granite dust as he dragged something large and heavy in.

147

'I've been waiting hours,' snarled Nabob. 'And being kept waiting is not what I need right now. Not with all these demands from the damned ferrymen changing every half hour or so. It's hard enough keeping those thick-skulled idiots out on strike as it is, but hanging around waiting for you . . .'

'Yeah, yeah, I get the message,' grunted Flagit, tugging hard on the large heavy something. 'Give me a claw with this, will you?'

'You could have left a message. Could have told me you'd be late. But, oh no, just go gallivanting off doing your own thing . . .'

'I had to move quickly!' growled Flagit.

'Enough excuses,' snarled Nabob. 'My proof. Have you got it? Did they say why the Flock Wars started. What rank d'you get? Captain General? C'mon, let me see.' The nine-foot devil almost skipped with eagerness.

'Patience, patience,' murmured Flagit. 'Give me a claw with this.' He tugged again at the large object and for the first time Nabob noticed that it looked like a very big body in a black hessian bag. It was.

Rubbing his claws together with relish he bent and the two of them hurled it on to the table with a thud. Nabob leapt forward and unzipped the black bag to reveal a bluish face almost totally hidden beneath a corona of facial hair.

'What rank is that?' he choked, wrinkling his nostrils in distaste. 'Looks like a common labourer.'

'Close, it's a blacksmith,' grunted Flagit, picking up a tiny infernite lattice and unzipping the rest of the bag. 'Pass that hacksaw.'

'A blacksmith!' roared Nabob. 'What about my proof?'

'You'll get it,' snarled Flagit. 'In the meantime give me a claw with this . . . ?'

'I haven't got time for this!' shrieked Nabob. 'I've got another strike committee meeting with Captain Naglfar and his cronies. They're convinced Seirizzim'll give in to their demands. How am I going to keep them out on strike?'

'I need a helping claw here . . .' protested Flagit.

'Not mine, you don't! I've got more important things to

do! And you've got proof to get me. You do want me to win this election, don't you?' And with that, Nabob spun on his heel and headed for the door.

'But, this is the future . . . .' objected Flagit.

'Yes, yes, I'm sure,' grunted Nabob dismissively. 'You can deal with the details, I've got a strike to maintain!' The door slammed shut and hooves clattered down the stairs.

Flagit growled angrily to himself, picked up the hacksaw, flexed his claws with a tattoo of cracking joints and proceeded to deepen one of the many furrows on Spam Smith's brow.

As metal ground bone, Unctuous was quietly sick.

Commander 'Black' Achonite ground his teeth just a little more loudly, snarled wider and angled the tallow candle closer to the prisoner's eyes. He growled as he cracked his knuckles and rolled up the leather sleeves of his armour. Normally Achonite loved a good interrogation, especially the 'terror' bit, but this wasn't going well. So far the huge assassin strapped in the chair before him hadn't flinched.

'I don't believe you!' shrieked Achonite, angrily slamming his fists wildly on the arms of the chair and glaring furiously into the killer's eyes. 'You murdered the smith! Admit it!'

'No!' protested the assassin wearily. 'I told you before. I've got an alibi!'

'Do you really expect me to believe that?' snarled Achonite, almost making the room vibrate with the sub bass frequencies.

'Yup. Ask the body in the Gutter if you don't. Or look in my top inside pocket, if you dare!' he grinned.

Achonite growled, tore open the assassin's armour to reveal a mat of curly black hair and delved in the said pocket. A moment later he revealed a map, a description of his target, a contract and a hefty down payment for a successful despatch. He snarled as he read the contract from the insanely jealous head of the Cranachian Family, Khar Pahcheeno.

Pahcheeno's reputation in Cranachan was deadly. Often even just the mention of his name to timid criminals could cause hot flushes and fainting. Everybody knew that nobody stood in the way of business that Khar Pahcheeno wanted doing.

'Not good enough!' spat Achonite. 'Anyone could draw up a contract like that. I need more proof!'

'How many times do I have to tell you, I'm an honest trader, I wouldn't kill anyone without a contract. Where's the profit? I spent all night in the Gutter,' snarled the assassin, startled by Achonite's cavalier disregard for a contract with possibly more power than a royal edict.

'The Gutter?' growled Achonite. 'Drinking what?'

'About three gallons of Hexenhammer.'

Achonite stepped back, raised the tallow candle suspiciously and stared hard at the killer. 'Stick your tongue out!' he ordered.

'What? For some new torture? No way . . .'

'Do it!'

The assassin lashed his tongue out for a second, and in that instant Achonite knew he was telling the truth. A carpet of furry greenish-yellow ran from tip to epiglottis which, from personal experience, Achonite knew could come from only one place – the unmistakable residue of a heavy night in the Gutter.

With a squeal Achonite hurled the candle across the room and smashed a guard across the back of the head, barking, 'He's free to go. *This* time!' and heading for the door.

'Wait,' snarled the assassin, glaring at the mat of black hair still in Achonite's gauntlet. 'I believe that's mine,' he growled. 'I would appreciate it if you returned it to me. Señor Pahcheeno's vary particular about his receipts.'

Achonite rumbled something unfathomable, hurled the scalp at the assassin, strode angrily across the corridor and kicked down the door of the other interrogation suite.

Captain Barak whirled around as the Commander exploded inside, stomped forward and grabbed Hack D'ripper around the throat.

'Well?' he demanded.

'I didn't do it! Wasn't there!' croaked D'ripper.

'Why should I believe you?'

150

''Cause I only do girls,' Hack confessed with a whimpering choke.

Achonite screamed, the muscles on his forearm bulging as he clenched his fist, lifted the prisoner and chair off the floor and hurled them into the far corner with an oath that would have melted cast iron at a hundred yards. Before the dust had settled he was out and striding down the corridor, fuming.

'I say,' beckoned a voice from a side corridor, 'I wonder could you tell me who's in charge.'

Achonite turned and snarled, his teeth tattoos glinting in the dim light as he scowled at the intruder in full camouflage cassock.

'Ah, Commander,' began General Sinnohd, recognising and interpreting the rank markings of his molars, 'I appear to have lost one of my chaps, wonder could you offer any assistance?'

Achonite stared and fought hard with the fulminating tempers surging within and barely managed to answer. 'RUC, Upstairs,' before vanishing around a corner and wreaking havoc on an innocent suit of armour.

General Sinnohd would never know quite how close he came in that instant to meeting his maker prematurely.

Flagit hurled a knot of miserable sinners out of his way and stomped on through the flamestorm.

'Y . . . you . . . you can deal with the details . . . ails . . . ails.'

The words rattled around his fuming head. Details! Hah! As if it were some trivial party arrangements. It wasn't easy lugging eighteen stone of unhelpful smith up a freshly chewed stalag-mite hole and dropping him on the outskirts of Cranachan. Details!

Strikes had details! Flagit's plan had grand sweeping strategies. How could the ferryman's strike take up so much of Nabob's time? It was pathetic!

Automatically Flagit turned and swept down the spiral stairs, his cloven hooves ejecting wailing sinners from this path.

'Y . . . you . . . you can deal with the details . . . ails . . . ails.'

151

Yes, he would. He'd show Nabob just how things should be organised. Flagit would make it happen. Now! And 'it' would be far bigger, far better than anything Nabob's wildest dreams could even dream about!

With a demonic shriek he kicked open the door to the storeroom, shook the ash off his cinderella and snatched his infernite lattice off the back of a stone chair.

In an instant it was settled in between his horns, his eyes had closed and his mind's claws had reached out to the sleeping man in a hammock, one thousand feet above.

The mental talons of Total Limbic Control locked around the will of two sleepers, swung one off his recuperative hammock and lurched him away through the hospital door, and leapt the other out of bed and out the back alley behind the printer's shop.

Guthry the dwarf didn't like it one bit. He stood with his hands on his diminutive hips and stared from beneath a vast array of red eyebrows and plumes of henna-coloured beard. Thoughts dashed and whirred beneath his floppy black hat as he scowled across the expanse of water.

'No siree, Bob. Ain't natural,' he complained inside the privacy of his mind, turned and spat a glob of saliva at a shovel. There was the soggy ring of a direct hit.

'No varmint in their right mind'll use it, no way. That just ain't the way things is done. Lived without it fer censhries, an' as sure as a hill'o'beans ain't a mountain, we sure's hell don't need it now!'

He took another deep draught of ale, chewed another mouthful of sticky tobacco and stared angrily over the night-darkened water. It was way after the end of the shift on the Cranachan Harbour development and Guthry, the Site Manager, glared hatefully at the Trans-Talpino Canal. Just because he was in charge of it all didn't mean he had to like it. That was one of the good things about being a dwarf; gold outweighed anything.

'Well, stands t'reason, don't it, ever since the very first cart was dragged 'cross them Talpa Mountains by the very first rhinoceros, everythin', dammit *everythin's* gone by track. You name it . . . food, lemmin' skins, armies, ale, tobacco. Shoot! Why, it's a perfect system! What damn' fool said, "armies march on they's stomachs?" Gods, sure's a gopher's got teeth, they were barkin' up the wrong trouser leg. Carts! Rhino carts, that's how it's done these days. I mean, hell's teeth, why else would the army have a cartillery division if that ain't so eh?'

He swigged again, chewed and launched another black gobbet shovelwards.

'An' they want to throw it all way. Bin all that heritage.'

In the still of the night Guthry hiccuped and failed to register the stealthy drop of a trained body over the site fence.

'There's gratitude,' he grumbled into his beer, 'an' after I'd spent months improvin' the Trans-Talpino Trade Route. Okay, okay, so it had a mighty few hiccups. Well, shoot, nothin' ain't perfect. Yeah, so it ain't winnin' top prize in the smoothest run civil engineerin' project ever. So it was late openin' – but whose fault was that, hmm? Sure took near three weeks clearin' up after them pesky Hauliers stopped riotin' over rights o' way in that hogwashed contraflow. Shoot! But feast yer eyeballs on it now, ye unbelievin' varmints! Three lanes o' damn fine gravel highway thrustin' through them mountains like a greased gopher on rails, each corner cambered t'perfection, each passin' place marked, an' as if that ain't enough these days, there's a six-lane drive-thru takeaway Happy Chef franchise perched in the top o' the Foh Pass. Holy moles! It's the pinnacle o' high volume goods relocation systems, *Triumphant Herald* said so, must be true . . . and they want t' replace it wi' that!'

He glared at the water-filled ditch that cut through the Talpa Mountains and snarled irritably.

Behind him a large shadowy figure almost slithered over a pile of stones whilst a tiny red-nightdressed girl skipped up to a vast stone-laden cart.

'A canal. Pah! Ridiculous. Ain't gonna work, never'n a million years. Things, 'specially heavy things, need wheels t' move 'em. Or maybe sleds at a push. Take away the wheels and it don't move, makes perfect sense. Y' *definitely* don't make things move by throwin' 'em in the canal! They reckon if you shape it properly yer c'n make steel float. Been drinkin' too much, or been out in th'sun too long, I say. I mean, you ever tried washin' a chain-mail shirt. It sinks! And they reckon you can bundle dozens of 'em together, throw 'em on a thing called a barge and they won't sink. Sheee-yoot!'

He shook his head forlornly and necked another half-pint.

'Still 'f that's what they's wantin', who'm I t'argue. Let 'em fill the damn thing wi' bundles o' chain-mail shirts, if they's wantin'. Sure be a lot safer. I mean, any varmint could easy fall in and drown.'

Tetchily he stared at the sheet of parchment curling before him and frowned at the plans for the port of Cranachan. The red-nightdressed girl grasped a long handle on the cart, depressed a small button in the top, and tugged.

'There y' go, see? Proves they was out o' they's cotton-pickin' heads when they thought o' it. Called it the' first thing that came into they's minds. Port! I ask ye? Drunken good f'nothin's. Tell you, this kingdom's on th' slide if it's run by people like that!'

Of course he'd never air those views in public. He'd be out of a job and up to his wrists in handcuffs and dungeons before he could say, 'Oi! . . .' That is, if he was lucky and Khar Pahcheeno *didn't* hear about it.

Not that it would make that much difference really.

The large shadowy figure moved silently through the site, creeping closer to the mournful figure on the canal bank, halting in a shadow ten feet behind him. He had to keep in the shadows, he didn't want to alarm the little fellow, especially if he caught sight of his scarred forehead. A glimpse of a cat-gut cross-stitched skull in moonlight did funny things to people.

Suddenly a stone-laden cart parked on the bank of the canal lurched forward as its hand-brake was released and a nine-year-old girl leapt free with a giggle of glee. In a flash, gravity's eager fingers had snatched it and pulled, adding to the cart's acceleration. At the first sound Guthry was on his feet and turning, 'Wh . . . what? Who's there? Who's it?'

He never got an answer. The cart thundered towards him, gaining speed, racing at the Site Manager on the bank.

Guthry screamed, frozen to the spot, watching powerlessly as the runaway truck loomed, expanding to fill his horizon. With a sickening, heart-stopping lurch the cart hit the canal bank and leapt into mid-air, arcing impossibly into the black waters with a plume of turgid liquid.

Guthry watched it describe an arc right over his head. Shaking, for once, in horrified relief that dwarves were of a naturally diminutive stature.

Behind the stones, the grin on Slamm J'hadd's face dropped, and contorted into a scream of defeat. In a second he was cannoning out of the shadows at full rugby sprint, SAS training coming quickly to hand. Still accelerating, he hit Guthry square in the stomach and carried both of them ten feet into the middle of the still writhing canal. They skipped once on the oil-dark surface and then vanished below, bubbles exploding from Guthry's mouth as he thrashed helplessly, pinned down by his attacker. Surprisingly, the more philosophical part of Guthry's brain took over. 'Hot diggity, I told ye,' it shrieked. 'Di'n't I say? I said some poor varmint'd end up drowned in 'ere, I said, canals, dangerous, I said . . . !'

Fortunately it was interrupted by a seething cascade of bubbles blasting to the surface a few feet away to his left in front of the upturned cart as a section of weedy rock erupted, a host of horrific claws scrabbled and thrashed into view and propelled an enormous shadow out of the silty bottom.

Guthry the dwarf's last vision was of a rapidly approaching nine-foot demon wearing a mask, flippers and a belt of lead weights.

Of Blueprints and Hair-nets

A flurry of rooks clattered irritably out of Abbey Synnia's bell tower, cawing and squawking their annoyance as the tinny matins bell shattered the still morning silence. And a sleeper in the hospital wing burst awake, screamed, fell out of his hammock with a wet slap and watched in horror as a trickle of muddy water dribbled away across the tiled floor.

'Nurse!' he squealed.

Images of swirling streams of silver bubbles blasted his memory, he had been running, sprinting, he had hit . . . something . . . and then . . . the water. It was a dream, wasn't it?

Another finger of opaque liquid slithered off to join the first. 'Nurse!'

It had to be a dream! *Had* to be . . .

So why did his lungs hurt as if he had held his breath for half an hour? And where had all the water come from?

'Nurse!'

'How many times do I have to tell you, there's no nurse here!' grumbled Pasterr around a huge yawn and a steaming slice of porridge. 'Now what are we doing down here?' he said condescendingly, staring quizzically at the sodden patient and wincing as he saw the string of cat-gut stiches holding the top of his head on. 'Pope Uri said you should be getting *up* and about. I don't think you should be down there.'

Slamm J'hadd squelched pathetically on the floor and shivered. 'The water!' he wheezed.

'Yes. I can see you're a bit damp. Tut, tut.' Pasterr bent and helped J'hadd on to his dripping feet. 'Dreaming again?' he asked as he hurled him back on to his hammock.

'Yes, I've . . .' began J'hadd.

'What about *this* time? No, wait, let me guess. You

imagined you were swimming, hmmm? With the Raft People of the Eastern Tepid Seas? And, half-crazy in love, you were paddling away a young girl called Dhay-See, in a coracle made for two. Am I right?'

'It was murky!' croaked J'hadd as he dripped as he swung. 'There was a struggle . . .'

'Ha! Didn't fancy you, eh?' letched Pasterr around another mouthful of porridge.

'What?'

'Dhay-See. Didn't fancy you. Rejected your advances. Chucked you in? Oh, never mind . . .'

'No! It was a building site, or something, and there was a runaway cart and I jumped in afterwards and . . .' blurted J'hadd in confusion.

'Did you save her?'

'Her? No, no. It was a "him" . . . and I wanted to murde—'

Suddenly a look of extreme disappointment flooded over Pasterr's eager face. 'Oh! Not again. Why can't you have decent smutty wet dreams, like everyone else?'

'Isn't *this* wet enough?' pleaded J'hadd, dripping for effect.

'Well, yes, but that doesn't count! Somniprescience is cheating, anyone can sweat that much if gripped in a firm enough somniprescient state. Says so in my lecture notes if you don't believe . . .'

'Sweat?' squealed J'hadd. 'Are you trying to tell me I smell like a canal when I sweat?'

'Er, yes . . . I think.'

'Come here,' pleaded J'hadd. 'Come closer. Taste it, come on. It even *tastes* like a canal. Not a trace of salt or anything else you'd normally find in sweat. C'mon, explain that one.'

'Easy. That's one of the first things you learn, that is.' Pasterr scratched his head and thought hard, back to the lectures. 'Yeah, I remember. "Normal physiological parameters cannot be used or trusted during, or immediately after, a prolonged somniprescient seizure." So your sweat

157

could be almost anything. Tomorrow night you should try dreaming you're a rose. Then we can bottle the stuff and sell it as perfume!' And with that Pasterr turned to leave.

'Hey! Where are you off to?' protested J'hadd. 'Aren't you going to give me a towel?'

'Hear that ringing? That's matins. Late for matins and it's messy . . .' He made a slicing movement across his throat, then shoved the last of the porridge into his mouth.

'But what about me, I'm soaking!'

'Ah, that's part of the cure. Should teach you not to do it again. See you later, we'll get you up and about.' And with that Pasterr vanished off towards the main chapel.

J'hadd crossed his arms huffily and cursed as he wrung another three gallons out of his pyjama sleeves and felt something wriggling in his top pocket.

'Let's see somniprescience explain *that*,' he growled to himself as he pulled a pair of gasping tadpoles out of his pocket and hurled them into the puddle beneath the hammock.

J'hadd, he thought, you're a failure. Can't even arrest yourself. What would Sacrosanct Sergeant Vertex – bless him! – have to say about that?

And suddenly a shaft of fear raced up his spine faster than a tadpole fleeing from a four-foot pike. Sacrosant Sergeant Vertex! he squealed in the privacy of his mind. J'hadd was letting him down, shaking and snubbing the faith invested in him. Right now Sergeant Vertex – bless him! – would be in his office in Cranachan awaiting his report . . .

J'hadd's head began to throb again.

. . . but his report on what? Why had the strings of fate been manipulated from that office, sending him to the SAS training under deep cover, attaching him to the only successful team *ever* to steal the Chalice of Wyndarland, and gaining entry to the SAS as a full Friar-Private? J'hadd knew it was something big. Something that only he could solve . . .

But what ever happened in an Abbey?

His head throbbed again. And it hit him. The Flock Wars! They hadn't got in the way of his investigations, they *were* his

158

investigations. In a flash of pride he could see it all, every detail of the vast scheme of things, the grand plan. And there, tiny but vital, the single cell of yeast that would leaven the bread of Truth, Justice and the Cranachanian Way; there was he, Pious Constable Slamm J'hadd. Oh, what faith and perfect foresight Sacrosanct Sergeant Vertex had shown – bless his woolly socks!

He, J'hadd, was the chosen one, the transgression seeker! And yea, though the path had been hard (especially the yomping bits), and verily though his hands had smarted much after the thirty-foot bell-rope climbs, and even though he had been flattened by a wild assault camel in the field of duty – boy did *that* smart! – this pain had focused his mind. He now knew with absolute certainty the critical nature of his delicate mission.

Now where was his hymnal?

Set in a quarter acre of prime Cranachanian stone cherubs, neatly manicured lawns and a shrubbery, the mansion 'Cosa Nostra' nuzzled affectionately at the outer walls of the Imperial Palace Fortress, as close to royalty as it could possibly be without a knighthood.

This was the mansion owned by Khar Pahcheeno, a vast bullfrog of a man who could make money out of anything there was to make money out of. Anyone who stood in his way would be summarily despatched and buried 'unofficially' in the foundations of some civil engineering project or other, or laid to rest officially via his very own Undertaker's Parlour on Pitt Street. Over the years, that had become a nice little earner.

Right now, Khar Pahcheeno wasn't very happy. He'd just received some bad news.

'Gone!' he screamed from behind his highly polished walnut table, which despite hours of scrubbing still sported a scratch in the shape of a pair of obscenely gesturing fingers. 'What a-you mean, gone?' he roared, trembling with fury in his midnight-black suit.

The Assistant Chief Underling to the Secretary of the Site

Manager, who had been unfortunate enough to draw the short straw, swallowed and answered, 'He's not there any more and a cartload of stones is missing and the plans are gone and we don't know what to do . . .'

The huge white rat on Khar Pahcheeno's lap squeaked as his grip tightened around its throat. He'd stood to make twenty-five thousand groats out of that port, and then there was the shipping surcharges to be had . . . every day lost was money! Pahcheeno growled, clicked his ostentatiously ringed fingers and held out his hand.

The Assistant Chief Underling to the Secretary of the Site Manager swallowed nervously and glanced around. It was a well-known fact that one of Khar Pahcheeno's finger clicks could mean anything. Carried in that single percussive blow could be the information to 'break hees legs, drop-a heem off a-da breedge, then breeng me one of Mama's special Espressos!' or much, much worse.

Terror swelled within the Assistant Chief Underling's chest as the enormous pin-striped bulk of Fhet Ucheeni the bouncer stomped forward, snatched him by the back of his neck and propelled him exit-wards. At the door, he stopped, handed him a copy of the plans and kicked him at a cherub.

'Feeneesh on a-time, we'll be happy, and you'll be alive. Have a nice day.' Casually Fhet Ucheeni hurled a small metal badge at the quivering Underling, bouncing it off his forehead.

It was only half an hour later, when his legs gave out in a darkened back street and he collapsed with terror that the Underling dared look at the badge. The metal star glinted two words at him, 'Site Manager'.

There and then he wet himself.

By now Reverend Unctuous thought he had heard all of the sounds which the Underworld Kingdom of Helian had to offer, most of which recently seemed to revolve around the incessant chewing of rocks. He was, albeit reluctantly, getting quite used to being regularly awoken by the scream-ing of tormented souls, or the eight-hourly squeal of the shift change Klaxon. The bangs and pops of the underfloor heating system were also becoming uncomfortably familiar. But so far he had never heard anything quite like the sound currently filtering into his earshot.

At first he had thought that the dark, malevolent chuckling was some form of seismic activity outside. It had come as a shock to realise that it was coming from Flagit as he pored over a vast sheet of blue Nognite Parchment, scribbling frantically with his boil-point pen and keeping up a low running commentary to a short, scarred, and profusely sweating, figure standing at his side. As Unctuous stared at the vast scaly back of the demon, watching its shoulders twitch uncontrollably and snatching tantalising fragments of commentary, a spasm of curiosity ran its probing fingers up and down his spiritual spine. What was Flagit up to? Who was he talking to? And why did he keep pointing at the tiny windmill-like device and the rest of the entrails of the air-conditioning system scattered all around the storeroom? It was no good, Unctuous simply had to know.

Silently, stealthily, almost dreading what evil scheme he would witness being hatched by Flagit's wicked mind, Unctuous padded across the floor and stood at his other elbow, peering at the pattern of interlinked lines scrawled across the sheet. Then he rubbed his eyes and squinted again, blinking incomprehensibly at the criss-crossed wounds on the forehead of Flagit's short but attentive audience.

Unctuous caught himself staring at the stitches and, embarrassed, squinted at the blue sheet on the smoked obsidian table.

Flagit had drawn what appeared to be a vast domed affair squatting on the top of a mountain and had annotated it with dimensions across the base, the apex and each of the seven internal walls. A pair of parallel lines dropped out of the centre of the dome appearing to plunge, according to the diagram, two hundred and sixty-seven ells through solid rock. Close to the top of this tube Flagit was carefully drawing a tiny windmill shape which, had Unctuous known anything about fluid dynamics in the context of air-conditioning systems, he would have recognised immediately as a main charging turbine.

Unctuous shook his head again and stared at the net skeleton of lines, his eyes tracing the domed curve, trying to wring any scrap of sense out of the sketch. Fortunately for Flagit, Unctuous had never seen the detailed blueprint diagrams necessary for civil engineering projects and wouldn't have recognised the complicated leisure complex plans if they had been festooned with neons. Baffled he scratched his head. And then, in the instant his fingers contacted the curve of his skull, he saw it for exactly what it was.

'Oh, that's lovely!' he proclaimed leaning forward to stare intently at the pattern. 'That's very kind.'

Flagit jumped at the sudden interruption, reflexively spreading his arms wide to hide his secret, looking alarmingly like a six-year-old caught drawing rude pictures in the corner of his exercise book.

'No, no, let me see,' insisted Unctuous. 'Don't be shy. It'll be beautiful. A very thoughtful gesture.'

Flagit and Guthry the dwarf stared bewildered at the Reverend. 'What?' they chorused.

'That hair-net. It'll be perfect to cover up those dreadfully unsightly scars,' said Unctuous pointing at Guthry's forehead.

'Hair-net?' yelped Flagit in the privacy of his seething mind. And then, in the way that a drawing of a black candlestick can flip into two white facial profiles, he saw his grand design in a totally different light. Guthry shook his head, 'Sheeeyoot, boy! I don' need no hair-net. I gotten me a hat . . . ooooof!'

'Er, yes, yes,' stammered Flagit, removing his elbow from the side of Guthry's head. 'Ha, hair-net! Must be your intuition, Unctuous. I just felt I had to cover this poor unfortunate's fatal wounds,' he raised a claw and whispered behind it, 'It's a surprise for him. Doesn't know.' He pointed at the dwarf and smiled as benevolently as he could manage. Which

162

wasn't very successful. Guthry emptied a bucket of simmering canal water over his overheating body and stood steaming gently.

'Oh, that is nice,' offered Unctuous. 'But there's just a couple of things I don't understand. It's not a criticism but, well, what does *that* mean?' asked Unctuous pointing at the dimension marking across the base. 'Sixty-five ells? I've never heard of that in lace circles.' In truth he had heard the word ell before, somewhere. He just didn't know where. It was a weight or thickness, or something. If he had in fact recalled at that precise moment that one ell was equal to a yard and a quarter he would have been even more confused. Who, in their right mind, would want a two-hundred-and-fifty-foot hair-net?

Flagit swallowed nervously. What could he say? Part of him wanted to smack the Reverend across the cavern and stand over him, laughing gleefully. 'Oh, idiot! You know nothing? Soon it'll be far too late to be of any concern to you!' The other part of him had more sense. It giggled casually and smiled unnervingly.

'That's my shorthand for stitches and er, needle size. It's sixty-five stitches along on . . . on size "e" eleven's, all right?'

Unctuous blinked, something about that didn't sound right, now what was it?

Guthry stared at the demon as if he had gone mad.

'Oh, of course,' answered Unctuous gullibly believing every word despite the twittering note of doubt in the back of his mind. One of the qualifications for becoming a practising devotee of St Absent, the Regularly Forgotten, was the ability to stamp on any feelings of overwhelming scepticism. 'And what's this?' he asked, pointing at the pair of vertical lines plunging out of the centre.

'Ah, er, chin strap,' answered Flagit through tightly clenched teeth.

'I thought as much. Oh, I do like the little windmill clasp, lovely!'

'Er, yes, he was a miller before he . . .'

'Miller? Holy moles! I was a drainage contrac—' blurted Guthry before receiving another elbow in the ribs.

Flagit feigned embarrassment, then leaned over to Unctuous and whispered, 'He's still a bit confused. Has these delusions, you know. Happens a lot with fatal head injuries,' he lied, tapping his forehead meaningfully. Then in a flash he stood, bundled up the blueprint hastily, snatched Guthry by the neck and propelled him towards the door. 'C'mon, c'mon,' barked Flagit. 'Time to go and pick what colour you want for your hair-net.'

The door slammed on baffled protests from the dwarf.

Reverend Unctuous scratched his head, a vague feeling of unease spreading fungally from the back of his mind. Somehow he felt that Flagit had just possibly been trying to hide something from him. Well, vowed Unctuous in his most righteous manner, when he came back, he'd jolly well find out what was going on. Devil or no, he just shouldn't go around telling lies to men of the cloth. It just wasn't right.

The light from a tallow candle reflected off the oil slick of grease on Fhet Ucheeni's hair as he leaned across the desk and scowled meaningfully.

'But, I don't *do* missing persons,' spluttered Commander 'Black' Achonite, shifting uncomfortably in his leather undies.

'This ees a missing dwarf. And Khar Pacheeno says a-you do eet,' snarled Fhet Ucheeni in pin-striped malevolence. 'And what he says . . .'

'Yes, yes, I do. I know, it's in my Black Guard Contract,' grunted Achonite, holding his teeth and praying that no one could hear him. Ucheeni grinned, stood and made to leave.

'Er . . . Just one question,' said Achonite.

Ucheeni frowned, then made a small sweeping gesture with his hand.

'Why such interest in a dwarf?'

'Competition,' growled Ucheeni. 'A cartload of stones, da port plans and a-da site manager deesappear at a-da same time. Da Boss, he's a suspicious, comprende?' The last word was spat out more as a command.

Mutely Achonite nodded and Ucheeni slammed the door

behind him. In the silence of his office, the Commander of the Black Guards dropped his head into his hands. Missing dwarves! As if he didn't have enough on his plate. A wave of anger coursed down his spine as he thought of rat-proof boots buckling in intense heat.

'Barak!' he shouted, slamming his fist on the desk and hurling himself upright. In a second he was out the door, heading towards Pitt Square and the answers that Barak had better have ready. For the sake of his teeth.

His stalag-mite clipped firmly into its cage and growling contentedly after another thousand-foot vertical feed, Flagit clattered down the crimson backstreets of downtown Tumor. He oozed confidence from every scale. Things were going well. Guthry would have appeared just outside the Cranachanian Civil Engineering Project's Meeting; he had a sack and the blueprints, he knew where the safe was and he had a deeply ingrained Total Limbic Control Programme buried irremovably in his infernite latticed brain.

Now, back to the storeroom, there had to be a way of getting a regular supply of cash, everything hinged on it. He galloped on.

Suddenly a side alley exploded with a growl, a host of wriggling talons locked around Flagit's throat and he disappeared with a grunt.

'Well?' snarled Nabob, staring at Flagit pinned to the wall. 'Where's my proof?' Smoke curled angrily out from Nabob's flaring nostrils.

'I'll get it just as soon as . . .' choked Flagit.

'You'll get it now! Today!' he shrieked, the pressure of the election mounting daily. 'Seirizzim's way ahead in the latest derision polls. If I don't have proof I'll lose . . .'

'Just let me . . .'

'No! I'll take that creature back up there,' snarled Nabob curling his lip at the stalag-mite.

'But, I . . .'

'Go! Take this,' he thrust a small pouch into Flagit's claw

and hurled him in the direction of the Phlegethon. 'Bring me a General!' he croaked and vanished into the shadows.

'Bring me a General,' spat Flagit miserably as he trudged off. 'Why can't he go, why is it always me?'

It was easier than he had thought it would be and it surprised him. Okay, so he'd been to all the lectures* but some things are easier listened to in the dark comfort of a warm lecture hall than practised on the windswept side of a hill just mere yards from the war-ravaged acres of the Ghuppy Desert.

Slamm J'hadd was very pleased that he had been able to track the paths of the shepherds this far. He was a living testament to the teaching standards practised by the Religious Undercover Crime Squad and this made him proud.

He stood in the middle of the ten-yard swathe of blackened boot-trodden grass that led directly from the main door of Abbey Synnia to the natural amphitheatre used for the annual Lammarch Wart-Hog trials and breathed a satisfied breath.

Now the real work could begin. He flipped open his tiny hymnal and stared at the now indecipherable smudges, readying himself to add to his invaluable wealth of evidence. Slamm J'hadd hadn't spent the last fourteen years in the Religious Undercover Crime Squad as Pious Constable without knowing that everything, no matter how much of a nothing it looked, everything meant something. The tiniest scrap of a bitty fragment of everything could just be the something he desperately needed . . . so where was it?

Right here, right now there were plenty of everythings, he was tripping over them. The whole place was heaving with screaming everythings all shouting to be that vital something! Overturned trestle tables, trampled scorecards, hurled sods of turf scattered randomly, the odd curved blade

* Well, nearly all of the annual lectures entitled 'Tracking. A Practical Theory of Surveillance. Pursuit and Sneaking-Up Unnoticed', anyhow. It was a source of personal discomfort to him that he had missed the most recent two due to the impossibility of getting time off from the SAS training since it would blow his cover.

of a ceremonial yataghan dagger . . . everythings everywhere.

But he couldn't find *the* everything. The single minuscule scrap that would tell him WHY!

As soon as he knew WHY!, he could work out WHO!, then WHERE!, possibly WHO ELSE! and quicker than any quick brown fox could jump over all the lazy dogs in the world he'd have it in the bag. He tugged the collar of his rain-cloak up tight around his ears and scuffed at the grass, deep in thought. He'd tried the ways suggested by the autumn series lectures on 'Thought Processing within the Context of Evidential Prioritising' but, since he hadn't even understood the title he had got nowhere. He'd tried a more culinary approach, letting his eager eyes hoover up naked facts, chop them and hurl them into the searing heat of inspiration, thrilling as vast plumes of sizzling irrelevance burnt off, cheering as clouds of unimportant impurities blasted forth and then sobbing as he had stared at the charred black glob of despair that remained caked to the bottom of his elucidatory wok. There was nothing else. Not even the tiniest inkling as to what was behind the recent spate of ram-raids perpetrated by the D'vanouin. There were no ransom demands . . . nothing. Just a war and a very painful headache.

He was running out of time and he knew it, but the answers just had to be around here somewhere, staring at him, winking seductively like a pouting strip-joint chanteuse, he knew it. It was a well-known saying that the answers always return to the scene of the crime . . . or was that murderers? Whatever, he knew that when a new kettle of fish turns up smelling bad, well, it's time to start looking for rotten apples. Was he right? Or was he right?

Haven't a clue.

In sudden frustration he grabbed his mind and spun it into the interrogatory chair in the darkened room and turned the ten-thousand-lumen spotlight on it.

'Who did it?' he demanded from the shadows.

'D'vanouin,' spluttered his mind, wincing beneath the photic barrage.

'Proof!' he yelled.

'Yataghan daggers and camel prints. Can you turn the light off?'

'No! Motive?'

'Stealing sheep. It's very bright.'

'Not good enough. Why steal sheep when you've got goats?'

'Variety?'

'I'm asking the questions! What's Reverend Vex Screed got to do with it?'

'Don't know. Now, about this light . . .'

'Liar! He's behind it, isn't he? He told them!'

'What would he stand to gain?'

'Feeling of power . . . revenge?'

'Revenge for what?'

'Maybe the Sheep Marketing Cartel of Southern Rhyngill bought up the land he was building a chapel on and destroyed it. Then, enraged by feelings of extreme frustration he set about systematically destroying the remaining flocks of . . .'

'Oh, come on. There's no such thing as the Sheep Marketing Cart—'

'OK! Try this. He was hurled down the front steps by the head of the Sheep Marketing Cartel for trying to preach . . .'

'NO! You'll never prove that! Haranguist Missionaries always get hurled down the steps while trying to preach. It's an occupational hazard!'

'He's a courier! Smuggling drugs from the . . .'

'You're clutching at straws. Face it. You haven't a clue!'

'Told you that before you turned the light on.'

Miserably, J'hadd took another dejected step forward, sighed and stood on a small book half-buried in the semi-circular imprint of a camel's hoof-print. It was in his hand in a second being mercilessly scoured, wringed and grilled for any tiny scrap of information.

After digesting twenty odd lessons he read aloud the phrase,

> Fear ye not the darkest depths of night,
> let ye lambs of devotion burn bright.

and grinned. He'd found a something! It was such a good job he'd attended lessons on advanced D'vanouin during his RUC training. He flicked to the inside cover. He knew that there was bound to be a name there . . . the name behind it all!

Spark . . . spark . . . spark . . . whoooooosh! The flames of inspiration blasted wildly inside his head and with a little skip of joy he wheeled around on his heel, leapt on to his llama and spurred it eagerly towards Cranachan.

Away across the crumbling bulk of the Imperial Palace Fortress, fists were pounding on tables.

'Order, order!' cried the chairman of the Cranachanian Civil Engineering Projects Council – a self-important body of three men whose self-appointed task it was to determine which, if any, of the requests for planning permission would be granted. They were the judges, and their decision was financial.

'I say a-no,' shouted a judge in a pin-striped tunic as he stared at the worth of the proposal. His slicked-back hair glistened in the sparse candlelight as he continued stroking a vast white long-haired rat.

'Do I take it, Khar Pahcheeno, that you are refusing Mrs Lidoh's request to build an outdoor swimming pool?' questioned the chairman.

Pahcheeno nodded slowly and continued staring derisively at the tiny heap of fiscal inducement before him.

'Upon what is that decision based?' asked the chairman as Mrs Lidoh fidgeted nervously before the semicircular table. A lot depended on her building this swimming pool. She'd told her neighbours she was going to have one. Oh, the shame if she was turned down.

Khar Pahcheeno ruffled his rat behind the ear, cleared his throat and answered in the dark accented whisper he had, 'Profeetabeelity.'

169

A rustle of shock echoed around the room; its epicentre, Mrs Lidoh. 'Profitability?' she shouted. 'But you're not investing anything.'

'Oh no?' breathed Pahcheeno. 'You're asking me a-to make a deceesion. For me to a-say "yes" I got a-to do a lotta soul-searching, I got a-to look atta pros and cons, I got a-to make sure it's the right a-deceesion. That takes a lotta time. Time ees a-money. It costa lotta money to a-say "yes". Not enough money there. I no make a-da profeet eef I a-say "yes",' he growled, staring fixedly at the pile of groats glinting on the table.

Mrs Lidoh sagged. She would never be able to look her neighbours in the eye when it leaked out that she was too poor to bribe the Civil Engineering Projects Council. She would be spurned. Oh, woe.

'Any other business?' shouted the chairman, throwing the meeting open to the floor.

'Oh yes,' answered a small man, kicking open the doors at the far end of the room and lurching in under the combined burden of a knee-length henna-coloured beard and a bulging sack. 'Lots of it!'

A ripple of sharply intaken breaths swept around the room as the dwarf stepped into the light and everybody clapped eyes on the ring of criss-crossed scars holding his skull together.

'You!' choked Pahcheeno, recognising his ex-site manager instantly, 'You should a-be drown—'

'Jumpin' Jiminy! Seems like them rumours is a bit exaggerated!' he grinned lurching towards the table. 'I bin busy!'

'Your for . . . forehead,' blubbered the chairman, cringing as he saw the pale tinge to his skin. 'Looks like you've had an argument with a h . . . hacksaw.'

'Sheeyoot! Don't be stupid,' growled Guthry, smoothing his stitches carefully. 'Cut myself shavin', so I did, that's all.' His time spent with Flagit had taught him how to lie easily.

A wave of murmured doubt washed around the hall.

'Since when has a-da personal health of anybody been of

eenterest to a-da counceel?' whispered Pahcheeno, intrigued completely by the bulging contents of the sack, some of which was sticking out of the top.

'Yup! My feelin's exactly,' gurgled Guthry, swinging the hessian holdall on to the floor and tugging a large blue parchment from beneath his tunic. 'Gentlemen, you's all familiar wi' my work on th' Trans-Talpino Trade Route Improvement Scheme an' are undoubt'ly aware o' the high standards t' which I tirelessly work. However, I've recently had a change o' mind, [a thousand feet below Flagit sneered cheerfully and stifled a chuckle] an' wish t' depart from schemes designed fer the benefit o' the masses. Instead I want t' concentrate on a personal projec' which'll be o' benefit only t' a select few o' the richest, most prestigious, members of Cranachanian Society. Shoot, folks not unlike yerselves, gentlemen.'

Guthry then unravelled the blueparchment of a vast hilltop complex, which, if looked at through the completely rose-tinted optimism of a vicar's naivety could possibly look like the plans for a hair-net. 'It'll consist o' bars, spas, jacuzzis, massage parlours 'n' water slides, all housed under a vast temperature controlled canopy.' His commentary never faltered, highlighting the exclusivity of the clientele which its anticipated three-hundred bikini-clad companions would be ready to serve; emphasising the constantly tropical environment that the Talpine weather could not destroy. Khar Pahcheeno leapt forward on his chair, clamouring for a closer view when Guthry announced the final facts. 'An' I's sure you's all will be rightly eager t' be knowin' why the internal design's split about a seven-fold geometrical axis. Well hot diggity, this is the key to th' projec's success. Each o' these sections'll be designed t'house one o' yer fayvrit deadly sins on a rota basis an' create th' perfec' atmosphere in which t' indulge yerselves t' the full, aided and abetted by our staff, thematically dressed as devils or demons or centaurs. Yup, there'll be food galore in our constantly restockin' Gluttony Suite; fawnin' lackeys in our Hall o' Pride; insatiable companions in the Vestibule of Lust . . .

171

Gentlemen, I stand before you beggin' that you grant me permission to start work on Centaur Parcs Debauchery Centre, now.'

The chairman was ready to agree even then, as he saw the preliminary designs for the Centaur Parcs waitress uniforms, all clingy, shiny red with claws and whips.

'But afore you'll be decidin', gentlemen, I have, ahem, brung you a little gift.' And with that he upended the hessian sack and smothered the table in what looked like crisp new hundred groat notes.

It was the quickest confirmation the council had ever given.

They moaned and grumbled and complained as they stamped their feet on the banks of the Phlegethon and warmed their talons over the curling flames of an infernal brazier.

Flagit peered at the ranks of the Ferryman's Picket line from behind a large rock and tutted at the slogans scratched clumsily across the slate placards they held high.

'Underpaid Underworld Underdogs!' proclaimed one in scrappily etched letters. 'Souls Not Dole!' yelled another. And there were more that Flagit had real difficulty in decifering.

'Good afternoon, gentlemen,' growled Flagit as he strolled up to the picket line, casually swinging a large black pouch.

Suspicious eyes from beneath cowled hoods stared mistrustfully at him. 'You come to negotiate?' snapped Captain Naglfar, pulling on his flaming pipe.

'In a manner of speaking, yes,' answered Flagit swinging the pouch a little more for effect.

'Pah! We of the Underworld Ferrymen's Coalition of Arguing, Shouting and Generally Being Narked don't negotiate!'

'Shame,' grumbled Flagit and made as if to leave. The pouch made the type of chinking sound that only vast amounts of obuls casually rubbing together can make. Thirty infernal tongues dropped longingly out of mouths at the seductive sound. A host of bony elbows jammed urgently into Naglfar's ribs.

'Er . . . but we can haggle,' he coughed to a gurgling of approval.

Flagit wheeled casually on his heels in a way that he hoped didn't look too interested. The bag chinked again.

'Three thousand obuls, or nothing!' demanded Naglfar, his voice booming arrogantly across the sluggish black of the river. 'Unless you take into account annual refits and pension rights, then we'd be happy with two k. Of course, phase in twenty days' annual leave, private health plans and productivity bonuses and we'll start back immedia— oooof!' A hail of elbows cracked against his ribs.

'Not interested,' grumbled Flagit, tutting under his breath. No wonder Nabob was worried about the strike lasting until the election.

'But, it's a good offer,' whimpered Naglfar.

'One day only,' added another ferryman.

'Never to be repeated,' added a third.

'I don't require a repeat,' oozed Flagit enigmatically.

'Eh?' grunted Naglfar scratching confusedly at his skull and producing a vast cloud of smoke.

'A one-off, er, favour from one of you good ferrymen is all I require,' said Flagit, twitching the bag like an expert trout fisherman with a freshly wound fly.

'What sort of favour?' nibbled Naglfar. 'I ain't doing nothing weird!'

'I need to book a ferry crossing. Me, return, and a single for a guest.'

Naglfar narrowed his eyes suspiciously. A discontented grumbling echoed over his shoulder. 'Er, what sort of guest? Damned or demon?'

'Damned,' answered Flagit, staring straight back at the inchoate eyes of the ferryman. 'It'll be well worth your while,' he added with a grin and tipped a huge pile of coins out on the rocky banks.

'What! Are you trying to use bribery to make me break the

bounds of the strike and, in so doing, undermine the solid strata on which our industrial action is rooted?' asked Naglfar carefully under the infernal gaze of the other ferrymen.

'Nope. I just want to hire someone's ferry for a bit.'

'Oh, that's all right then!' declared Naglfar stepping forward.

'No it's not!' shrieked the other ferrymen in solidarity to the cause.

'Why not? It's private enterprise!' argued Naglfar.

'Blackleg!' cried a voice from the mass of ferrymen.

'Who you calling blackleg? We've all got black legs!'

'Scab!' snarled another voice.

'You'll be covered in 'em if you carry on like that!' snarled Naglfar, his fists circling in the air.

'Strike-breaker!'

'Call me nose-breaker!' he screamed and launched himself into the throng, bony knuckles thrashing wildly into the skeletal remnants of what once passed as noses. In a second he was buried in a frenzied heap of scrapping Underworld Ferrymen.

Flagit closed his mouth, tutted disgustedly and began miserably refilling the bag.

Honestly! he thought, anybody'd think they'd never seen fifteen thousand obuls in one place before.

'Ferryman?' shrieked a voice from the mêlée. 'More like a fairy-man! Go on then, hit me! Properly . . . take a swing and . . . ooooof!' There was the sound of spitting teeth. 'That's it! Now I'm mad!'

'You've always been mad! Ha, ha, ha!' bellowed another demonic voice.

'Come back and I'll scratch your eyes out . . .'

'Too late . . .' screamed a reply.

Shaking his head Flagit stood and began to trudge miserably away down the banks of the Phlegethon. It was going to be impossible to cross the river now. Even if he had the correct vessel, and even if that did float, everybody knew that rip-tidal currents surged within the opaque glutinous torrents of the river. It was going to be impossible to get across. Totally, hopelessly, impossibly, unfeasibly . . .

'Ptht! That offer thtill open? whispered a hoarse voice as clearly as he could through three broken teeth.

'Er, I . . . you?' stuttered Flagit as Naglfar appeared from behind a barrel.

'Who d'you eckthpect?'

'But how . . . ? You . . . the fight?'

'Ahh. Oldetht trick in the book. Thirty on to one. Never ever keep track of who'th thumping who. Get in low with the firtht few wallopth and it blothomth ever tho nithely. The hard bit ith thneaking out without anyone notithing,' lisped Naglfar. 'Now, one thingle and one return, wathn't it?'

Captain Barak stood trembling outside the inferno that was once Spam Smith's Smith's Shop. Hundred-foot flames seared into the sky through the vast hole in the roof, licking and widening with every passing minute. He'd tried dozens of times to close down the forge, or at least bring the hellish scene under some form of control. Droves of bored onlookers hung around in Pitt Square, milling restlessly behind the blue and black tape of the Black Guard cordon.

Suddenly the crowd surged and, like some biblical scene, parted, spitting out a fuming Commander 'Black' Achonite.

'Barak!' he screamed as he picked himself off the ground. 'Barak, report!'

The Captain swallowed and ran forward. The crowd murmured in mounting interest. It looked like someone was about to be torn off a strip, and this crowd was definitely in the mood for a good strip-tearing, especially after staring at hundred-foot-high flames for a couple of hours. I mean, once you've seen one flame you've seen 'em all.

'Barak', growled Achonite with a rumble of fury. 'That fire is not out!'

Barak stamped to attention, fixed his gaze the regulation six inches above eye level and shouted, 'Correct, Sah! We are working on it, Sah!' Involuntarily, two of his fingers crossed, praying Achonite wouldn't ask precisely what this work entailed. It would surely mean the end of his enjoyment of crispy pork crackling if he were to tell the truth. He couldn't admit that they were all standing about and waiting for it to burn itself out, could he? He'd been in there, he'd seen it. Nasty, smelly, burny thing, sheets of flame everywhere. Terribly dangerous. He braced himself for the question, preparing his answer, his excuse . . .

'So I can hear. Good work.' Achonite scowled up at Barak and flashed his teeth.

'Sah, I . . . what?'

'The hammering,' growled Achonite, 'trying to close the forge grate, I presume.'

'I . . . I . . . er,' spluttered Barak as for the first time he realised that an incessant hammering was issuing from the inside of the smithy. Pounding blows rang out above the roaring of the flames. He shook his head and counted his men. They were all there, trembling nervously.

The crowd behind the tape shuffled a step forward with mounting excitement.

'Who's in there?' growled Achonite. 'Such bravery . . .'

'Well, it's . . .' flustered Barak.

Achonite wheeled around, snarled and glared up at his Captain. 'You mean, you don't know? First lesson in discipline, know where your troops are, man . . .'

'Sah, I know where all my troops are,' trembled Barak, pointing at a small group of matt-black-clad men. A motley selection of tooth tattoos grinned pathetically back.

Achonite boiled with rising fury. 'Are you telling me that in there is a . . . a civilian?' he roared, much to the appreciation of the crowd.

'It appears . . .'

'You don't know?' boomed Achonite, an artery beginning to pulse at his temple.

Barak shrugged.

'Then get in there and find out!' bellowed Achonite, his teeth grinding audibly.

'Are you joking? In there?' blubbered Barak.

'Look into my eyes,' snarled the Commander tugging down the corner of his left eye and glaring up at Barak. 'Do I look like I know the meaning of the word "joke"?'

Barak whimpered and shook his head, trapped between a thug and a hot place.

'Then get in there!' bellowed Achonite.

Before he realised it he was scurrying toward the smithy door. In seconds he flashed through it and was hit by two things. The first was an almost solid wall of intense heat blasting from the molten heap of metal that was once a top-of-the-range forge. And the other thing was the noise.

Above the constant roar of the flames there was a solid cacophony of pounding metal and anvil. He screeched to a stop, quivered, then screamed.

For there before him, engulfed in the inferno and seemingly oblivious to it, the deathly blue figure of Spam Smith battered several shades of shining fury out of a thirty-foot windmill shaped object. Spam looked up and grinned manically.

Barak took one look at the apparition's cat-gutted forehead, screamed and fled.

A few moments later, after the third bucket had been emptied over his face, Barak came round.

'Well, who is it?' roared Achonite. 'What are they doing?'

'Sp—' he croaked as a sliver of potato peeling trickled down his cheek. 'Sp—'

'How many letters in it?' heckled a voice from the crowd.

'Has it got a "j"?' yelled another, to a peal of raucous applause.

'Spam . . .' whimpered Barak and was rewarded with another bucket of pure Cranachanian street water. 'Spam Smith!' he finally spluttered around a host of mouldering cabbage leaves.

Commander 'Black' Achonite stood and laughed in the envegetabled face of Captain Barak. 'In there?' he mocked, pointing at the surging inferno of hundred-foot flames. 'Don't be so stupid. No blacksmith worth any amount of salt would be hammering away in there!'

177

'B . . . but . . .' began Barak.

'See that tape strung across the whole front entrance, eh? *That* says he's not in there. That says that this area is under Black Guard jurisdiction pending the completion of our investigation. Anybody that steps over that line without express permission from me is deemed to be interfering with Black Guard business and I'll have their head on a stick before the hour's out! I didn't give him permission because he's helping Thor Rensic with his post-mortem inquiries. Do I make myself entirely clear?'

'Y—'

'Excellent. So you'll agree, there's no blacksmith in there!' snarled Achonite.

Barak swallowed. He hated to disagree with Achonite, he knew the possible consequences of such an action. It had been Achonite himself who had introduced the Black Guard's Motto 'Disagree and Die!'

But Barak knew what he had just seen. He swallowed again, took a deep breath and attempted to phrase possibly the last question he might ever ask, 'Permission to speak, Sah?'

'Gods, what is it, now?' rumbled Achonite, the leather on his gauntlets creaking as his fists flexed.

'Well, I was thinking, Sah. Well, if there's really no blacksmith in there, then who's doing all that banging?'

Achonite's eyes rolled into his forehead as fury overtook him and, snarling, he leapt at Barak, clamping him around the throat, dragging him from the ground. The crowd cheered.

Barak was only saved from certain death by the sudden cessation of hammering from the smithy. Miraculously Achonite noticed the sudden absence of anything but the deafening whoosh of infernal flames. He looked around.

It probably would have been better for his long-term sanity if he hadn't. For at that very instant the door to the smithy was kicked open and a vast figure lurched into the evening air.

'You!' shrieked Achonite as his eyes fixed unbelievingly

on the pallid fizzog of Spam Smith as he lugged a freshly forged windmill arrangement into view. 'Why aren't you dead?'

The smith grinned, looked straight at Achonite and said, 'It would appear that rumours of my demise have been somewhat exaggerated.'

With a hail of squeals the crowd scattered, arms aloft, panic-stricken.

Achonite's face twisted in a way not normally associated with the head of the Black Guard as he saw the cat-gut cross-stitch holding the smith's head together. 'Y . . . your head?' he croaked.

Spam Smith smoothed his stitches carefully and, as straight-faced as he could possibly manage under the circumstances, answered, 'Cut myself shaving.' With an inhuman effort he continued to lug the vast turbine blades off towards the flat peak of Tor Khamada.

For the first time in his life Commander Achonite hadn't a clue what to do. Before his very eyes an entire murder investigation had simply unravelled. How can he possibly be investigating the murder of Spam Smith if he was still alive and well and smithying?

Okay, so maybe he didn't look too well, but if you'd been murdered you wouldn't look your best . . . What was he thinking?

He needed answers.

Almost absent-mindedly he rolled up the sleeves of his leather armour, flung Barak to one side and stomped off towards the Imperial Palace Fortress and a chat with Thor Rensic.

This time there would be no excuses.

Barak coughed, rubbed his throat and wearily struggled off after the fuming figure of Commander Achonite.

If the light had been even half a dozen lumens brighter, the colours would have given anyone a migraine in seconds. As it was, you could almost feel the air in Gravure's Print Shop dripping with supersaturated rainbows of hue, you could almost smell the envy of the greens as they watched cowardly yellows being smashed black and blue by marauding gangs of ultra-violent violet. But Gravure was immune to it all. He just balanced a pair of cut amber discs on the end of his nose and peered through them as he laboured away to produce the neon-bright illuminated manuscripts for which he was so famous. Not for nothing was he known as 'Dazzling Gravure' in the heady circles of the Lithographer's Guild of Master Printers. So far he hadn't come across anything in two dimensions that he couldn't reproduce brighter, flashier and downright more 'ooooh'-provoking than the original.

Right now he was poring over a vast stone slab, hooked nose inches away from the surface, adding the finishing touches to the last greased block that would reproduce all the pages of the parchment-back edition of the Book of Krill.

Behind him the door creaked open with a ring of a small bell and a long-haired man with a beard, wearing a beret and painter's smock, struggled in under a gallery of canvases. Gravure looked up and removed his amber glasses with a flourish. 'Can I help you?' he asked.

'Sure 'ope so, squire,' said the trembling artist in a thick brogue of an accent. 'These paintin's, see? I's got a double bookin' fer two 'sibition's, see?' He waved a canvas of water-lilies at the printer and patted himself on the back for invention.

'Oh? And what can I do about that, Mr . . . ?'

'Er, er . . .' flustered the artist, staring around him for inspiration. A name! He hadn't thought of a name! His eyes latched on to a few coins scattered across a small shelf. 'Money!' he declared. 'Yes, that's it. Money.' He thrust a water-colour of a ruined cathedral under the printer's hooked nose and breathed a sigh of relief.

'I'm a printer, not an art critic,' growled Gravure.

'Ha! Yes, 'spose you are. See, thing is, I can't show my paintin's at same time in two differen' places, now can I?'

'So?'

'So, 'ow much'ld you charge fer copyin' 'em all, eh? Good as new, mind. Same size an' stuff. 'Ow much, eh?' The artist grinned toothlessly.

'More than you can afford,' grunted Gravure irritably. It was unfortunate timing, he was always irritable when he was using tartrazine yellow. Secretly he wondered if he had an allergy to it.

'No, look at 'em!' insisted Money, quite surprised that he had been so forceful. Still, needs must when an arrest dangles in the winds, as they say. 'I want a proper quote.' He thrust the pile of canvases at the printer and peered insistently at him in the way curious marmosets have. Gravure shrugged, realised that there was no way this artist was taking a negative answer and began to rifle through endless pictures of different coloured haystacks.

Now, with the printer's attention distracted, the artist's gaze began to scour the criminally cluttered shelves, searching, probing every nefarious nook and cranny for the tiniest scrap of evidence . . .

'Fond of water-lilies aren't we, Mr Money?' grunted Gravure after squinting at the fifty-third example.

'Cheaper than payin' fer models,' answered the artist. 'An' far less distractin' if y'get my drift?' he added with a leer that surprised himself. Gravure shuddered and returned his attention to the canvases.

The artist carried on poking about in a vast pile of recently type-set frames. Trembling, his index finger tugged one out, seemingly at random. His face creased into a searing grin of immense satisfaction. Aha!

'These your type-setting frames, sir?' he asked with enforced casualness. Inside he was raspberry jelly.

Gravure grunted an affirmation and glared at another half-dozen haystacks.

'All work you've carried out on these premises, by your very own fair hand, sir?' pressed the artist, so pleased that he was framing his questions in *such* a professional manner.

Gravure nodded, failing completely to notice the artist had unceremoniously kicked off his thick brogue.

'And were you paid to produce these particular, highly specific arrangements of letters, sir?'

Gravure looked up. 'Yes, it is my job to. You ask an awful lot of questions.'

'Yes, it is my job to,' grinned the artist, snatching off his beard, beret and wig with an eager flourish normally associated with labrador puppies, 'and with the answers you have given, along with the evidence stacked oh-so-neatly in the corner here, it is also my job to nick you in the Name of the Lord.' Oh, joy! He'd said it! For real. Fourteen years' training could teach one *so* much!

'What?' shrieked Gravure and cringed as he saw the lattice of cat-gut stitches across the artist's forehead.

'I, Pious Constable Slamm J'hadd of the Religious Undercover Crime Squad, arrest you, matey-boy, in connection with inciting illegal religious uprisings, passing forged publications off as genuine, plus, there's eight hundred and fifty-six counts of second-degree agnicide *and* interfering with RUC business. In short, I'm nicking you for starting the Flock Wars!' J'hadd jammed a whistle into his mouth and blew hard. The door and three windows burst open, exploding with countless bodies of crack uniformed officers. In a second Gravure was buried under a heap of seething blue vestments. At least that's what would have happened if he'd remembered to liaise with headquarters, but, in the excitement it had sort of, er, slipped his mind . . . well, there was a lot to do before a big bust . . . especially his first.

'You have the right to remain silent,' whimpered J'hadd losing momentum fast. Now, what had he thought up for this bit. There was a threat, er . . . oh, yes. 'But you won't want to, remain silent that is, when you see all the lovely ways we have of extracting confessions! Take him away, boys . . . er . . . ahem, come with me down to the yard!'

Pious Constable J'hadd grinned feebly to himself, he wasn't really sure that'd had the impact he wanted it to, needed polishing a bit. But, still, he'd caught the perpetrator.

J'hadd poked Gravure in the small of his back with a handy

stick and marched him out, pausing only momentarily to pick up an armful of incriminating type-frames and a couple of lithographs showing a group of particularly hirsute angels.

And as he scuttled out of the workshop he seethed with emotions. He had him! The felon directly responsible for the Flock Wars, caught red-handed.

Well, actually it was more sort of bright yellow, but that was just being picky. He patted the camel-hoof indented copy of a certain 'holy' book and harboured only one tiny fragment of doubt. He hadn't been just a little *too* hard, had he?

'Stay there,' grunted Flagit as he stepped off Captain Naglfar's ferry on to the far side of the Phlegethon. The jet-black ooze licked at his hoof-prints. 'And keep quiet.'

'Sure,' grunted Naglfar, shutting the infernal combustion engine down to tick-over and settling himself against the mast. He tugged a long draught out of his flaming pipe and smirked. Flagit wouldn't last long, he thought. They never do on their first visit this side.

Keeping low, Flagit scrambled up the rocky bank, crouched behind a suitable boulder and peered out at the Immigration Hut as covertly as he could with three feet of viciously curly horns on his head. He knew he shouldn't be here. If the Malebranche caught him smuggling souls . . .

Nervously he skipped out from this rock and dashed the short distance to the hut wall, flattening himself in a shadow and listening. And then the sound hit him.

Now, over the centuries that Flagit had lurked in Helian he'd become somewhat used to the constant background screams of the hellishly tormented. Their wailing rang out all hours, pitiful, anguished, desperate . . . But the screams haranguing his ears now, blasting from the overcrowded confines of the Immigration Hut, were not so much miserable, more extremely miffed.

'For the fifth time of asking,' shouted a large man in a camouflage cassock, sporting an arrow through his eye. 'Where are we?'

'Told you,' grumbled a demon behind a desk boredly. 'All will be revealed on the other side.'

'And how do we get to the other side?' snarled Friar-Captain 'Tucky' Succingo (deceased). 'Paddle? Swim? Hire little floaty things with pedals?'

The immigration demon scowled at the suede-headed man and croaked derisively, 'We have advanced a little beyond that. We have ferries now, a whole blinkin' armada of 'em!'

Succingo peered through his arrow and declared, 'I see no armada!'

The demon groaned, 'Well you wouldn't, would you. They're out on strike, something to do with pay and conditions.'

'Dammit, man! If this is some kind of evil D'vanouin game, I'll . . .'

'You'll what, eh?' growled the demon.

'. . . I'll make you pay!' roared Succingo, gnashing his teeth.

'Tough cheese, matey,' tutted the demon and nudged his snoozing partner as he wound himself up for his favourite answer in these circumstances. 'It's you that's got to pay, one way on the ferry! Ha ha!'

Succingo growled something unprintable and shoved his way through the grotesquely dismembered mob.

An SAS monk once of the 18th Organ Division peered miserably down at the lance sticking from his chest, 'I told you,' he grunted. 'This *is* Helian.'

'No, no,' answered his colleague holding his head up with his right hand. 'This is Purgatory.'

'Can't be. The lighting's better up there, and besides, does that look like your average angel?' He pointed to the laughing demon.

'D'you get angels in purgatory?'

''Course you do. I had this near-death experience once and I saw a host of golden . . .'

'Psst!' hissed Flagit as Succingo approached. 'Want to know what's on the other side?' he growled and waggled an invitationary talon.

'Talking to me?' snapped the ex-Friar-Captain, scowling as menacingly as he could around his arrow. It was pretty effective.

'It was you making all that noise a moment ago, wasn't it? Want some answers or not?'

Succingo glared suspiciously at Flagit peering out from behind a convenient pillar, then shrugged and swaggered over. He hadn't achieved Friar-Captaincy without knowing how to swagger effectively, 'Okay, wiseguy, you tell me where we are.'

'Not so fast,' sidestepped Flagit. 'I don't just give answers away. We trade, huh?'

'What d'you want to know?' growled Succingo. His fingers itched for his trusty Uri 9mm Anti-Heretic Crossbow but somehow he managed to hold his gaze steady. Straight as an arrow, in fact.

'Why are you here?' whispered Flagit, somehow edging the four words with razor blades.

'Ha! You tell me where "here" is first,' grinned Succingo.

Flagit gnashed his teeth impatiently. 'I'll give you a clue. Hear that inhuman howling echoing with insatiability? Well, that's the sound of a very hungry guard-dog, one with a triplet of rumbling stomachs and a matching set of slobbering heads. Dear little Cerby's there to keep you in!'

'Oh, and I suppose that's the Phlegethon?' said Succingo sarcastically, pointing at the slithering river, knowing the painted backdrop of a D'vanouin artist when he saw one. He'd heard about these heathens' mental tortures and the way they treated prisoners of war. Well, he wouldn't get any information out of him, not with such a shambolic scenario anyway. How was anyone supposed to believe that they were really wounded so badly? Pah! There was no pain! The D'vanouin's would never break him. Everybody knew the first rule of torture – No pain; no gain. 'And I bet the Styx is due east of here?' added Succingo casually wondering where the zip was in that tacky devil costume.

'Bingo! So, now you know where you are, tell me why.'

'I would've thought that was obvious,' Succingo snapped,

pointing at the arrow through his skull. 'You don't live long with a few feet of willow jammed in your head.' He gave it an arrogant twang.

'Nice to see you still have a sense of humour,' growled Flagit dryly. 'You'll need it in the next few centuries of eternal torment! Now, tell me why you're here and I might be able to pull a few strings, get you a lighter torture rota, gloves for rolling rocks uphill, that sort of thing. C'mon tell me.'

'We lost,' admitted Succingo, staring critically at his inquisitor's devil costume and wondering again where the zip was.

'I know that! Look, just tell me why you were fighting.' Flagit's translucent patience was rapidly wearing even thinner. He had far better things to do.

'Those damned D'vanouin stole our sheep!' snarled Succingo, the flames of battle still smouldering inside.

'I know that!' tutted Flagit, rolling his eyes and starting to feel like a phlebotomist at a blood donor clinic for bricks. 'Why did they steal your sheep?'

Time for the truth! ''Cos they're heathen sheep-stealers!' fumed the ex-Friar-Captain.

Flagit wanted to scream. 'Look here. You ever heard of a guy called Gravure? Printer in Cranachan? Nine-year-old daughter? Inventor of chip-set typography?'

Succingo shook his head and shrugged.

Flagit's face turned crimson with frustration as he tried to hold in his scream, then he wheeled on his heel, sprinted over the horizon of the bank and bashed his forehead repeatedly against a rock.

'Hey, what about my rock-rolling gloves?' cried Succingo grinning, and was totally ignored by his inquisitor.

Pathetic! he thought, you just had to look at that costume to know it wasn't real. There is no way that devils have horns that curly!

But, despite his scorn there was a question he would love answered. How did he get his tail to move quite so realistically?

Deep in the bowels of the Imperial Palace Fortress of Cranachan a body groaned as it lay face-down on the cold stone floor. Nervously it licked its lips and felt the horribly familiar carpety texture of its tongue. Adaptive gyromancy had its hazards, the all-too-real possibility of severe bruising from the inevitable fall and the certainty of a screaming hangover. Thor Rensic groaned again, caressed his pounding forehead gently and pulled himself into some semblance of professionalism. Blinking, he carefully squinted at the chalk marks on the floor, rolled over and revealed his gyromantic conclusion regarding the cause of death of his most recent case.

Before he had a chance to think any further, the door to his lab was kicked open and a fuming figure in black erupted through it. Barely touching the floor Commander 'Black' Achonite swept across to the slab in the centre of the lab and screamed.

'Sssshhh!' whimpered Rensic, clutching his head and writhing on the floor. 'Please, not so loud.'

Achonite's fists slammed on to the marble slab, he wheeled on his heels, snatching Rensic warmly by the throat with the feral glee of a lust-crazed mantis. At that instant Captain Barak arrived at the door, doubled-up and panting.

Blinking through crimson-rimmed eyes, the semi-comatose coroner attempted to focus on the furiously molar-grinding Commander. 'Ahhhh, c . . . come for the report, have you?' he grunted around a shag-pile tongue and Achonite's vice-like grip. 'After extensive work I can conclude that the cause of death is . . .'

'What have you done with it?' roared Achonite, shedding enamel from his rear dentition at an alarming rate.

'Well at first I . . . I employed lepomancy, extispicy . . .'

'Where is it?' growled Achonite, swinging Rensic around and pointing at the naked slab of marble. 'Where's it gone?'

Barak peered worriedly into a cupboard. Rensic attempted to shrug, stared around the room and vowed there and then never, ever to try adaptive gyromancy again.

Things seemed to have happened that he hadn't a clue about. Normally it wasn't this bad. On previous occasions he had come around to find interesting collections of shrubs, or groups of orange and white Trans-Talpino Contraflow cones arranged randomly about the lab and was totally at a loss to explain their appearance, but he'd never lost a body before.

Achonite's mind whirled with horror-riven images of Spam Smith dragging a vast cast-iron turbine out of the inferno of his smithy and attempted to quell any feelings of nausea. 'You've got no right to release the only witness, without my permission!' he screamed.

'R . . . release . . . ?' spluttered Rensic, his feet barely contacting the floor. 'B . . . but he was in no fit state—'

'Tell him that! He's back at work. But you really butchered his head . . .'

Barak's stomach did a strange flip.

'Work . . . ?' Rensic stared at the slab. 'Well, tell him not to lift any heavy weights until that stab wound has healed up in his ribs . . . What am I saying? Is this a joke?'

'Do I look like I'm joking?' snarled Achonite. 'What stab wound?' he barked, dropping the coroner and pacing around the lab angrily. Thor Rensic stared at Achonite's clenching fists, shook his head and relaxed. It was all right, he suddenly realised. Everything was fine. He was caught in the grip of an extremely realistic, but none the less fictitious adaptive gyromantic seizure . . . he was still smashed. All he needed to do was relax and go with it. All would become clear later on in the morning when he actually *did* wake up.

'Ah, stab wound, yes,' he muttered, adopting his serious coroner's expression. 'Very unusual shape. Can't possibly have been caused by one blade.' He snatched a quill and a parchment off a desk and drew a single dot, an extremely narrow vertical elipse and another dot. 'Cross-section like that, never seen anything like it.' Barak and Achonite stared at the diagram and snatched in two sharp intakes of breath as they recognised instantly the section of a ceremonial SAS dagger.

'And that was between his ribs?' grunted Achonite, knowing the lethality potential of SAS daggers.

Rensic nodded almost cheerfully.

'Black' Achonite turned pale as his mind's eye flashed back to the smithy and came up with some extremely unsettling conclusions. Either Spam Smith had been murdered by an ex-SAS assassin, lain on Rensic's slab, come back to life and was back at work, or Achonite had imagined it all and Spam Smith really had cut his forehead shaving. Both ways it only had one course of action.

Commander 'Black' Achonite knew that he had a date with several very large frothing flagons of Hexenhammer. Gibbering only very slightly he spun on his heel and sprinted off towards the Gutter.

This was his biggest and best yet.

Fifteen on one gibbet had been good – well, once he had finally managed to get it to work without interference from the crowd it had been wonderful. And what interference. It was still a complete mystery quite how the red-haired girl in the audience had managed to smuggle a dragon into the Hanging Gardens of Rhyngill, but, smuggle it she did. All one hundred feet of the damned thing, swooping about the place torching all his wonderfully designed multi-gibbet just to save three of his 'clients' from certain death. Pah! Some people are *so* ungrateful.

But the second time he had laced up fifteen at once, well, it had broken all box-office records.

'A triumph of modern synchronised swinging' as the *Triumphant Herald* had declared. Fifteen sequentially triggered hangings at once, initiated by a single ratchet lever mechanism.

'Long-drop' Swingler thrilled as he thought about it, the smell of the black leather Balaclava of Executionary Office teasing his nostrils as he grinned. He still couldn't quite believe how miserable he had felt after the applause and the press plaudits had died down. Was that it? The peak of his career? Downhill from now on?

Not a chance! There was only one way to go after the showiest execution of fifteen hardened criminals at once,

189

well, apart from doubling the size of his royalties from t-shirt sales, that is. The only way was up. And now he was putting the finishing touches to the tiny one-fiftieth scale model of his best yet. Twenty-one at once! Three rows of seven, the first triplet initiated by hand, the subsequent drops triggered by ropes looped to their ankles. He could almost hear the crowd gasping and cheering in rapturous swirling applause . . .

Abruptly the door was kicked open, shattering his reverie like ice water on lust. With a shrieking whistle of air Gravure the Printer was hurled inside. The one-fiftieth scale structure of tiny pulleys, trap-doors and nooses trembled in the down-draught before the Printer hit in a devastating explosion of matchsticks, string and curses.

Swingler the Royal Executioner squealed, spun on his chair and leapt at the open doorway with a speed that defied his girth. 'Bang him up in . . . ooooh, sorry. I got a little carried away thuuurgghh,' gasped Pious Constable Slamm J'hadd as Swingler's hand snatched at his throat.

'How many times have I told you to knock when I'm working?' growled the Royal Executioner, pinning J'hadd to the far wall at shoulder height.

''Ncludin' this?' choked J'hadd.

'Including this time, how many?' fumed Swingler, cringing as another five gibbets crashed to the floor.

'One,' grunted J'hadd, turning purple.

'Er, oh. Well, if you ever muck up my prototypes again I will personally see to it that your execrable face will be burnt into the thrill-seeking minds of the general public for its requisite five seconds. Understand?'

J'hadd shook his head in confusion.

'Gah! Don't they teach you anything these days? In letters of one syllable for the hard of understanding. "Knock or die!" Comprehend?'

J'hadd grinned feebly and managed to nod once before he was hurled down the corridor. Swingler dusted off his hands with a sneer of distaste and strolled back into his workshop. For a few moments he stared almost wistfully at the crumpled wreckage crunching beneath Gravure's beetle-like attempts to right himself. Then he snatched the printer off the table and held him at arm's length for a moment, scowling and snarling thoughtfully out from beneath his black leather balaclava. 'Hmmm, eight stone four, five foot three, that's . . . oooh, eight foot six and a quarter of grade six Nostretch Dangl-Eezy hemp. Hmmm, you'll do, that neck's hardly worth sharpening an axe for,' he mumbled before almost absently tugging open a large reinforced door and hurling the whimpering printer inside. 'Funny the way skinny ones always need a longer drop,' he mused.

Then with a single expansive sniff he swept his vast arm across the wreckage on the table, reached on to a large shelf and carefully pulled down plan 'B'.

It was only a skeleton at the moment but, well, if the fates dictated that Plan 'A' was destroyed after all the work he had put in and with the deadline approaching for a really decent showy piece of justice, well, he'd just have to skip twenty-one and go for a full thirty. It would take a little bit longer to build up a large enough 'cast of criminal stars', but it would be worth it!

He rubbed his hands eagerly together as he reached for a bag of matchsticks and the pot of glue.

Thirty at one drop! Ooooh yes!

J'hadd lay in a crumpled heap in the corridor and moaned as his head and throat vied to see which of them could produce the most agony.

See what you get for not obeying the rules, he told himself with a wagging finger. Knock or Die! Good job he didn't throw the Book at you . . . The Book!

Suddenly, he was on his feet, sprinting down the corridor towards Sacrosanct Sergeant Vertex's office – bless him! – his head pounding only marginally harder than his feet.

Flagit fumed almost as much as Captain Naglfar's pipe as he sprinted through the backstreets of Downtown Tumor. 'Waste of time!' he snarled to himself, dashing around corners and hurling bodies out of his way. Not to mention a waste of obuls. Fifteen thousand for a trip over the Phlegethon and for what? Nothing!

Should've known that the chances of ripping anything even remotely useful out of a bunch of battle-crazed soldiers – 'holy' or otherwise – was so close to nil as not to be worth bothering about, especially *that* lot. What had Nabob been thinking sending him on a wild proof chase across the Phlegethon? What answers had he expected? 'Oh yes, Flagit, we were fighting because a nine-year-old changed the letters around to inflame the D'vanouin, a nine-year-old that was partially possessed by Nabob!' He howled and flung a few of the more sluggish pedestrians out of his path. Those damned soldiers had actually cheered when he had hurled the three hundred and eighth of them across the Immigration Hut and stomped out. Not only that, but they'd started stamping and chanting something about kicking D'vanouin and winning!

Well, Nabob had blown his chances of winning the election. It was up to him now to defeat the hated Seirizzim. It was all on his scaly shoulders, now.

Well, his, a nine-year-old girl's and a certain printer's.

He hurtled onwards, fervently hoping that his pet stalagmite was feeling hungry.

It was as if a vast tarpaulin of despair had been flung off Pious Constable Slamm J'hadd's outlook and replaced with the rose-tinted bedclothes of overwhelming optimism. Thirteen years, eleven months and twenty-eight days ago he had scurried eagerly down these self same corridors towards the offices of the, then, Sergeant Vertex, a gleaming future in the Religious Undercover Crime Squad beckoning. It had been a long and rocky road, but finally, like the ancient Prophet Pwarroh himself, he had reached the final stone and achieved everything. He couldn't wait to see Sacrosanct Sergeant Vertex's face light up with joy when he shared his good news with him. Ahhh, bless him!

J'hadd skittered around a corner, hurtled down a very short corridor, screeched to a panting halt and delivered a smart tattoo to the outside the Sergeant's door.

There was a growl from within, J'hadd took a deep breath, turned the handle and entered. He strode towards the vast desk, delivered his crispest crucifix of a salute and winced only slightly as he realised he hadn't removed his artist's smock. Still, this *was* the Undercover Crime Squad. Sacrosanct Sergeant Vertex would understand.

'With you in a minute,' mumbled Vertex through his ruddy sideburns as he scratched a quill absently across a stack of parchments.

J'hadd grinned and savoured the moment, his eyes lingering on the office walls lined with Vertex's trophies from his SAS training – first in the Individual Font Carrying, 1017; Outstanding Achievement Award for Yomping and Navigation, 1018; The Pope Uri Prize for Overwhelming Piety Under Attack, 1018 . . . it was an impressive catalogue. And there were more, but a grunt shattered the silence as Vertex flung his quill into a holder and looked up.

'Now what can I do for . . . ?' his voice faded as he stared at the grinning figure in the artist's smock. Vertex's face twitched uncontrollably as emotions wrestled within – loathing, detestation, the constant embarrassment of J'hadd soiling the name of the RUC with his incessant ineptitude. 'YOU!' he finished, the colour draining from his face as if a ghost were sticking fingers in his ears. 'I thought you were dea . . . ahem, er, so you survived the SAS training?' he spluttered looking crestfallen.

J'hadd beamed. 'Your Elucidarity, I have completed the task you so carefully laid before me. It was long in coming and difficult to decipher, but it was as you had foreseen.'

'. . . ?' spluttered Vertex.

'I was as an undercover pawn, tossed on the currents of destiny, but your faith in me was justified. I have not failed you.'

'What in the names of all the Gods are you . . . ?'

'I have him, Sacrosanct Sergeant,' J'hadd beamed.

'Have who? What have you done . . . ?' pleaded Vertex, dreading the worst, panic playing the xylophone with his nerves. Could J'hadd have actually arrested someone? Oh, cruel fates, three days before he would have washed his hands of him for ever and . . .

'The miscreant whose responsibility it was to create the Flock Wars. I have him in . . .'

No, don't say it! screamed Vertex silently. Don't say the 'c' word. Not you!

'. . . custody!'

Vertex sagged. An arrest, he made an arrest! Then he saw J'hadd's forehead and hopes swelled uncontrollably within. He could be hallucinating, suffering from concussive delusions from a wound like that.

'Your head,' croaked Vertex, trying not to sound too cheery as he asked, 'Does it smart?'

'It serves as a constant reminder, a gift received in the futility of war . . .'

Gods! He's turned into a martyr!

'. . . either that or I cut myself shaving. But, 'tis of no matter. Come I must show you my captive, my sinner, my enemy to justice, my miscreant from . . .'

'Shut up!' shrieked Vertex as he was dragged from his chair by J'hadd bouncing enthusiastically. 'Silence! Let me think!' he bellowed as he reluctantly followed the skipping Pious Constable out of his office.

If there's anything wrong with this arrest, any slip in the parchmentwork, one sign of impropriety, the merest hint of slapdash smudging of the Pristine Rules, his prisoner'll be out of the front doors faster than a rat in a catapult, scowled Vertex and raised a little prayer heavenwards. Please, please, please . . . just *one* spelling mistake.

Rubbing his talons together with a sound like a serial axe murderer honing his favourite weapon Flagit sneered diabolically to himself in the storeroom and prepared to take care of another of Nabob's so-called 'details'. He chuckled as he sipped a refreshing draft of lava martini on the rocks, shaken not stirred, then reached out for the shimmering silver-grey mesh of his infernite lattice.

In seconds it was perched expertly between his horns, the

crystal spectrecal lenses dangling before his eyes, and his mind's claws were limbering up for another session of total control, reaching out once more . . .

Bare feet skittered eagerly down a dark corridor in the deepest bowels of the Imperial Palace Fortress of Cranachan, twisting and turning expertly through the permanent gloom of the labyrinthine passages. It was as if she knew exactly where she was going, or perhaps someone, or something, was guiding her.

She skipped around a sharp left on one right foot, hopped and slapped to a neat half outside a huge oak door. A look of malevolence flashed across her nine-year-old face as she reached out and pounded on the wood.

'Go away!' came the shouted reply, slightly muffled by the triple-ply portal.

Alea raised her tiny fist and pounded again.

'Go away. I'm busy!'

Anger swept across her face, mirroring the seething snarl a thousand feet below, before she composed herself immaculately, donned her finest butter-wouldn't-melt expression and pushed open the door.

An enormous black balaclavaed man spun around on his chair and glared at the red-nightdressed girl peering through the cracked door. The model on the table behind him trembled as he bellowed. 'Get out. This is not the nursery.'

'Oh, oh, please, I don't want the nursery. I, I . . .' Alea looked down at her toes, pigeoning them five degrees for effect. 'Oh, oh, Mr Swingler, sir,' she whispered glancing up through her eyebrows and managing to produce a single glistening tear at the corner of her eyes. 'Please can I see my daddy, please,' she whispered at the edge of audibility.

'Well, I . . . er.'

Suddenly she caught sight of the nearly completed model on the table and Flagit sent a limbic command to show enthusiasm – total unfettered gushing enthusiasm.

'Oooooh!' she shrieked, pointing at the heap of matchsticks, string and old packing cases. 'Did you make that? It's lovely! Is that the next multiple hanging set-up? Thirty at once, wow! Where's my daddy going to be? I've seen all your finest . . .' she yapped, feigning eager enthusiasm as commanded.

Behind the black leather balaclava Swingler's face lit up. A fan!

'. . . loved the way that with just one lever you are able to set in motion such a stunning display of synchronised swinging. Gets me right here!' crooned Alea, punching her chest. 'And now, my daddy's going to be there, on one of your gibbets! Ooooh! It's so 'citing! There he is! Please, can I tell him how 'cited I am? Please.' Spotting a convenient sandbag by the cell doors, she fluttered her eyelids and Swingler melted.

''Course you can see him, dear,' he crooned as he unlocked the door to Gravure's cell and turned back to his model, touched by the simpering of his youngest fan. As he sat back down he failed totally to notice a slight whistling sound and a fifty-pound sandbag arced out of the air and thudded across the back of his head.

In the heat of Helian, Flagit shrieked with evil laughter, snatched his pet stalag-mite out of its cage and let it loose on the roof of his cavern.

'Daddy, Daddy!' squealed Alea, brushing sand off her hands as she sprinted into the cell and leapt into Gravure's arms, flinging hers tightly around his neck. Swingler hit the floor with a thud, blissfully unaware of the deviltry that now inhabited the red-nightdressed girl's face.

'Okay, pal. D'you want out of here? Or d'you wanna be part of that creep's roadshow?' growled Alea tightening her grip around Gravure's neck.

'Alea?' choked the Printer. 'What are you . . . ?'

'No questions! Swing or spring? You want out or not?' she snapped with an evil chuckle.

'Well of course, I'd give . . .'

'What would you give?'

'Anything. But how are you going . . . ?'

'*Absolutely* anything?' snarled Alea.

'Yes. Absolutely anything. What are . . . ?' pleaded the printer.

'Anything at all?' snapped the girl.

'Yes! Anything at . . .'

'Bingo!' growled Alea, leaping from his neck as the claws, legs and antennae of the stalag-mite erupted from the cell floor. It was followed by the talons, horns and head of Flagit as he sprang from the hole, snatched Gravure and vanished in a burst of fetid air and rubble.

Casually Alea swung a key out from the front of her nightdress, unlocked the cell door and strolled out past the bulk of Swingler, deftly rehanging the key on his belt as she passed.

Rapt in the wreckage of his latest model, the Executioner failed totally to notice that he would have to wait a little longer to complete his thirty-strong cast of criminals.

On the banks of the Trans-Talpino Canal, where there should have been several hundred workers toiling furiously under cracking whips and hails of abusive orders, nothing moved. The vast piles of stones, the ells of high-security barbed string fencing and the heaps of tools had all vanished within minutes of the arrival of Guthry the dwarf, a signed planning permission parchment and another sack of cash. It was as if the entire building site had hitched up its skirts, trudged up to the top of Tor Khamada and settled down again. And with the vast cash injection, work was proceeding at a cracking pace.

Labourers were surprising themselves as they faced up to strings of deadlines, stared them squarely in the eye, calculated the vast bonuses to be reaped from stamping all over them and launched gaily into full-steam-ahead mode. Already the purple sprigs of heather and local crocuses that made Tor Khamada famous had vanished to be replaced with bare rock and the hill was almost surrounded by high-security fencing. Fires had been lit to burn off the foliage and within the hour muscled shoulders would be whirling picks at the bald pate of the Tor. Already foundations were forming where vast on-site forges would be built to cope with the excessive demands of pick repair, shovel reforging and component manufacture.

197

In six hours they had achieved more than in six weeks of the dock project.

Guthry stared around him at the feverish activity and grinned. Such is the power of money.

Ell? . . . What is an ell?

The Really Reverend Unctuous' brain whirred and seethed as it tried to snatch a clue to the answer of the gloomy smog filling his mind. He'd heard of ells before. But where? It certainly wasn't in lace-making circles, how could he have believed that it referred to size 'e' eleven needles – everyone knows there aren't any needles in lace, just bobbins! Millions of them.

The chewing of a stalag-mite burrowing through the wall was really getting on his nerves. How much longer were they going to be fitting this air-conditioning?

Suddenly his reverie was shattered into a million spinning fragments as the door to Flagit's storeroom was kicked open and Flagit and Nabob burst in, babbling furiously. Unctuous dragged himself up to his full height and bustled forward ready and quite prepared to demand the truth from Flagit. Okay, it *had* been a long time since his last confession but he was certain he could remember all those subtle little questions that would tug the right answers out into the open. Especially regarding the gold-braid skullcap he was clutching in his hands. There was more to that than presents for demons' mothers, he felt certain.

'You expect me to believe they knew nothing about it?' snarled Nabob.

Unctuous raised a hand and made to tap Flagit on the elbow.

'Didn't know, wouldn't tell, what's the difference? They're mad, I tell you. Cheered when I hurled one of them across the hut!'

'So you found no proof that I started the Flock Wars?' pleaded Nabob. Unctuous's ears pricked up in alarm.

'What did you expect? Written statements, signed and witnessed?' growled Flagit.

'I don't need sarcasm,' snarled Nabob angrily. Before his very eyes his grand election plan was slithering apart.

'No,' grinned Flagit gleefully. 'But I know what you *do* need. Something infallible and quick-sharp or Seirizzim's in!'

'Three days!' wailed Nabob, gnashing his teeth.

'Be close, but we can do it,' sneered Flagit.

'What? Do what?'

Flagit took a breath and began to explain.

'What kind of a name is "Centaur Parcs"?' snapped Nabob desperately after half an hour.

'Perfect,' insisted Flagit. 'They won't suspect a thing.'

'Oh, come on!' snarled Nabob, pacing the storeroom, obviously flustered. 'Won't suspect a thing? Pull the other one! Anybody in Cranachan with half an eyeball won't fail to spot d'Abaloh's blinkin' great holiday palace being built next door. Have you gone mad?'

Unctuous trembled in a shadow. What were they talking about?

'If I could just finish,' smirked Flagit, pouring himself a lava martini and shaking it casually. 'They won't suspect a thing because . . .'

'This had better be good,' growled Nabob, snatching the drink. Unctuous agreed and quietly postponed his searing inquisition for a few moments.

Flagit scowled. 'Because,' he insisted pedantically, 'I've got planning permission.' The Reverend's jaw dropped as Flagit continued. For some reason he found himself thinking of the large blue parchment sheet again.

'Permission, in writing, from the Cranachanian Council themselves. As far as they know, Guthry the dwarf has started building a sixty-five-ell diameter dome to house a very innocent horror holiday theme park. What a genius I am! D'Abaloh himself could turn up on a site inspection and nobody would bat an eyelid. They'd just think he was one of the props.'

Unctuous shook his head and began to feel very odd in the stomach department.

Nabob drained the lava martini in one swallow, coughed and spluttered the question, 'How did you persuade them?'

Flagit's face creased into a demonic grin, 'Money,' he answered. 'They'll do anything for enough of it!'

'Where, in Helian, did you get it all?' spluttered Nabob reaching for the martini flask.

'Couple of minor safe cracking expeditions got the ball rolling, but . . .' Flagit stopped, twitched a beckoning talon and strolled jauntily towards a far door in his office. With a flick of a claw he swung it open and revealed a plethora of printing presses pounding out fortunes of groats, strings of them decorated the room drying on lines. Dimly, through the forests of notes the deathly figure of Gravure slaved furiously over a hot block.

Nabob's jaw dropped, he screamed and swung the curtains shut. 'Are you barking mad? How did he get here? You know what the Malebranche'll do if they catch you with an unauthorised torture shirker. They can easily trace . . .'

Nabob really didn't like the self-satisfied sneer that slunk across Flagit's face. 'No danger of a trace,' grinned Flagit.

'But how, he's . . . No! You haven't . . . ?'

Flagit nodded.

'A pact?' screamed Nabob. 'You . . . you know the rules!'

'Few pacts for a good cause never did any *real* harm . . .'

'A few!' Nabob's eyes bulged as if his head were about to explode. 'How many?'

'Including him,' began Flagit, pointing towards the curtain hiding the printer, 'well, I'm not sure the others really count as pacts, er, they're more sort of permanent possession, I suppose. Total Limbic Control, I tried to tell you about . . .'

'How many?'

'Three. Well, unless you count the Reverend . . .'

'A man of the cloth! Here?' Hysteria leapt off every consonant.

'Where d'you think that first telepushy net came from, eh? Mail order?'

Unctuous trembled in a corner as the two demons' tempers rose.

'Look, needs must,' snarled Flagit. 'You should be grateful.'

'Grateful? For putting my election prospects on the line? If anyone discovered this I'd be kicked out faster than . . .'

Something started to happen in Unctuous' toes as he listened to the mounting fury. His ankles flexed and the soles of his feet just suddenly got the urge to run. He tried to hold them down. Tried and failed. In a split second he was up on his feet and sprinting through the crack in the door, absently clutching the gold-braid remnants of his skullcap. He clattered down the stairs and out into the heaving streets of Mortropolis.

'Your election prospects died when you ignored tele-pushy . . .' snapped Flagit. 'And even if Seirizzim does win, we won't have to worry about that for ever. As soon as things are ready up top we will have freedom. Complete freedom!'

'What?'

'Er, er, d'Abaloh will be so grateful that we won't have to bother with fiddling petty things like jobs. We'll be made.'

'So long as nobody finds out about your little pet, in there,' reminded Nabob pointedly.

'No problem. The door's always locked. He can't escape.'

'And the vicar?'

'Yeah, he's over there,' Flagit pointed a curved talon casually across the cave.

'Where?' growled Nabob staring in vain.

'Over there!' Flagit's face contorted in several ways it was surely never designed to as he too stared at the horribly empty-looking storeroom. He trembled for a second before catapulting himself at the door, racing down the stairs and exploding on to the street, panting wildly. Legs spread, he lanced his gaze up and down the street, flinging tormented souls aside as he scoured the area for the fleeing Reverend.

In that moment something inside twisted and tightened. For the first time ever, Flagit's bowels shook hands with real terror.

The Suspicion Bells

If the Really Reverend Unctuous III had thought Flagit's office was an infernal mess, then his vocabulary probably wouldn't stretch as far as a running description regarding the rest of downtown Tumor. Within seconds of scarpering from Flagit's cavern the Reverend had found himself jammed in the midst of a flood of seething souls sweeping down crammed streets to destinations unknown, screaming. To his left and right he caught glimpses of eternal tortures in action. Grinning devils armed with flaming feathers jabbed their victims between the shoulderblades and placed a century of inaccessible itches there, whilst others laced bags on their hands. Sneering demons stared out over screaming crowds of damned lottery-ticket-clutching souls and tugged stubs out of a hat declaring, 'And the winner is . . . number . . . no, not that one.' Pet lovers watched in eternal horror as forty-ton wagon wheels thundered unstoppably towards their favourite six-day-old kitten pinned to the road.

Torrents of people surged onwards through the streets of downtown Tumor, racing madly towards their next torture shift, swirling round corners and dashing desperately down ever-narrowing alleys. Unctuous stared around him, horrified and yet fascinated by the myriad tortures swirling about him as he sprinted onwards. And then the gate-post of the Phlegethon Shipyard hit him in the face. At least it felt like a gate-post. Until it spoke.

'Passmort,' it growled.

Unctuous looked up and, with mounting trepidation, followed the alarmingly overmuscled arm that snaked away from the fingers currently wrapped around his throat. '. . .?' He whimpered.

'Passmort,' repeated the thing with the red-and-yellow-striped arm. 'C'mon, where is it? Need permission to toil in

202

there.' As if to prove who was in charge, the fist squeezed just a little more. 'No pass, no toil.'

'P . . . p . . .?' attempted Unctuous as he caught a glimpse of vast machines swarming with countless, regularly whipped bodies in an incinerating, sweat-stained heat.

'You 'aven't got one, 'ave you?' snarled the securi-corpse. 'Should've guessed. You don't look worthy of a treat in the shipyards. Clear off back to your own torture, sciver!' The arm made to hurl Unctuous away.

'W . . . wait!' he screamed. 'What torture?'

'Awwww, you lost?' grimaced the securi-corpse. 'Should I get on to the Malebranche?'

Something in Unctuous shuddered and ran in cold trickles. The Malebranche? So the tales they'd told him during his clerical training were true. They did have a security force of devils patrolling the place. Unctuous was stunned.

But he was more stunned by what he was about to do. Without even the slightest ounce of qualm raising its picky head, his mind assessed the position in which he found himself, checked around to see if anything else was watching and quite casually answered. 'Er, no. The Malebranche are quite busy enough as it is. I seem to have misplaced my direction. Thought this was . . . er . . . "Blasphemers".' Part of Unctuous' mind screamed, he must have been down here far too long. For the first time ever, he had actually told a lie. Worryingly, it hadn't been that hard.

'Blasphemers? I ain't 'eard of that. New one is it?'

Unctuous dangled pathetically a few inches from the floor. 'Y . . . yes,' he stammered. 'I . . . I've just been transf . . . transferred.' A second lie!

'Oooh, where from?'

'Er . . . er . . . arsonists,' he whimpered.

'Really?' blurted the securi-corpse. 'Well I never . . . D'you know Ryck "the Wick" Forks, great guy until that accident . . .'

'Er, no . . . it's a big place. Friend of yours?'

'Me? Ha. no. Used to keep trying to sneak in here for a scive.'

'I'll be back there soon,' lied Unctuous again. 'Want me to pass on a message?'

'Nah, just tell him I said "Hello",' grunted the securi-corpse and dropped Unctuous. In a split second it was staring at bare floor.

Unctuous sprinted into the seething crowds and was dragged and pushed along in the torrent of souls. His mind whirred, horrified at his new-found lying ability and attempting to make sense of where he found himself. Questions spun and screamed for answers. Where was he? Why was he here? And if he was where he thought he just might be, then why didn't he have a torture to go to?

He swept around another sharp corner at full sprint, lost his footing and was spun out uncontrollably. His ankle caught a small violin case, he tripped and came to rest upside down on top of a very annoyed musician.

'Get 'im!' cried an ageing artist, leaping up off his haunches and cannoning into Unctuous. He was followed a moment later by a wasted man wearing a fixed rictus of a grin. In seconds they had rummaged through the entirety of Unctuous's pockets, spat derisively and failed to find anything of any use.

'Well. I hope it was worth it,' growled the artist, squatting miserably back down in the tiny alley.

'Sorry?' asked Unctuous struggling upright off the violinist. 'Worth it?' He failed totally to keep the shriek of bewilderment out of his voice.

'Good pact, was it?' grumbled the man with the fixed grin of pleasure. 'Better than twenty-four years of every delightful experience a body can stand, eh?' he leched.

'Shutup, Phaust,' growled the artist.

Unctuous shook his head. 'Pact?' he whimpered.

As if in answer the violinist spun his bow dramatically between his fingers and sawed a screaming peal of arcing semi-quavers. The harmonics battered into Unctuous' ears, pummelling his eardrums with the final ear-splitting glissandic crescendo of Queazx's Erotic Symphony in B Minor. Anyone who knew anything about post-modernist neo-classical symphonic works would have recognised those four bars of nine-eight as the most technically difficult fingering in the history of the fiddle.

'Yeuch! What a racket,' grunted Unctuous, his palms slapping against his ears.

The goatee-bearded face of the violinist twisted into a sneer of distaste. ' 'Eathen,' he growled, prodding Unctuous in the nose with his bow. 'Ain't you never 'eard music?'

'I've heard more melody from a boiling cat.'

'Tha' was perfection, mate,' snarled the violinist. 'No one can play tha' better, can they? And nobody ever will,' he growled, kicking a bundle of rags on the floor. The rags stirred, waved a rude finger gesture and collapsed again. 'Hate t'admit it, don't you Queazx?' The finger waved again.

The artist stared at Unctuous, 'Sad really. He sold his soul to write the most technically difficult piece of music ever, he sold his to be able to play it, and they're both stuck down here without an audience to rub together.'

'B . . . but, how?' whimpered Unctuous, not wanting to trust his ears despite his decades of strictly disciplined 'Belief Training'.

'Easy,' grunted the artist. 'Way too easy. Just whisper your greatest desires three times down your local devil's earhole and "whoop!" you've been had. Before you know it you're down here, homeless, tortureless, with about as many rights as a comatose woodlouse in a euthanasia scandal. We're Helian's Illegal Immigrants.'

Unctuous's jaw was dangling limply against his sternum. 'What're you here for?' he mumbled.

'Acne,' admitted the artist, his skin gleaming as fresh as a baby's powdered bottom.

'You look fine to me,' answered Unctuous.

'Gah! It *was* dreadful. Couldn't get anyone to pose nude for me in case they caught anything. I was desperate, it was ruining my career. So, I did this,' miserably he tugged the cover off the painting in his hand to reveal a barely recognisable self-portrait buried beneath a festering heap of oil-painted pustules and sores. 'We get all sorts down here.'

He pointed to another heap of rags on the floor. 'That's the richest man ever. Sold his soul for a ten million groat note. Died penniless. No one ever had enough loose change.'

The question sprang into the Reverend's head at exactly the same time the violinist asked, 'So why are you here?'

'I . . . I . . .' he looked down at his sandalled feet. 'Lust,' he confessed.

'No,' chorused the pact-men in shocked disbelief.

'Yes,' answered Unctuous. 'Nubile Nymphs Ride Bareback Polo Ponies.'

'No!' repeated the artist.

Unctuous nodded.

'No,' insisted the artist. 'I mean, nobody has ever sold their soul for lust . . .'

'I did,' interrupted Phaust.

'You told me that was orgies,' butted in the violinist.

'Yeah, well there was a bit of lust in it,' grinned the wasted figure lasciviously.

The artist spun back to Unctuous. 'What's the thing you remember wanting most? The last thing you recall?'

Unctuous shook his head. 'A congregation,' he whimpered. 'I said I'd give anything for a congregation. All I ever wanted was to save one soul!'

Phaust burst out laughing and was kicked sharply in the ribs by the violinist . . . 'You've been had, matey!'

Suddenly a tail-like whip snatched out of the air, wrapped around the extended ankle of the violinist and pulled. The musician spun and shot down the alley towards the triplet of vast black-scaled creatures clomping purposefully forward on their cloven hooves.

'Malebranche!' shrieked the artist, snatching his portrait and sprinting away down a tiny alley. 'Hide!'

Unctuous stared about him in shock as the three nine-foot devils tossed the violinist between them, shaking him upside down as they searched for his passmort. The Reverend stared, horrified at their expressions, revelling in the sport of playing with the pact-man, their scaly faces splitting in raucous savage amusement, filling the air with screams of devilish delight.

Without warning a hand sprang out of a side-alley, grabbed Unctuous around the throat and tugged him into the gloom. 'C'mon,' barked the voice of the artist. 'Follow me!'

Unctuous needed no second bidding. In a flash he had hitched up his cassock and was legging it at full tilt, terror slamming its foot hard on the mettle of his convictions, sprinting away from the rampaging chaos of the Malebranche. Panic tugged hard at the strands of righteous indignation criss-crossing his fevered mind and the finger of outrage wagged long and hard at the fragment of his soul that was still his, challenging him – what are you, Man or Mouse? Reverend or Rodent?

In the instant that the violinist looped screaming over his head and flattened the artist into a far wall, something deep inside Unctuous tugged a metaphorical gauntlet out of his sleeve and advanced on the twee, timorous, namby-pamby part of his character, cheerfully cuffing it around the cheeks.

Unctuous found himself rolling up his cassock sleeves, clenching his fists and even gnashing his teeth for effect.

No matter how big they were, he vowed secretly to himself, no matter how much they shouted and stamped and complained and had bad tempers, he wouldn't let them build that Palace. Oh no. Somehow he would stop them!

After all, he was already in Helian, without a congregation, bereft of hope at the end of a wasted life talking to rats. It couldn't possibly get any worse. Could it?

Overhead, a vast sheet of fire exploded across the horizon and suddenly, without the slightest warning, it started to flame. Within seconds the streets were alight. It was flashing down again.

Unctuous ducked out of sight and waited the pyrotechnics out.

And it was there, watching sheets of crimson fire batter and toast the ground that he noticed something really strange happening in his cassock pocket. A weird warmth began to spread outwards against his body, seeping through the material as if a small rodent had snuck in, leaked and snuck out again double-quick. Oddly, it was glowing.

Nervously, he reached inside his pocket. His fingers touched hot metal and snatched it into the open. Barely stifling a squeak of astonishment he stared at the woven strands of gold-braid lying at his feet, shocked as it fluoresced cheerfully at him in the gloom of the flame-storm.

Deep within the quivering fear-laden heart of Flagit a host of nagging doubts huddled and gossiped like a fleet of fishwives, wagging accusatory fingers in grim relish. Unctuous had vanished into the outside underworld, could be anywhere; but it doesn't matter, he insisted to himself.

'It doesn't matter!' he also insisted to Nabob.

'What? How can you say that! What if he's caught by the Malebranche?'

'What if he is? Illegal Immigrants go missing every day. They can't trace him to us!' growled Flagit, hoping he didn't sound as unconvincing as he felt. 'We don't need him. He's served his purpose,' he snarled and shook his Total Limbic Control net significantly.

'But he'll talk,' blabbed Nabob. 'We'll be ruined!'

'Let him talk. Nobody'll believe him down here.'

'How can you say that?' whimpered Nabob, his talons fidgeting nervously.

'Because Reverends can't lie,' growled Flagit. 'Forget about him, he can't do us any harm. And once we get the Palace finished, we're made for eternity! Now get out, I've got some work to do,' he snarled, flipping his Total Limbic Control net expertly on to his scaly skull, settling it between his horns with a flick of a talon.

Nabob hardly needed a second bidding. He had to get away from this mad-devil. All this talk of Palaces and weird mental control was too much. He had to get back to something he understood. Time to tighten the noose on Seirizzim's chances. He'd have to act fast . . . he just hoped it wasn't too late to escalate.

In the storeroom, Flagit focused his eyes on the silver discs dangling from the net and reached out with his telepushic mind. Once again his thoughts exploded in a stream of active consciousness, ripped through a thousand feet of solid rock and snatched on to the sympathetic net wrapped around the central limbic system of a certain civil engineer. And Guthry the dwarf wasn't the only one to notice the blast of mental energy.

In a darkened room in a vast matt black tower at the far side of Mortropolis a demon stared boredly at a vast obsidian crystal. Tiny pin-pricks of luminosity glowed regularly as a vast green forefront swept around the screen, detecting and tracking any acorporeal cerebral activity moving between Helian and above.

This was the Voyeur Traffic Control centre of Mortropolis, the choreographic hub upon which hung the entire co-ordination responsibility for the whole of the Helian Tourist Industry. So many devils and demons were vacating their bodies for two to three weeks in favour of a resident possession of another that someone had to make sure they returned to their correct bodies. Every one of the tiny glowing pin-pricks represented an individual devil and carried with it a complex string of identification numerals. All that is, except one.

'It's back!' shrieked Daymyn the demon, pointing wildly at the screen. The fifteenth time this week. In a flurry of black scales his commanding officer was at his side staring at the bright unnumbered point.

'Give me triangulation!' he barked at Daymyn. 'Nail it down!'

Frantic talons scratched wildly at the control-screen panels and pull-down menus sprang up for immediate access.

'Damned backstreet tour operators,' cursed the officer. 'Get them!'

Daymyn the demon's talons flicked mad instructions and set off a whole string of search programmes. Behind him his commander fumed at the green point. And then it blinked out.

'Get him?' he snapped, shaking Daymyn by the shoulders. 'Well?'

'Didn't stay on long enough to get an accurate trace. Downtown Tumor, that's as close as I could get,' he admitted nervously.

The commanding officer screamed something harshly unprintable and whirled on his hoof. 'Keep your eyes peeled. I want him!'

'. . . and it was this vital segment of information that led me directly to him. The arrogance of the man, printing his name in the front of his inflammatory tomes. That's worse than leaving a calling card!' shrieked Pious Constable Slamm J'hadd righteously. He skipped through the winding passages of the Imperial Palace Fortress and urged Sacrosanct Sergeant Vertex towards his prisoner. It was traditional that a Sergeant attend the confession of a captured felon along with the apprehending officer. J'hadd thrilled as he looked forward to filling in the parchmentwork. Apprehending Officer . . . Pious Constable Slamm J'hadd! He'd practised it thousands of times, making sure that he could jam it all in the tiny rectangle and still keep it legible, but soon it would be real. His first arrest!

Bubbling with enthusiasm he spun around a corner and launched into a detailed description of the actual arrest. He'd kept up an incessant barrage of words for the last ten minutes, barely pausing for breath as he regaled Sergeant Vertex with information about this miscreant. And all the time Vertex's scowl had grown deeper and darker. It was a good case, he could find no technicality on which to release him. He'd just have to pray that J'hadd had cocked-up the parchmentwork.

'Here we are!' declared J'hadd, skittering to a halt and rapping firmly on the door. He heard a moan inside, turned the handle and burst eagerly in as Swingler was picking himself up off the floor. The Executioner rubbed the back of his head through the black leather Balaclava of Office, scowled at the wreckage of his model gibbets and groaned.

'Don't get up,' said J'hadd, oblivious in his self-importance. 'Carry on with your rest, we're here to see the printer, Gravure. This way,' he added to Vertex, as if he didn't know, and scurried eagerly towards the cells.

'Long-drop' Swingler attempted to shake life back into his fuzzy head and stared bewilderedly at a fifty-pound sandbag on the floor. His attempts to understand what had happened were rudely interrupted by a squeal of angst from the direction of the cells.

'Where is he?' screamed J'hadd, exploding towards Swingler, his fists circling. 'What've you done with him? Where's my prisoner?'

'Eh?' grunted the Executioner, staring from the fragments of matchsticks to the sandbag and back. 'Prisoner?'

'Yes! That's what I said. I brought a grade-one sinner here not half an hour ago and now he's gone,' shrieked J'hadd, sensing his life in the RUC slipping uncontrollably out of reach. What had he done to deserve this? He'd done everything by the Book. 'Where is he?'

'I . . . I don't remember,' grunted Swingler, a severe concussion taking effect.

Sacrosanct Sergeant Vertex slapped his hands across his mouth and barely held in a shriek of laughter.

'Was he wearing a red nightdress?' struggled Swingler through a miasma of spinning thoughts.

'I would have arrested him for something else if he had! I brought him in wearing an inky overall and yellow hands. Remember?'

Swingler shook his head and Vertex turned a shade redder, holding back his amusement, wishing he'd thought of it. What better way to stop J'hadd making an arrest: lose the felon. Brilliant! Swingler would get a pay rise for this.

'Who's in charge here?' demanded J'hadd, stamping an angry sandal on the floor.

Swingler scratched his balaclava, 'Er . . . Commander "Black" Achonite, but I don't think he'll be too pleased . . .'

'No! I shouldn't think he would be pleased to find out just how lax the so-called security is down here,' shouted J'hadd, then he whirled on his heel and stared at Vertex chewing at his fingers in crimson hilarity. 'Your Elucidarity, sir, there

211

has been gross negligence here. This matter *will* be dealt with, immediately. I can see how deeply this is affecting you.'

All Vertex could do was nod and pray that he would stop it, now! He couldn't guarantee how much longer he could stand up to the pressure inside his ribs and the urge to collapse on the floor, kicking his legs in the air and shrieking with uncontrollable hilarity.

Pious Constable Slamm J'hadd placed his hand on his heart, stared fervently at Sacrosanct Sergeant Vertex and declared, 'Worry not, sir. The faith that thou hast placedeth within this humble receptacle shallst not be spilled. I shallst recapture the printer, solveth my crime andst joineth thee onst thine right hand in the glorious illumination of the RUC! Farest ye well!' With a flurry of artist smock J'hadd was gone.

And not a moment too soon. Vertex exploded in a fountain of laughter, collapsing on to the floor, totally helpless.

Half an hour later, his ribs aching mercilessly, he stood shakily, tapped Swingler on the shoulder and told him to keep up the good work. Then, still tittering involuntarily, he staggered into the corridor and lurched away, musing on the fact that the Gods did indeed work in strange ways.

It is said that during times of extreme stress a person's life will flash across that person's eyes, every single important event blasting uncontrollably by in a wild fast-forward review. Something similar was happening to the Really Reverend Unctuous. Only the images bombarding his mind as he huddled in a tiny alley, lost and alone in downtown Tumor, were not of his past life, but his recently past death.

Pacts . . . scattering rats . . . claws . . . erupting floors . . . His mind buzzed with whirlwinds of blizzarding images. Endless interrogations about the rat-trick . . . lace lessons . . . snippits of devilish conversation . . . secreted printers . . . scarred foreheads . . . glowing lace hair-nets. It was all seemingly too much to comprehend. A booming torrent of nonsense.

212

But somehow, as he watched in the privacy of his own brain, whirling threads of logic began to snag on the curling of factual hooks. They caught hold, took up the slack and started to winch. Spinning fragments coalesced like dark matter at the dawn of the galaxy, drawn inexorably closer by the forces of supposition. And gradually, through a fitful nightmare of abstract cerebral representation, sense was squeezed out of the sponge of Unctuous' mind. He recalled the day in the chapel of St Absent the Regularly Forgotten when he had first plucked up the courage to attempt telepushy. He was bombarded by Flagit's incessant demands for the secret and his feeble attempt to emulate his mammalian control. And with a start realised that it was only after Flagit had mastered telepushy that his interest in Unctuous had waned – when he was no longer needed, he was redundant. The story of his life.

Suddenly a host of pieces tumbled out of his subconscious and dropped smartly into place like a synchronised stunt jigsaw. In a flash he realised the truth, he could see the picture in full.

Unctuous started to growl again as he fumbled with the remaining network of his skullcap, settling it carefully over his head. He closed his eyes, dredged up everything he could remember of telepushy and began to send strings of mental tendrils out through a thousand feet of solid rock. The angry bees of his aggressively suggestive imagination were free. And they weren't going to be ignored!

Away across Mortropolis, in the dark of a vast busy cavern, a talon pointed at a luminously crackling screen and shouted. 'Sir. They're back!'

It was as if a thousand lunatic druids had declared the crown of Tor Khamada a site of special religious interest, bought out every torch shop in three thousand ells, persuaded a gang of mates to join them on the best pilgrimage of their lives and were even now revelling in gay dervish abandon beneath countless searing flames, sacrificing virgins left, right and centre.

Sadly, the truth wasn't nearly as much fun.

All through the darkness of the talpine night, the torches had burnt bright, banishing shadows and feral ravings with equal ease. The work continued unabated; cement-mixers sweating eagerly to maintain target on their bonuses; kiln builders firing their ovens to bake the bricks to line the forges needed to heat the steel for the teams of smiths to work the iron to make the tools to keep the quarries digging the clay to make the bricks to build the . . .

Driven by countless flexibly friendly hundred-groat notes work was no longer a four-letter word: seething industry spread across the rapidly balding pate of the tor like an ambulatory slime mould on an apricot. The entire population of Cranachan was overjoyed . . . wealth beyond their wildest dreams. They sang as they dug as they forged as they . . .

Well, the vast majority of them did, anyway. There was a small group of decidedly conscientious objectors who scowled under a cloud of fulminating anger at the vast hive of heavy industry. Had anybody been bothered enough to ask this band of enrainbowed warriors to explain how they felt about all this environmental damage, it is doubtful if the inquisitor would escape without several hours of ear-chewing. But nobody had asked. It wasn't necessary. The vast forest of placards being furiously waved said it all.

'LEAVE THE LOVELY LICHEN ALONE,' yelled a rock-shaped notice covered in mycelial-green lettering. 'FUNGI HAVE FEELINGS TOO,' screamed another.

'SAVE THE SLUG,' blared a third. And there were dozens more, demanding that hands be left off their horticulture and a myriad other captions.

It had to be said that Mrs Olivia 'Green' Beece wasn't best pleased with the positioning of the building site. Tor Khamada was the only area within the nearest ten miles that could support the incredibly rare Variegated Crimson Jelly-Mould. Only here was the balance of cover and shade, temperature and acidity, sweetness and light just right to allow the bulbous red mould to thrive, lurking in hollows in the rock, quivering transparently.

214

From beneath an olive green battle bob-cap and furrowed eyebrows, Mrs Beece, the voice of a million downtrodden invertebrates, fumed and barked a series of final orders. Her dark olive waterproof jacket chinked and glistened with the badges and medals from a thousand campaigns. Whales mingled with gleaming enamelled rainbows rising, and button badges declared everything from 'Ammorettan Death Lizards are for life, not just barbecues' to 'I Luv Lemmings!'

And, as another team of Cranachanian rock-rollers sprinted eagerly towards a red-spotted boulder and began straining at the centuries of inertia, she screamed a hail of last orders and lead her team off at full sprint. Placards waving a constant hail of wordy abuse she stomped forward, her vast green boots rattling in wild irritation. In seconds they had swept across the scruffy tundra, skirted the mostly completed twenty-foot security fence and were locked eye to eye with the group of startled rock-rollers.

'Stand back!' she screamed.

The labourers looked up in alarm. 'Eh? What d'you . . .'

'Remove your filthy hands from this rock at once!' squealed Mrs Beece, striding purposefully forward and scowling daggers from beneath her bob-cap. Behind her a platoon of environmentally friendly water-pistols were expertly cocked. The safety valves snipped off. 'I am claiming this territory on behalf of the People's Front for the Liberation of Flora and Fauna. Now, back off!' If she'd had a flag it would have been jammed into some tiny crack in seconds. Instead she defiantly slapped her hand on to the boulder. There was a dull splatting sound as a three hundred year old Crimson Jelly-Mould was smeared across the granite surface. Mrs Beece winced and surreptitiously wiped her hand on the hem of her jacket.

With an enormous cheer of support from her pistol-toting troops a cart rattled up, screeched to a deft hand-brake turn and dropped a gangplank off. In seconds the rock was surrounded by Mrs Beece's troopers, palms slapped on to the granite and they pushed. Baffled the official rock-rollers watched as their intended target was shoved inexorably on to the cart, strapped down and driven off in a cloud of dust and a hail of victoriously thumbed noses.

Mrs Olivia Beece squealed with delight, and wiped her hand on her hem again. She had done it, she had led her team in, right under the noses of the enemy and swiped the Variegated Crimson Jelly-Mould from the very jaws of extinction. And all without a shot being fired.

It was a very good job that she hadn't looked at the crushed carnage smearing the outside of her trophy.

In the darkened room of the Voyeur Traffic Control a hail of curses accompanied the sudden disappearance of a single luminous spot.

'Lost it!' translated Daymyn the demon, helpfully.

'Did you trace its source? Where's the damn thing coming from?' snarled Dragnazzar. The shrugged answer didn't go down very well.

'It was too short . . . Oooh, wait a minute. It's . . . it's back!' he stuttered in disbelief and pointed at the obsidian screen.

'Get on it!' snapped Dragnazzar. 'I want whoever's responsible. They're not escaping voyeurport tax!'

'Er . . . I, think it's a different one. It's not in the same place.'

'You sure?'

'The other was definitely nearer to the Phlegethon . . .'

'What? Two of them!'

'Looks that way, I . . .'

Suddenly the screen froze, a vertical green beam lanced across it and was intersected by a horizontal. They crossed at the exact point of the green luminescence and started to flash a series of numerals.

'Got it!' shouted Daymyn and punched the air joyously.

'Well what are we waiting for?' shouted Dragnazzar wheeling on his cloven hoof and galloping out of the Control Room in the direction of downtown Tumor.

In a tiny clearing, surrounded by two and a half acres of the most perfectly coppiced alder anywhere within a hundred ells of the Talpa Mountains, there squatted a ramshackle woodcutter's hut.

Today, nothing stirred in the clearing. Thick silence gripped the scene tighter than a lambswool cod-piece after a thunderstorm.

It had been like this for hours. Wrapped in a quivering expectant silence. Waiting for something to happen and dreading the worst . . .

Suddenly an antique pine sideboard exploded from the hut's back wall, spun across the clearing and splintered against a row of pollarded willow. It was accompanied by the distorted screaming of twisted teenage vocal cords and a cry of 'Emily, stop that!'

The hut shook and dislodged a dozen tiles as a squealing growl bawled its angry reply from within. It was the type of protest a starving pack of wolves would be proud of had they been ordered to turn vegetarian.

'Emily, be good!'

Another inhuman squeal was followed by the ritual destruction of a treasured chest of drawers and the frantic galloping of a pair of panting horses.

Scattering gravel and woodchips in all directions they screeched to a rapid halt outside the hut. 'This is the place,' barked the taller rider pointing at the flashing Emergency Red Crucifix on the cottage roof and swinging off his panting steed. He covered the distance to the door in seconds, his white habit swirling impatiently around him. 'Come on, come on!' he shouted as the screaming and wailing echoed from within the hut and blasted around the forest clearing. Impatient panic surged around the back of his mind like a caged panther.

Trying frantically to ignore the furious tantrums, the other rider worked urgently at the clasps on the saddlebags. A difficult task as his hands were vibrating with excitement. *This* was what Xedoc had joined the Abbey for. *This* was what being a trainee priest was all about.

With a squeal of protesting hinges the hut door was flung open and a bearded face squinted out, focusing on the vast red crucifix emblazoned across the chest of the rider. ' 'Bout time too,' yelled the woodcutter. 'That what you call prompt service, is it? I could've 'ad five 'ectares of willow coppiced in 'alf the time!'

Swallowing with secretive apprehension as another wave of fetid green fog curled out from under the door, Sinnohd, the Exorcist General of Abbey Synnia rubbed his hands across the suede-length crop of hair nestling on his skull. With a grimace he tightened the laces on his thirteen-hole Prayer-Wear Boots and found himself yearning for the restfully predictable violence of the SAS and the Flock Wars. D'vanouin heretics! he thought, you knew where you were with D'vanouin sheep-burning heretics. But this. . . ! Suddenly he felt out of practice.

Three vases and a chamberpot crashed against the inside of the door and shattered noisily, raising a shriek of cacophonous delight from within, and a sudden flood of adrenalin from everyone gathered outside.

Adjusting his abbey-issue steel reinforced mail cowl, Sinnohd checked his array of anti-demonic candles, expertly lit the pilot-light on his incense-thrower and nervously pressurised the Uri 9mm Holy Water Dispenser. Xedoc was torn between sucking every detail from Sinnohd's actions or unloading the horses.

'Come on then!' snapped the woodcutter from behind the Exorcist General. 'Get on with it!'

'Patience is a virtue!' growled Sinnohd, checking his sights and furrowing his forehead with devastating effect.

'Patience? Not when I'm payin' you by the hour it's not!' snapped the woodcutter, eyes blazing, knuckles white around the shaft of his favourite axe. 'I can't afford to stand around here listenin' to my daughter bein' possessed! Good worker she is! Every hour she's in there tied to the bed that's fifteen elm that's still standin'! I'm losin' money!'

'Yes, yes, I'm sure the financial considerations are of vital importance . . .' began Sinnohd sarcastically.

'And look at all this sticky slime everywhere. . . !' bellowed the woodcutter, pointing wildly with the tip of his favourite axe.

'Ectoplasmic residue,' corrected Sinnohd, glancing at the yellowish goo and cringing.

'Don't care what it's called . . . I can't find anything! I bet my favourite rip-saw's under there goin' rusty! Wife's goin' mad tryin' to clean it up all day! And she hasn't had a decent night's sleep with all the bangin' and wailin' . . .'

'Who is it?' shrieked a cracked falsetto voice from within the hut.

'Red cross,' shouted the woodcutter over his shoulder.

' 'Bout time! . . .' answered his wife, appearing around a door post. 'I ain't 'ad a decent night's sleep with all the bangin' an' wailin' . . .'

'See!' snapped the woodcutter, embedding his axe in the wall.

'*Careful* with that axe!' snapped his wife. Eugene, the woodcutter, rolled his eyes, extracted the implement and turned to Sinnohd. 'Well, you goin' to do somethin', eh? I can't afford to 'ave 'er possessed any longer. Girl of 'er age lyin' around tied to that bed when there's all these jobs need doin', ain't natural!' he ranted.

'Well. I'm here now. If you could show me the patient . . .'

The hut shook around them as something extremely large and heavy was hurled at an internal wall, showering the woodcutter with plaster dust and a few startled woodworm.

'In there?' asked the Exorcist General brushing at his white cloak and pointing at the bulging door oozing far too much goo from its hinges. The woodcutter nodded, staring around him as a vast pile of equipment settled in the hut and Xedoc the trainee priest squeezed himself out from underneath and peered eagerly around.

Sinnohd rubbed his hands across the suede-length crop of hair and adjusted his Abbey-surplus chain-mail cowl. Then he pounced on a small white trunk, flipped it open and filled his cloak pockets with top-grade anti-demonic candles. With a flourish he lit the pilot light on his shoulder-slung incense thrower. Xedoc lapped up every detail and feverishly took notes.

'I'll, er, leave you to it then . . .' whimpered the wood-cutter backing away as wisps of fetid green smog oozed under the door. 'If there's anythin' you need . . . hot water, lots of towels, just . . .'

Sinnohd shook his head, gritted his teeth, grasped a large purple and white bulb firmly in his fist and ripped it off his belt, biting the head off with a private morale-boosting snarl. It was now or never. Counting three he smashed open the door with his thirteen-hole Prayer-Wear boots and tossed the sphere over-arm into the room, accompanied by a cheer from Xedoc. A second after the garlic bulb exploded. Sinnohd was in the thick of it, laying down a damping fire of Holy Water. He skipped over the wreckage, rolled neatly and lined both barrels of the incense burner at the girl strapped to the bed.

'Okay, the game's over. Get out!' he squealed, ducking only once to avoid a circling bedpan.

'No, no wait. Let me explain . . .' growled Emily in a voice that sounded as if she had just been on the receiving end of an emergency tracheostomy.

'I would prefer not to have to use force . . .' snarled Sinnohd, staring at the suppurating cheeks of the girl and concluding that mould-green didn't suit her. He also realised that he had forgotten quite how distasteful teenagers could be. Especially possessed ones. The room was a mess.

There was the patter of scurrying feet behind him as Xedoc sprinted in, dropped a large case at the foot of the bed and stared open-mouthed. It was his first real exorcism. He knew what to expect of course. Sinnohd had taught him well, albeit very hastily on the way here, but actually seeing it, in the flesh. Well . . .

A blast of icy air laced with the aroma of month-dead teenage girl slammed into the General, knocking him a few paces backward. With a yell of irritation he spun around, expertly emptying several pounds of incense at the face lashing tongues over the edge of the bed.

'Sorry,' whimpered Emily. 'I didn't mean to . . . Look listen to me. I've got a message . . .'

'Shut up and get out.' snarled Sinnohd loosing another few gallons of Holy Water.

'No, look hang on . . . she's being awkward. I don't want to hurt you . . . oh, keep still, dear,' growled the girl on the bed in a tone of voice completely at odds with the snarling face and writhing body. 'Stop struggling!' she admonished herself.

Emily thrashed frantically on the bed, tugging at her bonds, plumes of green smog blasting from beneath the mattress, lifting the bed off the floor. With a curse Sinnohd made a mental note to make his instructions a lot clearer in future. Next time he would insist that the bed was tied down as well.

'Look I'm dreadfully sorry about all this . . .' growled Emily as the bed arced into the air. 'Ooooh, I don't feel very well . . .'

Several gallons of the steaming contents of an overactive gall-bladder splattered across Sinnohd's pristine cloak as Emily swooped wildly about the room.

'Right! That does it, miss!' he shrieked, unclipping several catches around the edge of the case as Xedoc clutched at his mouth and fled the room.

'Oh dear, oh dear. I'm sorry I didn't mean to . . .' apologised Emily. 'I really didn't think it would be so much trouble.'

With a deft flick of his wrist Sinnohd tugged and erected a top-of-the-range Travel Altar complete with Abbey-surplus field Crusade-o-Fix and three dozen Eezy-Lite joss-sticks. 'Creature from the pits of depravity. Tortured ogre from below. You have been found to be cohabiting a ready occupied soul in a manner likely to cause offence, in direct violation of the Personal Sanctity and Inhabitation Bill, sub-section 195b.'

'Yes, I wouldn't normally but something nasty's come up . . .'

'You have the right to remain violent, but anything you do

221

with be taken down and revisited upon you a thousand times worse,' yelled Sinnohd.

'Oh, now really, you don't have to go to all that trouble.'

'Shut up!' shrieked Sinnohd, dropping the incense-thrower as if it was alive and with a dramatic high-elbow sweep snatched a very large weapon out of a hidden holster. The matt-black barrel swept upwards, following the circling bed with pin-point accuracy, throbbing eagerly with straining sacred fury. He squinted through the sighting cross and released the safety catch.

'You are now looking down the barrel of the latest in high-impact expulsion technology. Deliverance capability of fifteen rounds a minute, high-velocity aura-piercing missals.'

'Oh, please now, violence won't be necessary . . .'

Sinnohd settled his Prayer-Wear booted feet slightly further apart, bent his knees and readied himself for the recoil he knew the Exorcuter would deliver.

'If all things were equal,' he snarled in almost a whisper, ignoring the almost apologetic words – he knew from of old how they could sound so convincing, 'you could possibly whip up enough momentum to break through that wall before I shot you down and sentenced you to an eternity of charitable deeds and high-intensity prayer meetings. Now, what you have to ask yourself is,' he growled, sneering up at the possessed teenager circling above him on the green cloud-belching bedroom furniture, 'do you feel lucky?'

'Look, if you could possibly just pass on a message to Pope Uri . . .' pleaded Emily.

Sinnohd shook his head.

'. . . or even Sacrosanct Sergeant Vertex, I'd . . .' she continued.

What was this? What lies were wrapped up in such an innocent sounding request? Sinnohd found himself getting angry. He wasn't going to find out. 'You've got five seconds to get out!' he shouted, ducking. 'Or I'm coming in with this!' He patted the matt-black barrel affectionately and grinned with far too much relish for a man of the cloth. 'Four . . .'

The bed wobbled. 'Hey, what about five?'

'Three . . .' he shouted, tucking the stock firmly against his shoulder.

'That's not fair . . .'

'Two,' his index finger crawled closer to the trigger.

'Look here! I only want to . . .'

'One . . .'

'Uri won't be happy when Centaur Parc—' The bed stopped racing forwards, trembled and tumbled floorwards. With the nonchalance of a man stepping off a kerb Sinnohd avoided the bed's re-entry two inches to his left, began to polish his fingernails and was trampled a moment later by the sprinting woodcutter racing daughterwards.

'Emily!' he shrieked, unsure whether to hug her or hurl several buckets of disinfectant at her.

'And here endeth today's lesson,' grunted Sinnohd, staring at the very pale face of Xedoc peering around the edge of the door. 'Look, if you really want to become an Exorcist you're going to have to do something about that stomach of yours. I didn't get where I am today retching my guts up every time I saw a half-decomposed teenager. Think of it as really bad acne and it's all right, look!'

Emily was sitting up in bed, already looking a far more environmentally friendly shade of green.

'Oh, Mr Sinnohd,' oozed the woodcutter's wife. 'How can I ever thank you?'

'Please, call me General. Twelve groats fifty and a donation to the Abbey roof fund and we'll call it quits.' He forced a grin and held out his hand expectantly.

But beneath the relieved exterior Sinnohd harboured dreadful thoughts. He felt certain that the possessed had *never* asked to have a chat with the Pope before. An uneasy feeling settled in his kidneys as he pocketed the cash and left the hut.

In a tiny alley, not far from the Phlegethon, the Really Reverend Unctuous III snarled miserably, 'Exorcists! Far too power mad for their own good!'

A few hundred yards to the west of the Centaur Parcs

building site, three huge wooden barn-like structures had been thrown together in financially stimulated double-time. Inside each, vast forges had been erected next to massive benches and teams of swiftly trained blacksmiths had been assembled and armed with vast mallets. It was their job, under the command of Spam Smith, to forge huge plates of steel, roll them into cylinders and rivet them shut to form enormous conduits.

In the noise and hubbub nobody noticed the scratching of fevered claws beneath the ash pan of the forges, no one witnessed the emergence of the stalag-mite and no one even had the time to wonder who it was that had lit the scorching sheets of hundred-foot flames, or wonder why no one had thought to organise regular deliveries of coal.

In the dark triplet of satanic mills, a cacophony of hammering began.

Nabob exploded through the door to his cavern and slammed it behind him with a scathing scream of vitriol and a blast of sulphurous air. It was getting worse, every day it seemed there were more and more people lurching about on the streets. It had taken him an hour and a half to get home from the picket lines on the River Phlegethon. An hour and a half! Shouldn't take more than ten minutes. And all that after another exhausting day in the Sinful Service, processing the Immigration forms of the recently deceased.

He stomped across the cavern, past the little plate of coloured rock proclaiming 'Hole Sweet Hole' and poured himself a double brimstone and treacle on the rocks. And followed it swiftly with another. Trekking miserably through shoulder-deep rivers of damned souls was getting far too hellish, especially after listening to that damned Seirizzim in yet another round of talks, nay screams, with those damned ferrymen. He sneered as he recalled Seirizzim's face when, right on cue, Captain Naglfar had demanded double-time on Sindays. It was brilliant, another five hundred obuls well earned. Really made Seirizzim sit up and think for a moment. Nabob scratched his head and snarled noisily as he thought of how the conversation had gone then. He wrestled with the words and found nothing. He'd heard it, so had all the ferrymen. Somehow Seirizzim's tongue had moved faster than the ears of his beholders. Somehow he had agreed to Sinday double-time, but only if it was tied into increased productivity and a five-century no-strike policy.

Nabob screamed and smashed his scaly hand through the top of his osidian table.

Two days to the Election. Two days! It was so close and everything pointed to Seirizzim getting those ferrymen back to work. Nabob shook angrily with wild frustration. If the picket lines stayed solid, Seirizzim wouldn't stand a chance of winning d'Abaloh's favour and clinching the Undertaker-in-Chief's job. They had to stay out. They had to!

Everybody in Immigration agreed. The most unimaginative of Sinful Service Accountants were getting hotter under their collars about the vast loss of index-linked payments accrued over the centuries. Satanic Secretaries tutted and shook their heads sagely. Even the most inept of clerks could see the validity of Captain Naglfar's requests. It was as if a strange new disease were spreading throughout the Sinful Service, everyone in Immigration had come out in a rash of sympathy.

Suddenly Nabob sat bolt upright. Sympathy, that was it! Perfect!

He roared in almost cheerful anger and necked a third double brimstone and treacle.

He could see it all now, dreamlike before him. He would leap on to his obsidian desk in the headquarters of the Sinful Service and stamp his hoof down hard, ignoring the lightning crack of splintering mineral snaking away from his heel.

'Listen to me, Brothers and Sisters!' he would yell commandingly above the infernal hubbub after stirring their hearts to action. 'Search inside your stirring hearts and consider their fate. Frozen wages. The imposition of unfeasible quotas. They're bound to an outdated contract drawn up centuries ago. How easily could that be us?'

There would be interruptions and he would dismiss them

with a flourish of expert talon. Someone might shout, 'They get double-time on Sindays.'

He would snort derisively. 'A hollow victory. Double nothing is still nothing!' The opposition would crumble and he would ram home his gleamingly evil advantage.

'Seirizzim will treat us the same as the ferrymen! We need to show our solidarity! Join them on the Phlegethon picket lines! Strike!'

And suddenly Immigration would explode in deepest sympathy with the infernal ferrymen, carrying banners of support and creating an insurmountable election defeat for Sierizzim. It would be glorious!

For the first time in longer than he could remember Nabob was actually looking forward to a Chewsday morning.

Guthry the dwarf could barely make himself heard above the rapidly growing racket of the rapidly growing Centaur Parcs building-site. Vast slabs of shaped sand-stone rumbled and scraped noisily as they were hauled on top of others and mortared into place. Already the first two complete circuits of the dome were in situ, rising a good ten feet above the naked crown of Tor Khamada, the first tentative swellings of the planned carbuncular construction. A kilofoot beneath Guthry's tootsies, Flagit barked directions and thrilled as he witnessed crowds of labourers jump to the civil engineer's command. Flagit loved the power of Total Limbic Control. And his ego flopped and revelled in the warming currents of the anticipated day when he would have complete and direct dominion over the kingdoms he could, as yet, only glimpse via the crystal goggles of his control net. The day that was moving ever closer, with every raised stone . . .

Suddenly the cavern door was kicked in and five vast Malebranche guards stormed in. Flagit leaped to his cloven hooves in abject shock, his face contorting in deep anguish as he attempted to gather the threads of his consciousness back into the confines of his skull.

'What is the meaning of this. . . !' he began in what he

thought was a pretty impressive rallying of cognitive thought given the unexpected circumstances.

'Captain Dragnazzer, of the Malebranche,' growled the tallest demon, holding out a small rectagle of Nognite parchment with a less than accurate sketch of him in the top left-hand corner. His slitted eyes scoured the interior with alarmingly rough thoroughness. 'This your cavern?'

'Yes, I . . .'

'Search it, lads,' barked Dragnazzar.

'What. . . ?' Flagit shook his head, tugged off his infernite lattice and threw it casually over one of the long spikes rising vertically out of the back of his chair. 'What the Styx are you looking for?'

'Language, sir,' growled Dragnazzar as his men dived under beds and swarmed through cupboards. 'We have reason to believe that this cavern has recently been used as a base for illegal, non-scheduled mind-share tourism, sir. We are therefore, at present, engaged in a thorough search of these premises in order to locate the necessary equipment required for such a pastime, sir. If and when we do come across such equipment it shall be seized and any outstanding voyeurport tax will be collected in the usual extremely painful manner, sir . . .'

'But . . . I . . .' blubbed Flagit as his drinks cabinet was unceremoniously trashed.

'You have the right to remain silent,' continued Dragnazzar almost wearily, 'but you and I know you did it so spill the beans now and make it easy on us all, sir.'

'But I haven't . . . wouldn't . . . didn't!' whimpered Flagit as he tried to work out what was going on. 'Why pick on me?'

'Ho, ho, sir. Very good, sir. You'd be surprised how brightly unlicensed trips show up on the voyeur traffic control scanner. Now where's the equipment, sir?' He was of course referring to the huge transcendental hyperbooster which fitted over the head like a hairdryer and focused the tourist's psyche into the required destination.

At that moment the head of the search team strolled up to

227

the captain, saluted in the complex manner they had and held out Flagit's infernite lattice.

'Found nothin' but this, sah.'

Dragnazzar took the shimmering headgear on his index talon and squinted long and hard at it. 'And what might this be?' he asked Flagit.

'Er . . . I. Ahem, it's a lace hair-net,' he answered and then cunningly looked at his cloven feet.

'Lace? You make lace hair-nets?' Dragnazzer failed totally to keep the note of derision out of his voice. 'Wouldn't have thought a big boy like you would be into lacy things, would we lads? Still, what you gets up to in the privacy of your own hovel, well that's up to you.' He barely stifled a snigger. A chorus of disapproval chimed around the cavern and Dragnazzar flung the infernite lattice on to the floor as if he had just noticed a large green glistening glob of sputum on it, disturbingly near his talon. 'Anything else?' he growled, staring angrily at his team leader.

'Well, there was a curiously large number of these in a box in a back room, sah.' He held out a selection of hundred-groat notes.

'Ha! Now we've got you, counterfeiting!' Dragnazzar stared and then looked disappointed. 'Groats? What are groats?'

'I, er, made them up,' shrugged Flagit. 'It's for a new board-game I'm inventing called, er, called Mortropoly, yes! You go round the board and buy up all the major streets until . . .'

Dragnazzar rolled his eyes and cursed. 'Anything else?'

'No, sah.'

'Gah! You've been lucky this time, laddie,' he snarled, breathing hot breath on to Flagit's face. 'I don't know where you've hidden it, but next time we'll get you!' He wheeled around and stormed towards the door. 'Let's check out the other one!'

Flagit slammed the door shut after them and collapsed into his chair shaking. He had no doubt that he had just had a very lucky escape. Got away with it by the skin of his fangs.

His only problem was. Got away with what?

The matted tresses of flask-blonde hair cascaded down the bare shoulders of the teenager strapped spread-eagle to the bed. She writhed and spat, furiously tugging against her bonds in desperate frustration.

'How much more time are you going to waste?' she croaked, her chest heaving with the effort. 'I haven't got all day, you know.' She blinked pointedly through the three-inch raven-feather eyelashes and curled her lip. If she could have folded her arms and tapped her foot she certainly would have.

The cassocked man at the door averted his gaze from the straps of her lingerie and mumbled a quick rosary. What was keeping General Sinnohd? He should have been here by now.

'I'm not doing this for fun,' snapped the girl. 'Do you think I actually enjoy being strapped down, hmmm? Well, I'll tell you . . . Ahhh, about time!' She finished as General Sinnohd burst in through the door and began readying himself for another exorcism.

'Look, as I was trying to say before you so rudely exorc—'

'Shut up!' snapped Sinnohd.

'Well, that's *very* nice I must say . . .'

'Creature from the pits of depravity,' boomed Sinnohd clicking his Eezy-Lite joss-sticks into action. 'Troubled ogre from below. You have been found . . .'

'Yeah, yeah. We did all that last time. How is Emily, by the way?'

'. . . guilty of cohabiting a ready-occupied soul in a manner likely to cause offence . . .' fumed Sinnohd, working the pressurising foot-pump on his Uri 9mm Holy Water Cannon.

'There's no need for force. Promise me you'll get a message to Pope Uri and I'll . . .'

'I make no bargains with creatures from the Underworld!' bellowed Sinnohd, letting rip with a searing blast of Holy Water.

'Arrrggh! Not even if I'm trying to be helpful?'

'Hah, helpful? Don't even know the meaning of the word!' Sinnohd cried, laying an ornately carved crucifix on her stomach and pointedly ignoring her heaving bosom.

'An action or series of gestures designed to ease the burden of . . .'

'Silence!' screamed Sinnohd, snatching the safety catch off the Exorcutor and waving the weapon provocatively.

'I've got to tell you that Centaur Parcs isn't . . .'

'Get out!' His finger trembled over the trigger.

'Don't say I didn't warn . . . I'm gone! I'm gone!'

Suddenly the nymphomaniac blinked, fluttered her raven-feather lashes and stared at General Sinnohd. 'Hello, big boy,' she crooned.

'Another fine victory against the forces of evil,' smarmed the guard-monk at the doorway.

General Sinnohd growled irritably. Something funny was going on. Never once, throughout his entire career history of exorcisms had they requested an audience with the Pope. And now *twice* in less than twenty-four hours. It didn't make sense.

In a tiny alley by the banks of the Phlegethon the Really Reverend Unctuous III (deceased) fumed and snarled impotently.

The only sound in Flagit's search-destroyed cavern was the whooshing of the magma underfloor heating, the occasional ponderous sigh and the whirling machinations of his seething mind. Ever since Captain Dragnazzar and his band of Malebranche thugs had whirlwinded out of there he had been sitting on the edge of his chair, elbow on knee, chin on knuckles, thinking. What had it all meant?

He was a legitimate mind-share holiday travel operator, he had a job at the Transcendental Travel Company Ltd to prove it, so what had made them think he was running backstreet deals from here? Especially with some fictitious partner way across town. It was ridiculous. He would never work with anyone on something so unimaginative or easily detectable. Oh, no. Flagit only made pacts with those that

230

kept their mouths clean and their noses shut – there was nothing worse than some partner's bad case of the verbal trots after he's sniffed out something naughty.

Suddenly something moved. His head whirled with raptorial speed, his slitted pupil pouncing angrily on the motion. He stared at the wreckage of discarded boxes hurled by the Malebranche, a trickle of lava martini oozing from a broken flask, and . . . it moved again. In a flash he was on his hooves, snatching wildly through the debris like an ostrich in the final stages of dementia, hurling boxes of spherical crystal mortbles and bowls of cocktail cinderellas over his shoulder in explosions of colour. Then a flash of dull-grey lattice shot across the floor, accelerating and hit the wall with a tinkly splat. Flagit stared open-mouthed at the glowing lattice. Inanimate objects just shouldn't do things like that.

In ten strides he was across the cavern and snatching the lattice up in both hands. Did it feel just a little heavier than usual? He spun in a screech of cloven heels, dashed across to the far wall and dropped it, kicking frantically at the debris and trying to clear a path. The lattice shimmered and was on the move almost before it hit the floor, zapping across the cavern as if on elastic, its bid for freedom ending with the same tickly splat against the wall.

Flagit shook his head and stared open-mawed. The scientist in him wondered if the other lattice would behave in the same irrational manner, disobeying the standard laws of irrefutable physical behaviour in an, as yet, inexplicably non-fathomable modus operandi.

And the more sensible part of him told him to get real and remember that the search had only turned up one lattice.

Suddenly, and despite the fact that the cavern was currently a comfortably baking six hundred and sixty-six degrees Fahrenheit, a band of icicles ran squealing up Flagit's terror-stricken spine. This could only mean two things.

Unctuous had the other lattice.

And he was using it!

*

231

As Captain Dragnazzar and his Malebranche clattered further towards the Phlegethon, closing in on their second target, hurling tortured souls out of their path and screaming strings of choicest Helian abuse, he began to get the slightest feeling that perhaps something wasn't entirely right. He knew very well that transcendental hyperboosters cost hundreds of thousands of obuls to buy (eighteen thousand plus delivery and fitting if you wanted one stolen on demand) and he also knew that if all the occupants of the Phlegethon district were strip-searched and all their pockets emptied the total ready currency would probably amount to five obuls and a couple of favourite pebbles. So who was running a transcendental hyperbooster down here? And why?

'This way!' shouted the search team leader and whirled around a corner into a dark alley. An alley which, up until three seconds after he had cried 'This way!' had been entirely full of illegal immigrants.

Years of being on the receiving end of countless unprovoked beatings and a host of grossly unnecessary punitive exercises had honed the pact-men's early-warning system to very near perfection.

As the Malebranche screeched to a rapid halt the only thing that moved was a small fragment of Nognite parchment kicked up in the hasty exit.

Captain Dragnazzar made a very odd noise in his throat and scowled at the team leader.

'But . . . er, look, what can I say? I was told here. Captain, no, Captain! . . .'

The sound of a scream, the whistling of air and the percussive contact of scaly palm on scaly skull echoed across the banks of the Phlegethon.

Work on the Centaur Parcs dome had continued to rattle and crash along all night at a cracking pace. Masons, hired memorial makers and anyone with even a passing ounce of skill with a cold chisel swarmed over the enormous hemisphere in wild, greed-driven abandon.

Hours ago three hearty cheers had shattered the talpine

dawn as the last block was man-and-boy handled into place and leapt on by a host of frantic cement-wielding pointers. Almost immediately, and with military precision, teams of smiths flooded out of their triplet of dark satanic mills, each struggling under a vast heap of wrought-iron pipework. They swarmed through the high-security fencing, and disappeared into the vast stone igloo of the dome.

Inside, Guthry the dwarf was barking orders and waving his arms frantically, a grin splitting his face from earlobe to earlobe. He had never had a team of such enthusiasts. Ahh, the power of cash!

The stream of pipe-carrying smiths split and headed off in seven different directions under the expert direction of Guthry's wad-filled hand. In seconds they were connecting pipes into a vast spider-web of dully gleaming metalwork and suspending it from the curved ceiling with much wire and swearing.

In the centre of the dome a twenty-foot bowl had been excavated and the enormous windmill blade was mounted horizontally on a vast roller-bearing, precisely as the plans had indicated.

Guthry stood directing the proceedings, staring intently at the blue Nognite parchment plans for a few seconds then glancing up at progress, waving a few handfuls of scattered cash-highlighted directions before squinting again at the drawing. He had to keep a constant check. At this rate of construction, one slip, one single slip, and the entire thing could shoot off at an almost irreparable tangent in a matter of seconds.

A squeal of metal on rock and a host of grunted curses shattered the hubbub as a twenty-foot-diameter lid was shoved into place over the windmill blades, dropping the final few inches with a clang. It squatted like a vast whisky still, the only differences being that it wasn't copper, had a row of seven holes around its crown and there was nowhere to collect any freshly purified *aqua vitae*. Oh yes, and then there was the stange system of pulleys, levers and geared cam-shafts that connected a small water-wheel in a gushing cataract outside to the central gear on the turbine blade. When the entire system was up and running the septet of pipes would supply the necessary air-conditioning to each of the seven chambers of sin, pumped around by the torque generated from the water-wheel system outside. Each section could have its very own environment uniquely tailored to the specific sin – hot and sweaty for lust, dark and humid for sloth, that sort of thing. And at the current rate it would only be a matter of a few short hours before the air-conditioning was fired up.

However, that rate was about to take a dramatic turn for the faster.

The door of the storeroom of the Transcendental Travel Company Ltd slammed shut behind a panting Flagit clutching a gryphon-skin bag to his chest. So far so good, he thought.

After having snuck past the massed ranks of the Demons' Institute strapped into the hyperboosters on a package tour he was feeling happier. Not one of them had batted an infernal eyelid. How possessing a troupe of oiled muscle-bound dancers on a tour of depravity would be considered fun he'd never know. Still, they were hooked.

He took a nervous breath, fumbled with the clasps on the gryphon-skin bag and upended the contents on the table. With a flurry of talons and chitinous claws the stalag-mite righted itself and glared at him.

'Sorry,' grunted Flagit. 'Nerves,' he grinned and scratched the infernite lattice. For an all-too-tension-filled moment, he stared at it, fighting a battle of wills with himself on the brink of his biggest moment.

Look. Just put it back in the bag and walk away . . .

What? Back into the humiliating squalor of obscurity and subservience? Do me a favour!

No. No. I mean back to normality.

Boot-licking, toady subserviance more like! Pah! Come too far to give up now. Everything is ready! Just think of all that space . . .

But . . .

234

No, buts! Do it!

He fitted the lattice expertly between his horns and swallowed in terror as he ran through the plan once more. His mind whirled back a desperate hour, when, seething with panic and power-hungry madness he had tapped his nine-inch talons on his temples, his brow furrowing in intense concentration. Tiny green spots squeezed themselves into his vision as he screwed his eyes. Think, think! It had come as a terrifying shock to know he could be detected by the Malebranche at the Voyeur Traffic Control Centre. There had to be away round them, had to be! Everything depended on it! Seeking for a solution, mentally ripping up any cerebrally unturned stone, his eyes screwed tighter. Tiny green spots on thick black. They swirled and buzzed as the veins stood out on his neck. He had to find a haystack to hide his vital needle . . . Tiny green spots . . . !

And then he saw it. Haystacks were worse than useless for hiding needles if your opponent has a metal detector. But, hide a single needle in a case of pins . . .

Would it work? Would it? He pounded his forehead wildly as indecision scrapped mercilessly with the writhing tendrils of fury.

Face it Fagit, he snarled at himself. You've got no choice.

Shutting all thoughts of the danger of being traced away into the back of his mind, and pausing only long enough to whisper a series of complex instructions to the stalag-mite, he reached out an eager telepushic thought stream, thrust it straight into the limbic system of a certain civil engineer and hoped no one would notice. The stalag-mite disappeared through the roof in a shower of chewed granite.

Away across Mortropolis in the vast black tower, a tiny luminous green pin-prick of light appeared on the obsidian screen of the Voyeur Traffic Control scanner. It flickered, glowed dimly and then beamed out at full intensity in the darkened room.

And Daymyn the demon, eyes peeled even as they were, failed to spot it. Well, one tiny extra pin-prick amongst the numbered throng of fourteen Demons' Institute Tourists wasn't exactly obvious, and he had been on a double shift so his eyes were tired.

Unnoticed by the swarming teams of workers inside the Centaur Parcs dome, something strange was happening to Guthry the dwarf. His eyes had taken on a disturbingly distant look, almost as if they were no longer his. As if someone else was staring out through them. A someone, or something, that knew exactly what needed doing next and had no need to refer to plans. Absently Guthry's grip slipped on the Nognite parchment blueprint, completely failing to notice it flutter and soar away behind a small pile of rubble.

'You! No, not there! Bring it here!' bellowed Guthry, his voice naked in its accentless tone, somehow echoing forcefully above the cacophany as he gesticulated wildly at a clump of smiths.

'But you said . . .' began one of them.

' "Said!" Past tense. I am now saying bring it here, NOW!' he pointed dramatically between two of the larger suspended pipes, whirled and saw another group struggling under a crude valve assembly. 'No, NO!' he screamed as he sprinted at them. 'Other way round. Check your flows!'

'I thought . . .'

'You are paid to *do*, not think! Other way round!' he screamed, and then he was off to harangue another crew. Thrashing them verbally about the ears he skipped around the dome bellowing orders left, right and centre. And in the chaos nobody had the time to stop and think about what he was doing. Nobody noticed that once all the valves were swapped around and the ducting rerouted and the extra access vents were dug through the outer shell at the last minute, once that happened Centaur Parcs' air conditioning wouldn't work.

But, by then it was already too late.

Unseen below the central lid of the ducting system, hidden below the vast blades of the cast-iron turbine, rocks began to tremble unnaturally. It was as if something with a stack more claws than it needed and a far from healthy appetite for granite was gnashing its way upwards through the last few final feet of rock. It was.

With a shriek of delight Guthry dashed towards a handle positioned next to an array of pulleys, gears and rods, and tugged. A single spinning cam moved, locked in to mesh with a host of pinions, transferred torque through a series of enhancers and, in a flash, connected the water-wheel to the turbine. The ground rumbled as the huge cast-iron blades shuddered into motion and began to suck momentum from the waterfall.

At the very instant, claws and legs erupted beneath the windmill in a shower of rubble as the stalag-mite chewed its way through the last few inches. Hot on its tail came a whooshing eruption of superheated infernal gas, blasting upwards. As the momentum of the turbine increased, so the whooshing suction rose. Each swipe of the blade dragging more air out of the Underworld Kingdom of Helian.

Inside the Centaur Parcs dome, work came to a sudden terror-stricken halt. All around them pipes began to rattle, grumbling intestinally as they were force-fed with the atmosphere from below. Pops and bangs shook the system as the cast-iron expanded with the heat. And then suddenly, out of the seven freshly dug holes in the outside skin of the dome, like some vast pressure cooker about to explode, black and red gas erupted and shot skywards in vast tumbling billows.

Smiths, masons, pointers, joiners and all manner of other workers erupted from the entrance, tumbling over each other to escape, terror ringing in their ears as they sprinted down the scree edges of the Tor. Behind them the rapidly growing plumes of superheated gas billowed uncontrollably towards the stratosphere. And then it hit them. Like a fetid blast of eucalyptus oil boiling on sauna stones a searing wave of choking sulphur-laden heat blasted out, cooling rapidly from its initial six hundred and sixty-six degrees Fahrenheit.

At the top of the Tor, two figures heaved at the high-security gates and sealed them shut. It was only then, far too late to do anything about it, that some people noticed the uncanny similarity between the scars snaking across the foreheads of Spam Smith and Guthry the dwarf.

In the windswept storeroom of the Transcendental Travel Company Ltd, Flagit squealed with delight as he smashed the crystal window to the outside of the building. Helian air whirlwinded in, sucked by the vacuum created by the turbine above, and was followed by reams of Nognite parchment and all manner of sundry stationery whisked violently out of the room by the greedy fingers of feral vortices. In seconds the storeroom was bare. Flagit wheeled around the door his ears popping with the roaring pressure difference. He struggled frantically to heave it shut, locked it and sprinted out into the heaving crowds of downtown Tumor. It had begun.

Centaur Parcs was ready for business.

Of Beavers and Catastrophic Converters

'Another!' growled Commander 'Black' Achonite leaning over the bar in the alcohol-ridden atmosphere of the Gutter. 'Gimme 'nuther flagon of Hexenhamm— beer!' He'd already downed five and was really getting into the swing of it. Fifteen more and he might have almost forgotten the nightmare sight of that blacksmith lurching out of the inferno, skull stitched together . . . 'C'monnn!' He pounded impatiently on the oak bar.

'All right, keep your hair on,' said the barmaid and then cringed as she stared at the stubbly crown of Achonite's head. 'Er, what's your hurry?'

'Bad day,' Achonite growled seismically and gasped to show just how in need of a refill he really was.

'Oooh, shame,' she answered, paying little attention. With a flourish of her wrist the leather flagon landed on the bar, she snatched the money and headed off towards a vast clump of rock-rollers that had just been paid off from Centaur Parcs.

'Need cheerin' up, darlin'?' oozed a voice at Achonite's left earlobe. 'I 'eard you'd 'ad a bad day, lovey.' Maisy, part-owner of 'Daisy and Maisy's Pleasure Parlor' in Fort Knumm and professional 'cheerer-upper' winked far less than surreptitiously at him. 'I've got over one hundred and six different ways of cheerin' fellas up.'

Achonite took a huge swallow of Hexenhammer, wiped his hand across his mouth and asked, 'Know anywhere I c'n get rat-proof bootsss? Only, the smiffy I'd 'ired went an' got 'mmmself killed, I think, an' now 'e's makin' win'mills in 'is smiffy which is on fire an' 'e should be burnted but ees not cos of . . .'

Maisy shook her head, tutted something about getting all sorts in here these days, rearranged her blouse to display her curvature to the full and slinked off towards the rock-rollers.

239

It was at that very moment that the door was shoved open and a certain Pious Constable Slamm J'hadd entered seething with righteous irritation and dripping with talpine drizzle. Eight hours he'd been searching high and low for Commander 'Black' Achonite and he wasn't best pleased about it. He'd been sent an entire trawlerful of slapping red herrings, passed from one sniggering Black Guard to another and misdirected down every back alley and shady passageway in the whole of Cranachan. How many times he had cursed himself for not attending the courses on criminal tracking he wouldn't like to say, but he'd certainly be in the confessional a lot next week. It was only by sheer chance that, on passing the Gutter for the nineteenth time in a new and surprising direction, he had peered out from beneath his hood and spotted Achonite inside leering at Maisy.

'So this is where the head of the Black Guard is to be found nowadays, is it? What does a man of the cloth have to do to find you?' fumed J'hadd on extremely dangerous ground.

'Gemme a flagon of Hex—,' grunted Achonite.

'What?'

'—enhammer, or I'll pull orl your teeth out an' nibble you to death with 'em. Ha. ha!'

'I trust that is some sort of ribald greeting?' snarled J'hadd, scowling from beneath his dripping hood.

'Nnnope. Gemme a drink!' growled Achonite, snatching the sodden Constable firmly around the throat.

'Urrgh, 'ffff you 'nnnsist.'

'I do!'

'I am only carrying out this action under duress,' grumbled J'hadd, fishing in his cassock pocket and mumbling things about not being a suitable example of setting law and order. Choking he leant over the bar and ordered a flagon.

'Wherrz she gonn?' grumbled Achonite looking around for Maisy. 'She was goin' to cheer meeyup.'

'Your drink,' mumbled J'hadd. 'Now, to the matter in hand. I have uncovered a serious breach in the procedural apprehension of known felons to which I believe your attention much be drawn . . .'

Achonite wasn't listening. His mind, slipping the leashes of alcohol-sodden reality, was spinning over images of the lurching Spam Smith. It whirled and attempted to wring an ounce of sense from the feelings that he had definitely witnessed something which he shouldn't have. I mean, how could anyone have cut themselves so badly shaving. The yearning tendrils of Achonite's desperation stretched out, attempting to snatch comprehension from the swirling acres of embittered bafflement whilst he gabbled incessant rubbish.

'Are you paying even the slightest attention to a single word I am saying?' huffed J'hadd. 'That is the height of bad manners, you know. I'm simply asking a series of polite but firm questions in the convivial atmosphere of a licensed hostelry in order to ascertain the *precise* whereabouts of a recently apprehended felon and . . .'

'Finnnishd this one,' gurgled Achonite tipping the empty flagon over morosely.

J'hadd flipped back his hood and stared at the Commander with the expression with which one scolds an errant child. 'Very well, you can have *one* more and . . .'

It didn't really have the effect he had planned. Achonite took one look at J'hadd's glistening row of cat-gut stitches decorating his forehead, pointed and screamed.

'H . . . head,' he stammered, eyes wide, quivering.

'It's not as bad as it looks. I, er, seem to have cut myself shaving. Now where's Gravure the printer, my criminal?'

Fortunately for Achonite's long-term sanity (a term to be used with extreme care around him) mental knuckles were already pounding hard on his cerebral doors. For at that precise moment a certain Reverend, not to be put off by a little exorcise, was attempting to make another contact.

'. . . how c'n I 'ave a real murd'rinvestigashun if ees not murderrd no more . . .' slurred Achonite as pictures of Spam Smith waved windmills at him cheerfully.

A desperate tendril touched on something, wrapped around it and hauled. Out of the perpetual darkness of the unknown a shape appeared, grinned and began to rush uncontrollably upward.

'And how can I have a trial without a felon?' scowled J'hadd. 'Where is he?'

Achonite continued oblivious to the pleas. '. . . rat-proof bootssess they won't be able to . . . able to . . .' But before Achonite realised that anything untoward was happening a dark shape had roared out of the unknown, pummelled down the door and leapt into the driving seat of his resistance lowered mind.

'. . . able to . . .' Suddenly Achonite sat bolt upright, grabbed J'hadd's arm and lost all expression in his face.

'Are you feeling okay?' whimpered the Pious Constable wondering if a career in the RUC was *really* what he was definitely after.

'Ah! Hello!' Achonite's voice was the only thing cheerful about his entire appearance. In fact, just for an instant it looked like it was the only thing alive about him. 'Hello? Cooeee, can you hear me? Can I talk?' grunted the body of Achonite. Oddly, the voice sounded as if it had come from a very, very long way away. Beyond the grave, in fact.

'Er . . . yes,' answered J'hadd reluctantly. What was Achonite doing? Was *this* the fabled Black Guard sense of humour? Quickly he looked over his shoulders to see if any groups of sniggering people were taking an undue interest in his behaviour. Everything seemed on the reassuringly rowdy side of normal. 'Y . . . yes I can hear you.'

'Oh goody. Now, could you be an angel and do me a little favour?' Absently, almost zombie-like, Achonite's hand reached out for his flagon and raised it to his lips. Unaware, he kept talking. 'Can you tell me if there are any ex . . . uuuurgh!' A fountain of ale frothed out of Achonite's mouth as his drinking reflex steadily refused to lie down.

'I really think you've had *far* too much for . . .'

'Help, I'm drowning!' frothed Achonite.

People in the bar were beginning to look their way.

'Er, Commander, stop that,' stage-whispered J'hadd uncomfortably.

'Would if I could,' he gurgled and then mercifully the flagon was empty. 'Hasn't he . . . er, haven't I had enough already,' he growled and stared blankly around. The hand seemed to realise the flagon was empty, dropped it, slapped on to the bar and began rummaging around for other, filled tankards. 'Sorry about that, he seems to be a little difficult to control, who is he?'

'What?' grunted J'hadd.

'Oh, never mind, you wouldn't understand. Er, now about those exorcists? Any around, hmmm?'

'Exorcists?' whimpered J'hadd tentatively sniffing at the joke. 'Well, I . . . I can't see any.'

'Oh, that is a relief,' Achonite sighed. His right hand trundled along the bar in search of beer. 'I had never realised they were quite so bossy, you know. Shocking, it is. Still, only doing their job I suppose . . .'

'What's this sudden interest in exorcists?' J'hadd wondered aloud, playing along to see what Achonite was up to. If he *had* to go through a few small hoops to find Gravure, then so be it. He just hoped there weren't too many. 'I didn't think you were much bothered about the occult and possessions and stuff.' J'hadd sat back and waited, more than half-expecting Achonite to come back with some contrived line about possessions being nine-tenths of the law. But he didn't. Instead he swayed precariously, stared out of glassy eyes and cleared his throat with a sound like a boulder crashing into the bottom of a phlegm-filled well, all the time apparently totally unaware that his hand had casually snatched a flagon of ale from in front of a vast rock-roller.

'Yeuch,' growled Achonite, 'Did that sound as bad to you as it did down here?' he asked hollowly.

J'hadd nodded, baffled at the use of the word 'down' and for the first time suspecting that something wasn't entirely right about this.

'In that case I don't think I have long,' he grunted as his hand made a start on the return journey mouthwards. 'Seems I haven't got the hang of suppressing rejection, yet. Look, you don't know me, not many people do, I wasn't exactly popular, but, well c'est la . . .'

'What are you trying to say?' asked J'hadd, one nervous eye on the slowly moving flagon in his hand.

'I've got to warn you. It's all my fault. I should never have tried telepushy. I pray that St Absent the Regularly Forgotten will forgive my sinful . . .'

Suddenly two things happened almost simultaneously. The giant of a rock-roller reached for his flagon and for the first time noticed its marked absence. Achonite's hand jumped in alarm and scuttled along the bar in a bid for freedom.

'Oi! Gimme back my beer!' snarled the giant.

'. . . has enabled me to talk to you and save . . . uuurgh!' The flagon was a direct hit. It was followed a second later by the labourer's vast hands slamming into place around his neck and hoiking him off his stool. 'Gimme my beer!'

Achonite's cemetery voice echoed panic around the best part of a quart of ale, spluttering the words, 'Centaur Parcs . . . Beware!' It was the last thing he grunted before being hurled across the bar, bouncing on a table and skittering across the Gutter's floor to end in a crumpled heap in the corner.

J'hadd grinned sheepishly as he was rounded on. 'Gentlemen, please, ahem . . . allow me to reimburse you for . . .' He delved in his pocket, dropped a wad of groats on to the bar, scarpered through the door quick-sharp and kept on going towards the chapel. If *that* had been a joke by Commander Achonite, well – he didn't find it funny at all. All that fuss just to tell him that Gravure was in the Chapel of St Absent the Regularly Forgotten. Pah! Secretly Pious Constable J'hadd muttered a quick prayer to any Gods that might be listening to give Achonite a really stinking headache.

The Really Reverend Unctuous III shook his head and cursed as he snatched the gold-braid hair-net off his head and tried to stop his head from spinning. Beer! Horrible stuff! he thought with the taste of second-hand hops in his mouth. Why can't they drink communion wine like civilised people?

'Do be careful!' screamed Mrs Olivia 'Green' Beece as her enrainbowed warriors unloaded their liberated refugees from the cart. The planks creaked alarmingly as the huge crimson-smeared boulder was rolled on to a hastily requisitioned patch of the market square in Cranachan.

They arranged a plethora of placards around the boulder amid a hubbub of enthusiastic excitement and raised a huge attention-grabbing cheer as Mrs Beece hitched up her dark green overcoat, slapped her hand on the cart and vaulted up amongst the crimson stains. Surreptitiously she wiped her mould-smeared hand on the hem of her overcoat and hoped no one would notice. She was ready to make her point. Oh yes, everyone who was here in the market square whether it was to buy their weekly turnip or lay their hands on some cheap goat cutlets, *everyone* was going to be told about the shameful plight of the Variegated Crimson Jelly-Mould.

'People of Cranachan!' she yelled and pointed to the crimson-stained rock. 'Are you going to stand by and watch this slaughter? Are you willing to watch the destruction of one of your distant cousins? Are you . . .'

'You calling me a jelly-mould?' snapped one of the women wielding a large sack and a length of shopping parchment. 'How dare you stand there and call me a jelly-mould!' she bustled.

'I said nothing of the sort,' countered Mrs Beece. 'I was merely trying to show the extent of the cruelty . . .'

'I've got better things to do than stand around staring at crimson splattered rocks,' shouted the woman and scurried off towards the goat cutlet stall.

'Greed has ruined this entire . . .' shouted Mrs Beece gesturing wildly at the rock.

'What? Greed did that?' asked another woman armed with a host of shopping sacks.

'Yes!' shrieked Mrs Beece, wheeling round and fixing her with a sharp gaze as she pointed at the Centaur Parcs building-site. 'They have squeezed the very life out of that to line their own pockets with countless . . .'

'Must've squeezed mighty hard,' mocked another

shopper, nudging the woman next to her and winking. 'I ain't never seen anyone get that much blood out . . .'

'No, no!' shouted Mrs Beece above the peals of ribald amusement and hopping up and down on the cart. 'It's not the stone. It's the Variegated Crimson Jelly-Mould whose ecological niche has been . . .'

Unseen by Mrs Beece a few of her warriors had noticed something very odd happening at the Centaur Parcs site. Vast plumes of black and red smoke blasted skywards.

'Mould? She say mould? Euuugh!' blustered another shopper. 'That's not hygienic, is it? Especially with all this food about.'

'Don't you care about the environment?' shouted Mrs Beece, her fists clenching furiously as she ignored the tug of a hand on her overcoat hem.

'Can you eat it?' shouted a voice from the crowd. 'Not much use if you can't eat it.'

'No! We must preserve the ornate tapestry of nature's rich . . . what is it?' snapped Mrs Beece, staring down at the timidly tugging hand of a red-haired teenager sporting far too much forehead for her own good. Mutely she pointed at the massacred hilltop of Tor Khamada and the Centaur Parcs complex. Mrs Beece spun round and stared in acute horror at the growing plumes of smoke exploding skywards.

'No!' she screamed, 'they can't do that. The . . . the . . .' She fished around frantically inside her head for something, anything that would be endangered. 'The . . . ravings! Give me that placard!' In a flurry of olive-green overcoat and matching bobble-hat she sprang off the cart and fell upon the placard like an Ammorettan Death Lizard after a month of dieting. She scrubbed furiously at it with her sleeve, produced a stick of chalk from her pocket with a flourish and hauled the placard aloft a few moments later.

'Come on!' she cried, firing her troops up to complete picket-frenzy. 'We've got to stop them!'

In seconds she was muscling her way through the heaving Market Square, eyes blazing as hot as the fires of Helian, adrenaline surging as she waved her 'Save the Ravings!'

placard. This had gone too far. Killing moulds was one thing, but trying to inflict asthma, bronchitis and a whole host of other respiratory disorders on the entire population of the Talpa Mountains was really not on. Ravings had very sensitive lungs.

In the midst of a large scrubby forest on the banks of Lake Hellarwyl, to the west of Cranachan, something stirred. It paced restlessly around the inside its lair, slapping its vast flat paddle-shaped tail on the mud floor. Something wasn't right. It could sense it. It had a wife, two cubs and another litter on the way but . . . it just wasn't right.

Irritably, it tapped its powerful claws on the mud floor and ignored its largest cub gnawing at its left ear.

Unseen outside the confines of the creature's lair, a vast black and red cloud was gathering and spreading. Already, frustrated weather patterns were being muscled backwards across the sky and trade winds that had been established over countless generations, handing down their blustering franchises to son and grandson, building up a reliable following, even these were having their routes redirected by the brash, pushy, new clouds on the block.

The creature in its lair brushed his cub off its ear, made an incredibly discontented clucking sound through its two gravestone-shaped front teeth and ducked outside. With an expert flourish of its tail it vanished through the pool in the floor, pushed on through the passage and surfaced a few moments later in a large tree-lined pool. Three strokes of its tail and it had reached the edge of its very own dam.

The cloud spread ever further, casting an ever-expanding shadow over the vastness of the Talpa Mountains and pouring hundreds of degrees of heat into the air.

Clucking irritably once more, the creature hauled itself on to the wall of mud and sticks, built by its very own paws, and peered around. And then it knew why it was dissatisfied. When it'd finished its dam it had been so proud of it, it was the best in the colony, laced with gleaming spruce and fresh clay. But over the months it had been bringing up its cubs, tending to its wife and furnishing her with another set of offspring – that had been fun! – it had not been keeping an eye on its neighbours.

And now just take a squint at their dams.

It peered at them through aquatically rodenty eyes in a suddenly different and far from entirely rosy light. For the first time the beaver felt the bitter tang of acute jealousy. It had been left behind by its so-called friends. Well, it'd just see about that!

And in that moment it vowed by this time tomorrow it was going to have the biggest and finest dam in the whole colony. They would look up to it. They would want its dam . . . and they could go and whistle! With a splash, a flurry of waterproof fur and the desire for tree-trunk nibbling growing by the minute, it headed for the trees.

All around the colony other lodge-proud beavers were having similar, inexplicable thoughts of owning their very own vast acreage of envy-inducing dam.

Far below, Flagit giggled.

Pious Constable Slamm J'hadd slithered to a swift halt in the bowels of the Imperial Palace Fortress of Cranachan, knocked on the insignificant door of the Chapel of St Absent the Regularly Forgotten, folded his arms and waited. He would ride this out, rise above the infantile humour of the Black Guards, not let them see his quivering intestines begging for the return of his prisoner.

Hands slapped across grinning mouths, stifling roars of belly laughter. Teeth bit smirking lips, bottling bubbles of contained amusement. Faces leered from the opened door, childish victory writ large.

Surprisingly, none of it came.

Instead he was greeted by the cold, dark silence of a very empty chapel long unused to visitors' tootsies and totally devoid of anything even remotely associated with the Black Guard. It was the type of silence that always made J'hadd want to whisper nervously.

'Er, hello?' whispered J'hadd nervously.

The only reply he received was the skittering of ratty claws on shadowy stone.

So *that* was how they were going to play it, was it? A treasure hunt. How unimaginative!

He shrugged and, candle held before him at arm's length, began to scour the place; peering into the strangely pristine collection boxes; scrabbling behind the altar; ransacking the vestry. He even upended and shook every single hymn book hoping a scrap of self-congratulatory parchment would appear with a clue.

He found nothing. Well, not until his eyes locked on to the baffling array of unfathomable marks on the floor. In an instant desperation vanished without trace to be replaced by the screaming cacophony of the suspicion bells. Adrenaline-heightened awareness sucked images through dilated pupils, hoovering them into the dust-bag of his untidy mind, filtering, gathering. And staring in utter incomprehension. Okay, so it was a clue. But what did it mean?

He bent to have a closer look at this new evidence and found far more than he had expected. Lying face down under a pew where it had been hurled by flailing, panic-stricken arms in their last frantic moments on this mortal soil, there lay what looked like the type of tiny cheap parchment-back tome that the Scroll Club charge such ludicrous rates for. With a grunt J'hadd ferreted under the pew, tugged it into view and shone his candle over the gold-leaf lettering on the spine. He gasped in confusion as he read the title.

TEACH YOURSELF TELEPUSHY
Suggestive Mental Assertion in Twenty-Four Easy Lessons

A tiny clump of memory neurones scratched their collective selves and wondered where they had heard the word 'Telepushy' before. They were thoroughly ignored for J'hadd knew that here was the clue that the Black Guard had hidden. He grinned proudly, his face lighting up as he thought of how easily he had found it. Four hours. Piece of cake. Oh, he was officer material – Chaste Inspector here I come!

He opened the tome, placed his index finger under the first word and set to work cracking the fearsome code that simply *had* to be wrapped in its text.

'Congratulations on your choice of book and welcome to the future of almost limitless poss—'

. . . and there were three hundred and six more pages just like it. Oh boy.

Khar Pahcheeno sat behind a battered oak desk in one of his many warehouses on the edge of Cranachan and stared at the parchment list before him. It was a good list – eighteen dozen nine-inch stiletto heels, seventy-six bushels of finest whalebone corset stays, three hundred yards of the clingiest crimson leather, twelve cases of assorted whips, manacles and thongs – and that was just for the Chamber of Lust. There were another six lists like it. He had every item in stock in his warehouses (or readily swiped from someone else's, which was pretty much the same). He had the staff to load on to the carts and, most importantly for Khar Pahcheeno, he had a massive profit margin on absolutely everything, which would be generously tripled if he could deliver it all by tomorrow evening.

'How a-soon?' he squeaked in shock, staring desperately at Guthry. Well, at least his eyes stared, his mind was too busy watching countless groats winging their way out of reach.

'Shoot! I done said so. T'morree evenin', if you's'll be wantin' bonus.'

Khar Pahcheeno shook his head and stifled a tear of regret. Such a waste, all that money not going his way. It was so unfair! Sixteen forty-ton wagon trains at his disposal and more rhino fodder than you could shake a dozen sticks at and he couldn't complete a simple delivery to the Centaur Parcs site on time. He stared once again at the stack of parchments that was the 'Essential Provisions' List for the Chamber of Gluttony and his bottom lip trembled. The after-dinner mints alone would fill three carts. For two trips. The whole lot would take four days at least, working round the clock with the opposition's drivers hijacked at sword-point! He had to face it, it simply couldn't be done. Bye-bye triple-time bonus.

Guthry patted the lists significantly, grinned and skittered out of the warehouse. He didn't even slow down when a nine-year-old girl in a 'borrowed' dark blue jacket sprang out of a shadow and flashed him a questioning glance. He simply sprinted forward palm raised, jumped, slapped her five fingers and vanished with an evil wink.

That gesture said it all. Success! You got th'ball now girl. Go bag it! Go, go, go!

In the office of the warehouse Khar Pahcheeno stroked his pet rat and sobbed over the lost revenue, wallowing in a pit of deprofitability.

And then suddenly there was the sound of urgent footsteps slapping towards him at full sprint. 'Message for Mr Pahcheeno! Paging Mr Pahcheeno!' trilled the little girl in the blue uniform urgently, waving a tight roll of parchments.

The man in the jet-black suit held out his ostentatiously ringed hand, the roll dropped in and the page dashed off. It all happened faster than a world-record change in a sprint relay.

Pahcheeno blinked, wiped a moist eye and unravelled the parchments. Then he blinked again and stared at the complex diagram spread over the entirety of the sheet. He was stunned. It showed a crude but very recognisable sketch of a wagon train with a thick wax cross blotting out the haulage rhinos. On the next sheet was a series of parts, a whole complex array of calculations, pressure gauge read-outs and an illustration of a vast appendage bolted on to a rhinoless wagon train. On the next sheet was an exploded view of the device, parts linked by arrows in full orthographic projection.

Pahcheeno stared in utter bewilderment at the first-ever plans for an infernal combustion engine complete with catastrophic converter. Quickly, secretively, he rolled them up, grinned and sprinted off towards a mechanic who owed him a favour.

Unseen around a far corner, the page smirked, tugged off her peaked hat and 'borrowed' uniform and skipped off down the street: once more a red-nightdressed nine-year-old brimming with malevolence.

In the gloomily lit storeroom of the Transcendental Travel Company Ltd, Flagit sat back in his chair for a moment and allowed himself a self-congratulatory gulp of lava martini on the rocks and a cackle of satisfaction. Everything was going precisely as he had planned. Hyperheated smoke erupted gaily from the dome of Centaur Parcs; flames seared skyward from Spam Smith's infernal forge and the three dark satanic mills; a vast horizon-filling duvet cover of snuggly clouds spread ever more thickly above it all; minute by inevitable minute the temperature scrambled uncontrollably higher . . .

There were just a final few pressing matters that needed dealing with and his election victory would be totally complete. Well, how could Foul Lord d'Abaloh refuse him anything when he delivered the entire freedom of the upperworld? Especially at a perfectly delightfully balmy six hundred and sixty-six Fahrenheit.

He chuckled evilly and drained the last of his lava martini. Then checking his infernite lattice he reached out once more to the impressionable mind of Alea. Mental talons snatched at the tiny nine-year-old mind and blasted a host of final instructions into it – the last finishing touch of malevolent icing on a rich fruit-cake of ultimate evil.

Breaking contact with a scream of delight, he snatched the infernite lattice off his scaly head, mounted it on a length of No-glo string and stormed out of the door past the Demons' Institute Package Tour. The time had come to deal with matters a little closer to home.

Slamm J'hadd had scoured the entirety of the inside of the Chapel of St Absent the Regularly Forgotten a dozen more times looking for a hint of a clue as to how this telepushy tome could lead him to Gravure. He'd found nothing. And even after reading the thing cover to cover five times (once backwards) he was still clueless.

He knew that he had to be missing something, some diamond-like vital phrase buried in a slagheap of subtext, some code. It was either that or perhaps the clue was in the actual lesson. Was it possible that the only way he would find Gravure was by experiencing first-hand the awesome powers offered by telepushy? Could the answer only be uncovered by casting his brainwaves out across the surging seas of Suggestive Mental Assertion and there, bedraggled and parched on some distant cerebral shore, he would haul himself up the gleaming golden sand, open the chest and it would all be revealed in a blinding halo of truth?

Hmmm, beats scrabbling under pews again. Nothing to lose.

Shrugging his shoulders he flipped the book open at random, smoothed the palm of his hand across the spine and stared at the suggested mental exercise. In the chapter entitled 'Will Over Worms' he scowled at the section on 'Annelid Attraction', then shrugged non-committally. It seemed as good as any.

In fact, according to the paragraph at the top of the page, 'Annelid Attraction is a good all-round low-level telepushic procedure. Ideal for the beginner, or the keen-but-lazy fisherman who finds bait-hunting a chore, Annelid Attraction can give hours of harmless fun to even the most ardently serious of telepushic aficionados. So, try Annelid Attraction and watch those wrigglies come running!'

J'hadd read the operational procedure one final time, shut his eyes and began. He translated his every thought into a tiny bee, gave each wings and set them buzzing. He doused the walls of their hive with flames, melting its structure, tearing holes in its fabric and loosing his mind amongst the low-level mentality of the annelid worm. In moments his brow was wrinkling with the strain of concentration as he sent out concentric waves of mental urges, pulsing cerebral mind-waves which suggested that here, precisely where Slam J'hadd was now squatting, just here was the biggest pile of moist warm leaf-litter that any self-respecting worm would give its favourite body segments for.

He kept it up for hours, thoughtcasting on a single tight-beam wavelength without any distraction. As a first attempt at telepushy it was wonderful. Even old masters whose mental acuity and neuronal focusing ranked amongst the highest would have been proud of this effort of will.

But at the end of three hours' solid concentration, he opened his eyes and stared at the floor before him. Then he glanced around him looking for changes – a small piece of parchment here, a key there, a map with 'You are here' on it and an 'x' across Gravure's location. There was nothing. He tutted, scowled at the illustration in the book showing worms' heads poking eagerly out of the ground, glared again at the utter wormlessness of the expanse before him and, with a choice curse, hurled the book away across the chapel.

This had gone far enough. A joke is a joke, but when fourteen years of service to the RUC depended on it, and the entire foundations of Truth, Justice and the Cranachanian Way were being undermined by letting known war-mongers go free, it was time to get serious.

Slamm J'hadd bit his lip and snarled a tiny snarl. He stood, spun on his heel and stomped out of the chapel, fiercest determination raging through his spleen. It was about time that Achonite told him the truth!

Twelve and a half inches below the rapidly cooling spot of floor where J'hadd had been squatting, fifteen thousand annelid earthworms, ranging in size from one inch to nigh on a foot long, scrabbled and nosed frantically at the base of the chapel's foundations. And they were salivating.

They knew that just there above them was the biggest, moistest expanse of deliciously partially decomposed leaf-litter they could ever hope to lay their mouthparts on.

The Really Reverend Unctuous III fidgeted restlessly beneath the aging hull of a striking ferry and watched the Phlegethon slither malevolently by. Miserably he snatched at a nearby stone and hurled it towards the Phlegethon. It struck the surface, skipped once and disappeared in a gloop of steam. This was definitely not where he had expected trainee vicardom to lead. In fact, had anyone even hinted at the possibility that he would end up as an illegal immigrant in Helian, practising possessions left, right and centre and attempting to save the World, well, he would have laughed in their face. That was just not the type of thing clergymen got up to between services.

He probably shouldn't admit it, not even to himself, but secretly he was rather proud of the fact that he could actually possess people. Okay, so it wasn't the type of trick you should use at Papal Parties, but it hadn't half come in handy. Possession was, he decided, a necessary evil. Well, how else could he have warned them of the danger of Centaur Parcs?

Unctuous hurled another rock into the Phlegethon and suddenly realised that he really wasn't happy. He should be, but he wasn't. Somehow he had the sneaking suspicion that losing contact with Achonite in such a violent, and disturbingly airborne manner, wasn't the most effective method of warning people of the impending dangers of Centaur Parcs.

He had no choice. He definitely had to try again. But with whom? He'd tried a woodcutter's daughter, a nympho-maniac and a Commander in the Black Guard – and where had that got him? He needed a different approach. He needed someone whose voice would be heard by a faithful band of devoted followers, someone who was enthusiastic to levels above and beyond even the loudest calls of duty and above all he needed someone who was ever so slightly mad.

Now he only had one snag. Who could it possibly be?

He snatched at his gold-braid hair-net, slapped it on his head and tried for the thirtieth time in half an hour to raise some sort of response from anyone even remotely useful.

A hundred feet away, behind a stack of punitive boulders an infernite lattice spluttered into glowing radiance, twitched on the length of No-glo string and pointed to a spot directly behind the rotting hulk of an aging ferry. The glow lit a sneering scaly face for a second before a nine-foot monster leapt off its haunches and galloped forward.

Unctuous's brow furrowed and he screwed his face in intense concentration. He had to reach someone. He had to know.

'Cooeee, come in, anyone. Hello?'

'Hello,' barked a voice disturbingly close to his right ear. Unnervingly it seemed to display far more relish than Unctuous would have expected.

'Hello?' he whimpered and opened his eyes.

Nine feet of disturbingly familiar scaly black demon grinned for a second, then snarled, snatched Unctuous around the throat and sprinted wildly away with him tucked under his arm.

Flagit couldn't contain himself, he giggled uncontrollably as he clattered through the seedier streets of downtown Tumor, elbowing trudging souls out of the way and all the time staring out of madly mustard-rimmed eyes.

He had Unctuous back, the only bluebottle in the mayonnaise of his plan had been plucked out. Now there was nothing to stop him from total victory. Nothing!

'. . . that was no bacon tree. It was a ham-bush!' Yet another blast of raucous laughter exploded into the Gutter from the mob of pipe-rollers as the punchline was rammed home with far more drunken gusto than it warranted.

'Same again!' shouted Mahrley, the foreman, waving a wad of freshly earned fifty-groat notes at the barmaid. She leapt to it, gathering empty flagons and ramming them under the barrel of Hexenhammer. She also hurled yet another Twisted Lemming on to the bar for Maisy, who had somehow managed to wrap her buxom self around Mahrley's arm in as decorous a way as she could manage. 'That all, sir?' asked the barmaid, tearing her scowl of jealousy away from the fawning Maisy.

'Yeah, er, oooh no,' proclaimed Mahrley decisively as his eye fell on a small wooden box on the far side of the bar. 'Let's 'ave one o' them, too. I'm feeling flush tonight.' He pointed and Maisy's eyes lit up.

The barmaid handed him a single enormous cigar, stifling

a pang of jealousy as she handed over one of the most expensive bunches of leaves that money could buy – well, at least that money in the Gutter could buy. It was a Khuban Femur-rillo, hand rolled on the oiled inner thighs of nubile Khuban maidens. Each one cost the best part of one hundred groats.

'You gonna smoke that thing?' taunted one of the other pipe-rollers.

Mahrley nodded and the crowd erupted in whistles of mock admiration. 'Money's gone to his head!'

Maisy started to dribble. If there was one thing she really would do anything for, that was the smell of a Khuban Femur-rillo. She watched, whimpering and pouting as he held it up to his ear and listened as he rolled it slowly between his thumb and forefinger. Precisely why he did this he hadn't a clue, it was just the thing you did with Khuban Femur-rillos.

It was then that Maisy, the co-owner of Daisy and Maisy's Pleasure Parlor, saw the chance to do something that she had only ever dreamed of. It was the most extravagant flaunting of wealth that she knew of, an act that was only ever to be seen in 80mm Superthaumination at the local Magic Lantern Palaces. 'Allow me,' she crooned and pouted just a little deeper.

In a flash her hand lashed out, snatched a fifty-groat note from Mahrley's wad and curled it between her heavily painted fingers, just the way she'd seen the lantern goddess Fhulla Figha do. With a flourish she snatched the matches, struck one and held it up to the note.

'Oi! What are you . . . ?' For a second Mahrley's face flashed anger, then he caught sight of the look Maisy was giving him. The look that put him in mind of the infamous casino scene from last season's blockbuster *Groatfinger*. Maisy fluttered her eyelids, licked her lips, leaned closer and purred. And for a moment she looked exactly the way Ms Figha had. Mahrley grinned around his Femur-rillo and leaned forward. All those nights of practice pouting hadn't been wasted.

'Well all right then, darlin'. Go right ahead. It's only money,' crooned Mahrley, leering in a very poor impersonation of Rock Blurblurr. He knew the way that scene ended, all waves crashing suggestively on stormy shores. And so did the rest of the mob. They pressed forward eagerly, wolf whistling encouragement.

Mahrley grinned wider, the Femur-rillo trembling as he waited for Maisy to light the note and set the tip of his cigar smouldering with it. Somehow he found it remarkably exciting in a very naughty don't-ever-let-your-mummy-see-you-doing-it sort of way.

The flame of the match chewed cheerfully away at the stick, nibbling incendiary fangs closer to Maisy's delicately overpainted fingernails. Still Mahrley waited, his mind running barefoot towards the climactic, erotic, tension-building moment of the flame igniting the note, his entire focus of attention, as well as that of the rest of the mob, grabbed by the flaring yellow centre of destruction. Maisy touched the flame to the note and, with a squeak of alarm dropped the match, jamming her fingers in her mouth and looking hurt. The mob of pipe-rollers erupted in a fit of laughter and slurped away at their ale, the mood shattered. Maisy looked crestfallen, all her weeks of seductive practice blown. It shouldn't have happened like that. There wasn't a mark on the fifty-groat note.

Irritably Maisy snatched the note and struck a match beneath it. Nothing. She growled, tugged a hundred-groat note out of his wad and tried that. Not a scorch. 'Not fair!' she wailed. 'It won't light. How come it works in Super-thaumination?'

'Movie magic!' suggested one of the mob and was cuffed about the head by another.

Baffled now, almost as much as the rest of the mob, Mahrley snatched the matches, struck a couple of dozen and stared at the totally scorch-free notes. Incredibly he had failed utterly to burn any of the money they had just been paid with. Something was wrong.

'I know . . .' he began, and started rummaging frantically

258

in the bottom of his tunic pocket. After a few minutes' struggle and several bits of embarrassing-looking fluff, he tugged out a single battered five-groat note and was greeted with a wave of apathy. Instantly he noticed it felt different.

'Try this,' he said and handed it and the matches to Maisy.

'No, I . . .' she began, still nursing her finger.

'Try it,' he insisted, suspicions whirling inside his mind.

With a flick of her wrist that proclaimed how bored Maisy was with all this and wishing she had never thought of it in the first place, another match ignited and caught the note, torching it to a crisp with a shriek and a flash of carbon.

'Just as I thought,' snarled Mahrley and stood up, hurling his stool over behind him. 'Lads, we've been had!'

In that instant, not only was five groats and the vast majority of Mahrley's moustache consumed by fire, but so were the tempers of all the pipe-rollers massed around the bar. The word was out.

All around the rest of the Gutter small clumps of labourers could be seen attempting to torch their hard-earned . . . well what?

They'd been given something for their recent furious toils. And it wasn't money.

'What he goin' to do 'bout it?' snarled Mahrley. 'We goin' to let that damn dwarf get away with this, eh? Or are we goin' to rip his pathetic carcass limb from stinking' li—'

'Er, shouldn't we just tell the Black Guard about it?' asked a voice in the crowd. 'I mean, it's their job to solve . . .'

'Yeah, an' it's their job to charge for the privilege. There wouldn't be anythin' left by the time we got a look in. All be in their safe . . .' snarled a disgruntled voice in the mob.

'Get the dwarf!' came a shout of support.

'Get the Black Guard . . .'

Mahrley held up his hands. 'Get them both!' he shouted. 'Bring him!' He pointed at the crumpled form of Commander Achonite slouching in the corner and stomped towards the door. 'If nothing else we can use him as a battering ram.'

Maisy watched with a growing feeling of immense guilt as

the Gutter emptied, the labourers armed themselves with Achonite and stormed off in search of one dwarf called Guthry and a whole host of answers. Preferably bankable ones.

Just as the comatose figure of Achonite was hauled off towards Centaur Parcs, Pious Constable Slamm J'hadd screeched around the corner of the Gutter panting, questions fuming in his head. He whimpered desperately and sprinted off in hot pursuit.

'Well? Ees eet ready a-yet?' demanded Khar Pahcheeno as he swept into Ghaskitt's Engineering Yard and accosted the chief mechanic warmly by the throat.

'Sir, I . . .' spluttered the grease-splattered mechanic.

'Three and a half a-hours you said!' snarled Pahcheeno.

'Ah, well, that was an estimate wasn't it? Hit a few unforeseen snags when I started fitting the . . .'

'Ees that an excuse I a-hear?'

'Oooh, no, no, no,' he fidgeted with a pair of very large bamboo pliers and investigated his feet. 'It's . . . er, a reason.'

'How much a-longer?' growled Pahcheeno. 'Time ees expenseev! I want eet ready by a-dawn.'

'It'll be tight. It might take a while for your crews to get the hang of, er, to adjust to the new handling. It's a whole new way to travel,' admitted Ghaskitt.

'How do you a-know? What's deefferent?' blurted Pahcheeno, his eyes narrowing suspiciously as he squeezed Ghaskitt's throat a little tighter. 'You've got one feeneeshed, haven't you? One ees a-ready? Where? I want eet!'

'Few of the lads are out just giving it a last minute shakedown. Should be back any sec—'

Khar Pahcheeno didn't hear Ghaskitt's last few words. They were drowned in a vast roaring raspberry of belching smoke and noxious fumes as a forty-ton wagon train replete with full infernal combustion engine and catastrophic converter screamed into the yard and screeched to an abrupt halt. Clouds of black and yellow blasted skywards as the trainee mechanics tugged on levers, attempting unskilfully to calm the flatulent monster. It was, as Ghaskitt had said, a totally new way of yachting.

Pahcheeno couldn't believe his eyes. This was the answer to his dreams. With this he could make all the deliveries, with this he could travel. In short, there had never been anything like the infernal combustion engine. Well, not this far above the Phlegethon anyhow. It had been developed over countless centuries by one ferryman who, after becoming heartily sick of paddling souls through the sludgy gloop of the Phlegethon for millennia on end decided that there had to be a better way. There was. It was frighteningly simple and only involved the tiniest smattering of understanding of fluid dynamics.

Ask any avid hot-air balloonist and he'll tell you that if you heat air, it rises. Now, have you ever stopped to think about what replaces it once it's trundled a few feet higher? I mean, you can't have a hole left. It wouldn't be right, would it? Cold air scurries in to hold up the hot air and bingo! You've got wind. Stick a yacht in front of it and as if by magic you can go anywhere you want to if you direct the cold air inrush.

And so the basis of the infernal combustion engine was born. It had only been tweaked a bit from the original prototype, the air heating furnace had been expanded by about a thousand times and by slamming a catastrophic converter in front of it you could burn anything. Nowadays all ferryboats plying their trade across the Phlegethon, the Styx and even the Acheron were kitted out with infernal combustion engines.

There were only two major drawbacks. Unsurprisingly they produce a ton of heat and they crack most hydrocarbons to methane or some other really nasty complexes called 'Chthonic fumocarbons' or CFCs for short, strange gases that trap heat. Now with an ambient temperature of six hundred and odd degrees Fahrenheit to maintain, this isn't really a problem.

But in the comparatively arctic temperatures of the Talpa Mountains . . .

'I want a-da whole fleet kitted out by dawn!' screamed Khar Pahcheeno as he shovelled another load of prime alder into the catastrophic converter, fired up the infernal combustion engine and felt the suck of air batter against the back of his neck and push against the enormous sail. 'Dawn!' he squealed above the belching raspberry, released the handbrake and vanished out of the yard beneath a vast stinking cloud of chthonic fumocarbons.

Giant plumes of hyper-heated black and red smoke roared unstoppably into the once drizzle-filled talpine sky, swelling the vast cloud spreading like a deadly slime mould towards the horizon. And with every gaseous belch, the temperature rose. Already there were aerial casualties. Several ravings, three dozen Noleff Terns and a flock of extremely baffled cliff tits had passed out from heatstroke after flying too close to the fumes.

Sweating profusely and panting from the three-mile dash up to Centaur Parcs, Mrs Olivia 'Green' Beece led her enrainbowed warriors to the top. Suddenly she stopped, her jaw swinging open in horror.

'What is it?' panted Spruce, her second in command.

She choked, pointed desperately skywards and all eyes watched as a solitary bird swooped uncontrollably towards the spreading blanket of chthonic fumocarbons.

'Larch, Bindweed, Privet, follow me!' yelled Spruce, snatching a blanket from his pack. In a second four of the faithful band leapt into action, sprinting towards the tumbling body of the latest heatstroke victim. A hundred feet above certain death the screeching bird flapped limply, wiped its fevered brow with the back of its wing and fainted with the heat.

Mrs Beece shrieked as the bird suddenly gained all the aerodynamic panache of a feather pillow. Full of bricks.

'Faster!' she choked. 'Run!' Her faithful assistants scattered, tugging the blanket tight, dashing desperately hither and yon beneath the plummeting bird, like a fire team beneath a suicide jumper.

Barely a second later Spruce grabbed the limp bird. Privet's hand shot skywards as a flock of harfinches was engulfed in a plume of choking smoke and took a flap nearer to an almost certain rocky demise.

Mrs Beece cooed and clucked as she cradled the incredibly rare Hanbreak Tern, beak open, panting, its eyes rolling in the grip of another hot flush. As she fanned it with her battle bob-cap she determined there and then to put a stop to this ecological disaster. Somehow.

But it was already too late to prevent a hailstorm of harfinches. With a shriek of horror she lay the Hanbreak Tern carefully on a rock and turned her attention to the tumbling pink and green birds.

'Don't just stand there!' she yelled to her faithful band as she saved three in her cap, swooping them to safety inches above the ground. She leapt desperately for others, arm outstretched, squealing with relief as she cupped her fainted feathered friends in her diving palms. And all around her others were doing the same.

In a matter of minutes a heap of five hundred gasping harfinches, ravings and Noleff Terns littered the ground, their tiny tongues licking feebly at the rapidly heating air.

Away across the far side of Lake Hellarwyl a dozen spruce trees were being set about by a host of impatiently champing incisors. Fragments of woody flesh sprang in all directions as more and more beavers joined the throng, felling entire copses and dragging the trunks feverishly towards their very own dams. It was a hive of overactivity. Paddle-shaped tails slapped waterproofing mud up ever-expanding acres of enclosed shallows. Rivulets were re-directed into dead-end pools. All across the far side the beaver colony spread, matching the inexorable expansion of the vast black and red cloud banking above Centaur Parcs.

And as the cloud expanded, so came the heat, a dry baking sulphurous heat pushing up the ambient tempera-ture with terrifying speed. In the shallows of the ever-swelling beaver dams, leaf-litter sank and was pounced on by suddenly frisky algae and bacteria.

In the gradually warming pools of rapidly stagnating water, bubbles of methane began to rise, break surface and float towards the spreading cloud of chthonic fumocarbons.

Flagit bounded up the steps of the strata-scraper two at a time, his cloven hooves echoing on the hard stone. The Reverend Unctuous struggled wildly beneath his armpit but to no avail, resistance was utterly useless. In three giant bounds Flagit was at the top of the staircase, kicking open the door to the Transcendental Travel Company Ltd, checking there was nobody about and blustering into the storeroom. He flung Unctuous across the room snarling and sneering jubilantly, scowling briefly at the heap of pipes stacked in the corner. Damn those engineers, why'd they have to be so untidy. He cursed, spat and rounded once again on Unctuous.

'Nice try, Rev,' he mocked. 'Ten for effort. Shame it won't amount to much. Ha! Now there's nothing to stop me. Nothing! And even if there was it's too late. I am going to hand it all over to d'Abaloh and reap my just rewards. A place at his right claw, a pad in all the plushest volcanoes and all the lava martinis I can drink! Oh yes, very, very soon I'll be in charge!' Casually he hurled Unctuous' gold-braid net on to the back of an obsidian chair.

Flagit scowled meaningfully at Unctuous but instead of inflicting more fear in the Reverend's heart, it was his mood of excessive arrogance that dropped a few notches as he saw the unnerving expression. 'What?' he snarled, 'Have I got brimstone on my chin or something? What are you grinning at?'

Unctuous grinned wider. 'Nothing to stop you, eh? You absolutely one hundred per cent totally positive about that, hmmm?'

'What?' growled Flagit. 'What you on about? Course I'm sure!' he blustered. 'Your fate and the fate of the entire world is completely in my talons!'

Unctuous couldn't resist it. He knew that boasting was sinful, but he didn't suppose it really mattered any more. 'Oh, so you won't be interested in the name Achonite, then?'

Flagit looked blank, unsure what reaction to have. He was talking to a vicar – he wouldn't be lying, would he?

Unctuous grinned. 'Never heard of Commander "Black" Achonite of the Black Guard?'

Flagit's jaw dropped a fraction of an inch.

'Well, he's heard of you and your half-baked plan!' Unctuous knew that wasn't strictly true, but he thought it would sound better than 'Well, he sort of knows that Centaur Parcs isn't the friendliest of places and is being dragged there in a stupor.'

'They're on their way, even now, to destroy it and you!' shouted Unctuous.

That was it. Flagit had heard enough. It could be true, could be just a steaming pile of lies. He couldn't take the chance. Not now. Not with it all to lose.

With a terrifying turn of speed Flagit sprang across the storeroom, snatched his infernite lattice off the obsidian desk and jammed it firmly between his horns.

'J'hadd! J'hadd! Come in J'hadd . . .'

Unctuous saw his only chance and shrieking wildly he grabbed it. Where he got the acceleration he would never know, but somehow he sprinted forward, snatched his net off the back of the chair and dived at the pile of pipes. It was a perfect leap, with only the slightest winding he disappeared inside and squirmed deeper.

Flagit erupted with fury, lurching across the storeroom in four strides and thrashing wildly with his claws.

Unctuous screamed as talons scraped on metal scant inches from his toes and Flagit roared deafeningly. 'You fool! There is no escape! I have won. I have won!'

And suddenly he started hurling empty pipes around the storeroom, a stygian exterminator after a terrified Reverend rodent.

Mrs Beece was flapping a desperate fan over a heap of

panting harfinches and attempting to convince herself that things couldn't possibly get any worse, when, as if on cue, they did.

Vast tracts of thick smoke billowed over the horizon, advancing towards her from Cranachan. Moments later, accompanied by a heavy rumbling, eight forty-ton wagon trains sprang over the horizon each sporting a single enormous sail and a vast chimney spewing chthonic fumo-carbons in all directions. Mrs Beece's jaw dropped, convinced that her sanity had upped its skirts and fled. She stared bewildered at the rapidly approaching wagon trains speeding up the hill without hide nor hair of a rhinoceros anywhere to be seen.

Then she caught sight of Khar Pahcheeno proudly yelling directions to Magnus the cart-driver like some deranged figurehead and with a jolt of alarm realised they were heading directly for her heaps of helpless birds. Screaming desperately over the cacophonous raspberries of the infernal combustion engines she sprinted forward, waving her arms wildly above her head. The wagons thundered unstoppably on, devouring the distance as avidly as the catastrophic converters ate the fuelling mountains of peat. Mrs Beece rolled up her sleeves, snatched a placard off the ground, held it aloft and continued her dash, screaming at the top of her voice and wishing she'd taken off her organically knitted tank-top. A river of sweat torrented down her back.

Five yards from a disastrous collision Pahcheeno spotted the unmistakable green battle bob-cap surging forward on intercept course. He yelled a barrage of wild instructions to Magnus the carter and leapt for the mast. Huge biceps tugged on the wheel, slewing the forty-ton monster sideways in a sod-spitting curve, missing Mrs Beece and a clump of cliff tits by extremely scant inches. In less than a minute the other seven wagon trains had clattered by on either side, splattering the screaming woman with muddy turf and blasting her with plumes of hot choking smoke. Miraculously, the whirring wheels somehow missed the panting avian piles.

But they were far from out of danger.

Thousands of feet above their gasping beaks, the duvet effect of the clouds belching through the vents of Centaur Parcs continued to rise, mixing with chthonic fumocarbons, pushing up the temperature minute by sweltering minute.

'My birdies!' squawked Mrs Beece, dashing frantically between heaps of panting harfinches with a battered fan, her feet squelching in sweat-drenched boots. Above her, another Noleff tern cawed plaintively, passed out and plummeted soilwards in a flat spiral. Dripping sweat Mrs Beece pointed desperately skywards and kicked a clump of four gasping campaigners into life, sending them off with a catch blanket.

At her feet a tiny cliff tit flapped pathetically, looking forlornly up at her and licking its dry beak. 'Oh, my poor birdy!' she cooed, scooping the scrap of life up into her mud-splattered arms. 'Why here?' she wailed skywards in overly melodramatic style and fell heavily to her knees. 'If only there was some way to save my birdies. If only there was water!'

'Er, there is,' muttered a wiry youth lying on the ground close to heat exhaustion.

'What?' shouted Mrs Beece rounding on him. 'Water, where? And don't say under my armpits!'

'I . . . er, I don't know why I didn't think of it before,' croaked Bracket Fungus and licked his lips with a thick sound as he ignored Mrs Beece's vast oxters and thought of clean liquid. 'There is in fact a vast excess of water in the very near vicinity.'

With one hand cradling the cliff tit in caring gentleness, she wheeled around, snatched the youth firmly by the throat and barked, 'Where, dammit! My birdies need it!'

Pathetically, he pointed up and over a small hillock. 'Just up and over that small hillock,' he croaked. 'Lake Hellarwyl, the biggest expanse of fresh water to be found anywhere within the Talpa Mountains.'

Mrs Beece's glistening face lit up with joy.

Bracket Fungus grinned and offered, 'Er, I feel certain

that it may hold sufficient water for our feathered friends' cooling requirements.'

'Yes, yes!' shrieked Mrs Beece, panting rapturously.

'No one is certain precisely how deep the lake is and . . .'

Given any more encouragement he would have launched into a full two-hour diatribe outlining Lake Hellarwyl's false bottom, the legends about the various monsters that are said to dwell in its peat soiled depths and would have rounded off with a comprehensive list of sightings of the monster delving back over three hundred years, but he was swiftly set upon by Mrs Beece, bound, gagged and shoved out of sight behind a suitable bush.

Then she sprang soggily to her sweating enwellingtoned feet, sloshed three paces in the direction of the lake and stopped. Her faithful warriors halted in a shower of perspiration and stared at her, baffled.

'It's no use, Spruce!' she wailed, tears joining the flood of sweat racing towards her chin. 'Oh, fates, why deal me such a blow?' She stared at the sea of expectant faces. 'My birdies are doomed. Doomed! Leave them here and heat exhaustion will claim their tiny fragile lives. Carry them to the lake and they shall surely drown! Oh, woe, what a situation!'

'Er, what about if you had lots of buckets?' suggested a voice in the crowd.

Mrs Beece shook her head. The front row of the crowd wiped their faces. 'Get real! Where are we going to get enough buckets at such short notice? Nothing could get them here fast enough . . .' She stopped in mid-sentence, searching for something she knew she had in the forefront of her mind. Her eyes landed on a series of deep wheel-marks scoring the cracking ground. Suddenly her face exploded with determined delight as a plan snapped into place.

'You, you and you, follow me,' she shouted, the fire of action and inspiration burning in her eyes. 'You, grab this,' she barked at a bewildered follower as she tossed the gasping cliff tit in his direction. 'And the rest of you,' she shouted. 'Keep my birdies cool. I'll be back!'

In a flurry of green tank-top and wellies she was gone,

sprinting across the Tor, Spruce, Bindweed and Privet trailing frantically behind. It was a desperate idea, but it might just work.

Whistling tunelessly, Alea skipped up a small country track. It was difficult, she had recently discovered, to whistle in tune whilst wearing a sneer of malevolent mischief. But she didn't let this bother her in the slightest. She had already found that cows wouldn't know perfect pitch if it hit them in the teeth, and if they weren't bothered, then she certainly wasn't.

She reached the edge of a field, snatched hold of the rattly gate and vaulted cleanly over, hardly missing a quaver of the loose tune slipping between her lips. In a flash she had unfastened the top of a small pouch containing a yellowish powder and was generously sprinkling it hither and yon as she skipped a circuitous route between the unsavoury brownish disks that always seemed to follow cows around. She had stepped in one once, and that was more than often enough, thank you.

Barely slowing down she leapt over the far gate and was off to the next field of cows.

And even before she was out of whistling distance, a herd of large bovine tongues had discovered how remarkably pleasant the odd yellowish powder tasted, and. too late, found that it didn't really agree with any of their multiple stomachs. Etiquette took an embarrassed back seat as vast harrumphs of warm methane erupted uncontrollably from every beefy backside and floated up to join the great gaseous duvet in the sky.

Fortunately for the furious band of irate pipe-rollers storming towards the half-mile security fence of Centaur Parcs the air temperature at ground level was merely sweltering. They arrived at the gates of Centaur Parcs beneath a dense cloud of abuse and their tempers, as well as most of the rest of their bodies, were steaming furiously. Slamm J'hadd, eager to get some answers from Commander Achonite, struggled over the horizon and stopped dead in his tracks. The mob sprinted joyously on, brandishing their non-flammable hundred-groat notes and shouting.

J'hadd stared at the scene ahead of him and suddenly realised that something was most definitely up. And that something was a boiling black and red whirlwind of densely cavorting atmospherics, spitting shafts of fork lightning in all directions in meteorological mayhem. Rain tumbled out of huge cloudbanks, boiled off and evaporated before his very eyes. Now, meteorology really wasn't his strong suit, but he had a bit of a feeling that weather just shouldn't do that.

And then, in a knee-trembling revelation it struck him. No doubt about it, he was staring, face to fumarole, at an exact five thousand times enlargement of a page from the Vulgate Bible, in full glaring colour and in totally roaring, bubbling surround sound. He screamed and very nearly wet himself as the full meaning of the terrifying panorama slammed home and knotted his guts into the type of intestine macrame a medical craft fayre would be proud of. Somehow, five thousand times smaller, in two dimensions and fading colours, the End of the World hadn't looked quite as scary.

The words from the Vulgate spun wildly out of the memory of his RUC training and yammered into his ear-lobes.

. . . and smoke and lytenyng and thunder from ye Underwyrld shallst smyte mountains and blocketh out ye sun and yt'll get mighty hot and people won't lyke yt mutch, you'll see.

Ahead of him the pipe-rollers swarmed angrily towards the perimeter fence of Centaur Parcs. J'hadd struggled with terror and sprinted after them. They had to be warned! Nobody gets off lightly after stomping angrily up to The Gates of Helian and attempting to demand their money back.

Frantically trying to unknot his intestines so he could at least trot a bit, J'hadd stood, winced and struggled towards the End of the World.

270

Behind him a host of twenty-five thousand earthworms broke through the soil, blinked, squinted about for a juicy pile of leaf-litter that they had been certain was just here and sensed, in their own wormy way, that it was running away. That way. Quick. Come on.

Three seconds later a small patch of soil was pushed away by two shovel-shaped claws and a large pointed nose was thrust into the air. Two tiny, almost blind eyes peered about and looked immensely disappointed. Salivating messily the mole sniffed around, got a bearing and burrowed off in search of the biggest feast of earthworms ever to be seen in this neck of the woods, ever.

'Guthry!' screamed Mahrley, pounding his wad of hundred-groat bills angrily on the gate and wiping a river of sweat off his brow. 'Oi, dwarf, get your lying carcass out here, right now! I want some answers.'

It was far from being the most subtle of diplomatic opening gambits: the mob loved it, whooping and roaring wild support. Mahrley was always good in a dispute, he never used fancy words when plain honest-to-goodness insults would do. Nobody ever called a pipe a conduit in his earshot and lived.

'Guthry,' bellowed Mahrley. 'Oi, scarhead, get out here!' Another roar of approval.

J'hadd scratched his head as he sprinted into earshot. Scarhead? he thought, strange name for a dwarf.

A chant of 'Scarhead, Scarhead' rippled around the mob, gaining support and growing in volume. And then, abruptly, it hushed.

Through the slits in the high-security fence a body could be seen climbing wearily into the tiny crow's nest that overlooked the fence and the mob. 'Scarhead, Scarhead!' shouted the pipe-rollers again, trying to sound intimidating and all the while looking to Mahrley to sort all this out and get them paid in real, burnable money. It was hard to sound intimidating when you were so hot.

Seven fuming pillars of smoke continued to blast skywards through the dome of Centaur Parcs.

'Hurry up, Guthry! Get a move on,' jibed Mahrley moments before the figure stood in the crow's nest and stomped forward.

'What d'you lot want? You're not needed any more. Go away,' bellowed the hulking mass of Spam Smith from the crow's nest.

At the back of the crowd Slamm J'hadd screeched to a shocked halt and gulped. Even at this distance he could see the basketwork scars around his head. But he looked too big to be a dwa—

'Don't want work. We want the dwarf!' bawled Mahrley.

The dwarf's got scars too? J'hadd's mind whirled with the revelation. Something looked terribly familiar about that figure in the crow's nest.

'Ask nicely,' challenged Spam Smith with a wicked glint in his eye.

'No! We don't have to. We've got the Black Guards on our side,' yelled Mahrley angrily and the still comatose body of 'Black' Achonite was dragged forward like some pathetic mascot. 'And he wants to see the dwarf!'

'Tough. He's not in,' growled Spam Smith, turned on his heel and vanished behind the fence again.

The mob erupted, in anger and plumes of perspiration, chanting madly and hurling a hammering hail of rocks at the fence. A pair of blackened smith's fingers waved over the top, inflaming the tempers of the crowd even further.

Slamm J'hadd noticed none of it. He stood, trembling as the truth of his memories came screaming out of the sky and cannoned into the sudden revelations and exploded. He suddenly knew where he'd seen that smith before. Upside down with a knife in his side, swinging grotesquely whilst he banked up the forge. J'hadd whimpered as he stared at the burns on his hands. Memories of a dwarf assaulted him, too. Bubbles . . . cold water . . . his hands around the neck . . .

And all three of them were linked by one common factor. The cat-gut scars across the forehead.

Somehow he felt that talking to Commander Achonite right now might not be a good idea.

Mahrley was the first to realise that after the almost constant hail of stones the security fence was completely unmarked. After smashing half a ton of rocks at it he would have expected to see at least a slight scratch, or a teensy-weensy dent. There was nothing.

'Damn those smiths,' he snarled. 'Too efficient for their own good! But fear not. I have a canny plan to get our money back! Follow me, men!'

In a flash he stomped away towards the three dark satanic mills, growling and calculating trajectories, vector angles and how much force he could get out of various things readily available in your average, everyday smithy.

Several feet below Slamm J'hadd's feet twenty-five thousand eager worms squirmed forward, totally convinced that they were heading towards the finest example of heavenly leaf-litter ever. A few yards behind them a particularly ravenous mole's nostrils twitched and leapt for joy. Worms, thousands of them! With a desperate shove of claws into soil the mole dug off in hot pursuit.

'There is no escape!' shrieked Flagit, wrenching another pipe off the rapidly diminishing heap and flinging it across the storeroom. Unctuous trembled, clutching his telepushy net to his chest like a rosary. If he didn't act soon and escape from this pipe then that demon's words would become horribly true.

Suddenly talons plunged out of the sky, clamped on to the pipe and tugged. Unctuous' circular view spun as Flagit upended it and shook angrily. For a second the Reverend glimpsed hooves, the stone floor and knew it was time for action. Before Flagit realised what was happening, Unctuous erupted from the pipe, sprang between his legs and sprinted for a large conduit protruding from the wall and vanished inside.

Flagit screamed as his captive disappeared into the inaccessible interior of the unfinished air-conditioning system. 'Come out! There is no way out!

'And there's no way in, either,' taunted Unctuous, fighting

an attack of claustrophobia. Behind him he could hear Flagit raging and hurling anything hurlable that came to claw. Despite his bravado he knew it would only be a matter of time before the demon found a way in. He had to act fast.

With a flash of gold braid Unctuous jammed his telepushy net on to his head, slapped his eyes shut and tried to block the sound of Flagit's temper tantrum out of his ears. This would be his last chance to get the message through, so what did he need? A big mouth and an eager audience.

Somehow holding down a mounting wave of panic, Unctuous unleashed his swarming telepushic bees.

The beavers of Lake Hellarwyl had known it to be hot. Once. There was the summer three years ago when, for the first time in countless decades the curtains of north-westerly drizzle had drawn back, stopped and the sun had squinted myopically through, beaming on to their densely furry backs. For a day or two it had been glorious, basking cheerfully on the dam walls and flopping into your own private pool if it got too much. Hot, but never anywhere near this bad.

It was even getting too much for the swarms of mosquitoes that had seemingly sprung up from nowhere.

The beavers lay flaked out, panting and exhausted after the wild frenzy of dam improvements. For the first time in the history of beaverkind, their paddle-like tails were actually sweating. And it was no better in the pools. Where the heat was coming from they hadn't the foggiest, but then the average level of thermodynamic knowledge and understanding of heat transfer wasn't very high amongst beavers; but they knew it wasn't any cooler in the water.

And all around them bubbles surged relentlessly surfacewards. Every ten-degree rise in temperature doubled the rate of enzymic activity. Methane producing algae and bacteria chomped and digested their collective way through the tons of biomass on the dam floor, gleefully turning carpets of leaves into a thickening blanket of cosy, heat-trapping gas floating rapidly upwards.

*

274

Away across the Underworld Kingdom of Helian on a relatively peaceful section of the banks of the River Styx there squatted a vast pink palace complete with ornamental gardens, landing pad and stables. In the whole of Helian this was unique. This palace was the only structure to have been entirely built from rocks. Everything else had been carefully hollowed out of the very living strata using teams of carefully guided stalag-mites. It wasn't lack of space that made the strata-scraper so popular, it was simply the easiest way to 'build' them. Once hollowed out, droves of infernal internal decorators would swarm in and fit lava-lamps, underfloor heating, everything for a modern Mortropolitan Lifestyle.

And that had been where Foul Lord d'Abaloh had started as a young and eager demon. What he didn't know about Fissure-Fix crack filler, or the correct way to fit roar-bolts just wasn't worth knowing. He had memorised all of the manufacturers' instructions and price lists and was all set for a whole string of promotions. And then he had noticed the way of life enjoyed by higher ranking Sinful Servants and suddenly he was faced with a choice of doing a job he enjoyed and being paid a measly few obuls, or hating his job and living in the lap of luxury. With exquisite self-determination he chose the latter and set about greasing his way to the top. No palm was left uncrossed, no ego left unmassaged, no underdog left unstamped on in his frantic flight to the higher echelons. And now here he was in his pink palace, his pride and joy. Built by his own claws to an incredible profit since he had hired himself to do the job and paid himself out of the housing allowance for Rulers of the Underworld.

But today he was less than happy. The sound of deadly manicured talons drumming on diamond inlaid obsidian table top rattled around the inside of the palace. It was followed by a heavy grunt of extreme frustration and a roar of annoyance as, for the hundred and twelfth time that hour d'Abaloh lost at patience. Snarling and muttering a host of deadly oaths he snatched up the marble cards, shuffled them and dealt again.

It was obvious to anything within a hundred yards that

something other than patience was on d'Abaloh's seething mind. That something was his forthcoming trip to Mortropolis. He was looking forward to it with as much eager relish as a front fang removal. Without anaesthetic. Just the thought of pushing through the pressing throngs of Mortropolis's heaving creatures, the squeezing claustrophobia of them all, made his skin crawl. Was it all worth it? Such discomfort so he could preside in judgement over who should be 'elected' Undertaker-in-Chief for Mortropolis.

Well it would take a lot to bribe him this time.

He stood quickly, whirled to the left, kicked open a pair of enormous granite doors and pounded out into the gardens. Echoes turned to regular crunchings as he strode along the marble chip paths snaking between the acres of tightly cropped ornamental lichens. Above his crowned horns the dark, brooding atmosphere of Helian throbbed with heat and evil, emphasising the fragile innocence of a clump of mother-in-law's tongues and red hot pokers waving beneath a vast cooling fan.

In a few seconds he smashed open the door to the stables, stamped inside and was greeted by a deafening roar of affection.

'Saddle her up! Fast!' bellowed d'Abaloh to the stable demon and turned to the affectionately roaring creature in the stall. It flapped its thirty-foot wings eagerly and sent eddies of lichen bedding blasting everywhere. D'Abaloh scratched the dactyl's horned nose and casually held out a few chunks of coal-treats, dropping them on to Harpy's steaming crimson tongue with a flourish. The dactyl wagged its pair of tails rapturously and dislodged a few loose stones.

Grunting, the stable demon struggled out of the tackle room beneath a mound of straps, buckles and stirrups and staggered uncertainly towards Harpy. The beast roared cheerfully as it recognised the saddle, knowing instantly what it meant. It had been too long since she had been out for a quick hack about the place. Far too long. Especially on such a gorgeous day – clear, black sky as far as the eye could see.

An entire bucket of coal-treats was devoured in the time it took for the stable demon to fit Harpy's saddle. Then d'Abaloh took her reins, snatched at a large lever and opened the roof doors. Harpy whinnied and looked up at the widening expanse of miasmic black and red, aching for the feel of fire and brimstone beneath her air surfaces.

The doors clicked open and locked, d'Abaloh dashed forward, scrambled up Harpy's proffered leg and with a final spring settled himself in the saddle, making certain his tail wasn't tangled in the stirrups. And then, with the balletic grace of a rhino's *pas-de-deux*, Harpy fell into the air. Thirty-foot wings smashed downwards blasting lichen bedding hither and yon, and she lifted her six legs from the stable floor.

In five vast wingbeats she was clear of the roof, wheeling round and heading off for Mortropolis.

As if in direct competition to the constant belching of smoke from the Centaur Parcs vents, the hammering, banging, sawing and yelling of orders had been going on non-stop for hours. Every so often the massive doors of the dark satanic mills would be tugged open and a frantic figure would perform a lightning raid on the laden wagon trains waiting outside the security fence, snaffling various bits and pieces whose function could only be guessed at. Over the last three hours four carts, a waterwheel, five dozen of the Gutter's finest barrels and a very large bathtub had vanished inside to be greeted by shrieks of delight and a renewed cacophony of hammering, banging, sawing and yelling of orders.

But they weren't the only things to have arrived. The word had spread. Now everybody in Cranachan knew that the countless groats flooding in from the Centaur Parcs wages department were not, and never had been, the most legal of tender. Right now an enormous crowd of intensely irritated Cranachanians was seething around the perimeter fence, dribbling sweat and hurling rocks or insults as the mood took them.

Scuffles and sweat rashes were breaking out all over,

market traders accusing blacksmiths of deliberately buying thirteen pounds of sprouts with counterfeit money; card sharks knifing poker-faced punters who had gambled and lost; surf accountants piling the pressure on desperate debtors from the boxer shrimp leagues. Temper and temperature flared and soared respectively.

Suddenly there was a fanfare of grating doors from the satanic mills, a series of straining grunts and a vast device rumbled into the twilight gloom that passed as daylight beneath the ever-expanding duvet of chthonic fumocarbons. All eyes were suddenly on the emerging thing, baffled by the look of expectant victory on the face of Mahrley strutting proudly before it. It had eight wheels down each side, a huge hinged pole in the middle and a vast bathtub strapped to the far end. Just behind the hinge complex springs, knocked together from the straps of the barrels, strained against the tension applied by the rope which tugged from the bath down to the waterwheel. Hand-hurled stones hadn't dented the high-security fence, it was about time to see what a little mechanical advantage would produce. The crowd cheered and perspired as the makeshift catapult was hauled into position and eager hands wound hard on the waterwheel, dragging the bathtub down against the creaking barrel-springs. Rocks from all around were hurled into the tub, filling it in a matter of seconds. Under Mahrley's instruction it was lined up on the gate of the perimeter fence. Once breached they could get their hands on that dwarf and demand their real money. Or so the plan went.

An avenue of bare ground appeared between the catapult and the fence.

'Two more turns,' shouted Mahrley. 'Wind it in.' He wanted maximum power output from the catapult, he wanted that gate ripped off its hinges in a tangle of twisted metal and cheering applause. And he wanted it first time. Wood, metal and rope creaked in a symphony of increasing tension. The huge hurling arm bent and quivered, vibrating like a violinist with almost terminal first-night nerves. Mahrley raised his thumb and everybody backed away leaving him standing proudly by the catapult, the release lever clutched firmly in hand. All eyes were upon him. This was his moment of glory. He couldn't resist a few words of encouragement to the adoring crowds. Well, the occasion did warrant it. And besides, he wouldn't get another chance like this.

'Ladies and gentlemen, in five seconds I shall pull this lever and that fence will come crashing down. Please don't forget who is doing this. For all your plumbing needs call me, Mahrley for pipes. Showers are on special offer! Five!' he yelled and raised an encouraging hand.

'Four.' A few children joined in. 'Three,' bawled Mahrley.'Two,' answered the crowd. 'One!' screamed everybody. Then he pulled the lever. With a resounding 'twanng' the straining tension was released, there was a 'whoosh' as the arm was snapped upward, it arced to apex, flashed past its zenith and slammed into the ground, lifting the multi-wheeled base and hurling Mahrley twenty feet into the air.

Sadly his unplanned flight took Mrs Beece's blanket catchers totally by surprise.

'Not t'worry lads,' shouted Mahrley weakly from the ground. 'Back to the mills with it, I know just the thing to make it work!' Half a dozen pipe-rollers trudged forward and dragged him off after the catapult.

It was beginning to look like a taxidermist's paradise on the remains of the grass beyond the Centaur Parcs security fence. Countless hundreds of birds lay in clumps on their sides, sorted neatly into species by the enrainbowed warriors. The only movement of the heatstricken victims was the occasional pathetic flap of a wing and the constant desperate panting of dry tongues on beaks.

And it was getting worse, minute by minute more arrived, straining the now topless catchers and anyone with anything even vaguely fan-like to the limits of endurance.

If something didn't happen soon, there would be casualties.

279

'And you can shut up!' snarled one of the warriors as the wiry figure of Bracket Fungus, bound and gagged beneath a suitable bush began to wriggle and squirm desperately, trying to speak. 'Shut up, I said.' But there was something in the tone of Bracket Fungus's grunt that made him tug down his gag.

'She's coming!' he yelped. 'I had my ear to the ground, listen!' And sure enough there was a rumbling and a wild cacophonous raspberry of infernal combustion engine. Spirits rose as Mrs Beece sprang over the horizon on the front of the stolen wagon train, wind battering her as she brandished buckets joyously in each hand.

'I have return— Stop!' she managed to scream as the forty-ton cart thundered uncontrollably past the waiting ecological stormtroopers. Spruce threw it into a sharp turn, shutting off the infernal combustion engine and slewing it around wildly. Buckets and sods of turf showered out in a vast arc and the wagon thundered back at a barely diminished velocity.

'Grab a bucket!' shrieked Mrs Beece as she screamed past again.

It took fifteen more passes before the wagon train ran out of momentum and spluttered to a halt.

'Everyone. Grab a bucket!' she shouted at the top of her voice and untied Bracket Fungus.

In seconds he was clipped around the ears, told not to interrupt and listen and finally sent off towards the Lake. A string of eager soldiers of fauna tagged along, sweating but keen.

Mrs Beece shrieked with delight as she chivvied her minions into action, blindly handing out buckets to anyone who showed even the slightest interest.

'You!' she yelled forcefully at Slamm J'hadd who had just happened to glance bewilderingly in her direction. 'Yes you! Come on, save the birds! This is an emergency.'

Without awaiting an answer she slammed a bucket into his chest and pointed at the backs of hundreds of dripping helpers heading wearily over the horizon in the direction of Lake Hellarwyl.

In his state of shock he obeyed.

Unseen beneath his feet thirty-three thousand salivating worms wriggled eagerly in hot pursuit of the best pile of leaf-litter ever to grace the Talpa Mountains.

Not too far behind them sixty-eight moles scrabbled hungrily through the exquisitely worm-scented soil

Nabob had to admit it was an impressive sight. Placards and banners were raised high along the banks of Phlegethon by the chanting staff of Immigration as they added their support to the striking ferrymen. Captain Naglfar stood as imposing as possible in his peaked cowl of captaincy, a huge flame surging from his pipe every time he exhaled.

Nabob had only one regret; that he couldn't be yelling and jeering obscenities at Seirizzim with the rest of the mob. With the election only a couple of hours away, and the possibility that Foul Lord d'Abaloh could be winging his way overhead at any moment, it wouldn't do for Nabob to be seen actively supporting dissension without a very real and lucrative profit motive. Besides, if anyone was to find out that he had actually spent good money to start the thing in the first place. . . despite the heat he shivered.

Seirizzim drew himself up to his full nine-foot-six on tip-hoof and stared angrily at Captain Naglfar. His slitted pupils flashed with crimson fury and frustration. Negotiations shouldn't be this difficult.

'That's the typical suggestion I would've expected from a demon who never takes any notice of the working classes until we do something about it and stop work,' snarled Captain Naglfar around his pipe. A rumble of approval snarled out of the strikers. 'We don't want and never will need an Annual Refurbishment Programme for our ferries, including hull-scraping, sail enhancement and dry-cleaning. They're meant to look like death lingers on every creaking plank, our sails are supposed to hang like shrouds rotting on a crucifix. First impressions! Vital! Do you want them to enjoy themselves down here?'

Seirizzim fumed as yells of 'Hear, hear!' echoed across the

river. Nabob, standing in a position carefully calculated to look neutral, raised a surreptitiously supportive thumb as Naglfar tugged on his pipe. That was the longest speech he had given in centuries, he was quite puffed.

'Very well!' boomed Seirizzim arrogantly. 'Since you will not allow me to improve any of your squalid and archaic working conditions beyond that which I confess I find distasteful in the extreme . . .'

There was an irritable rumble of annoyance, Naglfar coughed and shouted, 'First impressions!'

'Yes, yes, so you say,' grunted Seirizzim with a dismissive gesture. 'And since you are still refusing to shift your belligerent carcasses and resume work, it would appear I have only two options at my talon-tips . . .'

Nabob stifled a grin. Got him! He's on the run now!

'I can have you all transferred to the excremental pits in downtown Tumor!' he screamed, tail lashing wildly and his eyes flaring with wrath. 'Or I can agree to your requests and implement them as soon as I achieve Undertaker-in-Chiefship of Mortropolis.' he added with a grin.

Suddenly the picket lines were in turmoil, fear and greed driving them all in the same direction. The second choice.

Nabob panicked. This shouldn't have happened. It was impossible, Seirizzim had agreed to their demands. Not only that but he had linked it to ensuring his election victory. Nabob felt the slippery carpet of his devious plan snatched out from beneath his hooves. Captain Naglfar almost swallowed his pipe. What was he do? Nervously he glanced at Nabob who flashed a fistful of five talons, four times. Naglfar understood immediately. Twenty thousand obuls for his continued support. It wasn't enough for this stress, he flashed back five times.

And Seirizzim shrieked, whirled on Naglfar and snatched him by the throat. 'So! Twenty-five thousand obuls is it? Is that your price?' The captain nodded. 'Pathetic! You placed your trust in him?' he snarled, pointing to Nabob. 'Laughable! It is good for all of you that he has shown his hand, as it were. What kind of Undertaker-in-Chief would he have made?'

'I'm perfect!' screamed Nabob, fuming now. 'I concocted that, the finest bribery scheme in Helian!' He boasted hollowly. 'I was in control. I had the ferrymen, the whole of Immigration and you were powerless against me, you couldn't stop me, I was . . .'

Seirizzim dropped Naglfar and turned menacingly on Nabob. 'Yes?' he growled, raising an arrogantly inquisitive eyebone.

'I was . . . bribing them quite well, thank you very much,' blubbed Nabob pathetically.

'Bribery!' shrieked Seirizzim hurling back his head and laughing. 'Is that what you call it? And what have you achieved with it, hmmm?'

Nabob's mouth opened and closed limply.

'Exactly,' supplied Seirizzim. 'Nothing. Shameful. You ought to know better than that. Bribery without gain . . . why that's charity!'

Hundreds of sharply intaken breaths were the only reply. The entire picket line scowled at Nabob and tutted.

Suddenly Seirizzim spun round, stamped his hooves angrily on the ground and roared. 'Right you lot, that's enough standing around. Back to work! Come on. Now!' His tail lashed whip-like as he bellowed them back to their ferries.

Seirizzim turned to grin victoriously at Nabob. But he was nowhere to be seen.

'Left, left! Come on!' screamed Mahrley, attempting to make himself heard by the catapult crew above the jeering and taunting mob of Cranachanians. Gradually the device swung around and was aimed once again at the vast metal gate.

'Take up the slack!' he yelled, feeling hs nerves tighten with every turn of the waterwheel. Creaks of woody protest sprang from the main projectile arm as the ropes wound in and the bathtub was tugged down to within reach. Eagerly Mahrley wiped sweat out of his eyes and hurled rocks into the now filthy enamelled receptacle, offering desperate psalms heavenwards with each added missile. This time they had to succeed, his reputation depended on it, and besides it was getting far too hot for this type of thing.

The tension increased, creaking stress bleating desperately from every joint and fibre. And that was just in Mahrley's nervy and dripping shoulders. The bathtub settled under the release arm and a few more boulders were piled in for good luck. Anyone within ten feet of the wound contraption could feel it quivering with masses of potential energy straining for release.

Mahrley checked the trajectory once more, diverted a river of perspiration across his brow, crossed his fingers and tugged the lever. Immediately, the launch arm leapt upwards, air molecules whooshing wildly out of its way in countless litres of absolute panic. The bathtub arced skywards, veered towards horizontal and the arm hit the stop. There was a resounding crack, whiplash and the half-ton of rocks zoomed unstoppably security-fence-wards with more than enough inertia to smash the hinges in a blast of screaming metal, kick the gate off its mounts and allow countless Cranachanians to swarm in and extract their monetary tokens . . .

At least that was how it should have been. Mahrley knew that, the gathered crowd knew that, even the jeering figures of Spam Smith and Guthry knew it. Sadly the catapult didn't. The projectile arm sprang upwards, hit the stop and lifted the entire contraption twenty feet off the ground, flipped it over on to its back and deposited it, upside down, fifty feet nearer to the fence.

Mahrley screamed a host of intensely scathing insults at anything that looked even remotely interested and several that weren't and began barking orders at everyone within earshot.

'It'll work! Trust me! We've just got to, er, anchor it properly, that's all, yes anchor it!' His upper lip twitched only slightly.

At the top of the watch towers Spam Smith and Guthry the dwarf clutched their ribs and collapsed in a heap of helpless hysterics. Had Mahrley been an enormous bull with an extra x-chromosome and a massive excess of testosterone and had he been on the receiving end of a malicious crimson handkerchief's taunting, he couldn't possibly have been more furious.

A twenty-five-pound lump of sandstone that he had in his hand dissolved in a cloud of fulminating fist clenching. This was a minor hiccup, this was a teeny-weeny fly in the ointment, this was surmountable. Soon, very soon he would be in there and then who'd be laughing, eh?

Slit-pupilled eyes peered out through the lenses of crystal goggles and squinted through what looked like a vast petrified forest of gigantic tree-trunks. The light from countless lava lamps winked out through the swirling miasma of black and crimson clouds that rose from the Phlegethon, peppering the strata-scrapers with gold beads of perspiration. Away to the left a flame-storm flashed down on downtown Tumor, sheets of heat blasting incendiary discomfort on anything caught without a cinderella or flame-cloak.

D'Abaloh patted Harpy on the side of her scaly neck and urged her around the storm. In minutes he would begin his descent into Mortropolis, ducking under the criss-crosses of walkways chewed out of the rock by generations of stalagmites, swooping around the clumps of strata-scrapers and finally settling into the stinking mess that so many demons called home.

The sooner this election was over and he could get back to a bit of palace improvement the better. His talons itched for the feel of a tube of Fissure-Fix as he swooped around the edge of a tower.

It was not a difficult task to tell when Mrs Olivia 'Green' Beece was feeling incensed about something-or-other's imminent demise. Neither was it hard to spot her in the grips of the fulminating glow of rich ire coursing through her veins whilst, for example, pondering a flagrant disregard of vermin rights. Mrs Beece in these states of histrionic activity looked pretty much as she did right now. And angry didn't come anywhere near the mark.

Her fists were clenched to white-knuckle tension, one around a placard handle, the other into a two-pound lump hammer of persuasion; her eyebrows semaphored v-signs of extreme irritation; her boots stomped; her tank-top crackled and her olive green knitted battle bob-cap fizzed and lanced waves of wrath into the clouding sky. She was not happy.

'What is the meaning of this outrageous discharge?' She shrieked, standing on a barrel with her bristling back to the Centaur Parcs building site. It ignored her and continued to gush countless volumes of black and red clouds in the sky.

'Doesn't anybody know the damage that airborne particulates can cause to the respiratory system of juvenile ravings. This is an affront!' she cried standing Britannia-like, her 'Save the Ravings' placard held high.

Over the years of her campaigning Mrs Beece has learned that by addressing her full vitriol away from the gleamingly impenetrable perimeter security fence and towards the band of mystified people she would achieve greater success. The reason was simple. She'd learned never to approach really big issues head on – way too risky. It was all well and good wanting to break down the gates, storm into the middle of Centaur Parcs and duff the boss up, whoever he might be, but she knew, from bitter experience, that big companies have lawyers and lawyers invariably mean tears before bedtime. Unless, of course, she had a lawyer of her own with an incredibly large soft spot for the current burning cause. So, by addressing her reasoned ranting at an ever-growing throng, she increased her chances of ensnaring a sympathetic knight in shining lawsuits ready to leap into the fray brandishing subpoenas and a host of writs. But right now, after saving countless birdies from an early roasting Mrs Beece was far from ready to hold back.

'. . . already destroyed a perfectly habitable environment for the Variegated Crimson Jelly-Mould and, not content with that, have added this festering eyesore of filth.

Environmental destruction on this scale can only end in one thing . . . bronchitis!' she squealed brandishing her placards with whirling overenthusiasm. She glared defiantly at the swelling crowds of dripping listeners, most of whom had simply popped along to see what all the fuss was about and were now regretting not bringing a drink.

But as Mrs Beece ranted furiously, her battle bob-cap lancing shards of deadly wrath in the air, she could never have envisaged the distance to which her messages would reach.

A thousand feet below, huddling in a semi-completed air-conditioning system the Really Reverend Unctuous III, sat up suddenly and narrowly avoided a nasty concussion.

'Yes,' he thought, stroking his chin as he eavesdropped on the conviction of the delivery and tried to ignore Flagit's threats.

'Yes,' he grunted feeling her work the crowd.

'Yes!' he decided. This is the one. And with that decision firmly locked into his mind he whirled the tendrils of his psyche in for the kill. It pulsed through the darkened depths of the underworld like some deadly squid homing in on a single helpless mackerel. Three pulses of the psychic cephalopod's body, a lashing of the two longest tentacles and it was nearly over.

'. . . cannot stand by and let this happ . . . oooh, I feel all . . . listen to me!' bellowed Mrs Beece, the sibilant edges of her voice swooping off into reverberative oblivion. The crowd looked suddenly shocked and stared up at her with expressions that somehow contained not a little sceptical awe. Some of her die-hard supporter's jaws dropped open. Never in all the campaigns they had fought side by side and in all the speeches she had delivered, never had they heard her sound like that. It was a neat trick.

Reverend Unctuous could feel, through Mrs Beece, the awestruck faces of an enraptured crowd. Row upon row of expectant faces hung on his every word. And suddenly Unctuous grinned. For the first time in his entire life, he had a congregation. Okay, so he had kidnapped someone else's but, well, all's fair in possessions. After all they are nine-tenths of the law.

Mrs Beece took a deep breath and despite looking a little glassy and distant around the eye regions, she launched in with both squelching feet. 'I'm going to tell you things about Centaur Parcs you just wouldn't· believe!' she echoed, sprouting Unctuous's remote thoughts with stunning effect across the gathered throng of hundreds. 'Pin back your ears, brethren and listen good . . .'

Unctuous's grin creased wider as he flashed telepushic commands up into Mrs Olivia Beece's limbic system, putting words into her mouth and swirling her arms in wild gestures. And as Unctuous watched the faces of his enthralled audience, so he enhanced on the details of Centaur Parcs threat, painting his smoke-belching backdrop in acute shades of sheer horror. And the audience, his congregation, started to get restless.

'. . . as you can see it is destroying the neighbourhood. Already in the last five minutes, cases of spontaneous bronchitis amongst juvenile ravings have trebled,' shrieked Mrs Beece to a wave of enthusiastic support. Several of the wilder members of Mrs Beece's flock bent and armed themselves with bricks and sticks, snarling as they glared at the belching site.

'Are you prepared to live next to such filthy neighbours?' she yelled, spurred on by the adoring gaze of her throng. 'Tell me, hutwives, are you happy to put up with streaky black stains on your favourite bed linen? It'll never be safe to hang washing out again!' There was a roar of support from the crowd.

And a roar of extreme anger from Flagit as he noticed the heated glow from his infernite lattice. He swore a hail of choicest Helian oaths and slammed his scaly claw on to the obsidian desk. So Unctuous was using his net? Well, he just wasn't going to stand by and wait.

'So what are we going to do about it?' shrieked Mrs Beece twirling the whisk of incitement and beating the crowd into a frenzy. And almost as one the crowd yelled back, 'Riot! Riot! Riot!'

Flagit screamed again. This had gone far enough.

'J'hadd. J'hadd! Come in, damn you!' he telepushed desperately.

This was a new sensation for d'Abaloh. His pulse raced, his eyes were jammed tight shut, his heart pounded, his claw palms were wet with sweat, and if he came much closer to another tower he wasn't entirely certain if he would be able to keep total control of his bladder. He hadn't a clue what Harpy was up to but he didn't like it one bit. For the first time that he could ever remember d'Abaloh was actually scared.

The dactyl had totally lost control. The whirlwind escape of gas blasting out through the office window in the Transcendental Travel Company Ltd sucked the vast creature wildly through the Underworld sky. Her legs thrashed, her wings pounded and she squeaked in absolute terror. Ahead, as she tumbled and spun, she glimpsed an enormous strata-scraper. And, unless she was terribly mistaken, after taking wind shear, perspective and allowances for panic action course corrections into account, in about fifteen seconds they would slam into it at about a hundred and twenty ells a minute. Harpy screamed and wished she was back in her stable.

Sweat seemed to be rolling down every part of Slamm J'hadd's body as he lugged a bucket of water down the hill from the shores of Lake Hellarwyl. This was his fifteenth such bucket and this time he was determined it would be his last. He was an officer of the Religious Undercover Crime Squad after all, not some servant of Mrs Beece whose only function in life was to fetch and carry coolant for perspiring birds.

Although it *was* nice to know that he was helping those poor little pathetic harfinches.

He looked ahead at the straggly column of people lugging similar buckets and then peered at the smoke-billowing dome of Centaur Parcs, belching hyper-heated black and red filth into the talpine air.

Terror rattled through his body as he thought once again of the image in the Vulgate Bible – the image of the end of the world. An image that looked terrifyingly similar to that fuming mess before him. Frustration snapped and jeered at him, he should be doing something about it. But how? he screamed in the privacy of his own head. What could he possibly do with an enormous security fence standing inpenetrably between him and . . . well, whatever was inside. He suddenly felt a wave of irritation at the chaps who'd written the Vulgate Bible. If they were going to tell folks about the end of the world, they could've had the decency to tell how to stop it, or at the very least offer some clues as to what was going on inside – detailed floor plans, modus operandi, that sort of thing. It wasn't much to ask for, was it?

Suddenly a shriek of anger blasted into the inside of his mind, shattering all thoughts but one. Murder.

'Oi, J'hadd. What are you playing at? Come in . . . Ahh, there you are! Now just stand still, this won't hurt a bit.'

The black scaly claws of Total Limbic Control snatched and scrabbled at the intimately squishy bits of his brain. He could feel the TLC tsunami surging through the valleys of his volition, washing away the very foundations of his higher faculties and whirling him downstream like a tiny chunk of mental flotsam. Just as he realised that something could quite possibly be wrong between him and his brain, his body was hijacked.

Below his feet thirty-nine thousand worms sensed a tasty snack suddenly sprint away. If they had possessed fists they would have smashed them collectively into opened palms in gestures of extreme frustration. They didn't, so they simply put on a quick burst of speed and wriggled off in hot pursuit.

One thousand and twenty-seven moles, however, sensed the sudden acceleration of their wormy lunch, slammed soily claws into open paws and tunnelled frantically onwards. In their moley minds they wondered irritably why these worms were giving them such a run around. Fifteen times they had suddenly spun around and changed direction and now this. It just didn't make any sense.

Flagit monitored J'hadd's every move through the crystal visors dangling before his eyes, thrilling and snarling wildly as he sprinted his way towards Centaur Parcs, his hooves stamping out every move like some deranged flamenco-phile in a dance to the death.

Mustard-yellow glinted around the edge of his eyes as he ranted and snarled to himself, convincing himself that he had won. Unctuous caught terrifying soundbites through the air-conditioning conduit.

'Victory for the Underdogs! . . . . d'Abaloh'll give me what I want . . . power! . . . Ultimate power!'

An artery pulsed at Flagit's neck with throbbing excitement, his claws flexed, curled and clenched as he stamped and bounded around the room. He was not going to let victory be snatched from his grip when he was so close to it.

Fifteen to twenty degrees hotter and all that would survive up there were scorpions and an occasional asbestos-based lichen. Ten degrees hotter still and even they would expire in a final gasp of desperation. And then there'd be nothing to stop it just getting hotter and hotter. Another twenty degrees, the seas boil and the ice caps melt. A hundred degrees up and grasses would ignite, another fifty and entire forests spontaneously combust, another two hundred or so and . . . it's sheer perfection. Charred black desolation of naked geography as far as the eye can see. And if it carried on at this rate it would be totally complete in a day and a half. Flagit's sneer grew ever-wider. Once d'Abaloh saw everything his devoted servant had done, once he witnessed it all . . .

Unseen by the seething nine-foot demon an inchoate blob soared before a black cloud in the distance.

Obliviously, Flagit's tail twitched and writhed like a cat in a hot tin nightmare.

Out through the window the blob metamorphosed into something with wings, ducked around a clump of pillar towers and began to head for the centre of Mortropolis.

291

Had Flagit not been so engrossed in the images from above and the task of telepushically doing away with the very vocal Mrs Beece, he would have been screaming wildly by now, desperately ranting that d'Abaloh had come too early and he wasn't ready and things like that. As it was, he didn't see the silhouette of Harpy and d'Abaloh form out of the shapeless blob on the horizon. He also didn't see the sudden and very unexpected course change that Harpy unwillingly undertook as a vacuum snatched at her wing, spun her round and tugged hard. Flagit was blissfully unaware of the fact that within seconds the vast dactyl and her high-profile cargo were caught in a whirling vortex of rapidly escaping gas and were being dragged inescapably towards the office next door.

For the first time in his life d'Abaloh screamed. Well, you would if you found yourself hurtling unstoppably towards a solid granite wall at a hundred and twenty ells a minute on the back of a six-legged monster with a sixty-foot wingspan and no brakes. Fortunately for his dignity nobody heard him, except Harpy – and she wouldn't tell.

He shouldn't have opened his eyes, it wouldn't have been quite so bad if he'd kept them shut, but, for some reason, just at precisely the wrong time he flicked them open. And there it was. Building. As far as he could see. And it was in his way.

What kind of a manoeuvre Harpy did he never asked, but at the last possible second, when all seemed as if it would end in a sad monolayer pasted to the outside of a strata-scraper, she tucked in one wing, spun around and hit the wall with him first. An inch or two either way and it would have been very messy, but incredibly Harpy managed to thrust d'Abaloh through the shattered window first and then splat against the wall, spread-dactyled and stuck, like a rubber Hallowe'en bat held across the nozzle of a vacuum cleaner.

It was only when d'Abaloh bounced off the back wall, ricocheted through the storeroom door and smashed Flagit to the floor in a flurry of hooves, tails and choicest blasphemies that Flagit noticed d'Abaloh was early. And it was only then that Flagit lost contact with J'hadd, his infernite lattice arcing off his horns in the fury of the collision. It was also at precisely the same time that utter chaos hit this tiny office.

Since Harpy was stuck to the outside of the building doing a wonderful job of sealing the shattered window and since the windmill blades nine hundred and fifty feet above their heads were still whirring wildly, then it follows that countless barrel-loads of atmosphere needed to come from somewhere.

The door to the corridor was sucked open and it started snowing. Plumes of blizzarding Nognite parchment notes whistled into the storeroom, splattered and slapped at faces and vanished through the ceiling next door. These were followed by carpets, sofas, filing-cabinets and would have been chased by a whole host of other objects from several floors below had it not been for the timely intervention of the vast obsidian table and a pair of filing-cabinets. Flagit barely managed to sidestep the bombardment of office furniture quickly enough, hurling himself sideways as two six-drawer upright storage systems roared past him. The table which, by a remarkable stroke of luck, just happened to be precisely large enough to fit over the hole, slammed into the ceiling and was held there by the two cabinets, miraculously sealing it tighter than a dactyl on granite.

A second or so later, Harpy squealed and dropped off the side of the building.

It took a long time for everybody's ears to pop.

Feelings of sheer detestation coursed hot through J'hadd's body, seething through his adrenal medulla and whipping into his bicep. With a scream he erupted from the crowd, SAS dagger raised high, his ears pounding wild blood fury, sweat dripping across his scars.

'. . . continues it will be such a senseless waste of . . urghhh!' J'hadd snatched Mrs Beece around the throat, dragging her to the ground, knife raised, snarling.

And suddenly he stopped.

At that very moment, unseen in the boiling miasma of

exhaust gases erupting skywards from the septet of fumaroles, an eighteen-inch-wide infernite lattice complete with matching pair of stereo scrying crystals erupted, spun end over end and landed half a mile away beneath a small clump of heather.

J'hadd shook his head as Spruce cannoned into the back of him, sending him sprawling. Everyone crowded forward a pace to get a closer look. Saving birds was one thing, but watching a punch-up was better.

Spruce leapt on to J'hadd, pinning him to the ground. And then looked about in complete confusion. He'd seen some strange reactions to people being flattened to the ground and, yes, laughing was one of them. But only if it was laughing hysterically. He had never, ever, heard or seen anyone roll on to their backs, point to the sky and shriek wildly as if they'd been told the most deadly joke in the entire world.

A filing-cabinet, a huge plume of Nognite parchments and a large sofa erupted from three of the openings in the dome.

And then something odd happened.

One thousand feet below, an obsidian table slammed against the opening in the ceiling and caused a very sudden, and almost total transient vacuum. This sudden drop in pressure sucked its way up the tube connecting Centaur Parcs with Helian and started the particular odd something happening.

J'hadd noticed it first. Well, he would since he was directly on top of it.

Fifty-three thousand worms, who up until that very instant had been licking what passes as lips amongst worms in anticipation of finally tucking into a tasty helping of well-rotted leaf-litter, suddenly lost their appetites and fled. Over a thousand moles followed in all directions.

The reason for this sudden and total mass evacuation was about to become graphically apparent to everyone gathered in and around Centaur Parcs.

For J'hadd, the earth moved.

The vacuum shock wave that had so recently ripped up

from the very bowels of Helian had loosened an already, almost terminally weakened expanse of ground. Fifteen passes of upwards of forty thousand earthworms and up to a good thousand moles does little for a soil's integrity. Especially when that soil was supposed to be holding back the entire combined weight of the largest expanse of fresh water in the whole of the Talpa Mountains.

Lake Hellarwyl burst its banks.

Countless millions of barrels of fresh water pushed their way through the worm-eroded strata and plunged through a guided channel down the side of the hillock.

'Run!' shrieked J'hadd, hoisting his cassock up around his knees and ably demonstrated the precise meaning of the verb. Mrs Beece and Spruce were hard on his heels in seconds.

The fresh water tidal wave smashed through the weakened soil, accelerated by the head of pressure above it, snatched by the forces of gravity below. The fifty-odd feet of soil that stood between it and the whirling windmill didn't stand a chance. Like some infernal aquatic bulldozer, the water shoved a couple of hundred tons of prime Talpine loam into the shaft and pounded it down a good thousand feet on top of a solid obsidian table.

And then, as if it were the beginning of some wonderful religious celebration, the windmill started to snatch at the incoming water. At first only a scant few drops were plucked at by the whirling blades, but, almost as if it were getting the hang of it, the windmill grabbed more.

'Look!' squealed Mrs Beece, alternately pointing and rubbing her eyes in sheer disbelief. 'My birdies!'

The seven fuming holes of Centaur Parcs coughed, choked and suddenly, gloriously, spat tens of thousands of barrels of clean fresh water hundreds of feet into the air.

Somebody else rubbing his eyes in disbelief was Flagit as he stared alternately at d'Abaloh, Harpy the hovering dactyl and the jam of filing-cabinets and tables in the room next door.

'How dare you!' screamed d'Abaloh, standing claws on hips and sneering imperiously at Flagit.

'I, I can explain . . .' Flagit whimpered, picking nervously at the ends of his claws and looking furtively for any sign of the infernite lattice.

'I don't need explanations. It's obvious what's been going on here,' snarled d'Abaloh, glaring meaningfully at the spray of tools and pipes scattered across the floor.

'It . . . it is?' gulped Flagit, shuffling his hooves apprehensively. What would d'Abaloh's reaction be? Flattered or furious?

'That'll teach you to use illegal immigrants, eh?' he growled, scowling at Unctuous. 'Should've used proper Mortropolitan Contractors, then none of this would've happened.' He shook a taloned thumb at the wreckage next door.

'Yes . . . I, er . . .' Flagit rubbed his head and felt for any signs of a sharp blow that may have caused concussion. It was the only explanation. He had been whacked over the head and now nothing was making any sense. Either that or he had just slipped silently into total barking madness.

'It's always the same with the likes of you lot,' growled d'Abaloh. 'Always complaining about lack of space, but you never learn.'

Lack of space? burbled Flagit's bewildered brain in the privacy of his owns skull. It was overcrowded down here but . . . what was he on about?

'With proper planning permission and correct site surveys you'd've been forewarned about coming across volcanic fissures unexpectedly. Ha, now what are you going to do about your extension, eh?'

'E . . . extension?' whimpered Flagit. Nabob scratched his head.

'Don't play the innocent with me. It's obvious you need extra storage space,' d'Abaloh sneered at the filing-cabinets. 'Now, if I were you, I'd slap a couple dozen bags o' Fissure-Fix up there, you'd need hyper-strength by the looks of it, multigrade just wouldn't do. Some folks swear by it, but me? I swear by the . . .'

And he was away, reeling off lists of trade names, methods of construction, the pros and cons of utilising roar-bolts in the attachment of vulcanised cladding to volcanic aggregates. His eyes clouded over wistfully as he recalled catalogues of building materials, his scaly upper lip trembling as he recounted the pack sizes of a hundred different types of grout. It had been so long since he had enjoyed such an intelligent conversation.

And even when the Malebranche came bursting through the door, thought Flagit, it wouldn't really matter. Incredibly there was no evidence of his misdemeanours, nothing to tie the printer or the priest to him. All it would take would be a few barefaced lies, the type at which he was exceedingly adept, and he'd quite simply be banged up for a few hundred years on various counts of extending property without planning permission, utilising non-standardised labour for said purpose and causing excessive trauma to d'Abaloh's personal transport.

Keep his nose clean, play the game and he'd be out in a dozen or so decades. Right now he could have kissed d'Abaloh.

But he was too late, with a cheery snarl and a muttering of something like not having had such a good time in years, d'Abaloh leapt out of the window on to Harpy's hovering back and soared off towards a pressing appointment with a couple of hopeful election candidates.

'Pull! Come on, pull!' yelled Mahrley attempting to whip his men into heady enthusiasm. 'This time it's perfect!' he cried as he leapt about on the top of the catapult. 'This time we'll . . . oooer.'

He stared at the scene before him and suddenly felt a little foolish. It was different to the last time he had seen it. For one thing, there hadn't been a vast swathe of a river torrenting down from Lake Hellarwyl, smashing its way through the gates he had been attempting to remove for so long.

At first nobody dared move, standing rooted to the spot staring at the septet of rapidly growing fountains pluming endlessly skywards, trying to fathom what was happening. And then they all realised that gravity was still working. It was difficult to miss. Simultaneously, like some perfectly choreographed aquatic entertainment, the seven fountains stopped rising, seemed to dither at their apex, made up their minds and plunged crowdwards. In seconds everyone was drenched. And a stack cooler.

Joyously, the crowds leapt and cavorted in the first water to fall from the sky in what seemed like an eternity. The fountains crashed on the surrounding hills, moistening the acres of parched trees, splashed into the lake and filled the streams, it banished the heat and the smoke. And just behind the security fence a small stream filled and grew, dashing eagerly down the side of the hill, spinning a small waterwheel as it did so, turning a shaft, winding a gear, twisting a pulley and powering a vast turbine that was set fifty feet below ground level.

The clumps of birds gasped and began to recover.

In fact, the only creatures in the entire Talpa Mountains that weren't entirely chuffed with the whole thing were the beavers. Having expended a lot of time and effort gnawing through trees and building bigger and better dams to irritate your neighbour, it was distinctly miffing to watch helplessly as fountain floodwaters babbled down the hill and washed it all away again. Still, it did smell a lot nicer.

Suddenly, Mahrley's arm shot out and pointed to two figures staggering out through a hole in the Centaur Parcs security fence. 'There's the dwarf,' he cried. 'Get 'im!' And a mob of irate pipe-rollers instantly forgot their catapult, screamed and dashed for the dwarf.

The sudden racket battered at the ears of a countless host of rapidly recovering birds. Water battered down from above, soaking all and cooling the fevered feathered brows of Noleff Terns, ravings and harfinch alike. One by one cliff tits shook themselves, preened randomly at ruffled flight feathers and took to the wing. Flocks of them clattered into the air watched by an open-mouthed and slightly dazed Mrs Beece. And, as if in that instant the weather wanted in some way to have its meteorological say, the sun came out. Millions of lumens of golden beams sparkled and flashed through the gallons of airborne water, reflecting and refracting joyously. And there, suddenly, framing the efflux of birds, a giant arcing rainbow appeared.

It was all too much for Mrs Olivia Beece.

With a whimper, she fainted.

Unseen by anyone as they all stared skywards a small red-nightdressed girl snuck out of a suitable bush and, with a grin, cheerfully set about tying Mrs Beece's bootlaces together.

The constant whooshing of the underfloor central heating rattled irritatingly by as the two candidates waited impatiently in the ante-room. A bead of nervous sweat squeezed its way between the scales on Nabob's forehead, breathed a sigh of relief at escaping the seething tumult within and leapt for the floor. It tumbled through the hate-charged air and hit the tiles with a final sizzle of steam.

Seirizzim looked up from a stack of Nognite Parchment ('Guaranteed not to burn, wrinkle or calcine in any way likely to impair information transfer . . . or your money back!'). Casually he licked the tip of his boil-point pen and scribbled a host of final figures on a set of tables.

Nabob scowled angrily at his opponent. He had hated Seirizzim before, but now that he had destroyed the ace card of his Phlegethon picket line, well, it was plain old fulminating detestation now. He had no choice but to go with the original plan. Damn Flagit for not bringing him any proof.

Suddenly the doors to the inner chamber were flung open and a terrifying figure stood beckoning, its arrow-headed tail flicking behind it.

'His Malevolence, Foul Lord d'Abaloh has been kept waiting long enough,' boomed the infernal lackey, 'Enter and state your case.'

In a flash Seirizzim was on his cloven hooves, stamping

forward, his curling horns trembling with pent excitement. Nabob stood, swallowed and wondered if he really did want to stand for Undertaker-in-Chief of Mortropolis after all. It would be hard . . . oh, but think of all that power to hurl around! Total control over the capital of the Underworld Kingdom of Helian, complete domination over the ever-expanding population, the opportunity to create new and ever more devious eternal torments . . .

A whirlwind of excitement tornadoed through his ruthless heart. Oh yes, this was a job he wanted. Head and shoulders above anything the Sinful Service could offer. He would never forgive himself if Seirizzim managed to slime his way into the post.

'Your Malevolent Majesty,' greased Seirizzim expertly as he oozed his way towards the black enthroned figure which sneered malevolently in a cloud of raw evil. One of the few aspects of being Foul Lord that d'Abaloh did enjoy was the sneering malevolently in clouds of raw evil. It always made such a satisfying first impression. 'I stand before you ready to outbribe, countercorrupt and profiteer my way into your favour and in so doing earn your eternal approval to become Undertaker-in-Chief of Mortropolis.'

Foul Lord d'Abaloh's scales creaked as he inclined his vast head and focused his full attention on the first candidate. Unblinking slitted pupils burned redly down from beneath the sweeping arc of his horns and the barbed brimstone of his fiery crown of office. The Lord of the Underworld's tail twitched and flicked with mounting malice. 'Speak!' he boomed, tapping a twelve-inch talon on the arm of the obsidian throne. He was proud of those talons, one of the things that he had never been able to do as a builder was grow them quite as long as he had always wanted. Seirizzim took a step forward and began. 'Make me Undertaker-in-Chief and I shall personally see to it that your vast Palace in Tumor will be completely refitted to the exacting depth of your specialised depravity.'

D'Abaloh snorted.

Nabob's hope leapt a notch. How dreadfully unimaginative.

'I shall also select the pick of the bunch of incoming female companions for your delight,' continued Seirizzim licking his lips and oozing closer.

Nabob tutted and rolled his eyes.

'. . . choose champions at all card games and gambling to compete with you, stock your kitchens with the finest chefs d'gluttony and have made a complete new set of riding tackle for Herpes,' ended Seirizzim after a catalogue of basest vitiation as long as his arm.

D'Abaloh glared and snorted derisively at Seirizzim. 'Her name is Harpy,' he snarled.

Nabob stifled a chuckle as Seirizzim swallowed nervously. This was going to be easy after all. As if d'Abaloh didn't already have full choice of the poor souls that ended up down here for eternity. Job's in the bag! Hardly needed to put all that effort in.

'In short,' purred Seirizzim, pulling himself together admirably, 'as deeply as you are debauched now, your Iniquity, it will be as nothing compared to the ripe plums of depravity waiting to be plucked if you select me.'

'Very bold, Seirizzim,' bellowed d'Abaloh. 'A dangerous claim since you have little idea of the extent of my current licentious profligacy. I do have very wicked tastes!' His huge lip curled lecherously back from his teeth. 'But enough.' He turned and glared at Nabob. 'You. What can you offer me in return for the Undertakership?'

Nabob took a deep breath. 'This!' he declared, producing a small gold-braided hair-net and crossing his fingers for luck. He really wasn't sure if it would work down here but . . . ahhh what the hell.

D'Abaloh fumed as he sat bolt upright and pointed angrily. 'You offer me an auric hair-net?' he bellowed, 'How dare you?'

Nabob winced and concluded that finger-crossing didn't work here. 'No, no!' he shrieked waving his palms desperately. 'You wear it on your head.'

'I know that! What ridicule is this?' bellowed d'Abaloh,

slamming clenched claws into the arm of his throne. Seirizzim giggled with devilish delight.

'Your Malevolence, this is a brand-new invention,' Nabob searched his mind for all the dubious technobabble that Flagit had come out with, 'Er, a . . . a creation of cutting-edge technology which, in the right talons can cause chaos and wickedness amongst the peoples of the world. It is a telepushy net!'

'What's that when it's at home?' grunted d'Abaloh.

Nabob grinned. 'My thoughts exactly when I first saw it. Your Iniquity, this device can control the actions of others, it can dictate the complex routes through which cause and effect are channelled. In short, this is the pipe that calls the tune!'

D'Abaloh growled a subterranean cacophony of irritation. 'And you are offering this to me?'

Nabob looked up at Foul Lord d'Abaloh and nodded. Then whimpered as the infernal entity screamed with rage. 'Have you failed completely to notice that I already call the tune. I already hold dominion over this miserable Underworld. I rule Helian!'

Nabob's vestigial wings flapped in the torrent of feral breath and silence fell in the inner chamber. Even the underfloor heating seemed to hold its breath.

'Ah,' simpered Nabob. 'It would seem that you have misunderst— er, that I have not made myself very clear, o Infinitely Debauched One.'

D'Abaloh trembled with rising fury. The obsidian arms of the throne creaked and splintered beneath the mounting tonnage of his grip.

'This controls people before they're dead, see?' finished Nabob.

Seirizzim's grin cracked and slid from his scaly face as he realised the terrible potential of what Nabob was offering. Armed with that machine, if it really did what he said it would, d'Abaloh would be able to pull the strings on both sides of the festering banks of the Phlegethon and beyond.

'What do you mean?' snarled d'Abaloh. 'What can it do? Why should it be of interest to me?'

'O your Hateful Nefarity, consider the pleasure of starting your very own war, or choreographing swarming plagues of rodents, or replacing police states with rampaging tyrannical dictatorships.'

D'Abaloh's face began to twitch into a sneer as he imagined himself ruling both the pre- and post-mortem worlds. Just think of the buildings he could build.

'You have proof?'

'Damn!' screamed Nabob inside his mind 'Damn, damn! He asked!' He nodded with devilish over-enthusiasm, trying desperately not to scream out loud. 'The Flock Wars!' he shrieked. 'The wild string of battles that raged along Rhyngill's southern border . . . your Dementedness, using this device, I started that!'

The inner chamber exploded with Foul Lord d'Abaloh's cacophonous bellow of derisive laughter, and seconds later Seirizzim was rolling about the floor helpless with shrieking mirth.

'I did!' protested Nabob unable to keep a whining note out of his voice. 'I used ths telepushy net two weeks ago and I made a nine-year-old girl paint moustaches on the angels and change all the letters in the New Field Edition Copy of . . . oh,' Nabob's voice wound down and croaked into a desultory stop beneath the torrents of derision. It really wasn't worth carrying on, he knew the way it was sounding.

'Your Magnificent Malevolence,' began Seirizzim gearing up to deliver the final blow to Nabob's job prospects. 'My Foul Lord, give me the Undertakership and I shall increase my offer. Everything I previously promised, plus! – every week, delivered straight to your own private hypercooler, three pounds of your favourite Rhyngillian delicacy!' He grinned and placed a small tub before the Foul Lord.

D'Abaloh stared at Seirizzim, then at the tub, then back and wiped his lips. 'Four pounds,' he demanded.

'Three and a half,' countered Seirizzim.

'Done!' declared D'Abaloh, slamming his claw on the throne arm and snatching the lid off the tub. For a second he stared at the pale frothy contents, his crimson eyes tasting, before his talon lashed out and scooped the lemming mousse into his salivating maw.

'But you can't give him the job!' squealed Nabob. 'He's unfit to rule, he can't control the ferrymen.'

'Do you honestly think I care if there is a modicum of extra suffering down here?' snarled d'Abaloh and took another languorous lick of lemming mousse talon.

Seirizzim jumped about leaping wildly high in the air and shrieking with devilish delight.

'Er what about this!' whimpered Nabob, snatching a small frame of balls on strings out of his bag. 'It's very relaxing! Or this. . . ' The wavemaker was completely ignored too.

Nabob turned and trudged miserably out of the hall, already plotting revenge against Seirizzim.

'Sheyoot, what money?' spluttered Guthry. 'I sure as hell ain't got no kinda clue what you're talking about. Fact I ain't never seen ya afore.'

'Pah! That the best you can do?' shouted Mahrley and spat derisively. 'Maybe I can help you remember. Okay, lads, pull!'

Four vast pipe-rollers spat on their palms and tugged on the rope looping over a hastily erected gallows. They screamed with wild delight as the dwarf spun around and was hurled aloft by his ankles.

'Remembered yet?' shouted Mahrley to the dangling dwarf. 'No? All right lads, duck!'

Guthry screamed as he plummeted towards the torrents of the new river, splashed through the surface and thrashed helplessly. The few seconds he was under seemed to last a lifetime. Why it seemed so familiar he couldn't tell.

'See what I mean?' snapped Captain Barak, twisting the Cranachanian Chancellor's head in the direction of the dwarf lynching mob.

'Well, I . . .' flustered Khenyth, stroking his chin nervously and attempting to look thoughtful. All around them people stared at knife-points beneath their chins as market traders ran wild attempting to extract proper currency from pouches and purses.

He knew that money had strange effects on people, he'd heard the screams from the masses when he invented another tax or hiked any of the others up a few points. But so far he had never found himself personally imperilled in the midst of a fully fledged riot.

Mahrley shouted at the dripping dwarf. 'If you don't give us real money soon we'll hang you the *right* way up!' Guthry screamed again as he vanished below a torrent of water.

'Okay, look at it this way,' snarled Barak, grabbing the Chancellor around the collar and waving two ten-groat notes at him. Khenyth's eyes snapped on to them, the plight of the dwarf forgotten for a moment. Barak held out a note as if he were handing it over. Khenyth grabbed, Barak tugged and the note shredded before their eyes in an irreparably soggy mess.*

'What are you doing?' Khenyth shrieked with shock.

'Hurts does it?' hissed Barak, releasing the Chancellor.

Khenyth nodded mutely at the loss of ten groats, looking suddenly like a little boy who'd just skinned his knees and was determined at all costs not to cry. His bottom lip trembled.

Barak held the other note at arm's length, one end in each hand and tugged his knuckles apart. Khenyth screamed as the note snapped taut, only slapping his hand across his bawling mouth in extreme embarrassment when he realised that it was still in one piece.

'See, still intact. C'mon, say yes,' pressed Barak as a mob of market traders spotted the dwarf and realised that in fact it was all his fault. 'Or else I'll charge you with wilfully not-stopping a riot and murder. That lot'll rip the dwarf apart! Agree and you're a hero, no and I'll hand you over to Swingler. Now what d'you say?'

There were an awful lot of things that Khenyth really wanted to say just then. Things which were far less than flattering about Barak, his parents, the company he kept,

---

* Unfortunately for Khenyth, transparent adhesive sticky tape was still centuries away from being invented.

305

things about his supposed unhealthy affection for sheep . . . a whole host of insults queued up for hurling.

'I . . .' he began. 'Er, I think that, er, owing to the improved resilience of these notes, er, and their demonstrable fire resistance, I . . . I shall declare these notes legal tender.'

Barak leapt for joy and sprinted off towards Mahrley and the dwarf lynching mob to spread the good news. That would surely stop the rioting and save him weeks of parchment work to boot.

Khenyth sobbed and bit his knuckles. That had hurt. All that money had been earned tax-free. It was criminal.

Still, he mused with dread, it probably wouldn't hurt half as much as the beating he'd get off Achonite when he found out.

Little did he realise it, but it also wouldn't hurt half as much as Achonite's head did right then. He crawled out from behind a pile of cartwheels and struggled towards the door and stared at the chaos. Before he could squeak in alarm a vast hand flashed out of the waterlogged sky and grabbed Commander 'Black' Achonite firmly by the shoulder.

'Now, about these rat-proof boots . . .' boomed the voice of Spam Smith, licking the end of his pencil and attempting to write on a small piece of parchment. 'How many did you say you wanted?'

In the midst of all the chaos swirling outside the wreckage of the Centaur Parcs security fence there was one small fragment of utter misery.

Slamm J'hadd slouched miserably against the wheel of the catapult and shook his head. He had to face it, he was a complete failure. With three hours remaining before the deadline for his acceptance to the RUC he hadn't a single arrest to his name. Fourteen years and nothing!

It's not that he hadn't solved a crime or anything, oh no, he knew very well who had started the Flock Wars and who had attacked Spam Smith and Guthry the dwarf. But that wouldn't do any good. He'd lost his criminal and he didn't really think that arresting himself really counted, besides, how could he investigate things if he was locked up? Oh, it was all too complicated . . . He'd just have to face it, the RUC wasn't for him.

Miserably he sighed as a cliff tit flittered out of the sky and perched on his shoulder. Strangely it looked as if it were waiting for something.

'Er, excuse a-me,' said a large bulk of a man in a sharply funereal black suit. Gently he stroked an enormous white rat. J'hadd looked up.

'I know eet's not a-really my beesiness, but should that cart be parked over a-there?'

J'hadd stared in the direction of the pointing finger and blinked. Strange, he had never noticed it before but a vast forty-ton-wagon wagon train was resting by the side of a double yellow line. Hope stirred, could this be true? Could this be a real offence? A legitimate collar?

He leapt to his feet, turned to the informant and saluted. 'Thank you, citizen!' And he was off at a sprint.

Khar Pahcheeno grinned and strolled away. Okay, so it would cost him a few groats in fines, but it was worth it to have someone so usefully gullible in the RUC in case he ever needed the favour returning.

The cliff tit landed on the sodden ground, cocked its head on one side as if listening, then snatched the head off a very surprised worm as it broke surface.

'Excuse me, sir, is this your vehicle?' began Slamm J'hadd feeling more confident already. 'Do you know you're not allowed to park it here . . . ?'

Beneath a small clump of heather half a mile from the security fence of Centaur Parcs a small mole was making a momentous discovery. It was very odd, but if he crawled under a large goldish net sort of thing that he'd found and thought about worms, well, it was funny, but they just sort of appeared at his feet.

307